IN *good* COMPANY

KAT SINGLETON

Copyright © 2025 by Kat Singleton LLC

Cover Design by Summer Grove @summerrgrove

Developmental Edit by Salma R.

Line Editing by Holly at Bird and Bear Editorial Services

Edited by Sandra Dee with One Love Editing

Proofreading by Alexandra Cowell and Briana Cohen

ISBN: 978-1-958292-18-1

This book is for my babes looking for the company of a rich, possessive, obsessed man. I hope you enjoy your time with Callahan Hastings.

Playlist

CHERRY - LANA DEL REY

CAN'T TAKE MY EYES OFF YOU - FRANKIE VALLI

HEAVENLY - CIGARETTES AFTER SEX

STATE OF GRACE (TAYLOR'S VERSION) - TAYLOR SWIFT

IMAGINATION - SHAWN MENDES

THERE SHE GOES - THE LA'S

YOU'RE GONNA GO FAR - NOAH KAHAN

FLICKER - NIALL HORAN

THIS - ED SHEERAN

WILDEST DREAMS (TAYLOR'S VERSION) - TAYLOR SWIFT

SUMMER LOVE - JUSTIN TIMBERLAKE

BEWITCHED - LAUFEY

HIGH - STEPHEN SANCHEZ

FALLING - TREVOR DANIEL

Author's Note

In Good Company is a billionaire, age gap, ex's brother, forced proximity, boss x employee romance novel. It is full of banter, sweet moments, and scenes that'll have you blushing. I hope that you love Lucy and Cal as much as I do. This is the first book in all-new series of mine called the Pembroke Hills series.

In Good Company contains mature content that may not be suitable for all audiences. Please go to authorkatsingleton.com/content-warnings for a list of content warnings for the book.

One
LUCY

I forgot how much I despised cooking for Laurent Hughes. When he asked me at the last minute to work the private dinner party he was hosting tonight, my first thought was to say no. I needed the money—desperately—but I knew preparing a meal for him would come with *many* challenges.

The main one being he might be the biggest douche in the Hamptons. Which is really saying something because this place is filled with pretentious assholes.

"When will the food be done?" Laurent comes stomping into his kitchen, his angry voice booming against the walls.

I take a deep breath and plaster on a smile, internally scolding myself for agreeing to be his chef tonight. "The main course will be done at the time I told you it would be. I will have the food ready for the staff to bring out at eight." My words come out rather tight, but they're still polite. It's all I can muster when dealing with a man like him.

He lets out a disgruntled sigh.

My smile remains stiff as I wipe my hands off on my apron and give him my full attention. I try to blow a piece of my long brown hair out of my face, but it does nothing. The stray piece falling over my eye annoys me *almost* as much as Laurent. "Has your party finished the prepared appetizers?"

Laurent shakes his head. "No. The guests are still eating."

I blink, at a loss about how to respond. I still have thirty minutes to get the main course ready to serve to his guests. I told him when he asked me yesterday that eight in the evening was the earliest I'd be able to serve the main course. I needed time this morning to hit the farm stands to pick up groceries and prep for the six-course meal he'd insisted on for the evening.

I bite my tongue, wanting to ask him if the four courses that I'd already served weren't enough.

Luckily, Laurent decides pestering me about the food isn't worth his time anymore. He turns on his heel and disappears from the kitchen, his heavy footsteps making it clear he's aggravated with me.

The moment he's gone, I let out a sigh of relief. The meal is almost over, and I've done my best to clean up after myself tonight. Hopefully, I won't have to stay long after dessert is served. The paycheck for the night will be great, but no matter how badly I need the money for me and my family, I make a promise to myself to never agree to work for the Hughes family again.

With Laurent gone, I'm able to return to finishing up the main course for the evening. He demanded the protein be lamb chops and that I serve it with some sort of potato dish and a salad.

I carefully place the lamb chops on a serving dish, garnishing the top with a sprig of rosemary. I kept the rest simple by roasting the potatoes and garnishing them with freshly grated parmesan and more rosemary. The lamb chops with the balsamic reduction sauce I made were supposed to be the star of the show. I wanted the sides to enhance the dish but not take away from the protein.

After plating the lamb chops, I work on finishing the salad. I stopped at my favorite farm stand this morning to pick up fresh tomatoes for the occasion. I was able to grab a few different varieties to make a beautiful tomato salad I hope everyone enjoys.

I continue to get everything ready for the meal. Soon, Laurent's staff will be back to grab all the food, and I want to make sure everything is perfect before they do so. Even though I regret saying yes to Laurent, I still want to give him and his guests a main course that wows them all.

I've been too busy preparing each course to greet anyone attending the dinner party, but Laurent is highly connected. There's always the chance that someone here could enjoy my food and decide to book me for their own private events.

The idea makes me smile. This summer is my last chance to make as much as I can before I return home to Virginia. It'd be huge if someone out there was impressed by the food tonight and offered me more dinner party gigs. I'm trying to pick up as many shifts as I can at Pembroke Hills, the country club where I wait tables, but being a waitress isn't my passion—making food is.

Kacey, one of Laurent's full-time staff members, walks into the kitchen. She huffs loudly, her palms hitting the granite countertop with a loud *smack*. "I wonder if Mr. Hughes has been in a good mood once in his life."

I rub my lips together to hide a budding smile. Judging by my interactions with Laurent Hughes, I don't think he's *ever* been in a good mood. I can't even picture it.

Lewis, another one of Mr. Hughes's staff members, walks into the kitchen with a wide grin. "You know, I've actually seen Laurent in a good mood."

Kacey dramatically gasps. *"Really?* When?"

Lewis props his elbows on the counter as he stealthily looks over his shoulder before looking back at Kacey. "His mistress comes over while Mrs. Hughes is at her golf lessons. Mr. Hughes is always smiling after that."

My eyes go wide as I try to pay attention to plating the skewers of jumbo shrimp next to the serving dish of lamb chops. The Hamptons feels like a small town, especially with the gossip that comes with working at Pembroke Hills Country Club. I'm used to the whispers of how the rich like to misbehave, but I try to stay out of it. Here, it's hard to tell the truth from rumors.

However, Lewis seems pretty confident that Laurent is, in fact, having an affair.

"I can't believe he invites his mistress to his house. That's diabolical," Kacey responds with a hushed voice. She shakes her head as she takes a step closer to me.

"It really is," Lewis agrees. He follows Kacey's lead, the both of them stopping next to me.

"Are these ready to go out?" Kacey asks, lifting her wrist to check the time on her watch. "We have two minutes to get these out before Laurent comes marching in here, all red in the face, accusing us of ruining his dinner party for serving the food late."

Kacey's comment makes me laugh. I take a step back and wipe my hands on my apron, giving the dishes a quick once-over. "They're good to go." I smile, letting out a small sigh of relief that I got the meal done in time. For pulling the meal together at the last minute and not having a lot of time to prepare, I'm impressed with how everything turned out.

"Hopefully it tastes as good as it looks," Lewis remarks, carefully picking up the plate filled with the lamb chops.

"You know it will," Kacey pipes up, grabbing the bowl with

the tomato salad and the basket of fresh bread I prepared. "Lucy always makes the best dishes."

I place my hand on my chest as I give her an appreciative smile. "That means so much to me. Thank you."

Kacey smiles before spinning carefully on her heel and walking right back out of the kitchen. I'm not close with Kacey or Lewis, but the few times I've cooked for Laurent, they've been incredibly kind to me. I make a mental note to wrap up the extra food we have from tonight and place it in containers for them.

I'm busy preparing a cherry tart with fresh cherries I picked up from the local market when Kacey comes hurrying in.

"Everyone is *marveling* about your food, Lucy. They'd like you to come out and introduce yourself."

There's a loud clanking noise as I drop the spoon I'd been holding. "Surely I don't need to introduce myself. Are they not all from the club?" Suddenly, my nerves take over at the prospect of going out there and speaking to everyone. Making connections with potential new clients is the main reason I accepted this last-minute job to begin with, but now that I'm faced with that opportunity, I'm overwhelmed with nerves. I've always been terrible about talking about myself. I'm even worse at accepting compliments—something that might have stemmed from growing up with two brothers who made it their mission to always humble me.

Kacey shrugs. "Even if they've met you before, they want to tell you how much they enjoyed the meal. Go talk to them." She waves her hands through the air to hurry me along, but I stand frozen, unsure of what to do.

Kacey snaps her fingers to get my attention. "Lucy." There's more snapping, this time her fingers even closer to my face.

I jump, my heartbeat speeding up. "Yes?"

Kacey's hands fall to my shoulders. "You're going to go out there and own that you just blew their fucking socks off. Now, go snag some more clients. All of them are nicer than Laurent, which is a total win for you."

I nod. Kacey has a point. Word of mouth is how to get new clients in the Hamptons, and anyone dining with Laurent Hughes can pay big money for meals. I need to own that I'm a damn good private chef and go make some connections.

I just might throw up first.

Kacey must see the fear in my eyes because she gives me a soft smile. "Laurent has dinner parties all the time. You're a far better chef than anyone else he's hired. Although, if you repeat that, I'll deny I ever said it until I'm blue in the face."

Her words make me laugh, easing some of my tension. "I guess I should get out there."

Taking a deep breath, I step around her. I give Kacey a nervous smile over my shoulder as I leave the kitchen, internally praying I don't make a fool of myself in front of Laurent's guests.

Two
CAL

I knew it was a bad idea to say yes to this dinner party. Laurent can be a raging asshole, which is truly saying something because I know I'm not always the nicest person to be around.

I only agreed because my best friend, Jude, was supposed to come with me. The fucker bailed last minute after something came up and he had to unexpectedly return to Manhattan.

I stupidly still came, and my night has consisted of listening to Laurent unnecessarily berate his employees and dodging the weird advances of Warren Simpson's wife as *he* ogles one of the waitstaff members.

I'm staring at my lap, trying to come up with an excuse for why I need to leave the moment after dessert is served, when Laurent clears his throat.

"Here she is," he announces. My eyes move from my lap to Laurent. Meeting the chef for the night might be the highlight of my evening. The food was incredible.

"I'd like everyone to meet Lily. You may have seen her waiting tables at the club, but she also cooks on the side." He laughs, pretending that anything that came out of his mouth was even remotely funny.

The soft clearing of a throat pulls my eyes from Laurent to the chef he found for the night. "It's—"

My eyes go wide as I sit straighter in my chair. "Lucy," I finish for her, blinking a few times to make sure my eyes aren't playing tricks on me.

I don't know who looks more shocked to see the other—me or her.

The last time I saw Lucy was at my family's home in Greenwich. Her dark hair is far longer than it used to be, but her warm brown eyes still look the same. It's a bit of a shock to see her standing there, her wide eyes pinned on me. For a moment, I don't even know what to say. I never expected to see her here in the Hamptons and especially never would've guessed she'd be working as a private chef.

"I was positive your name was Lily," Laurent pipes up. Neither Lucy nor I look at him. We're too lost staring at one another to worry about the host and his inability to remember the name of the person he hired for the night.

One question after another fires off in my head. It's been four, or maybe even five, years since I've last seen her.

Lucy pulls her eyes from mine and focuses her attention on Laurent. "It's Lucy, Mr. Hughes. Was the meal okay?"

I'm surprisingly annoyed that she won't look back at me. Instead, she just stares at Laurent, waiting for him to answer her. I fight the urge to ask how she ended up being a private chef. If my memory doesn't betray me, which it shouldn't because I typically have excellent recollection, she was adamant about being a business major in college.

"The meal was spectacular." Ida—Warren's wife, who has been a little too touchy-feely tonight—beats Laurent to the answer. "I'd love to get your information."

Thomas Boucher clears his throat. "Do you have a permanent job for the summer?"

Lucy pulls her lip between her teeth. "Um..." A nervous laugh bubbles from her chest as she looks from Ida to Thomas. "No, not really. I've just been taking private parties as they come in and working my shifts at Pembroke."

My head cocks to the side. How have I missed her at Pembroke? I only flew in for the season last week, but I've been at the club almost every day since returning. It's possible I just missed her. Besides, we've only met a few times, and it was years ago. But with her standing a few feet away from me, I know I'm staring at my little brother's ex-girlfriend.

And for some reason, she's pretending not to recognize me.

Rina, Thomas's wife, leans forward. "I feel like I've spent months doing different tastings with different chefs, and nothing's felt right for the summer. But your food tonight was delectable. I'd love to talk more about you being our chef this summer if you're up for it."

I frown, my finger tracing my top lip as Lucy's face breaks into a wide smile.

"Really?" Lucy questions, her voice full of doubt. Her fingers fiddle with the bow tied around her waist that's holding her apron in place.

Both Thomas and Rina nod. "Of course. Maybe I could get your number from Laurent, and we could set up a meeting?"

I watch the interaction, unable to stifle my curiosity about what brought her to the Hamptons and how long she's been working as a private chef. I haven't seen her since Ollie broke up with her. I don't remember the exact reason why he ended things, but it was right after that he started dating Sophia, who he's still with today.

I've always had the suspicion he cheated on Lucy, but I'm not confident about that. Just how quickly he moved on was odd. I still don't understand how he could choose someone like Sophia over Lucy. Our family loved Lucy the few times Ollie brought her home; it's been years, and my family *still* isn't sure about Sophia.

Lucy was easy to like. Even though I'd only met her a handful of times in the year she dated Ollie, I liked her. Who my family was didn't seem to matter to her at all, and that doesn't happen often. I'll never forget coming inside after taking a phone call and finding her casually talking business with my father at the kitchen counter. Sophia can't be bothered to have a conversation with any of us at any family gathering. My eavesdropping on the conversation between my dad and Lucy years ago is the only reason I remember her major being business. She'd told my dad all about how she was set to help her family business one day.

That's why it's such a shock to see her here cooking instead.

What's more of a shock is the fact that she's acting like she has no idea who I am. We met enough times that there's no way she wouldn't recognize me this closeup.

"Callahan?" Laurent's stern voice as he practically barks my name pulls me from my thoughts. I lift an eyebrow as I slowly drag my gaze to focus on him, unamused that he thinks he can talk to me in that tone.

"Do the two of you know each other?" Laurent asks, but I'm still too stuck on the brash way he spoke to me to even bother with giving him an answer. No one talks to me like that. I could buy his company out from under him, and it wouldn't even make a dent in my accounts.

"No," Lucy answers.

A corner of my mouth lifts as I look in her direction. I cock my head to the side. Oh, this is a fun twist. *Why is she lying?*

Ida taps her nails against the wood table in curiosity. "Then how did you know her name, Cal?"

My back straightens as I turn to face her. "It's Callahan," I say coolly. "And I guess you could say it was just a lucky guess."

I look back at Lucy, finding her wide eyes pinned on me. I'm not sure why she looks so confused by me playing along with her little lie. She started it.

"The meal was superb," I continue, picking up my bourbon and taking a drink. Laurent is cheap and doesn't stock the good stuff, so I try to hold back a grimace as I swallow it down. I manage another sip before I pull the glass from my lips and hold it in front of me. I stare at the amber liquid, twirling the glass in my fingers. "It *was* Lucy, correct?" I ask, suddenly finding myself enjoying this dinner party after all.

She twists her hands in front of her. "Yes. Lucy. And thank you."

I watch her for a moment, the rest of the room seeming to fade away as I focus on her. She looks so much older now, a far cry from the college freshman she was the last time I saw her.

I bring my glass to my lips and take a slow drink, deciding what I want to say next. For some reason, Lucy pretending she has no idea who I am has woken up something deep inside me. She's amusing me, and I'm not amused often.

Whatever game she wants to play, I'll play along, and I'll play it better.

"Now that you've been introduced, you're dismissed." Laurent waves his hand through the air dismissively.

Rina gasps, clearly taken aback by his sudden harshness toward Lucy.

I clench my jaw at his disrespectful tone. I knew he was an asshole, but before tonight, I didn't know how much it bled into how he treated the people who work for him. The way he's treated his staff during the party makes me want to never speak to the man again. It'd take one simple phone call and I could ruin the decades' worth of work his family put into their commercial real estate business.

"Actually, stay a minute, Lucy." I don't bother trying to hide the blooming smirk on my lips.

"Mind your place," Laurent hisses. He looks at me, red in the face, clearly not happy with the way I ignored his request.

Do I care? Not in the slightest.

The only reason I came tonight was because I thought it'd be great to speak with Thomas more. Hastings Inc. works hand in hand with the Boucher family. We handle all of their stocks, and I'll admit, I even like Thomas. Next time, I'll just invite him to my house and forgo having anything to do with Laurent.

"I'm talking to you, son," Laurent spits.

Despite the numerous people seated around Laurent's dining room table, the entire room is so quiet you could hear a pin drop.

A rough laugh comes from deep in my chest. If Laurent actually thinks he can speak to me this way, he's in for a big surprise.

"*Laurent, Laurent, Laurent.*" I click my tongue. What a disappointing man he is.

"It's time you go," he all but barks. I raise my eyebrows, thinking he's speaking to me. He isn't. His eyes are narrowed angrily but at Lucy, not me.

The nasty look he aims in her direction doesn't sit well with me. Rage bubbles inside my chest as I adjust my position in the dining chair. "Don't talk to her that way," I growl. My jaw locks, and my teeth angrily grind against each other as I see nothing but red.

Thomas coughs nervously into his hand, clearly trying to ease the awkwardness in the room. I don't pay him any attention. I can't look anywhere but at the pathetic excuse of a man that is Laurent Hughes.

"Excuse me?" Laurent roars. His face is beet red, and spit

flies from his mouth with every angry word he forces out. "What did you just say to me?"

I cock my head to the side, attempting to keep my temper at bay. He isn't worth getting worked up over. "I thought I spoke pretty clearly. You've spent the entire night berating your own staff, and quite honestly, I'm sick of it. So let me say this nice and slow for you. Do. Not. Talk. To. Her. That. Way." My words remain calm and composed, but they have the effect I want them to. There's venom laced in every word, and the way Laurent's eyes get wider with each one tells me they're hitting home.

I pick up my bourbon to take a drink but decide against it at the last minute. I'll wait and have the good shit when I make it back to my house. With a loud sigh, I push the glass in front of me and meet Laurent's gaze.

"I don't want to waste my breath arguing with you any longer. Don't be a dick. Treat your staff with decency, and maybe, for once, you'll be respected." I laugh. "Although, after spending the evening here and seeing how you treat others, I don't see you ever earning anyone's respect. But *anyway...*"

My eyes move from Laurent, and I focus once again on Lucy.

Meeting her tonight would've been something I didn't think much about if I hadn't been so impressed by the meal she cooked...and if she hadn't pretended not to know me. But both of those factors combined make me want to know more about the woman I thought I'd never see again.

She watches me carefully, her lips slightly parted and her chest falling with her quick breathing. The look on her face gives nothing away about what's going through her mind right now. It bothers me that I can't figure her out. I normally have an excellent read on others, but she's unreadable to me.

"Lucy, could we please have the dessert? I'm *dying* to know what you so kindly prepared for us this evening." I keep my tone polite, not wanting to let my anger with Laurent bleed into how I speak to her.

She smiles, her shoulders seeming to sag with relief that she's been given an out to get away from this interaction. "It'll be my pleasure," she hurriedly answers before spinning on her heel and retreating to the kitchen.

I don't blame her for wanting to get far away from the awkward tension in the room. Laurent places his balled-up fists on the table. He scowls, opening his mouth to no doubt scold me for what's transpired in the last few minutes.

I hold up my hand to stop him. "Save it. Quite frankly, I don't give a fuck what you're about to say. Hold your tongue, or I'll hold all the stock for Hughes Enterprise in my hands by Monday morning."

His mouth snaps shut, and to my surprise, he actually listens.

I grin, letting my eyes travel over the people seated around the table.

I lift my eyebrows and coolly sit back in my chair, pretending nothing has happened after all. "The host is certainly lacking, but the meal has been fabulous. Anyone else agree?"

It's quiet for a moment as everyone awkwardly looks around the table. Eventually, Thomas lets out a deep laugh. "Damn, I love summer in the Hamptons. There's truly never a dull moment."

I nod. My eyes wander to the doorway where Lucy disappeared. Thomas has a point. There's never a dull moment when spending the summer here.

And it just got a whole lot more interesting with Lucy now here.

Three
LUCY

I'm delicately balancing a tub of cooking utensils and my bag with additional supplies while I walk out to my car when a shadow pushing off the side of Laurent Hughes's house takes me by surprise.

I stifle a scream. "Oh my God." I take a deep breath, trying to calm my racing heart. If my hands weren't full, I think my fist would've connected with a face out of sheer panic and surprise.

"Need a hand?" Callahan asks, already taking the tub from my grasp before I can even respond.

"I've got it," I snap, trying to pull it back against my body.

What's worse is he doesn't even apologize for coming out of nowhere and scaring me. He lets out a low sound of amusement as he effortlessly tugs my things out of my hands completely.

"Callahan!" I yell, watching him walk down the driveway, acknowledging nothing I said to him. "Give me my stuff back."

"Which one is yours?" he calls over his shoulder, pointing to the cars parked neatly up the driveway.

Annoyed he's ignoring what I'm saying, I stop. My hands find my hips as I wait for him to realize I'm no longer trailing behind him. It gives me the chance to take a few calming breaths. My heart still races in my chest from the way he took me by surprise.

It takes him a few more seconds, but eventually, he glances over his shoulder. He sighs as he stops and turns around. "Lucy? Which one's your car?" he asks, his tone firmer this time.

I take a moment to look at the man in front of me. His hair is so dark it almost looks black. He's over a head taller than me, with broad shoulders and a narrow waist. He wears a white, crisp button-down and a navy sport coat with a pair of chinos. Every item of clothing he wears is perfectly tailored to his body. The light from the moon catches on the expensive gold watch on his wrist. Everything about him screams wealth.

He looks good. But no matter how good he looks, right now, he's getting on my last nerve. I'm tired, my feet hurt, and the last thing I want to be doing is dealing with Callahan.

I let out a slow sigh, trying to pull my gaze away from the frustrating man in front of me.

It's been years since I last saw Callahan Hastings.

Well, sort of.

Sometimes late at night, I'd look up the Hastings family to see what they were up to. Not because I missed Callahan's brother, Oliver, who also happens to be my ex-boyfriend. Our year together was fun, but there's something about your ex breaking up with you and immediately dating who you thought was your best friend that quickly makes you fall out of love with someone.

Or realize that you were never really in love with them at all.

But naturally, I'm a curious person. It isn't a sin to google your ex after a breakup. Everyone does it. It's a right of girlhood.

And sometimes...I'd stumble upon pictures of Callahan.

Sometimes I couldn't help but be more interested in what he was doing than what Oliver was doing. Oliver didn't speak much about his older brother. Callahan seemed like some mythical creature in the year Oliver and I were together. Even at family functions, my ex-boyfriend did everything he could to not be in the same room as his brother.

Which only made me want to know more about the mystery that was Callahan Hastings.

Time has been kind to him. He looks even better in person than any photo I could find of him online. Seeing him seated at Laurent's dining table tonight was something I didn't expect. Finding him still here long after the dinner ended is even more surprising.

"Were you waiting for me?" I ask before I can stop myself. The thought just occurred to me.

Callahan's lip turns up in the cockiest of smirks. "Yes." One word. So simple, yet for some reason, it sends a shiver down my spine.

"Why?" The night feels way too quiet as my question lingers in the space between us. Can he hear my racing heart? I blame it on the fact I'm still recovering from him taking me by surprise in the dark. My heart *definitely* doesn't beat erratically because I'm standing alone in the dark with Callahan Hastings.

He adjusts his grip on the tub, reminding me he's still waiting for me to tell him which car is mine. The cocky smirk on his lips disappears before he opens his mouth to speak. "Because I felt like it. Now, which one is your car? Don't make me ask again."

My cheeks heat at the commanding tone of his voice.

Because I felt like it.

I try not to read too much into his answer. Instead, I point to my parked car. "Right there."

A slow laugh rumbles deep in his chest. "I like the baby blue."

I can't help but smile, following him to my car. "I wish I could say it's mine, but I'm only renting it for the summer. A little treat to myself before I have to return home."

Callahan balances my work supplies in one hand as he opens the trunk. I try to rush and close the distance between us to help him, but he beats me to it. Instead, I just end up standing too close to him as he slides my items into the back.

I'm immediately hit by the smell of him. Bergamot and sandalwood. It's incredibly masculine and makes me want to inhale deeply and bask in the richness of his scent.

"It was a surprise to see you here tonight." Callahan's deep voice breaks me from analyzing what other notes I'm getting from his cologne.

I let out a nervous laugh before taking a step back. Now that my supplies are safely tucked in the back of the Bronco, it doesn't seem necessary to stand so close to him. "Yeah. You were the last person I expected to see tonight."

His head cocks to the side. "Did Ollie not tell you we summered in the Hamptons?"

My teeth dig into my bottom lip as I try to decide how honest I want to be with him. "It seems there were a *lot* of things Oliver didn't tell me."

Like the only reason he ever talked to me in the dorm dining hall was not because he was interested in me...but because he wanted to talk to Sophia. She didn't give him the time of day, and I did. He dated me because I was convenient. The entire time, he was still interested in Sophia.

Callahan stares at me for a moment, his dark eyebrows drawn in. I fidget underneath his intense gaze. I wish I knew what was going through his mind. Does he think it's pathetic that I dated his brother for an entire year and feel like I barely knew him at all?

"Are you looking for a full-time position for the summer?"

I blink, trying to catch up with his total change of subject. *"What?"* I figured he was going to ask me another question about Oliver or even stick up for his brother, but instead, he took me by surprise with his line of questioning.

"Do you prefer splitting your time between Pembroke and dinner parties, or are you looking for something more stable this summer? Like what Thomas and Rina were asking?"

I think about his question for a moment before answering. "I'd prefer not to split my time if I didn't have to. Cooking is what I want to do this summer. Waiting tables at the club is just a way for me to make a nice paycheck."

"What if you could make a better paycheck doing more private chef work? And it'd be more stable? Would you want that?"

I nod slowly, wondering why he cares so much. Thomas gave me his card before they left the dinner party, so there's a chance I'll be able to do a test cook for them and see if it'd be a good fit. I'm hopeful they were serious about wanting to hire someone for the summer, but I can't be sure. I don't want to get too excited about the prospect and get disappointed in the end.

"The entire reason I came to the Hamptons was to get a more permanent position." I laugh, pushing stray pieces of my hair out of my face. "Well, as permanent as something can be when I only have a summer left here."

Callahan is quiet for a moment, his eyes scanning my face. The intensity of his gaze makes me shift on the balls of my feet. What is he thinking, and why does he have to be so intense about it?

I don't know how long we stand there quietly when he

finally clears his throat and keeps his striking blue eyes pinned on me.

"Become my private chef for the summer." His words don't even come out as a question. They come out like a demand, as if he's already decided on my answer without my input. Maybe that's normal for him. It's possible he's used to always getting what he wants. He's going to quickly find out that it won't work with me.

"What?" I ask, trying to read his features to see if he's joking. He doesn't seem like the joking type with his rigid posture and brooding stare. "No," I add, shaking my head. The idea of working for him is crazy. "Absolutely not."

Four
CAL

I blink a few times, trying to replay Lucy's response back in my head. I analyze every one of her words, trying to figure out if I heard her wrong. "What do you mean, no?"

She crosses her arms across her chest. "It's a pretty easy word to understand. I mean *no*. Not happening. Absolutely not."

I frown, wondering why her immediate answer to my proposition is no. She just told me that becoming a private chef for the summer is exactly what she wants.

My jaw clenches as I try to figure out how to respond. People rarely tell me no, and because of that, her immediate denial hits harder than I care to admit. "Did you not just say you'd rather be a private chef for the summer over working at Pembroke?"

She looks at the ground, making me wonder if this conversation is making her uncomfortable. Her next words are directed toward the driveway as she answers my question. "I said that, but I thought you were asking about your friend Thomas. Not about *you*. I can't work for you."

"Why?"

She lets out a nervous laugh as she buys herself more time

to answer by closing the back of her Bronco and stepping even further away from me. Her wide brown eyes look at me as she shakes her head at me in disbelief. I stare right back at her, waiting for her answer. I didn't think hiring her on as a private chef is as crazy as she's making it out to be.

"There are tons of reasons I can't work for you," she finally answers. It's another moment where I can't get a good read on her. I can't tell if she's just surprised by my offer or if she's upset by it. With anyone else, I'd be able to tell. I'd know how to proceed because I'd have a good idea of where their head's at.

But with Lucy, it seems like I'll have to work harder than I thought. Her immediate no comes as a surprise, one I hadn't quite prepared for.

I run my hand over my mouth, trying not to let my frustration with the situation show. I thought she'd jump at the opportunity to work for someone somewhat familiar. She knows me—kind of—and doesn't know Thomas or his wife at all. If given the choice, I was confident she'd choose to work for me instead.

"And what are those reasons, Lucy?" I ask, my lips pressing into a thin line. My entire body feels tight as I wait for her to answer. This isn't going how I thought it would. I thought I'd offer her the job, she'd excitedly accept, and we'd spend the rest of our time tonight ironing out when exactly she could start.

Lucy's mouth opens and shuts a few times, as if she didn't expect me to ask for her reasons for saying no. "You're Oliver's brother."

"So?"

"I can't work for my ex-boyfriend's older brother. There must be some kind of rule against that somewhere."

I laugh, holding my tongue about telling her I don't think Oliver would care at all. The eleven-year age gap between me and my brother made it so we were never close. Who I employ is none of his business. And even if it was his business, he still wouldn't care.

"That's a terrible reason."

Her head rears back defensively. "No, it isn't. It's inappropriate."

My lips twitch in amusement as I tuck my hands into my pockets. Why do I find her so interesting? With anyone else, I wouldn't waste my breath trying to convince them to work for me. Matter of fact, anyone else would *jump* at the opportunity to work for me in any capacity. I don't need to be wasting my time with someone who clearly isn't interested.

Yet here I am, determined to get her to change her mind. She's told me no, which has backfired because now I'll do just about anything to get her to say yes. "I wasn't aware that asking you to prepare meals for me was inappropriate."

She rolls her eyes. "You know what I mean, Callahan. It doesn't feel right."

If it didn't feel right, I wouldn't be so insistent on convincing her to work for me. Unfortunately for me, the moment Thomas asked her to be his private chef for the summer, I wanted her to work for *me* instead. If she was going to be anyone's private chef this summer, she was going to be mine.

I wish I could explain why I feel this way, but I can't. It's incredibly frustrating because this never happens. It's a foreign thing to me. I hold my tongue from admitting to her that to me...it *does* feel right.

What doesn't feel right is having her call me by my full name. It feels too formal...too impersonal.

"Call me Cal."

She tucks a piece of her dark hair behind her ear. "You said at dinner to call you Callahan."

"I didn't say that to you. *You* can call me Cal."

It's taken forever, but I finally get a smile out of her. Her shoulders relax a little as she slowly lets out a deep breath. "It feels more professional to call you Callahan."

I rub my lips together to hide my own smile. "And why would things have to be professional if you aren't accepting my offer? Seriously. Call me Cal. Please."

She raises a dark eyebrow. "How'd that word roll off your tongue? Did it feel weird?"

I cock my head to the side, eyes roaming over her soft features. "Did what feel weird? My name?"

She laughs, and for some reason, I love the sound of it. Strands of her hair fall into her face as she shakes her head. "No. *Please.* You don't strike me as the kind of man who uses the word a lot."

I place my hand on my chest, feigning hurt. "Lucy, are you saying I don't have manners?"

She takes a step forward as she rolls her eyes. "Are you saying you *do* have manners?"

I'm quiet for a few heartbeats as I just stare at her. People don't take me by surprise often, yet here she is, continually saying things I don't expect. "I'm a little disappointed you think so low of me, Lucy," I begin, taking a step toward her.

I halfway expect her to match my step with her own step back, but she doesn't. She stays where she's at, allowing me to bring our bodies closer. Her eyes dart to the space between us before meeting mine again. I don't know why, but I'm drawn to her. I want to get as close to her as possible to talk without infringing on her personal space.

She lets out a sigh of resignation. "I don't think low of you. It's just that you give off this vibe that you don't have to have manners. People just do what you want before you even have to think of being polite."

Her words hang in the air for a moment as I stay quiet, too

busy trying to figure her out. She clearly thinks she's got me figured out perfectly, and it bothers me that the more I stand here and talk to her, it seems the less I have her figured out.

"Plus, it's obvious you don't care what people think of you. Don't try to pretend that even if I thought low of you, which I don't, you'd even bat an eye."

I play with the clasp of my watch, my eyes narrowed on her. Do I admit to her that she's right? I don't typically worry about what other people think of me, but tonight, with her, for some reason, I care. "Seems like you don't have me completely figured out. I do care about what *you* think."

Her nose scrunches as she looks at me in disbelief. "Why?"

I laugh, the sound of it vibrating my chest. "I keep asking myself the same thing."

A breeze dances between us as we stare at one another, neither one of us saying anything. Seeing her again tonight was a surprise but a welcome one. I can't explain why I want her to work for me so badly other than she's a phenomenal chef...and I'm intrigued by her.

There's something about her that makes me want to know more. What else will she call me out for? What witty remarks will come out of her mouth?

No one tells me no. The wealth and allure of my name get me anything I want. Yet Lucy seems to want nothing to do with me.

My determination to get her to agree to the job offer might also have something to do with the fact that I've been reunited with her again. For an inexplicable reason, I'm interested to know what the last five years have been like for her.

"Give me your phone." I reach my hand out.

She stares at my open hand. "Don't you have a phone?"

I shift on my feet as I try to stifle an annoyed sigh. "Obviously, I have a phone. I want yours."

"Why do you need mine if you have one?"

"So I can put my number in it."

"I dated your brother. You shouldn't be asking for my number."

I smirk. "I'm not asking you for your number. I'm giving you mine. I'll pay double whatever Thomas and Rina offer you. Once you think about it a little longer, you'll realize you'd be stupid to not take mine." I wiggle my fingers to remind her I need her phone.

She lets out a dramatic sigh, but she does pull out her phone and unlock it before placing it in my hand. She keeps hers on top of it for a moment, our fingertips just barely brushing.

I move first, shocked by the electricity I feel at the small connection of our skin. I pull my hand back and pull up her contacts. "Good girl," I whisper, the words taking me by surprise. Luckily, it seems like the praise came out low enough that she didn't hear me.

She's quiet as she waits for me to type my number in. I hand it back to her when I'm done, holding it in the air between us with my thumb and pointer finger. She takes it and tucks it into her pocket, her eyes never leaving mine.

"It was nice to see you tonight, Lucy," I tell her, tucking my hands in my pockets. I step away from her car, allowing her room to go to the driver's side.

"Goodnight, Callahan."

I click my tongue. "What'd I say about calling me that?"

"You told me you prefer Cal. Doesn't mean I have to listen."

I shake my head, unable to hide the blooming smile on my lips. "I really hope you change your mind about the job offer, Lucy." I resist the urge to tell her she *will* be changing her mind about it. I'll make sure of it.

Any hope I have that she'll make it easy on me and change her mind tonight leaves me when she gives me a polite smile and whispers, "Goodnight, Cal."

I stand in place, watching her get in the Bronco and drive away, wanting to make sure she makes it out of the driveway safely. I don't move until after her headlights disappear down the road.

As I walk to my car, I hope that it's only a matter of time until I hear from her again.

If I don't, I'm not afraid of taking matters into my own hands.

Five

LUCY

"So, are you going to tell me how your test cook went with the Bouchers, or am I just supposed to be left wondering all day?" Charlotte, my closest coworker and best friend, asks, resting her elbows on the bar and looking around the empty club restaurant.

I meet her eyes, lifting my shoulders in a shrug. "They offered me a position for the summer, so I think it went okay."

Charlotte lets out a loud squeal as she pushes her body off the bar and runs to me. "What? We're two hours into our shift, and you're just now telling me this?" She grabs my shoulders and gives me a shake. "Well, get on with it. Did you accept?" She pauses for a moment, her bottom lip jutting out in a pout. "Does that mean you'll be leaving me?"

I laugh before shaking my head and softly pushing her off me. Luckily, our boss, Loretta, is nowhere to be seen. If she saw us acting anything but prim and proper, she'd be threatening our jobs.

"I haven't accepted the job yet. I still have to think about it."

Charlotte narrows her eyes as she scans over my face. Her

fingers twist in the long strands of her ponytail as she processes my response. "What do you have to think about?"

I bite my lip, thinking of Cal's offer from a week ago. "It's just a big decision. If I take the job with them, I have to cut my hours here at Pembroke Grill. They want me Wednesday mornings to Sunday afternoons. Who knows if Loretta will even let me go that part-time or if she'll make me quit."

Charlotte waves her hand through the air dismissively. "Loretta has a terrible way of showing it, but she loves you. She'll let you work whatever hours you want. You have to take the job, Lucy."

My eyes scan the restaurant, making sure no one's been seated in the time Charlotte and I have been lost in our own conversation. This afternoon has been rather slow because the weather outside is so beautiful, but it'll get busy the moment people finish their rounds of golf. Until then, I'm left with a bit of downtime to talk with Charlotte.

"I think I'm just nervous," I answer honestly, focusing on neatly folding a crisp green napkin in case Loretta walks in.

I keep it to myself that something inside me is still considering Cal's offer. Part of me feels bad for even thinking about it. It doesn't quite feel right to accept a job from my ex-boyfriend's brother, but the other part of me feels silly for feeling that way. Cal is just asking me to cook for him, not marry him.

Yet, something has still stopped me from texting him for the last week. I've typed something out every single night but always end up deleting it. I can't explain why I can't just say yes to him, but I need to make up my mind soon. Part of me wonders if it's less about Cal being Oliver's brother and more about me feeling the need to tell Cal no. The shock on his face was evident when I denied his job offer. It's obvious he's not used to it. It'd be good for him to hear it every once in a while.

Plus, something about the conversation outside Laurent's

house felt different. I'm not normally one to get sassy or really argue with anyone, but Cal pushed my buttons enough that I couldn't help it with him.

Maybe working for him would be a bad idea regardless of who he's related to. If he can get on my nerves like that in one night, I can't imagine what would happen over an entire summer.

I sigh, wondering why I'm thinking so hard about it. The job with Cal might not even be on the table anymore since I've taken so long to get back to him.

And the Bouchers want me to make a decision by the end of the weekend, leaving me only two more days to decide what the hell I'm going to do for the rest of the summer.

"That might be the most neatly folded napkin ever," Charlotte comments, breaking me from my thoughts.

I jump, looking up to meet her eyes. A nervous laugh escapes me. "I got a little deep in thought."

Charlotte tosses her blonde ponytail over her shoulder. Her eyes soften as she pins her full attention on me. "I gathered. Tell me where your head's at. What's stopping you?"

I sigh, chewing anxiously on my lip for a moment. Charlotte has become my best friend. We started here at Pembroke at the same time and immediately clicked on the first day. I should be honest with her and tell her about Cal's offer. Maybe she'll be able to talk it over with me and help me make a decision.

I'm about to tell her when the familiar sound of Loretta's heels stops me from continuing the conversation.

"Lucy!" Loretta's tone is hushed but serious. It makes my spine straighten as I spin to face her.

"Yes?" I ask nervously. I smooth out the pleats of my skirt, hoping there aren't any wrinkles in my uniform. Loretta takes the dress code very seriously.

"You've been requested at table eight."

I look over my shoulder to see table eight, but it's out of view from where we stand at the end of the bar. "Table eight? Isn't that Charlotte's section today?"

Loretta gives me a tight smile. "The patrons at table eight have requested you. You'll take it today." Her words come out strained, but her tone leaves no room for discussion.

I nod, running my fingers through my hair to smooth it out. I have no idea who's requesting me, but I know if I don't show up looking fully put together, Loretta will have my job. I've seen her fire people for less. And with my inability to commit to either one of my other job offers, I might need to keep hold of this gig. "Yes, Loretta."

Charlotte gives me a reassuring smile. Luckily, it doesn't seem like it hurt her feelings to have someone from her section request me.

"Well, get going," Loretta scolds, giving me a curt nod and shooing me away.

I shuffle away from them, still trying to make sure my hair is tamed. I hurriedly make sure my polo is completely tucked into my skirt. If someone is going out of their way to request me as their server, I want to make sure I'm looking my best. I'm busy adjusting the waistband of my skirt when the table comes into view.

Cal's eyes immediately meet mine, and my steps falter for a moment.

I should've known the moment I'd been requested that he was behind it, but for some reason, it hadn't even crossed my mind.

"Lucy!" His voice carries across the empty restaurant. He holds his arms out, gesturing for me to come to the table.

I swallow, closing the distance until I'm standing above Cal and a man I vaguely recognize as a member, though I don't know his name.

"Mr. Hastings." I give both of the men a polite smile, trying not to stare at Cal for too long. It's impossible to not notice how handsome he is. His hair is one shade away from being jet-black, and it's styled to near perfection. An unwelcome thought pops into my mind, wondering what it'd feel like to run my fingers through his perfectly tamed locks. I swallow, trying to push the thought to the *very* back of my mind.

Cal's dark eyebrows raise on his tan forehead. The smug look on his face is infuriating. "So, now I'm Mr. Hastings? You're *really* keeping things professional, aren't you?"

"Hi, I'm Jude," the man sitting next to Cal pipes up. He sits up straighter, holding out his hand for me to shake.

"Lucy," I respond, placing my hand in his. It's a firm hand-shake, but he's gentle. Some men—especially here, where egos are through the roof—squeeze far too hard when shaking hands.

"Lucy, what a *beautiful* name," Jude tells me with a smirk. He emphasizes the word "beautiful" with a mischievous glint in his eye.

I give him a cautious smile, wondering why he keeps looking at Cal out of the corner of his eye with each word he says to me.

Cal rolls his eyes at his friend. "Ignore Jude. He flirts with everyone."

The casual tone of Cal's voice eases some of my nerves at seeing him again. I let my body relax a little as my eyes shift between the two men sitting in front of me.

Cal can only be described as tall, dark, and handsome. He keeps his cards close to his chest, his icy blue eyes almost always narrowed on you like he's trying to figure you out. Jude couldn't be more opposite. He had a smile on his face before I even made it to the table. His brown eyes are warm and inviting, even crinkling at the corners, which makes him appear a little more boyish.

Jude is approachable. Cal is anything but.

Both men stare right at me, one with an expression that gives nothing away and the other with a wide grin. I focus on Jude, plastering a polite smile on my face. "And here I thought the flirting was because I was special."

Jude throws his head back and laughs, the sound filling the quiet restaurant. He playfully elbows Cal. "I like her."

The heat of Cal's gaze on me forces me to meet his eyes. His thumb traces over his bottom lip as he thinks over his friend's comment. Eventually, he smiles, but again, it doesn't reach his eyes. "Good, because you'll be seeing her a lot this summer."

What does he mean by that?

Jude leans forward, rubbing his palms together in his lap. "I can't wait, Lucy. You work a lot of shifts here?"

I'm about to answer him when Cal clears his throat. "That's not what I meant. You'll be seeing a lot of her because she's my new private chef."

My jaw drops as my head snaps in his direction. "What?" I ask in disbelief. I haven't given him any indication I was going to accept his offer. In fact, the last time I saw him, I'd adamantly denied the offer of working for him for the summer.

"What happened to Randall?" Jude asks, his eyebrows furrowed in confusion.

Cal ignores Jude completely. He keeps his focus on me instead, his head cocked to the side and his eyebrows raised as if he's just waiting for me to argue with him.

A strangled sound leaves my throat as I scratch at the back of my neck. "I'm actually not his private chef," I explain to Jude, even though I can't pull my gaze away from Cal.

Cal's smile widens, showing off his perfect set of white teeth. "*Yet.* I'm here today to convince you."

I roll my eyes at his confidence. I'm sure he's used to getting everything he wants. Even though I know the best thing for me from a financial standpoint is to accept his offer, I want to continue to tell him no just so he gets the taste of being denied for once.

"It's a waste of breath," I finally reply.

Cal shakes his head. "Accept my offer, Lucy."

"No."

Jude lets out a low whistle. "This meal is about to be far more interesting than the nine holes we just played."

Six
CAL

I hadn't heard from Lucy in almost a week, something that bothered me more than I thought it would. I thought if I left her alone, she'd change her mind about the job offer.

I thought that she'd come to the right conclusion and come to work for me.

Apparently, she isn't in the mood to make the right choice.

Jude excitedly looks between Lucy and me, clearly having the time of his life with his front-row seat to the disagreement between us.

I sigh, pinching the bridge of my nose between my thumb and pointer finger. "I don't understand why you won't accept my offer. It's exactly what you want and is the logical choice."

Lucy plasters on a fake smile. I don't miss how her eyes soften slightly when she looks at a snickering Jude. A pang of annoyance runs through me at the way she glances at him. Maybe I shouldn't have forced Jude to tag along with me to convince her.

I bet if it was Jude offering her the job, she'd accept immediately.

I brush the irritating thought away when her eyes meet mine again, they're narrowed and full of defiance. She lets out a long sigh, not bothering to hide her annoyance with me. "You don't have to understand, Mr. Hastings. It's *my* decision, after all."

Even though her words are frustrating, I can't help but smirk. Her stubbornness is frustratingly endearing. Unfortunately for her, the more she refuses the job, the more I want to convince her to accept it.

"What drinks can I get started for you two?" Lucy changes the subject effortlessly, making the tone of her voice sickeningly sweet as she focuses her attention on Jude.

The bastard eats it up. I know the moment she leaves our table, he's going to hound me to know more. "Oh, I'll just take water for now. We had our fair share of beer on the course."

Lucy nods, her eyes finding me. "And for you?"

I lean back in my seat as I run my hands down my thighs. This little game with her is far too amusing. "Water for me too, *please*." I emphasize the word, hoping to remind her of our conversation last week.

A choking sound comes from Jude. "Did you just say please?"

My lips twitch as I look at my friend for a moment. "I did. Trying to be more polite so Lucy will accept my offer."

Jude's wide eyes meet Lucy's. "Cal's been my best friend since boarding school. I can't recall a time I've heard him say please. I don't know what's going on here, but you should accept his offer."

Lucy frowns. "Just because someone uses manners for once doesn't mean they can get whatever they want."

Jude lifts a shoulder as he moves his head from side to side in thought. "I see your point, but Cal's very determined. If he's saying please, it's only a matter of time until he'll have you working for him."

Lucy's eyes meet mine as I lift my shoulders and shrug. "I really want you to come work for me, Lucy."

She lets out a disgruntled sigh as she shakes her head. "I'll go grab your waters." She turns to leave, but I can't let her go. Not yet.

Before I can think better of it, I reach out and grab her. My fingers gently wrap around her wrist, applying just enough pressure to get her to stop for a moment. Her skin is soft and warm underneath my touch. I ignore the way the small connection sends a rush of heat through my entire body. "Have you at least considered it?" I ask, needing to know the answer.

Lucy looks at my fingers around her wrist. She stares at where our skin meets for a few moments before she looks up at me.

I'm surprised she doesn't pull out of my grasp. I don't pull away either, wondering why it doesn't feel wrong to feel her skin against mine.

The long strands of her hair glide along her back as she slowly nods and sighs. "Yes. I've thought about it," she finally responds.

A genuine smile takes over my lips. "Good." If she's been thinking about it, it's only a matter of time until she accepts. I'll make sure of it. I drop her wrist and say nothing else, letting her walk away to get our waters.

A few seconds go by before Jude clears his throat. "I must know more about Lucy." I close my eyes for a moment and throw my head back, wishing I'd showed up at Pembroke Grill alone so my best friend didn't bear witness to me practically begging Lucy to accept a job as my chef.

When I open my eyes, I find his gaze pinned on me. His eyebrows are practically to his hairline as he waits for me to respond. I want to avoid his question altogether and instead reach across the table and wipe the shit-eating grin right off his face.

"Lucy's a phenomenal chef, and I want her to prepare my meals for the summer," I reluctantly answer, steepling my fingers underneath my chin. He doesn't need to know how much her telling me no has gotten under my skin. "That's all there is to know."

Jude slowly nods, his lips stretched wide in a grin. "I've always thought Randall was a *great* cook."

"Well, Randall is getting some deserved paid time off."

The problem with having a childhood best friend is they can read you like an open book. I've always taken pride in being able to keep a poker face, especially since in my career, being unreadable is a must. It's key for you to be able to read anyone while you yourself stay completely unreadable. Yet Jude doesn't even have to open his mouth for me to know he sees right through all of my bullshit.

"Tell me the real reason you're hell-bent on getting that cute server to be your private chef."

I grunt, hating the way he called her cute. Cute doesn't even begin to describe her. She's breathtaking, with her big brown eyes that are hard to look away from and her high cheekbones that are pink from the sun.

"Don't talk about her that way," I scold, running my hand over my mouth.

He raises his arms defensively. "Since when do you care if I call someone cute?"

"She's Ollie's ex-girlfriend...and my future chef."

"*Ah.*" Jude's eyebrows pull in on his forehead as he thinks my response over carefully. "You still haven't answered me."

I narrow my eyes at him. He doesn't normally question me about things. Of course, he chooses this instance to analyze something I want.

"Her food is incredible, and Thomas was also impressed. So when he asked if she was looking for something more permanent for the summer, I got the idea that she should be my private chef instead of anyone else's."

"And when you get an idea in your head, there's nothing that stops you."

This makes me smile as relief washes over me. I know him well enough to know that'll be enough explanation for him—at least for now. "Exactly."

He reaches out to clap me on the back. "I'm looking forward to watching this play out. She's not convinced so easily, is she?"

I bark out a laugh. "I gave her my card a week ago and told her I'd pay double whatever Thomas offered. Haven't heard from her all week."

"So that's why you were determined to sit in her section? So you could talk to her again?"

"Yes, I thought after thinking about it for a week, she'd say yes when I asked her again. I was obviously wrong."

Jude runs his hand through the short strands of his light brown hair. "I like her already."

I fall back in my chair with a sigh. I don't tell him I've only had two encounters with her this summer, and I'm right there with him...there's something about her that intrigues me.

Even though I know I probably shouldn't be.

Seven

LUCY

"I'm mad you didn't tell me you knew Callahan Hastings," Charlotte scolds, slamming the door to her locker. Luckily, we're the only two people in the employee locker room, so no one else can hear her.

"I don't know him. Not very well, at least." I look at my reflection in my locker mirror, wiping underneath my eyes from where my mascara has smudged from the long workday.

Charlotte laughs, grabbing the corner of my locker and opening it wide so I'm forced to meet her eyes. "He specifically requested you. Clearly, you know each other. Anytime I've ever served him, he barely looked me in the eye, let alone cared enough to remember my name."

I sigh, my shoulders sagging a bit in defeat. I know if I tell Charlotte that Cal has also offered me a job for the summer, she'll think I'm crazy for not agreeing to it right away. Especially if she finds out how much I've been offered. "Cal's my ex's brother. We met a few times. Got along fine. There's not much to it."

Charlotte's green eyes widen. "Wait, you've never mentioned an ex."

I laugh. "For good reason."

She slowly nods in understanding. "I get it. We all have those asshole exes we prefer not to mention."

"Exactly. Cal's brother isn't even worth discussing."

She raises a blonde eyebrow excitedly. "But Cal *is* worth discussing. So tell me the deets. Why would he request you to be his waitress? Just being his brother's ex doesn't make sense."

I take a seat on the cherrywood bench between the sets of lockers. I'm used to being on my feet for long hours at a time, but the shoes we're required to wear at Pembroke aren't the most comfortable. My feet ache, but I know Charlotte won't let me leave until I tell her more.

"He offered me a job as his private chef."

Her jaw flies open as she hurriedly sits down on the bench in front of me, straddling the bench as her eyes bore into mine. "Callahan Hastings offered you a job as his private chef? When do you start?"

I look down, my fingers playing with the hem of my uniform skirt. "I haven't accepted it yet," I answer quietly. For some reason, saying it out loud that I haven't said yes already does sound a little crazy. Maybe the fact he's my ex's brother isn't a good enough reason to turn down the job. The money he's offered would be enough to help not just me but my family as well.

I keep it to myself that another part of the reason I've told him no is because it seems like he's never been told no. It'd be good for him to be denied for once.

"Why haven't you accepted it?"

I shrug. "It's weird for me to work for my ex's brother, right?"

Charlotte reaches between us and grabs my hands. She gives them a squeeze, a smile spreading across her lips. "No, actually, I think it's weird that you won't take it because of a shitty ex. If Cal's brother isn't even worth your breath to discuss, I don't think he should get in the way of you accepting a once-in-a-lifetime job offer. Not many people can say they worked for *the* Callahan Hastings."

"Thomas Boucher is well-known too," I counter before pulling my lip between my teeth because even I know it's not the same.

Thomas Boucher is well-known in his own right. Anyone who has a membership at Pembroke Country Club is wealthy beyond measure. They've excelled enough in their careers to not only afford what I'm sure is a hefty yearly membership fee at the club but also the notoriety to even be invited to join the club to begin with. You can't just have money to be a member at Pembroke. To be a member, you must also have *power*. People must know your name.

Pembroke's for the best of the best, and Cal is one of its most prestigious members.

Charlotte drops my hand and rolls her eyes. It's clear she thinks I'm crazy for not accepting the offer. *Maybe I am crazy for not considering it more.* "The Bouchers are great," she begins, her voice sweet. "A lovely family, actually. They tip well and are always very kind, but Thomas isn't Callahan. Having Callahan Hastings on your resume could open you up to any job you wanted after this. You want to be a chef for Scarlett Astor? Winnie and Archer Moore? The king? Having a recommendation from Callahan would get you a foot in the door with any of those people."

A laugh escapes me as I shake my head at Charlotte. "Royalty? I'm not so sure about that."

Charlotte tosses her long, blonde hair over her shoulder and shrugs. "Working for Scarlett Astor would be cooler, anyway. Did you know her family are members here? Maybe Callahan knows them."

"The Astors are members here?" I ask in disbelief. Scarlett

Astor is one of the most famous actresses in the world right now. You can't watch a movie or see a brand campaign without seeing her face. The Astors are film royalty. I don't know how I've missed them.

Charlotte nods confidently. "At least that's what I've been told. I've never seen them here, but imagine if they are. You could become a celebrity chef."

I roll my eyes at my friend. She's a big dreamer, and I love that about her. But even if the Astor family were members at Pembroke—which I doubt they are—I'm not looking for another private chef position after this summer. Once fall arrives, I'm on a flight back to Virginia to help with the family business. I'm supposed to take it over from my father. My resume as a private chef won't matter.

"I haven't even taken the job with Cal. Let's not get ahead of ourselves," I respond, my tone a little sad. I wish I could plan for the future I want, but I can't. I'm lucky my family's even given me the time I've had now to live out my dream career.

"As your friend, I can't let you turn down the job. Unless..." She pauses for a moment as she purses her lips. "Is the pay shit? Did he lowball you?"

I laugh at the question before letting out a sigh. "He said he'd pay double what Thomas offered."

She tilts her head to the side. "Then why are we still talking about this?"

My head falls back as I let out a loud whine. "I don't know. Because it still feels like I shouldn't take a job from my ex's brother. What if Oliver visits?"

"Then you poison his food."

My eyes widen. "*Charlotte*," I scold, hitting her on the thigh.

She shrugs, clearly not seeing anything wrong with her

solution. "Don't worry about stupid Oliver. Take the job, Lucy. Or I'm going to take the job for you, and I'm a terrible cook."

I laugh, remembering when we had a movie night, and she almost burned down my tiny apartment just by making a frozen pizza. Mr. Fred, the owner of the shop my apartment is above, came to our rescue in his pajamas with a fire extinguisher. "I'll never forget the one time I let you cook for us."

"I thought the plastic piece under the pizza was supposed to go in *with* the pizza. Sue me."

I shake my head. She can't cook at all, and her sense of humor is a little dark sometimes, but Charlotte is the best of the best. Making friends when you're an adult is hard, especially when in an unfamiliar place. I'm lucky to have found her, and although I won't be poisoning Oliver anytime soon, maybe she's onto something.

Am I overthinking this?

I scrub my hands along my face as I let out a groan. "Am I thinking too much into this? Should I have already said yes?" I wonder if I'm being a little childish by wanting to deny the offer just to tell him no.

Charlotte scoots forward, placing her hands on my shoulders. "Yes, you should've already said yes, but that's beside the point now. It's not too late to say no."

I nod, meeting her green gaze. "What if it is? I accidentally wasn't the politest to him at lunch today..." I cringe a little, remembering how short I was with Cal. I think he left the restaurant still wanting me to take the job with him with the way my responses only made his smirk even wider, but I can't be sure.

Charlotte quickly jumps up and claps her hands. "Up!"

I stay sitting. "Why?"

Charlotte rolls her eyes before grabbing my hand and

pulling me off the bench herself. "It's time for you to go find Cal and tell him you accept!"

"How do you know he's still here?"

"Because where else would he be?" she counters, making it seem like my question was dumb in the first place. She might have a point. Most members spend their entire day here in the summer. They have nothing better to do with their time. Their work is play, and their play is work. And it's all done here at Pembroke.

Before I can respond, the door to the locker room flies open. Charlotte and I both look in that direction, finding a woman in a black pantsuit leaning against the door.

"Don't mind me," the woman says, her palms flat against the wood door as she takes a couple of deep breaths.

I take a step forward in concern. "Are you okay?"

She gives me a tight smile. "I'm fine. Just babysitting and at the end of my rope."

Charlotte and I share a look. Charlotte's the one to speak up. "I love kids, but they can be a handful sometimes."

The woman laughs, pushing pieces of neatly curled, dark hair from her face. "Oh, I wish my problem was a child. Unfortunately, I'm tasked with babysitting a grown man who's currently making me contemplate committing murder."

"Men will do that," Charlotte pipes up.

This time, when the woman smiles, it actually reaches her eyes. "Yes, they will. Especially this one."

"Ditch his ass," Charlotte offers.

I shake my head at her, not bothering to hide my smile at her words. You never know what's going to come out of her mouth. It's one of my favorite things about her. "You can't say that to people you don't know," I scold. This woman clearly isn't a Pembroke employee, but something about her already mentioning wanting to commit murder tells me she won't rat on Charlotte for cursing in front of a member.

"It's fine," the woman gets out with a sigh. "I'm Camille. And *trust me*, I wish I could ditch him. I dream about it every night, but tragically, my job depends on babysitting a self-absorbed asshole who wants to make my life miserable any chance he gets."

"That sounds awful," I remark, feeling bad for her. She looks about my age, maybe a little older. Her stress is evident in the rigid set of her shoulders and the slight wrinkle on her forehead.

"Is he hot, at least?" Charlotte asks, letting out a yelp when I smack her shoulder with the back of my hand.

Camille tucks a piece of her dark hair behind her ear as she lets out a sarcastic laugh. "Unfortunately, yes. And he knows it."

Charlotte lets out a low whistle. "The worst combination."

"You're telling me," Camille responds, pushing herself off the door with a groan. "I've got to get going. I snuck away for a moment while my client talked business with Beckham Sinclair, but I've got to get back to the table before he runs away and I get fired."

"Good luck. If all else fails, give him a nice kick in the balls to keep him in line!" Charlotte says sweetly, twisting a blonde strand of her hair around her finger.

"Nice meeting you, Camille," I say, trying to keep a straight face after Charlotte's comment.

Camille opens the door before tossing one last smile over her shoulder. "I'll be dreaming about giving him a good kick in the balls."

"Are you in there gossiping about my balls?" a deep voice croons from the other side of the door.

Both Charlotte and I lean forward to sneak a peek. Unfortunately for us, the door slams shut before we can see the culprit behind Camille's annoyance.

It's quiet for a moment before Charlotte turns back to me, her eyes roaming over my face and hair. "Back to business. Let's get you cleaned up a little from your shift, and then you're going to go find Callahan and tell him you accept the job."

I nod, anxious butterflies taking flight in my stomach. Is that my final decision? Am I going to accept? Charlotte fusses with smoothing out my hair as I try to convince myself it still isn't a good idea to accept it.

But I can't convince myself it's the wrong decision. I think down the road, I'd be upset with myself if I turned down this opportunity.

"Purse your lips," Charlotte demands, holding up a tube of lip gloss.

I laugh. "I'm saying yes to a job, not asking him on a date. Is lip gloss necessary?"

She scoffs. "It's always necessary. Now, listen to me so you can get on with taking your dream position this summer."

I do as I'm told, allowing Charlotte to fuss over me as I muster up the courage to find Cal and tell him I accept.

Eight
CAL

I take one final drink of my bourbon before setting it on the table. "I should probably get going," I tell the men gathered around the table.

"Stay a little longer," Jude counters, taking a puff of his cigar.

I shake my head before standing up. "Can't tonight. Try not to get into too much trouble without me."

Jude laughs. "Can't make any promises."

Beckham Sinclair, someone I've gotten closer to in the last year, leans forward and places his hand on Jude's shoulder. "Don't worry, Cal, I'll keep an eye on him."

"He needs it." I love Jude. I'm closer to him than I am my own brother. He works hard and is damn good at what he does, but he enjoys having fun—sometimes a little too much. Unless he's sitting in a board meeting, he isn't taking life too seriously.

Jude smiles as he shakes his head. He pretends to be offended by my words, but the forced frown doesn't linger on his lips for very long. "I'm not stupid. I don't need anyone babysitting me. Not like hotshot Ryker over here." Jude lifts an eyebrow, staring right at our friend Ryker, daring him to respond.

"Oh, fuck you," Ryker responds, glaring across the room where his so-called "babysitter" is watching him from the bar. "My dad will stop being an asshole any day now, and I'll ditch her."

Ryker is known to be more reckless than Jude. He's made one too many bad decisions recently, which has reflected poorly on the Davenport empire. His dad hired Camille's father's PR firm to help clean up after the mess Ryker's made. As his publicist, Camille has been assigned to spend the summer with Ryker to ensure he doesn't make any more of a mess. Ryker is less than thrilled with the setup.

I turn from the table and walk away while they continue their conversation, otherwise I'd be here all night. Jude and Ryker are very similar. They would argue for hours about which one of them needs to be babysat.

I keep my head down as I walk the halls of Pembroke to the front entrance. Leaving the club can take an hour sometimes because of the number of people you run into. Everyone wants to stop and talk business, disguising it as shooting the shit. Typically, I tolerate it, but right now, all I want to do is get home.

The fact that Lucy still hasn't accepted my offer is bothering me. It's eating away at me more than it should. I offered her double what Thomas did. I gave her an unlimited budget for kitchen supplies and ingredients. I tracked her down at her job to try and convince her again that the best choice for her is to work for me. Nothing has worked, and I can't move past it. I'm stewing over her refusal to just accept my offer and coming up with another plan to make her say yes when I hear my name being called.

The front entryway to Pembroke is bustling with members. I look up and follow the sound of the voice, meeting the eyes of the woman who's been on my mind for the last week. Lucy gives me a timid smile. She anxiously twists her hands in front of her. "Can I talk to you?"

I cock my head to the side, wondering why she looks so nervous. "Sure."

"Okay." She looks down at her feet for a moment. "Do you have time? We could go for a quick walk?"

I nod, too interested in why she sought me out to refuse her. "You have my attention." My hand hovers over the small of her back as I guide her toward the door. "After you."

Lucy doesn't hesitate. She turns and walks out the front entrance. It's a lot busier now than it was when Jude and I first showed up earlier this afternoon. I ignore the curious gazes from familiar faces as I fall into step next to Lucy.

"Have you filled the private chef position yet?" she asks, her eyes trained ahead.

"You mean, have I filled it in the few hours since I last saw you?"

"Yeah."

It's quiet for a moment as we walk along the wide sidewalk of the country club grounds. To our right is the golf pro shop and the start of the course, where golf carts are neatly lined up. We head in that direction, following the path that'll eventually take us to the back of the club and the private beach.

"No, I haven't filled the position yet," I tell her, trying to keep my eyes pinned ahead instead of staring at her.

"You haven't?"

My heart picks up speed by the smallest amount at the excitement in her voice. Maybe she's rethinking her decision.

"Playing this cat-and-mouse game has been far too entertaining for me to give up that easily."

"Okay," she mutters, her hands still twisting nervously in front of her with each step she takes.

We pass the spa, neither one of us paying attention to the people walking past us.

"I'm assuming you tracking me down means you've changed your mind." My words come out more as a statement than a question. I can tell that I've finally won. I just need to hear it from her.

Lucy stops and turns her body to face me. "I'm more open to accepting the position now than I was when you first offered it, that's for sure."

I can't help but let a corner of my lip lift. I tuck my hands in my pockets, resisting the surprising urge to reach between us and tuck the strand of her hair that sticks to her freshly glossed lips behind her ear. I don't know why I feel the need to find some kind of physical connection to her, but I know it's best I don't act on it right now. I need to focus on getting her to finally agree to the job.

I fight a smile, thinking it's kind of cute that she's trying to pretend she doesn't want the job when I know she wouldn't have taken the time to track me down if she wasn't planning on taking it.

"More open?" I press. "What do you still need convincing of?"

Lucy sighs. She nervously twists a strand of her hair around her fingertip as her eyes dart around. "I need to know more details. What are the days? You said the pay would be double what Mr. Boucher offered, but you don't even know what he offered. What if double is too much for you to pay?"

The smirk falls from my face. I push my shoulders back and cock my head to the side. I try not to be offended that she thinks any number would be too much for me to pay. "Name any price and it's yours, Lucy. I assure you, I can afford it."

She pulls her bottom lip between her teeth as she mulls

over my words. A few moments pass before her brown eyes lock with mine again. "What days would you need me?"

"I'd love five days a week. The days might shift a little depending on the week. Sometimes I host parties, sometimes I don't. But no matter what, you will get two days a week off. I want to make sure of that."

She nervously wipes her palms along the pleats of her skirt. My gaze lingers for a moment longer than it should where the skirt ends, revealing the sun-kissed skin of her thighs. I swallow, trying not to spend too much time wondering how soft that exposed skin is. I pull my gaze to hers just in time for her to take a deep breath before opening her mouth to speak. "How far ahead will I know the schedule? That way, I can pick up shifts here at Pembroke on those days."

My lips press into a thin line. Being a private chef is a lot of work. It's early mornings and sometimes late nights. There's no way I'm going to allow her to use the two days off she gets a week to work even more. "You won't need to work at the club on your days off. You're to use them as rest days."

Lucy folds her arms across her chest as she looks up at me with a defiant glint in her eye. "I'll have to talk with my boss. I don't want to suddenly quit and leave them down a staff member during the busy season."

"Speak with Loretta, then," I offer. I know they won't have any trouble finding a replacement for her. Pembroke is one of the most prestigious country clubs in the country. One of the hardest to become a member of. Because of that, there's probably a long list of people who'd love to take Lucy's job. And if it's an issue, I'll arrange a solution.

She rakes her top teeth over her bottom lip, contemplating my words. We're close enough that I can see a small splatter of freckles underneath her thin layer of makeup. I don't remember seeing them last week, but then again, it was dark when we were reunited. The new freckles make a constellation along her cheekbones. I want to get closer so I can study every single one of them, something that takes me by surprise and elicits a foreign feeling in my chest.

Someone calls my name from afar, but I ignore whoever it is. I keep my attention firmly on Lucy, eager to finally get her to accept my job offer. "Any other excuses you'd like to use, or are you ready to accept my offer? We both know it's the best thing for you, Lucy."

"How do you know what's best for me? You don't know me."

"I'd like to, but you're making it rather difficult."

A small gasp falls from her lips at my response. I don't say anything else, letting my words hang in the air between us.

Finally, her cheeks puff out as she lets out a long breath. When her eyes find mine, it's obvious she's out of excuses. "As long as Loretta is fine with it, then I'll take the job. But I can only work until the week before Labor Day. I'd like to take a week off to enjoy the Hamptons one final time before I leave."

I can't help but wonder what she means by final. Does she not plan on ever returning back here?

"That's fine with me." The season typically ends around Labor Day, anyway.

Lucy focuses on a group of women walking out to the tennis courts. They all laugh loudly at something their tennis instructor said. She continues to watch them as they make their way to the courts, the sound of their voices and laughter getting further away with each passing second.

With her attention on the group, I use the opportunity to rake my gaze over her. The sun reflects off her dark, shiny locks of hair. Despite having worked a full shift at Pembroke, her hair is smooth. I want to run my fingers through the strands. For just a moment, I let my eyes linger on her lips. They're shiny from lip gloss, making it impossible not to wonder what she'd taste like if I leaned in and took her lips in mine.

I blink, shoving the thought *far* from my mind. I don't know where the idea came from in the first place.

Finally, Lucy looks back at me. Her lips pull into a shy smile as she smooths out the pleats of her skirt. "Then I accept your job offer, Callahan Hastings."

I hold my hand out, and she timidly places her cold hand in mine. I wrap my fingers around hers, shaking her hand a few times. I try to fight the thought nagging in my mind...it feels right to hold her hand in mine.

Lucy blushes at the contact of our skin. *Fuck.* Why do I love the specific shade of pink her cheeks turn so much? Her glossed lips spread into a wide smile. "Then it's settled. But only if you call me Cal."

She rolls her eyes at me. "What if I prefer to call you Callahan?"

I give one curt shake of my head. "You don't. You just like pretending you do to get on my nerves."

Her fingers twitch against mine before she pulls her hand free. Our handshake lasted longer than it needed to, but I couldn't let go. Not until she did. I can't explain why, but I wanted to feel her skin against mine as long as she'd let me.

"That would be very unprofessional of me," she whispers, her cheeks getting pinker by the second.

I smirk. It's adorable how she thinks she wants to play the game, but she can't fully follow through. "If you insist on calling me Callahan, so be it. But just know, I'd much prefer you call me Cal."

My words make her smile. "Before we do anything more than shake on it, are you sure you don't want me to do a test cook for you first? What if you hate everything I make other than what I prepared at Laurent's party?"

I scoff. "You're talented, Lucy. I don't think I could ever hate anything you do." I cock my head toward the path. "Let's keep walking, and we'll talk more details."

She doesn't argue. We spend the next hour walking around the grounds at Pembroke and discussing the details of her new position. I think I'm going to enjoy having her around more. She's different. Who I am doesn't seem to matter to her, and that's incredibly refreshing.

Nine

LUCY

"Good morning, Mr. Fred," I call as I descend the stairs from my upstairs apartment to his souvenir shop.

Mr. Fred stands in front of a shelf full of different Hamptons-themed magnets. He turns to look at me with a wide smile. "Good morning, Lucy. You're up early."

"It's my first day at a new job. I didn't want to be late." I take a deep breath, trying to ease my nerves. I feel like I barely slept last night because of how anxious I was to start with Cal today. I don't regret accepting the job. I'm glad I did. It's been a long time since I've been so excited about something that I couldn't sleep, but with the excitement comes a lot of nerves.

What if he realizes he hates my cooking? Although it isn't likely I'll ever need him as a referral once I'm back home after this summer, it'd be nice to have just in case.

"Need a cup of coffee, dear?"

I jump, focusing back on Mr. Fred. He holds a magnet in his hand as he looks at me over the top of his thick wire glasses. I shake my head. "I'm going to grab some here in a bit. Sorry, didn't mean to space out on you...what did you say?"

He patiently nods in understanding, not seeming to be

annoyed at all by my distractedness. "I asked where the new job was."

I push my shoulders back, faking confidence, although my stomach twists with anxiety. "Today is my first day as a private chef. I'm riddled with nerves, so instead of lying in bed worrying, I figured I'd get an early head start on my day."

He gives me an affectionate smile. "Whoever you're working for is lucky to have you."

I let out a deep breath. "I hope so." My conversation with Loretta a few days ago went surprisingly well after I told her I was offered a job with Cal. I thought she'd be upset that I couldn't work at Pembroke anymore, but she wasn't. She understood the offer was one I couldn't deny. I realized Loretta was a little less uptight than I gave her credit for. Or maybe she has a soft spot for Cal. Most of my meeting with her was spent listening to her fawn over him.

"I'm going to try and be the first one at the farm stand this morning. I want to get the best produce for the meals I have planned today."

Mr. Fred raises his bushy white eyebrows. "Make sure to tell Dolores hi for me."

I laugh, fixing the strap of my bag on my shoulder. "Or *you* could tell Dolores hi yourself." Mr. Fred has been a widow for a decade now. I've learned that in the last year, he's developed a bit of a crush on Ms. Dolores, who runs my favorite farm stand and also lost her spouse a few years ago. Mr. Fred has only mustered up the courage to say a few words to her, but I'm trying to get him to ask her on a date. They seem good for each other, but Mr. Fred is being stubborn.

"I think I'll let you tell her hello for me today." He gives me a wink before returning to stocking the shelf.

I laugh, shaking my head at him as I walk toward the front door. His store doesn't open for a few more hours, but once it does, he'll be busy all day. "I snuck some meals in the store fridge last night," I tell him, stopping at the door. "Make sure to take time to eat, even if today's busy. Okay?"

Mr. Fred doesn't look at me, but he rolls his eyes. A few weeks after I started renting the apartment above the shop, I started preparing meals for him. I couldn't help it. Once I learned he was surviving off frozen meals, I knew I needed to step in. He's been like a grandfather figure to me since I moved here. Plus, he charges me way less than he should for rent. Cooking for him is my way of showing my appreciation.

"You don't have to feed me," he grumbles.

"I know I don't have to. I want to. Just don't forget to eat them today!" I press my back to the glass door and slightly push it open before he can argue more about the food.

"You're too good to me, Lucy!" he calls out as the door shuts behind me.

I laugh as I walk to my car. I'd prefer to ride my bike to the farm stand, but I haven't gone to Cal's house yet. I know his house isn't far from my place or Dolores's stand, but I don't want to risk taking longer than needed to get to his house. After today, I plan on riding to work as often as I can. But today, I'm going to drive just to be safe. Besides, after I'm done getting items from the stand, I want to stop by his house and get situated in the kitchen before running back out and getting the rest of the groceries needed. Today, I'm only preparing lunch and dinner for Cal, giving me more time this morning to get ready.

The entire drive to the stand, I go over my recipes for the day in my head. I have a rough idea of what I want to make, but I also want to give myself the flexibility to change my mind if I see something at the farm stand that sparks an idea. Cal didn't give me much to go off of except explicitly stating he despises capers.

It'll either be amazing that he didn't give me any guidance

on his favorite foods or what he's craving, or it'll be tragic. I guess we'll find out.

Dolores is busy neatly arranging cartons of strawberries when I pull up to the stand. I put the car in park, giving her a warm smile as I grab my mesh produce bags from my passenger seat and open my door. Warmth from the sun heats my cheeks as I walk up to the stand. It's a beautiful morning with not a single cloud in the sky. The weather's so beautiful here I try to get outside as much as I can. I'm excited to make stopping by my favorite farm stand a daily routine.

"Lucy," Dolores croons, giving me the biggest smile. "You're here early this morning."

"I wanted to be one of your first customers this morning so I could get the first pick." My eyes roam over the vibrant colors of the fruits and vegetables. There are many local farm stands here, but Dolores's is my favorite. The quality is unmatched. Plus, she's sweet as can be. She reminds me of my own grand-mother, who passed years ago.

Dolores puts her hands on her hips as she watches me with a kind smile. "You're my very first. What are you looking for today?" She tucks her hands into her apron pocket as she waits for me to answer.

I glance at my options, immediately overwhelmed in the best way. Everything looks amazing. Different ideas for meals come rushing to my head as I mull over my choices. "Well, for starters, I accepted a private chef position. I'll be preparing meals five days a week."

She gasps, her hands flying to her mouth in excitement. "Oh, Lucy, I'm so happy for you. That's perfect."

I let out a nervous breath. "I'm really excited. Just don't want to mess it up."

Dolores scoffs and swats at the air. "You won't. Who are you working for?"

She follows me as I peruse the assortment of fruits and veggies. I want to grab one of everything, but that'd be wasteful. Cal's assistant gave me a credit card to use for food purchases, but I don't want to overbuy. "Callahan Hastings," I tell Dolores, picking up a carton of strawberries and blueberries.

"Cal? Really?" she asks, her voice full of disbelief.

I keep a hold of the fruit cartons as I narrow my eyes a little. "Yes...why do you sound so shocked?"

She shakes her head, plastering on a smile as she fixes a zucchini that's out of line. "I just thought he already has a chef, is all. Ignore me. At this age, I can't trust my memory half the time."

I stare at her for a moment, wondering if something happened with Cal's last chef. Dolores seems so confident that he already had someone. It makes me curious what might have happened. Had he been without a chef for a while before hiring me? Or was the loss of his last chef new?

I guess I could just ask Cal, but I don't know if that's something I have the right to know. I haven't spoken to him since last week at the club when I finally accepted the offer, and he made no mention of another chef. Since then, I've only coordinated with his assistant about the job.

"Anything I *have* to leave with today?" I ask Dolores, changing the subject before I can think too hard about what happened with Cal's last chef.

She nods her head in my direction. "You've got the berries. Excellent choice." The wind rustles the ends of her white hair as she slowly makes her way to the other side of the stand. She picks up a bushel of asparagus. "We've been selling out of these by mid-morning."

I nod eagerly, my mind already bustling with ideas about how I can shift the menu today to accommodate some of the fresh items from the farm stand. "I'll take it."

"How about I take these and set them by the cash register for you?" She nods to the cartons of fruit in my hands.

"That'd be perfect." While she takes the berries and asparagus to the register, I continue to look around. There's so much to choose from. I work through my meal ideas for the day in my head, trying to come to a final decision about what I want to prepare.

Dolores and I make small talk as I pick out a few more items and pay for the food.

"Thank you for helping me decide," I tell her, carefully placing my haul in my bags. I'm eager to get to Cal's house and get to work. "You'll be seeing a lot more of me now. Hope you don't mind."

She smiles, the wrinkles of her face getting even deeper with the movement. "I hope I do. I can't wait to hear all about your first day with Mr. Hastings."

I give her a nervous smile. My stomach flip-flops at the reminder of it being my first day. "Wish me luck!"

She rolls her eyes and playfully swats at the air. "You don't need luck."

Oh, but I might.

I'm confident in my ability to prepare mouthwatering meals for Cal and his guests. What I'm not confident about is putting up with Cal. His witty remarks and need to have everything done his way are something I don't know if I'm equipped to handle. I'm not normally one who likes to argue or toss out sassy comments, but there's something about the interactions between us that makes me unable not to.

I walk to my car and carefully put my haul in the passenger seat. The drive is short from the farm stand to Cal's house. I know my way around East Hampton fairly well, so the general directions I was given by Cal's assistant get me to the correct street. From there, I pay close attention to the numbers on the mailboxes until I find the one I was given as Cal's.

"Oh my God," I whisper, taking in the pristine white gate. I'd been given a keypad entry code, but for some reason, I thought it was to get into the house, not to get onto the property.

Owning a house in East Hampton is expensive. Every house is beautiful and worth more than I could ever dream of, but Cal's has to be one of the nicest on the street, and I haven't even seen the entire house yet.

I bring my rental to a stop and roll down the window to punch in the key code. It takes a moment, but a loud beep rings out from the tiny box before the gates push open, revealing a neatly paved driveway and one of the most stunning homes I've ever seen.

"You're joking," I whisper, stepping on the gas before the gates close on me and my rental gets crushed because I'm too busy gaping at my new place of employment.

The house looks like it was pulled right out of a catalogue. It has gray siding and navy blue shutters that appear to be freshly painted. Even the double front doors are painted the same vibrant navy blue.

Every window on the first floor has a flower box attached to it. Inside sit beautiful arrangements of flowers that bring even more character to the stunning home. I pull my car off to the side, parking next to a large black SUV.

Grabbing my phone from the cup holder, I read over the email from Cal's assistant that lays out all the details of the job. Apparently, the house has a chef's kitchen, something I'm thrilled to see in person. Cooking for private events here in the Hamptons has given me the chance to work in drop-dead gorgeous kitchens, but just by looking at the outside of this house, I'm fairly confident this kitchen is going to be the best one I've worked in yet.

And it's mine for the summer—kind of.

I'm busy memorizing the email from Cal's assistant when the sound of a knock against my car window startles me.

"Fuck!" I scream, my hand immediately covering my mouth when my eyes meet Cal's.

He smiles. "Well, good morning to you too, Lucy."

Ten

CAL

Lucy lets out a yelp as her hand drops from her mouth to her chest. She pushes the Bronco door open. "I'm so sorry. I didn't mean to curse...you just scared the shit out of me." Her eyes go wide as she realizes another curse word slipped out. "I mean, you really scared me."

I pull my earbud from my ear and give her a wide smile. "I didn't mean to scare you. It was just a bit of a surprise to see you. Wasn't expecting you until this afternoon."

Her breaths still seem quick from the scare, but she manages a timid smile in my direction. "I wanted to give myself plenty of time to prepare. I hope you don't mind..." Her words trail off for a moment, and so does her smile.

"It doesn't matter to me at all." I point to the bags of food in her passenger seat. "Need any help bringing those in?"

Lucy looks toward the passenger seat. "No, I can get them. I don't want to make you help me. You can finish..." She looks back in my direction, her eyes traveling over me for a moment. "Your run?" Her words come out as more of a question.

I look down at my shorts and old college T-shirt. "I try to get out every morning I can for a run along the beach."

Time seems to tick by slowly as her gaze roams my body far

longer than necessary. She focuses on where the fabric of my shirt clings to my skin from sweat. When she realizes she's been caught, her cheeks turn the perfect shade of pink.

"The weather is perfect this morning," she rushes to get out. She manages to keep eye contact with me for a few seconds before the embarrassment of getting caught is too much for her, and her gaze whips to the bags in her passenger seat.

I let out a slow chuckle. "Yes, it is." I don't say anything else, instead choosing to prop my elbow against the door of her car as she gathers all her things from the front, her cheeks still flushed. She seems to be so reactive. It's amusing. I can't quite put my finger yet on why I find her so fascinating, but I've been looking forward to her first day all week.

Lucy sticks a leg out of the Bronco to get out, but I step closer, caging her in slightly as I reach for the bags. "Let me bring these in."

She keeps a grip on them, being stubborn just like she was the first night I saw her at Laurent's. Tiny frown lines appear on her forehead with her concern. "You're my boss. I can't make you take in your own groceries."

I scoff, annoyed she thinks I'm incapable of helping. Or maybe it's that I'm annoyed she thinks I'll walk inside empty-handed as she carries everything in on her own. Either way, she's barely begun her first day, and she's already finding ways not to listen to me. My teeth grind together with frustration as I attempt to take a deep breath. "I'm fully capable of helping whether you work for me or not."

When I reach out to grab the bags from her a second time, she lets me. Her mouth opens and shuts as she tries to find the right words. Her shoulders sag in defeat as her eyes meet mine. "It just doesn't seem right to make you carry in food when it's my job to do it."

I take a step back, allowing her to step out of the Bronco. "It doesn't seem right to make you carry in bags of food when I have two perfectly good hands that can help you."

Lucy grabs a bag I hadn't seen from the floorboard of the passenger seat. The way she clutches it to her chest tells me it'd be best if I didn't argue and at least allowed her to carry that one in.

"Why do I feel like working for you is going to be incredibly different than any other chef job I've taken?" she asks, her tone more playful than I was expecting.

I can't help but smile at the easy way she gives me shit. I think that's why I'm fascinated by her. People rarely talk back to me, yet she does it so effortlessly—even if it makes her cheeks turn a little pink when she does. I'd guess that she's not typically defiant, and that smart mouth of hers is reserved just for me. "Because I'm better than anyone else you've worked for, obviously. Wickedly charming. Incredibly handsome. Pays well..."

"You do pay well," Lucy responds casually. She follows behind me as I walk to the side entrance. I want to give her a full tour of the house, but the door I lead her to is closest to the kitchen, so we can put her bags down before doing anything else.

"Weird you didn't mention anything about what else I said..."

She laughs. "No comment."

I glance over my shoulder with a raised eyebrow. "You don't have to say it out loud. I know I'm better than anyone else you've worked for."

She lets out a deep breath as I hold open the side door for her. The playful smile on her lips and narrowed stare tell me nothing about what's going through her head. "I guess we'll have to see about that."

I shake my head as she steps into the small mudroom.

Yeah, having her here every week is going to be fun.

As soon as she's far enough into the room, I shut the door and gesture to the hallway. "The kitchen is right this way."

I carefully brush past her, making sure to keep my distance despite the narrow opening of the room. We're both quiet as I guide her to the kitchen.

"Here's where the magic will happen," I tell her, setting the bags of food on the large kitchen island. I tuck my hands in my pockets and turn to face her, wanting to gauge her reaction to the space.

She's silent, her big brown eyes slowly assessing the room. I wait for a few moments, wishing I could get inside her head. It's a high-tech kitchen. There's not much more she could want for in here, but her silence makes me nervous. Is it missing something? I'll buy her whatever else she could want.

I tap my knuckles against the counter as I watch her closely. "Everything look okay?" It isn't hard to miss the uneasiness in my question. I clear my throat, not used to having to question things. Uneasy is not a tone I have often.

Lucy's eyes find mine. Her wide smile could thaw even the most frozen of hearts—including mine. "Of course," she answers, her voice breathless. She pulls her eyes from mine as she looks around the kitchen. She runs her hands along the quartz countertop, her bright smile never once leaving her lips. "I don't even have words. Cal, this kitchen is stunning."

I try to ignore the way my chest constricts ever so slightly at the way she says my name. "It should have everything you need. If you happen to find something it's missing, just purchase it with the card you were given."

Her top teeth rake against her plump bottom lip as she tries to keep her smile from growing. "Thank you. Really. I appreciate you giving me the job when things could be awkward because of Oliver."

I grunt. As much as I love hearing *my* name from her mouth, I loathe hearing his. "Shouldn't be awkward at all. He's stupid and didn't deserve you. I'm glad you didn't let him hold you back from accepting the job. That would've pissed me off."

Her jaw drops, but she can't be that upset because there's still a hint of a smile on her lips. "That would've pissed *you* off?"

I fold my arms across my chest. "Yes."

"Why?"

I take a step closer to her. There's still enough space between our bodies that we aren't inappropriately close. But even with an acceptable distance between us, the air still feels thick with something. "Because my brother should never be the reason you pass on a great opportunity. You honestly shouldn't spare him a second thought anymore."

Her head tilts to the side as her eyes track my face. She doesn't shy away from our sudden close proximity. "Do you not find it cold to speak of your brother that way?" Her question comes out unsure. She doesn't ask it judgmentally. It's as if she truly can't comprehend how I'm able to talk about Ollie that way.

"Maybe I'm a cold person." I keep the thoughts running through my mind about my brother to myself. I'm indifferent toward Ollie in a way that probably could come off as cold. But it isn't just me. I know he feels indifferent about me as well. The blood shared between us doesn't mean we have to be close.

"Maybe you just *want* people to think you're cold," Lucy offers. She shrugs, taking a step back and rounding the large kitchen island. She runs her fingers along the knobs of the range, completely oblivious that her comment has left me speechless.

Eleven
LUCY

My stomach twists with nerves—and maybe my hunger—as I put the finishing touches on Cal's lunch. His assistant told me, as a general rule of thumb, to prepare enough food for four people for lunches and dinners and two for breakfasts. If numbers change, I'll be told the evening before or early the morning of.

This is the first official meal I've cooked for Cal. I want him to love it. I don't want him to regret hiring me.

When I showed up this morning, I wasn't expecting to find him home. And I certainly wasn't expecting him to give me a tour of the house himself. I imagine he's a very busy man. You don't get to a place of power like him—and have so much money—without committing yourself to work. But he'd taken his time showing me every room.

It meant more than it should.

Cal's house is breathtaking from the outside, but it's even more incredible on the inside. It's common knowledge that he's a big deal. But to afford this home as a summer house...he's beyond rich.

"It smells incredible in here," a voice calls from somewhere in the house. I smile, recognizing the voice from the club. I'm busy drizzling the top of the salad with dressing when Jude strides into the kitchen. He wears a golf hat with the Pembroke logo on it and a green polo.

"I hope it tastes good," I remark, using a napkin to wipe the edges of the plate clean.

Cal walks in right after him, the scowl on his face a stark difference from Jude's wide grin. He's wearing an all-black outfit, his blue eyes seeming even brighter as he stares at me from under the brim of his hat.

Jude rests his elbows on the counter, putting his focus solely on me. "I have no doubt whatever it is will be delicious. What'd you make me?" He lets out a yelp as Cal's elbow finds his ribs.

"She didn't make anything for you. She prepared lunch for *me*. You just happened to come over." Cal's voice is a little tight as he glares at his friend.

Jude doesn't let Cal's grumpiness deter him. He rolls his eyes in Cal's direction before looking at me once again. "So what'd you make *me*, Lucy?"

This makes me laugh. I take a step back and wipe my hands on my apron. I cast one more look over the food before looking at the men standing across the counter from me. Spending more time with both of them is going to take some getting used to. Before I started working at Pembroke, I'd never really met anyone with extreme wealth and power. The club and working side jobs introduced me to this world of old money and deep pockets, but I've still never spent this amount of time with people who hold the power they do. I don't even want to think about the net worth of the two men standing in front of me. They're just two normal guys. One who I work for and one who it seems I'll be cooking for a lot. They both just *happen* to have money...and both look like they walked out of a Polo Ralph Lauren catalogue.

I clap my hands together and shake my head to rid myself of the distracting thoughts, remembering that Jude had asked me a question. "I marinated chicken thighs all morning and then prepared them on the grill. For the sides, I made thick-cut french fries and a summer salad with fresh berries from the farm stand this morning."

"That sounds amazing, and I'm starving," Jude notes. He dramatically rubs at his stomach as if he's actually been starved.

Cal aims a dirty look in Jude's direction. "Why are you here again? Get your own private chef. You can afford one."

Jude snickers. "Maybe I should reach out to your old one. I heard he suddenly has a ton of free time."

The muscle along Cal's jaw ticks angrily as he appears to grind his teeth. I stand by quietly, wondering what's going on between the two of them.

Cal lets out a long sigh, staring at his friend for a few more seconds before looking back at me. His eyes soften ever so slightly. "This all looks—and smells—incredible. Thank you."

The sincere way he says thank you makes me smile. "Just doing my job, boss."

Jude whistles. "*Boss.* Way to butter him up before he eats his meal, Lucy. I knew I liked you."

Cal rolls his eyes. "Do you really have to comment on every single thing?"

This makes Jude beam. He nods. "Yes. And it's the reason you stick with me. I do most of the talking while you do the brooding."

I can't fight the giggle that escapes from my chest. I try to play it off with a cough, knowing it's probably unprofessional for me to laugh at a joke that's at my boss's expense, but I can't help it. Jude's comment took me off guard.

I turn toward the oven range, trying to make it seem like I have to clean something up so I can attempt to wipe the smile from my face. It doesn't work. I know I've been caught by the deep, rumbly growl that comes from Cal.

"Aw...look, Jude," Cal declares, an unexpected teasing tone to his words. "Someone *finally* finds you funny."

My stomach growls loudly at the different smells filling the kitchen, and I hope no one can hear it. I try to ignore my hunger and turn back around, only to find the biggest grin on Jude's face. He reminds me of a golden retriever—goofy, loyal, and incredibly lovable.

"Lucy, I'm calling it now. We're going to be best friends."

I gesture to the plated food in front of us. "Try this and make sure you approve of my cooking first." I look over at Cal, who, surprisingly, has the smallest whisper of a smile on his lips. "Then you can decide if I'll take Cal's spot as your best friend."

"You don't have to tell me twice." Jude reaches across the counter and grabs one of the plates. I'd prepared enough food for four people but only plated enough for two. Jude and Cal had popped in earlier for a minute to grab drinks before going to the backyard to talk some kind of business. I didn't know if anyone else was joining and didn't want to plate food that wouldn't get eaten.

I try to clear my throat over the sound of my stomach growling again. Going forward, I really need to be better about making sure I eat in between preparing meals. I got so busy getting familiar with the kitchen and preparing lunch that I completely forgot.

Jude is already seated in the kitchen nook taking his first bite while Cal just stands on the other side of the counter. He stares at the plate that's left with a frown.

"Does the food not look good? I can prepare something else if—"

Cal's piercing blue eyes meet mine. "Where's yours?"

I straighten my back as I look around for a moment, a little confused by his question. "Um...what?"

He sighs as he angrily folds his arms across his chest. The position brings way too much attention to his tan, defined forearms and the way his polo shirt fits his frame perfectly. "You didn't make yourself a plate?" he pushes, his voice tight.

I shake my head. "No. I don't typically eat the food I prepare. Sometimes my clients let me if there's a lot of food left over and..." My words trail off when he rounds the counter and wraps his large fingers around my wrist.

"Come," he demands, pulling me toward where Jude sits.

I try not to stumble over my feet as he leads us across the kitchen. "Cal," I scold, trying to pull my arm free but failing. "What are you doing?"

He sets the plate down in the spot next to Jude. He thinks about it for a moment before sliding it to the other side of the table, away from where Jude sits. "Sit down and eat. Your stomach has been growling like a damn bear since we walked into the kitchen."

My mouth falls open as I look at him in shock. "I made that plate for you, Cal. This is my job. I'm going to eat as soon as you both are d—"

Air hisses through his teeth angrily as he loudly and dramatically pulls out the chair in front of the food. "Are we really going to argue about this? Eat. Now."

"No."

Jude chuckles through a mouthful of food. "Might as well just listen to him, Lucy."

I know Jude's right. It's not like I've had the chance to get to know Cal really well, but the little I do know about him tells me there's no way I'll win this battle. Right now, I don't care if he'll win. I have to at least try to prove to him how crazy he sounds.

"You know you pay me to cook for you, right?" I throw out, trying to take a step back. His fingers gently tightening around my wrist reminds me that he's still got a hold on me.

His eyes darken underneath his furrowed eyebrows. "I'm aware."

Jude continues to shovel the food into his mouth, completely unbothered by the battle happening between Cal and me. I nod my head toward the plate. "Then it should be obvious that I made the food for *you* to eat, not me. Eat it."

He smirks and lifts his chin before sticking his tongue out to wet his parted lips. "It's kind of cute you're still arguing with me when it's useless. I'll make myself a plate as soon as you do as you're told and sit down and start eating."

A choking sound comes from my throat. I shake my head, trying to rack my brain over whether he was this stubborn the few times I met him while dating Oliver. I think I was too busy doing whatever Oliver asked of me to pay much attention to Cal.

I stare at the stubborn man in front of me in disbelief, wondering if he was like this with his last chef. *Maybe that's why his last chef no longer works for him.* "You making yourself a plate while I eat the one I prepared for you makes absolutely no sense," I argue, my last-ditch effort to get him to see reason.

He drops my hand to pull out the chair in front of the plate even farther. His knuckles turn white from how hard he grips the chair, giving away his frustration with me. "It doesn't have to make sense to you," he grits.

"This food is to die for, Lucy," Jude interrupts, his demeanor still carefree despite the bickering happening between Cal and me. "Just listen to him. Sit down and eat this amazing food you made."

"*Ugh.*" I roll my eyes but finally concede. I angrily fall into the chair Cal had pulled out, keeping my mouth shut as he pushes me back toward the table.

I almost jump out of the chair I just sat down in when Cal's hot breath tickles the back of my neck. I stare straight ahead as he lines his mouth up right next to my ear. "Careful," he warns, his voice deep and throaty. "It might hurt my feelings that you listen to Jude and not me."

I snort. "Some might wonder if you even have feelings."

He laughs, his breath caressing the back of my neck in a way that sends tingles down my spine. "Everyone has feelings. I'm just good at hiding mine. Wasn't it you who pointed out my cold demeanor might just be a front? Did you change your mind about me already?"

Before I can respond, he backs away, cold air hitting my back immediately. My cheeks feel warm as my eyes meet Jude's. He stares at me from across the table with the biggest smile on his face. I'm starting to wonder if he's ever *not* smiling.

"I thought we were best friends now?" I mumble, picking up my fork. My stomach growls again as I look at the plate of food that was supposed to be Cal's but is now mine. "You were supposed to be on my side," I finish.

Jude laughs. "Trust me. I'm absolutely Team Lucy. I was helping you by telling you to not waste your breath."

I take a bite, my eyes fluttering shut for a moment because the chicken turned out perfectly. I quietly take a few more bites, not bothering to argue with either of them anymore. It's my first day, and I've already learned my lesson.

Glimpsing over my shoulder, I find Cal making his own plate of food. It feels weird to sit here eating while he does it, but I don't say anything. I know it's no use. It doesn't take him long to load up his plate and take a seat between Jude and me.

I watch him nervously as he takes his first bite. As if he can feel me watching him, his eyes find mine immediately. His chiseled jaw moves up and down as he finishes the bite.

My heart sinks when he sets down his fork, his eyes never leaving mine.

Does he hate it? Oh God, he hates it.

"Is it okay?" I muster up the courage to ask, forgetting all about my own plate.

It's almost like he can read my mind because his gaze flickers to my plate before meeting my eyes once again. "The food is perfect—just like I knew it'd be." He reaches across the space between us and taps his knuckles against the table by my plate. "Now, keep eating. And from here on out, when you prepare a plate for me or any of my guests, you will prepare one for yourself to eat too. Got it?"

I blink a few times, not knowing what to say. I have no idea why he's so insistent on me eating. With this job, a normal eating schedule during a workday isn't typical. You fit in snacks when you can. Never have I had a client insist I make myself a plate at the same time I make theirs.

But of course, Cal is different. I shouldn't even bother trying to figure him out or understand his reason behind things.

He stares at me with a lifted brow. He doesn't have to say a word for me to know he's waiting for me to agree with him before he eats anything else.

I let out a loud sigh that earns me the slightest of smirks from him. "Got it," I mutter under my breath before stabbing a piece of spinach and strawberry with my fork and aggressively putting it into my mouth.

He chuckles, picking his own fork back up. "She *does* listen to me after all. Good girl."

Twelve

CAL

I step out of my home office to the smell of lemon filling the house. It smells incredible, and I'm not even that close to the kitchen. The faint sound of music travels down the hallway. With each step I take toward the kitchen, the smell of lemon and herbs gets stronger, and the music gets louder.

It's Lucy's third day on the job, and I'm already wishing she could come back to Manhattan with me after the summer ends to continue working for me. Her cooking is that good. She prepares meals that feel like home-cooked comfort food but with unique flavor combinations and fresh ingredients that make my mouth water. Never have I cared about when I'd be eating my next meal. If we're being honest, meals were more of a social affair for me most of the time.

Now, I find myself counting down the minutes until I get to taste whatever she's thought up.

Today was a busy day. I'd been out all day golfing with seven other guys, and we did all eighteen holes, leading to a long day. It was both a mix of business and pleasure. I'm always with Jude, so spending the day with him was nothing new. And talking with Thomas, Ryker, Beck, Preston, and Archer is always a mix of business and pleasure. I actually like the men and would call them friends, but we're all about finding ways to work together for financial gain. Lucy had been out gathering dinner supplies when I finally returned from golfing, so I haven't seen her since breakfast early this morning.

I can't help but smile as I round the corner and find her at the stove. Music from the record player in the living room filters into the kitchen, masking the sound of my footsteps. It gives me the opportunity to watch her for a moment without being caught.

I lean against the wall, crossing my arms over my chest and taking in the sight in front of me.

Lucy's back is to me. She sways slightly on her feet to the sound of the music as she bends over and stirs something on the stove. It hasn't even been a week since she started working for me, and I'm already getting used to her company. It's refreshing to be around someone who doesn't want to talk business or use me for gain. In fact, she's been so quiet I wonder if maybe she's only tolerating being around me.

I don't move, fascinated by watching her as she reaches into the apron tied around her hips. She pulls out her phone and sets it on the counter in front of her, using the backsplash to keep it propped up. Her shoulders rise and fall as she appears to take a deep breath.

I watch closely as she opens up her camera and sets it to record. She takes three more deep breaths before she begins to talk. "Now that my lobster tails are off the grill and wrapped in foil until I'm ready to start plating, I'm going to finish my lemon butter sauce and toss the noodles in it, and then I will..." She pauses for a moment, shifting her weight on her feet. She's quiet for a few seconds before she talks again. "I'll just edit that part out," she mutters. "So once I've got my lobster tails and fresh asparagus grilled, I focus on finishing the pasta and sauce. The sauce has been simm...*ugh*." She hurriedly reaches in front of her and grabs the phone from the counter before angrily shoving it back into her apron.

For another minute or two, I stand there silently, watching curiously as she continues to prepare dinner—this time not talking to her phone. She takes out her phone once again and seems to take photos of whatever she's doing, but she doesn't ever attempt to record again.

I fight the urge to make my presence known. I want to ask her why she was recording herself. More than that, I want to ask her why she seemed to clam up the moment she started talking to the camera. I sat at the table yesterday as she explained to Jude in perfect detail how she made the teriyaki salmon dish we had for dinner. Jude knows nothing about cooking, but he'd spoken out of his ass and said the dinner was so good he'd have to make it sometime. Lucy was so excited and told him all about the recipe, so he just pretended to be interested.

I'm too swept up in wondering why she got nervous the moment she started recording herself that I can't even pretend to play it cool when she turns around and her eyes immediately land on me.

She gasps. "Cal!" Her voice comes out strangled as she places a hand on her chest. "How long have you been standing there?"

I push off the wall and close the distance between us. The delicious smell of whatever she's making is so strong it makes my stomach growl in anticipation of the incredible meal she's prepared. "Not long," I answer, stopping when I reach the island.

Her brown eyes quickly scan my face. I wonder if she's trying to figure out if I saw her record herself, and I don't know if I should be honest with her that I did. The polite thing would be to pretend I didn't. It was clear she was frustrated with herself after being unable to get her thoughts out correctly. The problem is...I might not have the best manners. I know if I don't ask her, I'll wonder all night about it.

"Okay," she whispers, her voice a little shaky as she turns and opens the cabinets behind her. "Will anyone be joining you tonight for dinner?"

I sigh, dropping the questions running through my mind— for now. "You're the only one joining me tonight."

She grabs two plates from the cabinet and sets them on the counter. "If you'd rather eat alone, I don't mind. I don't expect to eat with you when you have guests...I definitely don't have to when you don't have any."

I grip the edge of the countertop, watching her closely as she plates the food. She doesn't look at me. I wonder if it's because she caught me watching her or if it's because she's nervous about dinner alone with me. "Would you rather eat alone?" I ask, curious to know her answer. If I didn't want to eat dinner with her, I wouldn't have said it.

She looks up from unwrapping a lobster tail from its foil. A piece of hair falls into her eyes, but she doesn't try to move it. Instead, she just stares at me with a look of indifference. "I'm used to eating alone."

I swallow, letting her answer sink in. As much as I prefer to have alone time, I rarely eat alone. There's always some kind of function, event, or business meeting to go to. If I do have a meal to myself, it's typically while working or on a call. For some reason, the mental picture of her eating alone doesn't sit right with me.

"Tonight, you won't be eating alone." I run my hand along the countertop to keep busy. "You'll eat with me."

"You really don't have to do that," she whispers.

I rub at my temples with my fingertips. "Are we going to keep arguing, or can you accept that I'm well aware I don't have to do anything? Maybe I just want some company tonight."

Her lips twitch with the bloom of a smile. "It seems you always want company. I'm just throwing it out there that you don't have to settle for *my* company tonight."

I cock my head to the side. "Who said anything about settling?"

The lights of the kitchen are dim, but not dim enough to hide the blush that spreads across her cheeks. I probably find too much pleasure in making her blush, but I don't care. It's just so easy to make her skin turn the perfect shade of pink. Of course, I can't help myself.

She watches me closely for a moment before looking down. "Okay, well..." Her eyes scan the food she has laid out across the countertop. "I'm just going to finish plating the food, and then we'll eat."

I smile even though she doesn't even look at me to see it. "Perfect."

"You can go take a seat, and I'll bring the food over when it's ready."

I lean in a little closer to her. "Do you not like me standing here?"

Her eyes find mine. She gives me an apologetic smile. "You're my boss, so I probably shouldn't say this because you can do whatever you want, but...it does make me a little nervous to have you...hovering."

I hold my hands up in surrender. "Not trying to hover. I'll do as I'm told, for once." I mutter the last part under my breath.

This makes her laugh as I back away from the counter. I take a seat at the small table and pull out my phone. There's a comfortable silence between us as she finishes plating the food and I go through the emails I've received since leaving my office.

It isn't long before she's setting a plate in front of me.

"As always, this looks incredible," I tell her. As she said when she was recording, she's made a lobster tail, homemade pasta, and asparagus. Everything smells so good I don't even know what I want to take a bite of first.

She sets her own plate down and slides into the chair across from me. "Hopefully it's good. Just a simple lemon butter sauce with the noodles and grilled lobster tail and a vegetable. Nothing too hard."

I twirl a noodle around my fork and take a bite. My eyes fall shut with the flavor overload. I'm not the best cook and I can still tell this sauce is bursting with ingredients that aren't just butter or lemon.

I hold my hand over my mouth as I finish chewing. "These might be the best noodles I've ever had."

She rolls her eyes. "You seem like the type to have had fresh noodles in Italy. Don't lie to me in an attempt to flatter me."

I finish the bite of lobster tail I'd taken as a chuckle rolls through me. She's so sweet sometimes and sassy at others. "As I'm *sure* Oliver mentioned, my mother's family is Italian. We visit Italy often. It's one of my favorite places to travel. But that doesn't take away from this pasta...it's like I'm there again, eating on a terrace with the Italian breeze blowing around me. My nonna would be very impressed if she were still here." I smile, thinking of all the memories with Nonna. I wish she was still with us. Something tells me she'd adore Lucy.

Lucy shakes her head with a wide smile. "Don't lie to me like that. And I wouldn't know. I've never been to Italy, but I'd love to someday."

"You should."

"It's a dream of mine, actually, to take cooking lessons there." There's so much excitement in her voice I can't help but smile. "I know there's so much technique I could learn first-hand. Maybe even new recipes that have been passed down from family to family that'd be shared with me." She waves her fork in the air dismissively as she turns her attention down to her plate. "Sorry, I probably got a little too passionate there."

I shake my head as I set my fork down, wanting to give her my full attention. "Don't ever apologize for being excited about something, Lucy."

She rubs her lips together as she bashfully fights a smile. "Sorry. Oliver just hated it when I talked about cooking. He said it wasn't *refined enough.*"

I laugh at the way she mockingly imitates my brother. She's not too bad at it. "Then he's stupid and jealous because the man has never been passionate about anything in his life."

"He was about Sophia." Lucy's eyes widen the moment the words leave her mouth. She places her fingertips to her lips, as if she's in shock she even said the words in the first place.

I lift an eyebrow. This dinner is already getting more interesting than I was expecting.

"Sorry," she mutters, shoving a bite of food into her mouth to buy more time for her to think. "I don't know why I said that."

"What he did was shitty," I point out, keeping my voice as composed as possible. Anger pulses through my veins at the thought of my brother and what he did to Lucy. I'm still getting to know her, but she's a good person. It's hard to come by people who are actually genuine to their core anymore. It's obvious she cares about others, and I still don't understand how my brother chose Sophia over the woman sitting in front of me.

Lucy finishes chewing and lets out a sigh. "I know. And hopefully that didn't come out wrong. Sometimes, I just say things before thinking. I'm happy for them. *Really.* He didn't deserve me, and the moment we were over, it was obvious I deserved a love that was..." She looks away from me and instead looks around the kitchen for a moment before returning her gaze to mine once again. "Well, I deserve a love that's actually love."

I nod, hanging on her every word. I hate hearing her talk about my brother, but something inside me loosens at hearing her say that she didn't actually love him.

My thumb traces over my bottom lip as I try to think of what to say to her. Finally, I come up with something. "Did you know he's terrible with money? He keeps trying to get into crypto and has terrible intuition when it comes to investments. One of these days, Dad's going to stop throwing money at him to bail him out, and he'll be fucked. Sophia too. You dodged a bullet."

She shrugs before stabbing a piece of her asparagus. "Sucks for them." She lifts it to her mouth and takes a bite.

I chuckle, relieved it's obvious that she no longer harbors feelings for my brother. He's too immature for her. She deserves far better.

It's quiet between us for a bit. The only sounds are the clink of our utensils hitting the plate and the music pouring out from the record player. Many different things fly through my mind. None of them have anything to do with work or the things I typically think about. Instead, it's all questions about her.

One more than others.

I push my empty plate away from me slightly and sit back. "Can I ask you a question?"

She repeats the motion, both of us done eating. Part of me wants to ask for more food just to keep her here with me. I won't say it out loud, but I'm enjoying spending the quiet time with her.

"Callahan Hastings, you surprise me. You don't seem like

the kind of man who asks if he can ask a question. You seem like the type to just ask."

A corner of my lip lifts at her comment. She's not wrong. "Maybe I'm trying something new."

Lucy sighs before lifting her arms and waving them in the air. "Ask away."

I stare into her brown eyes for a few seconds, wondering if I have any right to pry. I already know I don't, but I still want to ask her anyway. Call me curious. "Earlier, why were you recording yourself making the meal? And why'd you stop?"

Her shoulders sag a little with my question. She sucks in a breath and looks at her lap for a moment. "Before I answer that, I think a glass of wine to finish off dinner would be great. What do you think?"

Without waiting for my answer, she's sliding out of her chair and beelining for the wine room.

I sit back and wait for her to return. If she needs wine to answer my question, so be it. At least she didn't totally disregard what I asked.

Thirteen
LUCY

Cal hasn't moved since I ran out of the kitchen to fetch wine. I probably should've asked him if it was okay for me to grab a bottle in the first place, but I was too surprised by his question to think straight. Plus, he made it clear where the wine room was when I needed to serve it with dinner. After dinner still counts...I think.

I set the cheapest bottle of wine I could find on the counter —even though I know it's still so expensive that I'd never be able to afford it myself. It doesn't take me long to open the bottle.

"Would you like a glass?" I ask, my words coming out faster than I intended.

Cal smirks. "Of course."

I nod, grabbing two wine glasses from the cabinet and pouring us each a hefty serving of wine.

My hands shake a little from nerves as I take them to the table and return to my seat.

It must be obvious how nervous I am because he sits forward and puts his hand over mine to comfort me. "You don't have to tell me." His words are said low and slow, as if he doesn't want to say them but knows it's the right thing to do.

I shake my head and let out a long sigh. "It's fine. I'm just being dramatic." I lift the glass to my lips and take a large gulp of wine...and then take another.

He watches me with a curious look on his face as I drink about half the glass before finally mustering up the courage to answer his question. "I'd love to get my recipes out to more people. Nothing would make me happier than to know other people are cooking up recipes I came up with."

"So you record them?" he asks. He leans forward, his thick fingers wrapped delicately around his wineglass as he pays close attention to me.

A laugh bubbles out from inside me. "I try. It turns out I have a little bit of stage fright. Every time I try to record myself, I clam up and can't think straight."

"Could you share photos?" he offers before taking a drink of his wine. His barely has a dent in it, while mine is already more than halfway gone.

"According to my friend Charlotte—who is way better at anything online than I am—video content is where it's at. I'm just terrible at it."

I shift awkwardly in my chair, trying not to think too much about the fact he saw me making a fool out of myself trying to record tonight. I wish he'd say something, but instead, he stays quiet, just giving me more time to get more and more embarrassed by the whole thing.

I set my glass of wine down and cover my face with my hands, letting out a long whine. "It's silly, I know. Videos or no videos, no one's ever going to see what I post. My recipes are meant for me to make, and that's okay."

I'm so lost in my own pity party—or maybe it's an embarrassment party—to realize he's left his chair. His fingers softly wrap around my wrists as he pulls my hands from my face.

"It isn't silly," he says, his voice softer than I've ever heard it.

My heart hammers in my chest, but it isn't because of embarrassment. It's because Callahan Hastings is standing so close to me I can feel his breath against my cheeks. I can see the different blues of his eyes, how they're darker around the iris and lighter around the middle.

Why does he have to smell so good?

Why am I learning that dark hair and light eyes might be my kryptonite?

Did he just look at my lips?

My mouth suddenly feels dry. I sweep my tongue across my bottom lip to wet it, all too aware of the sudden proximity between Cal and me.

He must realize it at the same time because with one quick movement, he's back in his chair across the table from me.

Cal takes a large drink of wine. I sit, trying to process what just happened. Why did my body react like that to Cal? He's my ex-boyfriend's brother...and more importantly, he's my boss. He shouldn't make my heart race. Not like that. I don't know if anyone's ever made my heart race like that just by a simple touch and standing close to me.

I shake my head to clear myself of the thoughts. My heart rate was up because I was nervous. That's the only reason.

I'm grateful for the music I put on before beginning to cook. At least because of the record player, we aren't left in complete silence as we both sip on our wine.

Cal clears his throat. "You shouldn't feel silly for wanting to share your recipes with the world. They're amazing and deserve to be enjoyed by people everywhere."

"I haven't even been cooking for you for a week. Maybe I've just gotten lucky."

He lets out a grunt of disapproval, making his feelings

about my comment known. "I've had countless people cook for me, Lucy. I know talent when I see it, and you have it. I knew it from the meal at Laurent's. Why do you think I was so adamant about you ditching private events to work for me exclusively?"

I shrug as I bite back a smile. "Maybe you just felt bad for me."

He scoffs. "I'm not known to do things from the goodness of my heart, Lucy. I'm strategic. I act on logic and what will benefit me. While the decision to ask you to be my private chef was a little hastier than I typically am, I did it because I hated the thought of you using your talent on anyone else but me this summer."

I swallow, his words having more of an effect on me than I was expecting. He uses every opportunity he gets to point out that he isn't sweet or thoughtful, yet he says things like that? Cal has more of a heart than he thinks he does; you just have to read between the lines a little to find it.

At least, that's what I think. It's still a little early to tell.

"You should post the videos. Who gives a fuck about what anyone else thinks?"

I laugh before picking up my wine and polishing off the glass. "I care about what others think. Plus, I haven't even been able to stop stammering enough to even complete an entire recipe video to share in the first place."

"What about when you described the recipe perfectly to Jude? You didn't fumble over your words once. You had him locked in, and that asshole hasn't cooked a day in his life."

I gasp. "What?" Jude seemed so interested.

Cal rolls his eyes. "He was flirting with you. You were excited to tell him about it. Of course he pretended to care."

My body heats at Cal's words. It isn't because he talks about Jude. I haven't gotten to know Jude very well yet, but it's clear that flirting is just a personality trait of his. No, what makes my skin flush is the way Cal's eyes darken when speaking about his best friend flirting with me. It almost seems like it's jealousy, but I know it can't be that. Right?

"So, why can you tell Jude so easily but not the camera?" His voice is tight. He keeps his eyes locked on mine, waiting for me to answer.

I anxiously chew on my lip, trying to come up with an answer that doesn't sound ridiculous. The truth is, I don't know why it's easy for me to tell someone how to prepare a meal step-by-step in person. There's something about talking to myself while the camera records that makes me freeze.

I lift my shoulder in a shrug, feeling like I'm under a microscope with his intense gaze. "I don't know, Cal," I get out with a sigh. "There's just something about teaching someone who's there with you rather than teaching a person you can't see."

He runs his fingertips along his jawline. For some reason, I want to know what his stubble feels like against my skin. Would it scratch my skin, or is it soft?

"Then record yourself teaching someone."

I'm so deep in wondering what his stubble would feel like that I don't even process his words until a few moments after he's said them.

"What?" I ask. I sit up straighter in my chair, wondering what he means.

"Teach someone the recipe, walk them through it, and just happen to press Record while you're doing it. Maybe then it'll feel more comfortable."

I smile as I mull over his words. "Your idea isn't terrible."

This makes him laugh. I love the sound of it. It's deep and throaty and feels like a caress against my skin. "You're so sweet, yet it's so hard to get a compliment from you."

My entire body feels flushed under his gaze. I blame it on the wine. Things are meant to be professional. I'm the one who told him it was unprofessional for me to take the job in the first place. I'd be a huge hypocrite if my body was warming under his icy blue gaze.

It's the wine, Lucy.

"I give plenty of compliments," I offer, twisting the end of my ponytail around my finger. "Plus, it's rich for you to say that. Do you ever give compliments?"

Cal shifts his body in the chair. His legs are so long that his leg accidentally bumps against mine under the table. "Should I be offended you think so low of me? I've complimented your cooking plenty of times."

My mouth snaps shut. He's right. I narrow my eyes on him as I attempt to hide the upward curve of my lips. "You're right."

He winks.

My stomach tightens.

I realize that despite his hard, grumpy exterior, he's extremely charming. And that charm is working on me.

"I'm always right," he points out as he stands up. "About time you realized that."

I roll my eyes, following his lead and grabbing our empty plates. His arm softly brushes against mine as he reaches for the empty wine glasses. "It's impossible for anyone to *always* be right."

"Fine. I'm right almost all of the time." He follows me into the kitchen. I set the plates in the sink and look around to determine how much of a mess I made. I try to keep my workspace as clean as possible when preparing a meal, but it's impossible to keep everything pristine.

It's quiet for a few seconds as we both get lost in our own thoughts.

I enjoyed tonight. I enjoyed spending time with Cal, something I never thought I'd say. There's more to him than I thought. He's got layers, layers I'd love to peel back and learn about, even though I know that isn't the most professional desire.

"Thanks for not letting me eat alone tonight." My voice is quiet and rushed, not sounding anywhere near as confident as I hoped it would be.

"Thanks for the meal. It was delicious. And it was nice to have a normal conversation and not talk about business for once."

"Didn't you golf all day? Is that really all business?"

Cal lifts a shoulder as he tucks his hands into his pockets. "Everything is business here, Lucy."

I pull my gaze from his and focus on the sink in front of me. I turn the water to its hottest setting, letting it rinse the plates and utensils in the sink before I soap them. "I'm happy to not talk business with you anytime."

He smiles wide and freely, the gesture even reaching his eyes. "I'll have to take you up on that."

We stare at each other for a few moments, both of us locked in the moment. He's the one to look away first. He pulls out his phone and looks at something on the screen for a moment before looking back at me.

"I've got to get back to the club. See you in the morning."

I smile. "See you then."

He doesn't say anything else before leaving. The moment he's out of view, I let out a dramatic breath, grabbing onto the edge of the countertop to steady myself on my feet.

I tell myself the reason I'm feeling light-headed is because of the hefty glass of wine. It wasn't because of the butterflies that took flight in my stomach at Cal's wide smile.

It absolutely wasn't that. Right?

Fourteen

CAL

The moment I open the back door to the house, I'm met with the sweet aroma of banana and something else.

"Good morning," I call as I enter the kitchen, giving Lucy a genuine smile after not seeing her over the weekend. It was her first weekend off, and the house felt a little empty without her here.

She looks up from where she places a waffle on a plate. Her smile is warm and genuine. "Morning."

"Have a good weekend?" I ask, fighting the urge to ask her everything she did.

She nods before turning around and grabbing a pan from the stove. "I did. What about you?"

I frown, wishing she'd give me more details. What did she do? Did she take time for herself and rest? Do something she enjoyed? Maybe even film some videos of herself cooking? I happened upon her Instagram account and her blog where she posts her recipes, but so far, I haven't seen any videos from her.

Lucy looks up from where she scoops some kind of banana mixture on top of the waffles. Her eyes roam over me, reminding me that she asked me a question.

I clear my throat, stopping at the edge of the counter.

"Yeah. It was a busy weekend. The Sinclairs hosted a dinner Saturday night. Their chef was talented but nowhere near as good as you."

This earns me a smile as she moves to pour the banana mixture on the next plated waffle. "I do like the Sinclairs. They were always polite at the club. Great tippers."

I round the counter and open the fridge, grabbing a glass water bottle from it and unscrewing the top. "Considering how hefty the membership and annual fees are for Pembroke, everyone should be good tippers."

Lucy lets out a sarcastic laugh as she places the pan back on the stove. She wipes her hands on the apron she's always wearing. "You'd be surprised. I've had some not even tip at all."

I pull the water bottle from my lips before wiping them with the back of my hand. "Are you serious? Who?"

She shakes her head. "I'm not telling you. Charlotte calls them the wannabes. She secretly flips them off from the kitchen every time."

This makes me laugh. "They deserve much more than that. I can't imagine paying two hundred thousand dollars for a membership fee, and fifty thousand every year to stay a member, to not tip the staff at the club you so desperately want to be a part of."

Lucy looks at me wide-eyed. She grabs the countertop to steady herself. "I'm sorry...it's that much to be a member at Pembroke?"

I set the glass water bottle down on the counter. "I figured you'd know the cost since you worked there."

"Nope. I knew it was expensive, but I didn't realize it was *that* high." Her eyes roam over my body for a moment. She stares like she's looking at me through a whole new lens. "I knew you had money but didn't realize it was that kind of money. That membership price is worth as much as my child-hood home." Her voice breaks at the end from shock.

"I haven't tried to hide from you that I make a lot of money. Why do you think I was insistent on doubling whatever Thomas offered you? If I remember correctly, my exact words were, 'I could more than afford to.'"

I don't know how I feel about the uneasy way she looks at me. She stares at me like I'm a whole new, different person to her. I don't like it. She just started to warm up to me.

I take a step closer to her, hoping to get her attention. "Lucy?" I say her name slowly. When she still stares at me with a lost look in her eyes, I reach out and grab her arm. "You okay?"

Finally, she snaps out of it. She blinks a few times before nodding her head. "Totally fine. Just having that kind of money is hard for me to process, so I spaced out a little. I grew up with kitchen-table bills, coupons, and only eating at restaurants where kids under ten ate for free. It's just a little jarring to learn how differently other people live."

My fingers twitch against her skin. I should probably let go, but I don't want to. Maybe it wasn't just her cooking or her presence I missed over the weekend...maybe I missed *her*.

A boss can miss his employee, I convince myself. *It can be absolutely professional to have a personal connection with someone on your staff.*

Totally.

"Now you understand why it infuriates me to know there are members at Pembroke not tipping. Every staff member should get tips."

Lucy's eyes focus on my grip on her arm. The moment her gaze lands on it, I pull away, realizing how unprofessional it was to keep hold of her far longer than necessary.

"Anyway," Lucy begins, turning to face the stove. She stares at it, her body still.

"Anyway..." I finish, taking a step back. I lift the bottom of my shirt to my forehead, wiping off the dampness along my hairline from my morning run.

"What's for breakfast this morning?"

Her shoulders loosen as her lips turn up in a smile. Her eyes rake over the plates lined up on the counter. "I made bananas Foster waffles."

"Did Jude request these?" I ask with a laugh.

Her perfect, plump lips part as her hand flies to her chest. "And why would you think that?"

"Jude would do questionable things for waffles. He used to beg our cooks at boarding school to put them on the menu every week."

"Did he?" She's a terrible actress. It's obvious Jude got to her. She made bananas Foster waffles for him.

I scoff as I shake my head at her. "I can't believe you made waffles for Jude."

"Did you say my name?" Jude asks, strolling in from the side entrance.

I point at my best friend. "Your pockets are almost as deep as mine. Get your own private chef, and stop telling mine what you want to eat."

The asshole snickers. He ignores my comment and walks straight to Lucy. "Did you really make me waffles, Luce?"

"Luce?" I don't even bother to hide the jealousy in my voice at the nickname. Are they really to the point of using nicknames?

Jude wiggles his eyebrows at me before reaching across the counter and swiping a piece of banana from on top of one of the waffles.

"Hey!" Lucy scolds, playfully slapping Jude's hand. "That one's now yours."

"I wanted that one. It's the biggest." He winks at her, and shockingly, for the first time in my life, I consider hitting my best friend.

"What's going on here?" I ask accusingly. My gaze travels between my best friend and my private chef.

"We're about to eat breakfast," Lucy points out, my jealous tone going right over her head.

"Yeah, Cal, we're about to eat breakfast." Jude looks me up and down with a lifted brow. "You sure you don't want to shower before eating?"

And leave the two of them alone together? Hell no.

"The food's already done. I'll shower after."

"Do you want whipped cream?" Lucy asks, her doe eyes focusing on me. The question is asked so innocently. I really don't think she even notices that the thing between her and Jude is rubbing me the wrong way.

"Uh, sure," I stammer.

She walks to the fridge and pulls out a bowl before setting it on the counter. No one talks as she grabs a spoon from the utensil drawer and scoops a large dollop of what must be homemade whipped cream onto the waffle.

"I'd love some too," Jude pipes up.

I toss an angry look his way, only making him grin harder.

"Is that enough?" Lucy asks me, gesturing to the large clump of whipped cream sitting on top of my waffle.

While she waits for me to answer, she spoons the whipped cream onto Jude's waffle and what must be hers.

"Shoot," she hisses, accidentally bumping her elbow against a discarded pan. The movement makes the heaping dollop of whipped cream splatter.

"I'll clean it up, I promise," she assures me anxiously, even though most of it is already covering her fingers holding the spoon.

Before I can say anything, she lifts her hand to her mouth and sucks the whipped cream from her finger. It feels like the air is sucked from my lungs, and I can't breathe as I watch her tongue peek out to lick more of the whipped cream off her hand.

A strangled noise comes from my throat.

Lucy's eyes go wide as her eyes meet mine. Her hand immediately drops to her side. "Oh my God. That was so unprofessional. I'm sorry. I'll wash my hands."

She steps closer to me to reach the sink.

I can't move.

I'm replaying the image of her pink tongue flattening against her skin and lapping up the whipped cream.

My body heats. My pulse spikes.

And what's highly unprofessional are the thoughts running through my head.

Her tongue.

My body.

My tongue.

Her body.

"Say something," Lucy pleads, finishing washing her hands and wiping them on her apron. It's obvious she's taken my silence as anger when it's the opposite.

I'm having very dirty thoughts about a woman on my payroll. A woman who's also my brother's ex-girlfriend.

"Yeah, Cal, say something," Jude chimes in from the kitchen table. I hadn't even noticed that he'd already taken his breakfast to the table and was busy shoveling it into his mouth.

Instead of saying anything, I turn on my heel and rush out of the kitchen like a bat out of hell.

I need a cold shower. Immediately.

Fifteen

LUCY

"I can't believe you talked me into this after barely talking to me for three weeks," Charlotte tells me before swiping a tube of pink lip gloss along her lips.

I give her an apologetic smile. "I know I'm the worst friend. I've been trying to get into a new routine working for Cal, and I just..."

"Abandoned me?" Charlotte finishes with a raised brow. She can't hide the smile on her face. I know she understands I've been busy adjusting to my first few weeks working for Cal. She doesn't hold me not being able to see her against me. I do feel bad for roping her into doing this today though.

"If you don't want to do this, just let me know. Jude asked last minute on his and Cal's behalf, and I didn't have any plans for the day, so I just—"

Charlotte holds up her hand to stop me from talking. "Of course I want to spend a day on the course with two of the hottest billionaire bachelors the Hamptons has to offer. I just wanted to give you shit about ignoring me."

I smile and shake my head. When Jude showed up yesterday morning begging for help with the charity golf event at Pembroke today, I couldn't tell him no. Both he and Cal just needed someone to drive their golf carts and stand in as a caddy, although I was assured we wouldn't have to carry their bags. They had entered the event as a pair but volunteered for the singles event after some members pulled out unexpectedly.

"Thank you for saying yes. I know there are tons of things you could do on your one Saturday off this month." I look out my windshield, watching people walk toward the golf course from the Pembroke parking lot. We still have about ten minutes until the time we're supposed to meet up with Cal and Jude. For some reason, I'm nervous, which is odd because I've seen both Cal and Jude almost every day during the three weeks I've been working for Cal. It just seems different to be out at the club with them, away from the professional setting I've been used to.

"You don't have to thank me. Today, I get to experience Pembroke the way a member does. I'm ready to soak it in, baby."

I laugh at Charlotte before opening the door to the Bronco and stepping out. The only golf experience I have is from when I was young and used to go with my brothers. I was there purely for moral support, which is hopefully all the skill I'll need for today as well.

Charlotte gets out of the vehicle and stops next to me with a beaming smile on her face. "We look hot as hell, Lucy." She holds up her hand for a high five.

I roll my eyes but slap my palm against hers anyway. "This golf skirt is a little shorter than the Pembroke one I'm used to," I tell her, looking down at the black fabric that falls against my upper thigh.

Charlotte scoffs. "Our job today is to look cute. I love your outfit." She loops her arm through mine as we head toward the pro shop, where we're meeting Jude and Cal.

"Your outfit is better. I want that pink."

Charlotte smiles as she looks down at her matching set. It's bubblegum pink and stands out enough that I'd be able to find her in any crowd. She even has her blonde hair pulled back in a ponytail with a black hat to fit with today's task. I opted to wear my hair down and keep the hair out of my face with a thin pearl-white headband to match the shirt I'm wearing.

The closer we get to the pro shop, the more people there are. It's a little odd to see people I'm used to waiting on, but I try to push the uneasiness of feeling out of place from my mind.

Like Charlotte, it's my day off, and I'm going to enjoy Pembroke the way all the members do. It'll be a fun day in the sun with some golfing, my best friend, and the guys, and it'll be in the name of charity.

"There they are," Charlotte exclaims, tugging on my arm. I search the sea of people for Cal and Jude but don't see them yet.

I follow Charlotte's lead until we walk up to our company for the day.

"Luce! You made it, and you brought your very pretty friend. I knew you wouldn't let me down." Jude closes the distance between us, his eyes locked on Charlotte and barely sparing me a second glance.

Charlotte eats up the attention as Jude takes her hand and places a soft kiss to the top of it. Because he's a complete flirt, he lets his lips linger against her skin for a little longer than necessary. She pulls her hand from his and places it on her hip. "Don't get any ideas, playboy. You're a member at the club, and I don't date members. You're cute though."

Jude's eyes light up with Charlotte's denial. He licks his lips before placing his hand over his chest. "What a shame."

The rest of the conversation between them fades away as Cal steps right in front of me. He wears a cream-colored polo and a pair of chinos, and he pulls it off too well.

"Good morning," he muses. His shoulders are pushed back confidently as he keeps his hands tucked into his pockets, his focus on no one but me.

"Morning, Cal," I respond. His familiar smell immediately hits me. I try not to take too deep of an inhale at the rich scent of the bergamot and sandalwood of his cologne.

"Thank you again for showing up this morning. I know you worked late last night because of the dinner party. I tried telling Jude to let you off the hook, but he insisted that you and Charlotte would have fun today."

I give him a reassuring smile, trying not to stare too long at him. His blue eyes look extra vibrant under the sun this morning. A man with eyes as light as his and hair as dark as his shouldn't be possible. It's a lethal combination, paired with the intense way he stares at me as if there isn't a horde of people around us, that makes my skin heat. "Charlotte's been excited about it, and coffee exists for a reason, right?"

Cal takes a step closer to me to let a group of men holding their golf bags through. His eyes don't move from mine. "What about you?" he asks, his voice deep.

Charlotte laughs at something Jude says, but I can't look away from Cal's piercing blue eyes.

I cock my head to the side. "What about me?"

"Are you excited about today?" He takes another step closer to me, completely surrounding me in his scent now.

He towers over me, having to curve his back slightly so his eyes stay connected with mine. I'm so distracted by his sudden nearness that I briefly forget he asked me a question. "Yeah, I guess," I mumble, wincing at how awkward my words come out.

He smirks. "You guess?"

I shift on my feet, wondering why he feels the need to stand so close. Not like I'm making any attempt to back up. There's something about him that pulls me in, even when I don't want to be. "It'll be fun to experience a Pembroke event like this. But I've never been very good at golf." I playfully swat at his midsection, the back of my hand meeting hard muscle. "Hope you don't expect me to play."

Before he can answer, his attention moves to a group of people walking up to us.

Sixteen
CAL

I can't help but laugh at the sight in front of me. "You look like hell, Davenport."

Ryker groans before leaning forward and massaging between his eyes. "I was going to just donate double today and nurse this wicked hangover at home, but someone wouldn't let me do that." He looks behind him where a group of our friends is standing.

Camille, Ryker's babysitter for the summer, plasters on a smile after hearing Ryker's words. "Nothing cleans up an image more than a charity event. I've told you for a week you were participating. It's not my fault you drank too much last night."

Ryker tosses a dirty look her way. "Maybe I wouldn't feel the need to drink if you'd leave me alone."

Camille opens her mouth to respond, but before she can, her eyes land on Lucy. "Hi, again," she says excitedly, sounding friendlier than I've ever heard her.

Lucy returns the smile, making me wonder if they know each other through Pembroke. "Hi, good to see you again," Lucy responds, taking a step closer to Camille.

Charlotte catches wind of the conversation and steps next

to Lucy before giving Camille a knowing smile. "Is this who you're having to babysit?" Charlotte asks playfully.

Everyone but Ryker smiles. His eyes shoot to Camille as his mouth falls open. "You've been telling people you're babysitting me?"

Camille shrugs before nodding. "Of course I have. I *am* babysitting you. I ran into these two when I was escaping you a few weeks ago. They talked me down from plotting your murder."

I raise an eyebrow as I look over at Lucy. Her eyes meet mine with a growing smile. She tries to rub her lips together to hide it, but it doesn't work.

"First off, you're not my babysitter," Ryker grits. His eyes are angrily trained on Camille. I have to give her credit—she doesn't back down under his stare. If anything, it seems like she finds his anger funny. "And second," he continues, "don't tell people you are."

Camille pretends to pick at a piece of lint on her skirt. She wears an all-black outfit, the fabric almost as dark as her hair. It's hilarious how seriously she takes her job of keeping an eye on Ryker and how little she actually cares for him. She rolls her eyes before focusing on Lucy and Charlotte again.

"So are you guys here for the couples event too?" She hooks a thumb over her shoulder and gestures at Ryker. "Unfortunately, I'm stuck with this asshole because, despite his protests, he's very much stuck with me as his babysitter."

"Couples event?" Lucy asks, her eyes moving to me.

"We're here," a voice calls from behind Ryker. Margo, Beckham Sinclair's wife, pops her head around Ryker's large frame.

"Hi," Camille says, proving she does know how to smile, just not when dealing with Ryker. "I didn't know you guys were going to be here too."

Margo smiles before looking over her shoulder, where Beck comes to a halt. He runs a hand through his blond hair and gives everyone a smile.

"We're excited to take home the prize. Almost missed it because our nanny was running late this morning," he explains, wrapping his arms around his wife and pulling her body against his.

"Winnie and Archer and Emma and Preston should be here soon too," Margo explains, her eyes finding Lucy and Charlotte. She breaks free from Beck's hold and steps forward, holding her arms out for a hug. "Charlotte, Lucy, it's so good to see you out here with us today. It's about time you took some time off work and enjoyed the other side of Pembroke."

Lucy steps into Margo's embrace. "It'll be fun," she responds before pulling away. Her eyes meet mine as Margo goes to pull Charlotte in for a hug as well.

"Although," Lucy begins, looking around at the crowd of people who've gathered around us, "I didn't know this was a couples tournament. I thought you just needed a caddy."

Before I can respond, Jude chimes in with a shit-eating grin. "That was my fault. I thought the word 'couples' would deter you from saying yes, and you deserved a day of fun...so I told a little white lie." He does seem sincere as he watches Lucy closely for her reaction. "Don't be mad at me, Luce. It's going to be a fun day. Pretend the word 'couple' has nothing to do with it."

Camille reassuringly grabs Lucy by the arm. "It definitely isn't *couples* couples. I'm stuck with Ryker...the last person I'd ever want to couple up with."

Ryker coughs, his eyebrows lifting to his hairline as he looks at Camille. A sinister smile crosses his lips. "You sure about that, princess?"

Jude whistles, catching my attention as Ryker and Camille

continue to argue. He loops his arms around Lucy and Charlotte before pulling them to his sides. "So which one of you wants to couple with me?"

For a moment, I see red. I can't stomach the mental picture of Lucy riding around with Jude all day, undoubtedly laughing at his stupid jokes and blushing at the way he flirts.

Stepping forward, I grab Lucy by the wrist and pull her to me. "Lucy will be with me." The direct tone of my voice leaves no room for discussion.

At least, I thought it left no room for discussion.

Jude snickers. "What if Lucy wants to be with me?"

Lucy takes a tiny step closer to me as my fingers stay firmly wrapped around her wrist. I know that Jude doesn't actually want to pair with Lucy for the day. Anyone with eyes can tell he's interested in Charlotte. He's just doing it to piss me off—and it's working.

"Lucy?" Her name leaves my mouth tight, almost like a question. "Would you like to ride with Jude or me today?"

"Is it riding or playing?"

I press my lips into a thin line for a moment. "Technically, you're supposed to play two holes. But just two of the nine."

Lucy's mouth falls open as she shakes her head. She looks at Jude with wide eyes. "I can't believe you lied to me, Jude. Because of that, I'll play with Cal for the day. Is that okay with you, Charlotte?"

Her friend bites back a smile as she looks from Lucy to Jude. "I'm along for the ride today. Jude doesn't seem like terrible company...as long as he knows nothing will happen between us."

Jude playfully pouts. "Why stop the fun before it even starts?"

I finally drop Lucy's wrist, missing the small connection the moment it's over. "Now that it's settled, let's go check in and get our cart."

Lucy follows my lead as we leave my friends behind. Stopping for a moment, I place my hand on the small of her back and guide her through the large group of people that are gathered outside the pro shop. I tell myself the only reason I found a way to connect our bodies again is because I don't want to lose her in the crowd.

When she looks at me from over her shoulder with a wide, nervous smile, something weird happens in my chest. The sight of her hesitant smile is stunning, and it's like I feel it throughout my entire body. "I hope it doesn't ruin your day if we lose. I'm a horrible golfer."

My fingers twitch against her back as I guide her to one of the staff members helping coordinate the event. "I get to spend the day with you. My day could never be ruined."

Seventeen
LUCY

"I think I like golf more than I thought I would," I offer before looking over at Cal. We're about an hour into the charity golf event and have only been able to play two holes.

I don't mind that it's taking longer than what Cal says is typical. I'm actually enjoying spending time with him. He seems more at ease than normal, and it's exciting to see him outside of his house. I'm used to our only conversations being in his kitchen over a meal.

"Is it my excellent company that's made you change your mind?" he asks smugly. His lips twitch with the beginning of a smirk.

I shake my head and can't help but smile at his comment. "I don't know if I'd describe your company as excellent, but what I meant was I understand why people like golf." I look out the side of the golf cart, taking in the breathtaking view of the Pembroke Hills world-famous golf course. There's a reason people pay big money to keep their membership at Pembroke, and the golf course is one of the biggest ones. You can't play it unless you're here with a member, and even then, from what I understand, the club has to approve it.

Cal keeps the golf cart stopped as we wait for one of the

couples in front of us to finish their round. I was shocked to find out that it was Preston Rhodes and his influencer girlfriend, Emma Turner, only two people ahead of us. My dad's a huge Manhattan Mambas fan. He'd be shocked to know I've served them before at the club. The two are very nice. And clearly very in love because they're too busy making out on the green to quickly take their turn at the hole.

I don't mind. The extra time with Cal is...nice. Things don't feel like they have to be as professional between us. Not that our constant bickering is very professional in the first place.

"What have you liked most about golf so far?" Cal asks, breaking me from my thoughts. I lean back in the seat, crossing one leg over the other while I think about his answer. I throw a look in his direction, finding his gaze on my legs. His eyes snap to mine immediately, his jaw getting tight after being caught.

"What's not to like?" I counter, holding my arm out of the cart. "The view is breathtaking and one of a kind. The weather is beautiful. It's relaxing. Maybe I need to take up golf as a hobby."

This makes him laugh. I'm learning to love the sound of his laugh—the real one. He has a sarcastic one he uses often, but this real one, the one that rumbles deep in his chest...it's kind of sexy.

Can you find a man's laugh sexy without finding *him* sexy?

I bite my lip before looking at him out of the corner of my eye. He *is* sexy, no matter how much I don't want to admit it. I just have to remind myself that no amount of good looks or charm can cover up the fact that he needs to be off-limits to me for multiple reasons.

"Anytime you want to come golf at Pembroke, you let me know, and I'll get us a tee time." The golf cart we're in isn't very wide, so when he shifts his body, his knee bumps against mine.

I let my gaze travel over his face, trying to figure out if he extended the invitation to be polite or if that's something he wants to do. Deep down, I know he wouldn't have offered if he didn't want to; it's just hard for me to accept that answer. If I accept it, I might think too deeply about what it means.

I might find it cute...charming...a sign that maybe he and I are developing a friendship, no matter how crazy that might sound.

Cal reaches between us and presses his fingertip to my temple. "What are you thinking about? I didn't expect the offer for us to golf together again would take so much thought."

His hand drops to the leather between us as I give him an apologetic smile. "I was thinking that you haven't even seen me swing a club yet. No matter how much I enjoy being a passenger princess while you expertly hit the ball, I'm actually terrified to do it myself."

He taps his fingers against the space between us, his pinky just barely brushing against my bare thigh. I freeze at the feeling of his skin against mine, trying not to let my body shiver in pleasure from the softest touch. "Don't be scared. I'm here to help you." His words are soft and sincere, something I didn't know he could be.

Neither one of us moves for a moment, too busy staring into each other's eyes to do anything else.

What is happening?

My heart races, no matter how many times I try to tell it to stop. Even though he can be perceived by those who don't know him as cold and cunning, I now know better. He's charming and charismatic when he wants to be. The way he's looking at me right now, it's like nothing else I've ever felt before.

I tear my gaze from his just in time to realize the line of golf carts ahead of us has moved. He notices too, both our bodies jostling a little as he presses on the gas and guides the cart to the next hole.

Cal puts the golf cart in park and looks at me. "Want to give this hole a try?"

My eyes widen. "Not really."

This makes him laugh. He slides out of the seat and stands up. I don't know why, but the way he adjusts his golf club is kind of hot.

Is golfing supposed to be this hot? Or is it just because Cal's doing it?

I shake my head. Maybe the summer sun is getting to me. Why am I having these thoughts about Cal?

"Lucy Rae Owens, come out here and show me your golf swing," he commands, his voice thick.

I stare at him in shock, my butt staying planted in my seat. "How do you know my middle name?"

He lifts his hat and runs his fingers through the longer tendrils of his hair at the top before placing it back on his head again. "It was on your resume. Now, come on."

Even though I'm still a little stunned about how my full name sounded coming from his mouth, I follow directions. My feet hit the pavement, and I meet him where he now stands at the front of the golf cart.

He smirks and cocks his head toward the green. "Let's see what you've got, Lucy Rae."

Eighteen
CAL

So Lucy wasn't lying. I stand off to the side as I watch her swing the golf club in a third attempt at hitting the ball.

She misses...again.

A crease appears on her forehead as she looks at me. "Ugh," she whines. "I suck at this, and it's embarrassing."

I uncross my arms from in front of my chest and take a step closer to her. "How about I help?" I offer.

"I don't know if your help will do anything. I'm hopeless." She looks over her shoulder at the line of golf carts waiting for us to finish our turn. She closes her eyes and lets out a groan. "And everyone's watching me make a complete fool of myself."

I close the distance between us, trying not to focus on how good she smells. I'm becoming far too fond of her sweet scent.

I'm becoming far too fond of *her*.

I reach out and let my fingers trail down her back reassuringly. "All of this is for charity. No one's judging you, I promise. Everyone in our group is my friend. They're just here to have fun and raise money. Stop getting in your head."

"Easy to say when you're so good," she protests. "You make it look so easy to hit the ball and have it go exactly where you want it."

"It's only because I've had decades of practice. Here, let me show you." I step behind her and line the front of my body to her back.

She doesn't shy away from the closeness of our bodies. I don't know if that's a good or bad thing. Probably bad. I can barely think straight when her ass softly brushes against my cock as she adjusts her position.

Air hisses through my teeth as she pushes her hips forward and away from me. "Sorry," she mumbles, trying to take a step forward.

I wrap my arm around her middle and place it against her stomach. Her stomach tightens underneath my touch. "Stay still," I demand, my throat feeling thick while uttering the word.

Before she can say anything else, I push my foot between her feet and tap her shoe with mine. "First, you need to spread your legs a little wider. They should be shoulder width apart."

Lucy does as she's told and inches her feet a little farther apart.

I look down, finding the distance acceptable. "Perfect," I note. My hand slides down her stomach before landing on her hip. My other hand follows suit, both my hands resting at the narrow of her hips. "Now, your body should be perfectly aligned with your target." I look over my shoulder to make sure she's lined up correctly. I lean a little closer, placing my lips close to her ear. "And your target is the hole over there on the green."

"Okay," Lucy whispers, her body tense against mine. "Feet shoulder width apart, body lined to target...what next?"

I chuckle at her eagerness to learn. I don't make her wait to continue the lesson, too excited to keep teaching her. "Next, we're going to talk about the swing itself."

My fingertips trail over her skin and down her arms. "Your arms should be nice and loose." I nod to her left foot. "Turn your toes out here, ever so slightly toward the hole."

She's a good student, doing everything I tell her to.

"Now, your lead hand goes right here." I keep my arms wrapped around her as I grip the top of the golf club. She places her right hand where I tell her.

"Good. Now, just grip it naturally. Don't think too much about it."

She sighs, and I can feel it from the press of my front against her back. It feels natural to teach her like this, and I don't care to read too much into what exactly that means.

"See how you're forming a triangle?" I ask, keeping my lips close to her ear because I love the way it makes her shiver.

She nods as she adjusts her grip on the club. "Mm-hmm," she hums as extra confirmation.

"Good. You want to keep that triangle." I place my hands over hers so I can help her guide the club correctly. I still wear my golf glove on my right hand, so there's no press of our skin against one another there, but there is with our left hands. I keep my grip on top of hers, firm but not too hard.

I test swinging our joined arms a little. She moves freely with me, giving me complete control.

"Now, keep your back completely straight and your knees slightly bent," I command. Air seems to be ripped from my lungs as she does exactly as she's told, but the change of her position has her grinding perfectly against me.

My entire body is tense as I try not to react. She innocently did exactly what I told her. I need to keep things appropriate between us, but all I can think about is what it'd feel like to have her ass pressed against me with no barrier of fabric between us.

I squeeze my eyes shut, trying to rid myself of the mental picture of her bent over in front of me.

Where are these thoughts coming from? And why are they coming at the most terrible of times?

"Everything okay?" Lucy asks, her voice quiet and unsure.

I clear my throat, hoping she can't feel the way my cock hardens at the press of our bodies. "Yes," I manage to get out despite the hard clench of my jaw.

It's a natural response. It isn't her. I repeat the words over and over in my head, but I don't believe myself for a moment.

As much as I want to deny it, it *is* her. With each passing day, the more I go from being interested *by* her to being interested *in* her.

"What next?" Lucy asks, pulling me from my thoughts once again.

"Make sure you keep your weight on the balls of your feet. Remember, your back stays straight, and so does your left arm." I guide our arms backward to show her what it should feel like for the proper swing.

"And hit just like this," I finish, taking her through the full motion. From the backswing to the downswing, I show her how to go through the entire motion. "Let your hips lead at the end, and then your torso follows. And just like that, you've done it."

She lets out a sarcastic laugh. "It isn't that simple for the rest of us, Callahan. But okay, I'm going to try."

Before, it bothered me to have her say my full name. But this time when she says it...it excites me. It's said intimately, like she knows me well enough to feel comfortable calling me whatever she wants.

I allow one more moment of feeling the press of our bodies from chest to thighs before taking a step back and giving her the chance to practice what I just taught her.

"Now, put it all together and hit the ball that way." I point to the hole.

Lucy stares at me, her eyes wide with worry. She pulls her plump bottom lip in between her teeth as her eyes dart from mine to the flag on the green and then back to me. "What if I mess up and make us lose?"

"It doesn't matter how many chances it takes, Lucy. We're here for the fun of it and to make a charitable donation. Now, hit the damn ball," I add, keeping my tone soft despite the words.

The bluntness must ease some of her nerves because a beautiful smile spreads across her cheeks. Her shoulders rise and fall with a deep breath. "I've got this," she says quietly, putting herself in the proper swinging position once again.

"Line up your left foot with the ball," I instruct.

She nods. I'm impressed with how much she remembers from our little lesson. She spreads her feet perfectly shoulder width apart and keeps her hands in the correct position on the club.

I watch closely, my palm running over the stubble on my cheeks as she pulls back on the swing. My stomach drops as it seems like her swing happens in slow motion. I don't know why I care so much about whether she hits the ball or not. It doesn't matter. I don't give a damn if we place last during this event because I'll still feel like I won by getting time alone with her.

But I don't want to see the disappointment on her face again. I can't stand to hear her cry of protest and frustration at completely whiffing the ball.

So I watch, my entire body tight, as she attempts to hit the ball.

Her form is perfect.

She seems concentrated but relaxed.

She's got this.

By the time it's time for her downswing, I know it's a perfect swing. The club hits the ball, and it goes soaring into the air—right in the direction she meant it to.

The golf club falls to the ground as she jumps up and down. "I did it!" she yells excitedly, her arms waving in the air as she looks ahead of her.

The smile I give her is genuine. Joy courses through my veins as she closes the distance between us. She leaps into my arms, and I immediately catch her, pinning her body to mine as her wide, excited eyes meet mine.

"Was that good?" she asks, her arms wrapping around my neck.

"That was incredible," I assure her, spinning both our bodies around in celebration. Her legs swing in the air as the cutest giggle leaves her, making her entire body shake.

"I thought I'd miss it," she confesses, a little out of breath from her laughter.

I smile, unable to resist directing my gaze to her lips for a brief moment. Our faces are so close it'd be easy to lean in and kiss her, but I can't, no matter how much I can admit that I want to.

There's nothing I want more at this very moment than to kiss Lucy Rae Owens.

I don't care that she's my employee for the summer. And I certainly don't give a damn that she's my brother's ex-girlfriend. Nothing matters more than the desperate desire to feel her lips against mine.

Her breathing gets shallower, and she leans in just a little closer, her lips slightly parted. I know she's mine for the taking.

It takes everything in me to put her back on the ground.

I take a step back and clear my throat. I stuff my hands into my pockets as I try to calm my racing heart. "Let's go see how close you got," I get out hoarsely.

Lucy smiles before turning to walk toward the golf cart. With her back to me, I'm able to close my eyes for a moment and take a deep breath to calm myself. Desperate longing courses through my veins, but I push it aside, reminding myself that there are a multitude of reasons I can't kiss her.

The problem is, I'm still deciding if just because I can't kiss her means I won't.

Nineteen

LUCY

"This is too much boob, isn't it?" I ask Charlotte, adjusting my bikini top as we walk up the driveway leading to Cal's house. After the event wrapped up and we were enjoying lunch with the large group of Cal's friends, Cal had offered to have everyone over for a swim. It was so hot we thought about just hitting the pool at the club, but Cal was insistent on something more private at his house.

He asked the whole table to come over, but his eyes had been pinned on me when he said the words. Charlotte said yes before I could think better of it.

"Is there such a thing as too much boob?" Charlotte asks, her tone completely serious. She throws a glance in my direction and looks my outfit up and down.

I laugh nervously, looking down at the oversized linen button-up shirt I'm wearing as a dress. "There is when you're at your boss's house," I mutter under my breath, feeling anxious. The offer from Cal came as a shock. I'm used to the members at Pembroke having dinner parties with formal attire and a full menu; a pool party seemed so...casual. But everyone's excitement at going back to Cal's to hang out after the tournament took me by surprise. Maybe despite their deep pockets and lavish lifestyle, Cal's friends are more normal and laid-back than I'd thought they were.

After we were done at Pembroke, everyone had gone their separate ways to go home and get refreshed. I'd thought about canceling. I work for Cal; I shouldn't be attending private events at his home unless I'm working one. But Charlotte was insistent we go when she showed up at my apartment dressed and ready to attend the last-minute pool party. Jude's constant flirting must've not been a total turnoff to Charlotte because she was excited to keep hanging out with him.

Charlotte lets out a dramatic sigh as she turns and stops in front of me. There are already plenty of cars in the driveway—most of them so expensive I can't imagine driving something worth so much—but Charlotte doesn't look at anything but me. "Cal is cool. He's not *really* your boss."

I cock my head to the side. "Then who is?"

Charlotte rolls her eyes at me and lets out an exasperated sigh. "Okay, so yes, technically, he's your boss...but it doesn't really count. You're cooking for him for the summer, and then you'll go back to Virginia and never see him again. If he invites you to a pool party, you attend the pool party. Don't make it complicated."

I narrow my eyes on her. "Says the girl who makes it obvious she's got a crush on Jude but wouldn't ever date him."

She gasps before excitedly leaning forward and grabbing my hands with hers. "Are you saying you have a crush on Cal?"

My heart plummets with nerves. "No," I rush to get out. I shake my head adamantly. "Not at all," I lie, realizing a crush is exactly what I have. "Plus, we changed the subject to you and your crush on Jude."

Charlotte's nose crinkles as she waves her hand through the air dismissively. "It's not a crush. He's hot, and it's easy to flirt with him, but he's a member at the club, and I don't date members. Plus, I think he's actually fun, and he mentioned he's here a lot, even in the off-season. It'd be nice to make a friend out of him since I'm here all year."

I click my tongue and nod. "Mm-hmm, sure. I *totally* believe you."

She lets go of my hands and swats at my stomach. "I'm serious, Lucy. I can't let his charm get to my head. I want him to be my friend. That's it. Although, a little playful banter never hurt anyone."

I roll my eyes before hooking my arm through hers and pulling her up the driveway. It isn't my place to keep pushing her on it. Not when she's just made me realize that I might have the smallest, tiniest, barely there crush on Callahan Hastings.

The same man opening the gate to his backyard and walking right to us.

"I was worried you were ditching us and found something far better to do," Cal points out.

I should form words and respond to him, but I can't. My throat suddenly feels swollen and my mouth incredibly dry as I take in the sight in front of me.

Cal. Shirtless. Each and every one of his abs is on full display. They even glisten as the sun reflects off what must be sunscreen that he's applied. My gaze travels down, finding him in a simple pair of navy swim trunks. They hit his lower thigh, giving me the slightest peek of his strong, muscular thighs.

A sharp elbow jab to my stomach makes me yelp. I wince, my eyes darting to Charlotte. "Ow!" I grumble, rubbing the spot where her elbow just hit me.

Charlotte ignores my protest and looks from Cal to me with a smile. "We wouldn't dream of missing this pool party. Lucy had to wait a long time for me. I had to get home and shower and all. I've never been fast at getting ready," she explains.

Cal nods as he comes to a stop in front of us. "Glad you

both made it." He nods his head in the direction of the pool in his backyard. "Everyone else is here."

Charlotte excitedly claps her hands and walks in the direction he just gestured to. "The pool parties I've been to have never been at houses this nice. I'm ready!"

She quickly walks ahead, and I chase after her, not wanting to be left alone with Cal while I'm still getting used to the sight of his perfectly toned body on display.

"Oh my God, your boss is hot," Charlotte whispers to me, leaning in close as we link arms once again and walk in the direction of his backyard.

"Charlotte," I scold, looking over my shoulder to find Cal right behind us.

The smirk on Cal's face tells me everything I need to know. "Thank you, Charlotte," he drawls, keeping pace with us as we reach the gate.

I groan, my eyes snapping forward as a blush creeps up my cheeks. "I hate you so much," I whisper, making sure my voice is actually only heard by her. I wish she could've afforded me the same luxury when talking about Cal's looks. Her whisper was a terrible attempt at being quiet.

Luckily, the sight of everyone we had lunch with at the club distracts me from the embarrassment.

"There you are!" Emma excitedly calls from a pink flamingo floaty in the pool. "The girls and I were worried that we'd scared you off somehow."

"If anyone scared them off, it'd be you, Em," Margo points out from where she lies on a pool chair.

"Rude!" Emma calls out, keeping a smile on her face. She screams when Preston dives into the pool right next to her, splashing water all over her.

"Happy you guys made it!" Jude pushes himself from the pool in one effortless move and walks up to us.

"Hello again, Charlotte," Jude pretty much purrs. He wraps his arm around Charlotte and pulls her body close to his.

"Jude!" Charlotte screams, attempting to push him off her. "You're getting me all wet."

Jude cackles, wrapping his other arm around Charlotte and pulling her flush against his body. "I'd be honored to get you wet," he tosses out, a mischievous smile on his face.

I laugh, stepping around them to search for a spot to set my bag down.

"Jude, don't even think about it," Charlotte yells. I look over just in time to find Jude picking Charlotte up off the ground and throwing her over his shoulder. Her bag drops to the patio just in time for him to run to the edge and jump into the pool with an unwilling Charlotte in tow.

Cal's shoulder brushes against mine as he steps next to me. "Should I be worried that Charlotte might retaliate against Jude?"

I laugh, watching as both Jude's and Charlotte's heads pop out from the water.

"She'll pretend to be mad at him, but I know she actually isn't."

"Want to set your bag down?" Cal asks as if he can read my mind.

I nod as Charlotte begins to yell at Jude even more.

I take a look around, smiling at the familiar faces all hanging out. Jude, Charlotte, Preston, and Emma all swim in the pool. Winnie and Margo lie out on pool loungers, the two of them looking at magazines while their husbands sit at a small table drinking beers. Ryker sits with Beck and Archer, but he doesn't pay any attention to the conversation between the two. His eyes are glued across the backyard where Camille paces back and forth next to one of the raised garden beds, her phone pressed to her ear as she appears to be having an intense conversation with someone on the other end of the line.

Cal's hand finds the small of my back. "You can come sit by me. Jude won't want his chair back anyway." The thin layer of fabric between our skin feels like nothing. It's like his fingertips sear my skin with the slightest pressure as he leads me to a set of pool loungers on the other side of the ones from Margo and Winnie.

"Are you sure?" I ask nervously, missing the warmth of Cal's touch after he removes his hand and takes a seat on the one next to mine.

"If I wasn't sure, I wouldn't say it to begin with," he mutters, his tone playful as he grabs the towel I assume Jude was using and folds it neatly before placing it at the end of his chair.

I nod in response, slowly placing my bag down on the lounger. I grab my own towel out from the bag and work on getting it laid out nicely across the chair before taking a seat.

I can feel Cal's gaze on me, more hot and intense than the summer sun. I try to ignore it for a moment and pretend to focus on watching Emma attempt to pull Charlotte onto the flamingo floaty with her.

Finally, I can't take the feeling of Cal watching me any longer, and my eyes meet his. My heart jumps in my chest at the playful smile that graces his mouth.

He's been so carefree today. Different. Maybe this is how he typically is on the weekends, not bogged down with work calls and meetings in between the social events of summering in the Hamptons. No matter what, this carefree Cal is dangerous. This version of him makes my skin flush and my heart pound.

"Why are you looking at me like that?" I whisper, unable to keep my thoughts to myself.

His smile grows wider. He lifts a shoulder in a casual shrug. "I was just wondering if the way you stared at my abs earlier meant you shared the same sentiment as your friend."

My eyes go wide, and my body jolts with embarrassment. I feel hot all over, and it isn't because of the summer sun or the way he looks at me. It's from embarrassment.

He did catch me.

Hurriedly, I grab my oversized sunglasses from my bag and slip them on. Maybe the size of them will hide the blush creeping over my cheeks. "I have no idea what you're talking about," I mumble, my heart racing at being caught.

He laughs. "I'll take that as a yes, then, Lucy Rae."

Twenty
CAL

This is torture.

I've already been struggling to fight my attraction to Lucy, and being around her all day in a bikini might be one of the worst ideas I've ever had.

And I never have bad ideas. I have great judgment. It's the reason I thrive at my job and the reason I'm able to not only uphold but catapult my family's legacy with Hastings Inc.

But inviting Lucy over was a terrible idea.

She wears a baby pink bikini that I can't stop staring at. I've never been a fan of pink before, but it might now be my favorite color.

The two little pink ties at her waist.

The tiny triangles that hide parts of her I'm suddenly desperate to see.

The color her cheeks turn from the little comments I make.

I squeeze my eyes shut as she walks in front of me, deep in conversation with Camille about something. I need to look away from her.

I need to not be attracted to her.

"Are you listening to a word I'm saying?" Ryker asks, breaking me from my thoughts.

I jolt, pushing my body up in my chair and turning my attention to him. "No. Sorry, I was thinking about work. What were you saying?"

Ryker lifts a sandy-brown eyebrow at me before rolling his eyes. "By work, do you mean you were thinking about the woman who works for you?"

My jaw flexes at the way he blatantly calls me out. Apparently, my attraction to Lucy has been a little more obvious than I thought. "What were you saying again?" I press, not wanting to discuss Lucy with Ryker.

I don't want to discuss her with anyone.

I've never seen the point in fighting my attraction. I haven't had to. It's hard to catch my attention, and every time a woman has, I haven't had a reason to fight it. I get what I want.

But I haven't been in a situation like I am right now. I haven't ever been attracted to an employee of mine. It's wrong, I understand that, but the more I deny it, the deeper the attraction gets.

Ryker laughs at my change of subject, but he lets me do it. "What I was saying is I've got to find a way to ditch Camille. My dad won't let up. I already agreed to fly under the radar here over the summer. I don't know why he's so insistent she be a part of it."

My eyes pull to where Camille and Lucy speak. I tell myself the only reason I'm looking over there again is because we're talking about Camille, but that would be a lie. I want a glimpse of Lucy again.

I've noticed over the past few weeks that if she's not right next to me, giving me the soft smile I'm so fond of, I miss her presence. I'm getting far too used to the way she blushes when she talks back to me or the way conversation is so easy with her.

"Camille really doesn't seem that bad," I offer. As much

shit as I give him for being assigned a babysitter for the summer, I definitely think things could be worse for him.

Ryker scoffs dramatically. I look away from where Lucy and Camille continue to talk about something and focus on my friend. "Not that bad? She's horrible. I have no peace. She follows me around like a damn dog. But at least dogs are cute and lovable. Camille is the complete opposite."

I sigh before pressing the tip of my beer bottle to my lips and taking a drink. "She's just doing her job, Ryker. And as much as it bothers you, you can't blame her for it. You fucked up, her dad's PR firm had to get involved, now you're suffering the consequences."

Ryker scrubs his hands over his face as he lets out a long groan. "She drives me fucking crazy. I won't survive this summer if I have to spend it with her."

I roll my eyes at his theatrics. "It isn't that bad."

I miss whatever he says because I notice that Lucy has moved from her conversation with Camille and is walking toward the pool house with a stack of bowls.

"One second," I tell Ryker, standing up and heading in the same direction as Lucy.

She's busy dumping out the remnants of the snacks in the trash can when I open the door to the pool house.

"What do you think you're doing?" I ask, closing the door behind me.

Lucy jumps a little as her wide eyes meet mine. "Nothing," she answers, her tone guilty.

I take a step closer to her, trying not to think about the fact she's wearing nothing but a bikini. "Today's your day off," I remind her, taking another step forward. My heart thumps erratically inside my chest at being alone in here with her, which is odd because I've been alone with her plenty of times. It's just that those times, we weren't wearing next to nothing.

Lucy sets the bowls on the small kitchenette counter and lifts her hands in the air, her palms facing me. "I'm not working. I just thought that while I had some downtime, I could clear out some of the empty snack bowls."

I cross my arms over my chest as I come to a stop on the other side of the counter from her. My head feels fuzzy, and I'm wanting to make terrible decisions now that I'm alone with her, so I keep my distance, knowing that's the safest choice for both of us. "That sounds an awful lot like work."

Lucy rolls her eyes at me. It's adorable. "Says the man who is always working."

Her sass makes me smile. She has a point. "We're not talking about me right now. I invited you over today as a friend, not as an employee. I don't want to see you working."

The word "friend" sounds odd coming out of my mouth, but I don't know what else to call her. Friend seems like a safe word, even though the thoughts running through my mind right now are not ones I'm used to having about my friends.

"Callahan Hastings...my friend...those are words I never thought I'd say," she jokes. She props her hip against the counter and watches me with a smile.

I stare at her for a moment. The air in this pool house feels thick. It feels small and cramped despite the open floor plan. Neither one of us speaks. Each second that passes by makes the surrounding air seem even more electrified.

What would happen if I just closed the distance between us? If I kissed her, would I regret it? I doubt it, but I keep my feet planted so I don't risk it. I should leave, but I don't want to. I've had to share her with everyone else since the charity golf event, and although I shouldn't, I want her to myself, if only just for a few minutes.

I sigh, pulling my gaze from Lucy's for a moment, needing a second to gather my thoughts. There's one thing that's been on my mind a lot. I just haven't known if I should ask her or not. "As your friend, can I ask you a question that's been on my mind lately?"

Lucy shifts on her feet, her fingers running up and down her arms.

Is she cold? Surely not. It feels like a furnace in here—or maybe it's just me. Maybe my deep attraction to her is burning through my veins, making me feel far warmer than I should.

"You can ask me anything." Her voice comes out barely above a whisper.

I know I shouldn't, but I round the kitchen counter and stop a few feet away from her. I'm still going to keep a bit of distance and not do anything that'd make her uncomfortable, but I want to be as close to her as possible when I ask her the question that's been plaguing my mind for weeks so I can read her every reaction.

"Why haven't you posted a cooking video on your account? You've uploaded photos and recipes but still no videos, even after our last discussion about it." I swallow, remembering the jealousy that ripped through me at the thought of her asking anyone to help her with the videos. Every time I've gone to her profile, I've braced myself to find a video of Jude or someone else on there with her.

Lucy's eyes go wide before she turns to face the sink. With her back now to me, my stomach sinks. Maybe I shouldn't have asked the question.

I close the distance between us. Worry sets deep in my bones that I've upset her.

"I'm sorry, I shouldn't have asked," I begin, reaching out to comfort her. I let my hand drop before our skin connects.

Lucy shakes her head. The ends of her wet hair dance across her lower back with the movement. "It's fine. I just wasn't expecting you to ask, and I guess I got embarrassed. I didn't know you paid enough attention to my account to know."

I grimace, realizing that my question gave away how often I'm checking her account. It's been every day. I can't help it. I've been waiting to see who she posts her first video with. I want to hear her explain her recipes and see the passion in her eyes when she does something she loves.

"Did you not like my idea?" I ask, wishing she'd turn around and look at me.

"I haven't had the courage to ask anyone to help," she whispers. Her voice comes out a little shaky, making me feel guilty for asking in the first place.

I run my hand over my mouth. This is probably another one of my terrible ideas. The last thing I need to do is find ways to get myself alone with her even more, but the next words come out of my mouth anyway.

"Teach me, then."

Twenty-one

LUCY

"What?" I ask, turning to face Cal. I didn't realize how close he'd gotten, but now that we're face-to-face, the distance between our bodies seems so small.

It doesn't seem to bother Cal. He keeps his determined eyes on me. "Teach me to cook and record it. You don't have to muster up the courage to ask anyone because I'm offering myself."

I shake my head. My cheeks heat with embarrassment that he felt obligated to offer to begin with. "Cal, you're busy. You're not taking time out of your day so I can teach you to cook for a silly little video."

The strong muscles of his cheek feather underneath his skin as he angrily clenches his jaw. "What have I said about calling anything to do with your dreams silly?"

My mouth snaps shut for a moment. I don't know how to respond to him. I wasn't trying to diminish my dreams at all with my comment. It was supposed to be funny. He has far better things to do than take time to help me record a video. "I'll ask someone else. I'm sure Charlotte will do it with me. I just haven't asked."

Cal takes another step closer. My heart leaps in my chest

with adrenaline. He's so close that our bodies are *almost* touching. It wouldn't feel so intimate if either of us wore more clothing, but the lack of anything more than swimsuits between us makes the proximity so much...more.

"I don't want you to ask anyone else." His words come out slow and composed until the very end, where they break off with the mention of other people.

"I can't ask you to help me." My words come out so quietly. I'm too focused on the closeness of our bodies to form coherent thoughts.

Cal's blue eyes bore into mine. "You didn't ask. I offered." His eyes cut from mine and travel over my skin.

My breath hitches. He's so close, and the pool house is so quiet that I wonder if he can hear the pounding of my heart. My skin breaks out in goosebumps under his intense stare.

"Cal, you really d—"

Before I can finish my protest, he presses two of his fingers to my lips. The pads are rough against my sensitive skin. He drags them across slowly, making my pulse spike and my thighs shake with desire.

"It's settled. We'll start next week," he states, his voice husky. "I'm looking forward to it."

I can't say anything. Not with him this close.

Time seems to stand still as his eyes stay locked with mine. The sun shines in through the small window behind me. Luckily, the pool house faces in a direction that shields us from the view of anyone at the party.

"Lucy." Cal groans, his gaze falling to my lips.

I can't help it. My lips part in desire at the sound of my name in his husky voice.

He traces over my lips, intently staring at them like he's starved.

"We shouldn't," I mutter, knowing exactly what's going through his mind. It's the same thing that's going through mine.

All I can think about is kissing him. What would his lips feel like against mine? Would they be strong and demanding or soft and gentle?

Cal's fingers move from my lips, but they don't leave my body.

They run down my throat. He presses his fingertips to my racing pulse and leaves them there for a moment. I should be embarrassed that he can obviously feel my reaction to him, but I'm too caught up in the way he stares at me to feel anything but pure desire.

"We shouldn't do this." His tone is normally confident and full of conviction. Right now, it isn't. It sounds like he doesn't even believe the words he's saying.

"Yeah, we shouldn't," I echo, my back arching with plea-sure when he runs his fingertips along the swell of my breast.

"This pink bikini has taunted me all day." He stares, tracing along the string between my breasts.

"I'm sorry," I whisper, not knowing what else to say.

This is inappropriate for so many reasons.

But I want to kiss him—desperately.

The rough skin of his fingertips drags along my ribs as he continues to torture me in the most delicious of ways.

Screams of joy and laughter break out from outside the pool house, but neither Cal nor I move to stop. We're both too caught up in what's happening right here between us.

My head falls back as a faint moan falls from my lips when Cal's fingertips dance along my hip.

"These strings especially. The thought that one simple tug at either bow on your hip and they'd be off drove me wild. It still does...and it shouldn't."

I close my eyes, trying to muster up the courage to stop this.

Not because that's what I want but because it's the right thing to do. "Cal," I whisper, my voice hoarse. "What about Oliver?"

Cal's fingers disappear from my skin in an instant. I open my eyes to find his face closer to mine. The crystal-blue color of his eyes is clouded with what looks like anger. "What about him?"

I shift on my feet, wondering if I shouldn't have said his brother's name at all. It's the effect Cal has on me. I can't think straight and said the first excuse that came to my mind as to why we should stop.

"Lucy." My name comes out like a growl. He leans closer, grabbing the counter on either side of my hips.

God, he's so close.

He smells like sunscreen and his cologne, a mixture that's overtaking my senses.

"What?"

"Don't talk about my brother when I'm seconds away from finally kissing you after I've been thinking about doing it for days...maybe even weeks."

Before I can respond, he grabs me by the hips and places me on the edge of the counter. It's cold against my skin, but his heated stare does plenty to keep me warm.

My skin flushes as his words sink in. Has he really been thinking about kissing me for that long?

Should I feel bad for wanting the same?

So many thoughts run through my mind as Cal's fingertips dig into my skin.

"You've wanted to kiss me before today?" My words come out breathier than I intended them to, but I can't help it. My heart beats so fast and so erratically it feels like it might just beat right out of my chest. It feels like my thoughts are jumbled, and the only thing that makes sense is the heated look in Cal's eyes and the possessive way his fingertips brand my skin.

"Much to my dismay...yes." Cal spreads my thighs open before stepping between them. I try not to stare at the obvious bulge in his swim trunks. Wetness pools between my thighs at the realization his reaction is because of me.

"Really?" The word leaves my mouth before I can think better of it. He's just often so composed it's hard to know what's going through his head. I've felt a connection with him, one I wasn't expecting but can't deny. I just didn't know he was feeling the same.

His thumbs trace circles along my inner thighs, making my nerve endings combust with pure need for him. His hands are dangerously close to the most intimate part of me. There isn't much fabric between us. It'd be easy for him to slip his fingers into my bikini bottoms.

Cal leans in close, our faces now just inches apart. His lips are so close all I'd have to do is arch my neck a little to bring our lips together.

"From the moment you pretended not to recognize me, I was interested in knowing more about you. I wanted to find out what led you here to the Hamptons, but with every discussion we have, I've become interested in so many other things about you, too."

A small moan falls from my lips when his fingers reach up and tangle in my hair. He weaves his fingers through the long, wet strands and uses his grip to tilt my face up, making it so our lips almost graze each other.

"Like what?" I breathe. I feel dizzy with the anticipation of kissing him.

"Lucy Rae, there are so many things about you that I'm interested in. But right now, there are two I can't stop thinking about."

"And what are those?"

"I'm dying to know what you taste like," he answers, his

voice hoarse. "And even more, I want to know if you're going to keep giving me excuses or if you're going to give in to what you want and let me kiss you."

I know this isn't a good idea. There's a list of reasons why I shouldn't let Callahan Hastings kiss me. None of them seem good enough to deny myself what I want in this moment.

It can be only once. One little taste, and then we can create boundaries.

With a deep breath, I meet his blue eyes before wetting my lips. "Close the distance and find out."

twenty-two

CAL

I don't waste another second.

After weeks of wondering what she tasted like, I lean in and press my lips to Lucy's. I'm hesitant at first, wanting to make sure she's okay with this happening.

She doesn't pull away or make any move to end the kiss. Instead, her lips eagerly meet mine. For a moment, we just stay there, locked in the sensation of finally feeling the joining of our lips.

But I need more.

My lips part as I wait to see if she'll let me deepen the kiss. My fingers tighten the grip they have on the strands of her hair, and I pull her body into mine.

Lucy reaches up and places her trembling fingers against my face. Something deep inside me relaxes at the simple touch of her fingertips along my cheek. It's a comfort to know she needs to feel the connection of our skin just as much as I do.

Desperate for more, I let my tongue dance along the seam of her mouth. When she moans, I taste it, and I swear time seems to come to a standstill when her tongue brushes up against mine.

The gentleness is gone. I can't hold back anymore, and it doesn't seem like she can either.

Our chests press against each other as our tongues meet in a wild frenzy. Hands pull at hair, and fingertips dig into skin as we get lost in the kiss. We swallow each other's moans greedily, never once breaking for air.

"Cal." Lucy moans my name, and the moment she does, I know I'll have to hear her moan it again. I want to discover what other sounds I can get from her as I explore her body. Maybe even discover what other ways she can moan my name.

I kiss along her jawline, letting the fingers not gripping her hair explore her body. I want more of her—I *need* more of her—but I don't want to take this too far.

Even *I* know I shouldn't be kissing her right now. I need to be careful that I don't cross the line more than I already have.

But fuck, it's tempting.

My lips trail along her neck as I try to taste her any way I can.

"Everything about you is so fucking tempting," I tell her, my lips dancing along her skin with the words. She tastes like salt from the saltwater pool mixed with something else. Something sweet and delectable. Maybe it's just her.

"Oh my God." Her back arches as my teeth nibble at the sensitive skin of her neck. I guide my tongue over the spot my teeth just dug into, wanting to ease the sting.

Her hands move down my back, and it feels like my skin is on fire everywhere she explores.

"I never want to leave this pool house," I tell her, fighting the temptation to coax the tiny triangle covering her tits to the side and taste her there too. Even her pebbled nipples fight against the fabric, showing their protests over being hidden.

"Why does this feel so good if we shouldn't be doing it?"

she asks, her eyes finding mine when I bring our faces together once again.

"Because even if you think this shouldn't be happening, this thing between us is undeniable." I lean in and kiss her slowly for a moment. My tongue works leisurely against hers, like I have all the time in the world to kiss her.

When she opens her mouth for more, I pull away with a smirk.

"And because I can't imagine anything else I'm meant to do at this very moment other than taste your needy moans."

Her eyelids flutter shut for a moment as she rocks her hips. I think if I dared, she'd let me untie the strings at her hips and press a kiss to her center.

I don't. As much as every part of me wants to do just that, I don't want to scare her away. I thought that maybe if I kissed her once, I could get it out of my system. I tricked myself into thinking it'd be lackluster and all these sudden urges I had for her would disappear.

I was so fucking wrong.

Now that I've kissed her, I want to kiss her again. I want to kiss her everywhere. I can't scare her away before I get the chance to do that.

Apparently a glutton for torture, I trail my fingers over the bow on her left hip. "It'd be so easy for me to pull on this," I toy, not really needing a response from her. My body betrays my desperation for her in many ways, the thickness of my voice being one of them.

"Cal." My name falls from her lips like a plea. I fucking love how many times she says my name. Hopefully, I'm infiltrating her mind like she is mine...like all she can think about is me, and that's the reason my name keeps falling from her lips.

"If I pulled on these strings, would I find that you're wet for me, baby?"

Baby.

The pet name falls from my lips so effortlessly I don't even question it. I can't question it, not after seeing her reaction to it.

Her teeth rake against her bottom lip as she circles her hips. She's seeking some kind of friction, and it's sexy as hell.

"I bet I would," I answer for myself, tugging on the string ever so slightly.

Needing to do something more, I let my fingers dance along the top of her bikini bottoms. My fingertips slide underneath the fabric, but only by a little. Just enough to tease her.

Her moan is everything to me. It's proof she wants this just as badly as I do.

Lucy's hands find either side of my face as she directs me to look at her. I commit the sight of her flushed cheeks and swollen lips to memory. I can't ever forget the sight in front of me. I wouldn't forgive myself if I did.

"Kiss me," she demands, her gaze falling to my lips. "Kiss me again before I feel guilty for letting you kiss me in the first place."

I laugh before doing as she asks. Leaning in, I press my lips to hers, loving how her mouth is open and ready for me the moment our mouths meet.

Her legs wrap around my middle, bringing my straining cock right against her core. She moves against it with a moan, her tongue circling mine inside her mouth.

For a split second, I think about freeing myself and ripping her bottoms off and joining our bodies. I don't, knowing it's far too soon for that.

But the temptation is there. Fuck, it's there.

Lucy tilts her head to the side, opening her mouth wider to deepen the kiss. Even her thighs part more for me, like she's trying to get our bodies as close as physically possible.

I grab onto both sides of her so my hands don't roam anywhere else. I'm so lost in the kiss that I don't even hear the sound of the pool house door opening before it's too late.

"Oh, whoops," a voice calls.

Lucy presses her palms to my chest just in time for both of us to see Margo's wide eyes staring at us.

"Don't mind me." Margo laughs nervously, her eyes awkwardly moving between Lucy and me.

I look at Lucy, finding her cheeks red and her fingers pressed to her lips guiltily. Her bikini top is slightly off-center, and her hair looks a mess. I'm sure mine looks the same.

"Oh my God," Lucy mutters, sliding off the counter.

Margo pulls the door shut without saying anything else. Lucy's panicked eyes meet mine for a moment before she races after Margo.

I step forward, trying to grab Lucy's hand. "Wait," I call after her, wanting her to stop.

When her eyes find mine, my stomach fills with dread. Regret is written all over her face, and I hate it.

"I have to go talk to her," Lucy explains, her voice shaky. She anxiously runs her fingers through her hair in an attempt to tame it. "We shouldn't ha—"

"Don't," I cut her off, the word coming out harsher than I intended. I sigh, trying to soften my voice with my next words. "Don't say we shouldn't have done that."

Her eyes soften slightly. For a moment, I wonder if she's going to stay and talk to me instead of running after Margo.

She doesn't. "I've got to talk to her," she explains before running out the door.

I sigh, dread running through me. My intuition is almost always correct, and the look in Lucy's eyes told me everything I needed to know. She regretted what just happened between us.

Hell, *I* should regret it. I just got caught kissing one of my employees.

But I don't regret it at all.

Instead, I'm hoping it happens again.

Twenty-three

LUCY

My heart races with anxiety as I open the door to the pool house and step outside. Part of me wants to glance over my shoulder and look at Cal, but I can't. I'm too embarrassed about us being caught to do anything but look for Margo.

Part of me expects everyone to be staring at me as I step back outside, as if Margo told everyone what she caught Cal and me doing in the time it took for me to chase after her.

No one pays me any attention. They're all too wrapped up in their own conversations to notice me step outside and beeline for where Margo sits alone on a pool lounger.

I close the distance to her, my cheeks heating with every step closer. It feels like I'm doing a walk of shame, but luckily for me, only one person knows about the shame. *At least the entire group didn't catch us*, I remind myself as I step up to Margo.

"We really don't need to talk about it," Margo gets out before I can say anything. She gives me a reassuring smile. It doesn't help ease my nerves about being caught at all.

"That wasn't what it looked like," I say, wincing as soon as the words come out. I sound incredibly guilty, telling her it's exactly what it looked like.

Margo laughs. "Listen, Lucy, I promise you there's no judgment from me. Trust me. We don't have to talk about it."

Despite her words, my entire body feels tight with nerves. It's like I'm hit in the face with the memory of everything that just happened, because mixed with the embarrassment of being caught is the heat of how right it felt to feel Cal's lips against mine.

Margo narrows her eyes on me before patting the open space on the pool lounger next to her. "Okay, maybe we should talk about it? Is that what you need?"

I groan, running my hand over my face before plopping down next to her. Our backs are to the rest of the party—and the pool house. Maybe just talking to her about what just happened with Cal since she knows about it will help.

"I don't know what I need," I answer, rubbing my eyes with the heels of my hand. "What you saw in there...was a mistake." The comment doesn't feel right leaving my lips, but I don't know what else to call it.

I shouldn't have let Cal kiss me. It's completely unprofessional.

"It doesn't have to be a mistake if you don't want it to be," Margo offers.

I realize I probably shouldn't be airing out my drama to a Pembroke member, but it's too late. She'd already witnessed Cal and me with our tongues down each other's throats. There's no coming back from that. Plus, in the time we've spent together today, I've learned I really like Margo. She's laid-back and down-to-earth, something that isn't always common with people in this town. Especially ones with her status.

"Oh, but it is a mistake. I just made out with my boss."

Margo shrugs, her shoulder bumping against mine. "I married mine."

I give her a curious glance, not knowing that little tidbit of information. "Well, the boss I was just making out with is also my ex's brother."

Margo throws her head back and laughs. "You're messing with me, aren't you?"

I narrow my eyes at her for a moment, briefly glancing behind us to make sure no one's eavesdropping. It doesn't seem like anyone is, but I don't look behind me for long, not wanting to meet Cal's eyes if he's also left the pool house. "This isn't a time for me to make jokes," I whine. "Cal really is my boss *and* my ex's brother."

Margo shakes her head, the smile on her face conveying that it's no big deal. Doesn't she see how stressed I am?

"Beck was also my boss and my ex's brother, so trust me when I say I'm not judging what I just saw. And I won't tell a soul."

I gasp. "Really?"

Margo nods. "Yes. I'm shocked you didn't know. It was all over the internet when we first got together. You could say we didn't have the most conventional start to our relationship."

"I had no idea," I answer honestly. Unless Charlotte tells me the gossip or I overhear it at Pembroke, I don't really know the backstories of many of the club members.

The only person I knew some things about was Cal, and that's because of my...occasional innocent Google search.

"So Beck was really your boss and ex-boyfriend's brother? Tell me more so I don't feel totally guilty that I was seconds away from letting mine have his way with me."

Margo giggles. The sound makes me relax. Maybe, just maybe, I don't need to feel as guilty as I do. I'm at least assured enough that she won't tell a soul about what she found Cal and me doing. "He was. My ex was horrible though, so it really shouldn't matter who Beck was. And my guess is your ex is an ex for a reason, so you shouldn't be sparing him a second thought either."

I shrug. "Mine got with my best friend as soon as we broke up. He'd been in love with her the whole time."

Margo gasps. "Shut the fuck up."

Charlotte screams behind me, catching my attention for a moment. I look over my shoulder to find Jude's hands on the small of her waist as he tries to place her on a hot pink floaty that hadn't been out before.

I pull my attention from my friend and look back at Margo. I don't have to look around to know that Cal is back outside. I can feel his gaze on me, but I don't look in his direction.

Instead, I angle my body toward Margo. "I wish I were kidding, but I'm not. The thing about it is I learned I really didn't love him. Not like I thought I did. I did love her though, so that part hurt."

Margo nods in understanding. She folds her arms across her chest and listens to me intently. "I get that. A best friend breakup can be harder than a boyfriend one."

"Exactly."

"So, if your ex was terrible—and so was your friend—why do you seem so nervous about kissing Cal?"

I let out a long breath, really thinking over her question. It isn't a bad one. She kind of has a point in asking it. I fight the urge to look over my shoulder again, knowing the man who's the topic of our conversation is still watching me closely. "Because I don't want it to seem that the only reason I kissed him was because of what Oliver did. I didn't do it as some kind of revenge, and I feel like if anyone found out that it happened, that's exactly what they'll think it was."

"As long as you know that's not the reason, why does it matter what anyone else thinks?"

I chew on my lip for a moment. It shouldn't matter what

anyone else thinks because no one else will know it happened. I can't kiss Cal again. I mean, I really shouldn't. Except, I want to.

When it comes to him, I feel like I'm losing all sense of reason.

"It matters what people think when they find out he's also my boss. Making out with him would be a HR violation if we were in a typical office space."

Margo tosses her hair over her shoulder. "Your situation is different. As long as he isn't using his power over you, I don't think you should feel guilty about kissing him. It can work out, and no one will care, I promise. Beck and I are proof of that. We're married with the most beautiful daughter. It can work out. Don't overthink it."

I laugh. "Well, I can promise you I'm not overthinking it that much. I go back to Virginia at the end of this summer and will probably never see Cal again. I just have to decide if we should kiss again." I shake my head before running my hands through my hair. "I'm probably getting ahead of myself. He's Callahan Hastings. He probably won't want to kiss me again, so I shouldn't even be worrying about it."

Margo clicks her tongue before bumping her knee against mine. "Listen, I'm saying this as a friend. We're friends, right?"

I nod, smiling at the thought. Today was the first day we really got to spend together, but I really like her. I want to call her a friend. "Of course," I answer.

"Then as your friend, I'm telling you I know an obsessed man when I see one. And that man right there..." She cocks her head in his direction, trying to be discreet, but it still makes me blush because it's a little obvious. "That man is obsessed with you. He wants to kiss you again. I'd bet all my money on it."

I risk a glance over my shoulder, finding Cal staring at the two of us. My cheeks heat at the look on his face. Ryker talks animatedly next to him, but he doesn't seem to pay any attention to his friend. He's focused on me and only me.

"There's no way he's obsessed with me," I offer, quickly turning around so he can't read my lips.

Margo rolls her eyes with a smile. "Enjoy the summer with him, and don't get in your head."

Her words run through my head even after she gets up to FaceTime with her daughter and their nanny. I know I should listen to her and get out of my head about what happened with Cal.

It was the best kiss of my life. Nothing has even come close to making me feel the way I did with his lips against mine. But I need to be careful when it comes to him. It's not just the fact he's my boss and my ex's brother. There's a more important reason why kissing Cal can't happen again.

I have to return to Virginia at the end of this summer. There's no way around it. I can't have a reason to want to stay in the Hamptons. And something tells me if I feel the press of Cal's lips against mine more than I already have, leaving when summer comes to an end will be almost impossible.

I can't kiss Cal again. No matter how badly I might want to.

Twenty-four

CAL

I tell myself it's totally normal for me to start my morning by working at the kitchen counter, even though it's not something I typically do. If I need to work, I do it from my office.

Not today.

Today, I'm sitting at the counter with my laptop open in front of me, staring at the side door, just waiting for Lucy to walk through it.

She hasn't said a word to me since Margo caught us kissing in the pool house. I tried speaking with her during the pool party, but it was clear she didn't want to talk to me. She avoided me at all costs, and I didn't want to make anything obvious by forcing her to speak to me.

But I can only handle the torture for so long. Today, we're going to talk about what happened.

So I sit at the counter and wait.

And wait.

I try to work to pass the time, but I can't concentrate. My mind is too full of Lucy.

I'm seconds away from losing the battle with myself and calling her to make sure she's okay when she opens the door.

"Lucy." Her name comes out strained as I push myself from the chair and walk to her.

"Morning," she responds, her voice quiet and tight. It isn't as cheerful as normal, making my stomach sink.

"Let me help you." I close the distance between us and reach out to take the bags from her. Normally, she only walks in with one from the farm stand, but it seems like she has more of a haul today.

When she smiles at me, something loosens in my chest. The tenseness that's been in my body since the moment she ran away from me in the pool house eases ever so slightly. "Thank you," she mutters, not arguing as I take the bags to the counter. I set them down gently and try to help her by pulling out the contents.

"You really don't have to do that," Lucy protests. She steps closer and places her hand over mine to stop me.

I freeze, looking down at her hand over mine. My eyes close for a moment as I try to push away the memory of my lips against the hollow of her throat. It's burned into my mind, the feel of her skin against mine, and once again, I do nothing to fight off the memory.

Lucy pulls her hand back quickly. It drops to her side as she takes a step back.

I hate the awkwardness in the air. It's never felt like this with her. Even from her first day on the job, things felt natural between us. Right now, it feels strained, and I don't know how to fix it.

I stand to the side, my jaw flexed and my body tight with worry, as Lucy unpacks the groceries for the day. It seems like she's brought way more today than she normally does, but I resist the urge to point that out.

Maybe she's making the most elaborate meals she can think of to keep herself busy and avoid me.

It's silent in the kitchen for another minute or two as she finishes unpacking, lining everything up neatly on the counter.

I sigh, unable to deal with the silence any longer. I'm a direct person, never one to beat around the bush. I was hoping she would walk through the door and want to talk about what happened Saturday, and when she didn't, I held my tongue.

But I can't hold it in for another second.

"Lucy, we should—"

"There were so many options at the stand today that I bought extra," she cuts me off. "I was thinking, if you wanted to, you could host a dinner party tonight. What do you think?"

There's a tightness in my chest at her determination to not have a conversation about what happened, but also because she won't even meet my eyes.

Regret isn't something I ever feel. I always own my decisions. But just this once, regret might be seeping into my bones at what happened with Lucy. Not because I regret kissing her. To be honest, I want to do it again. And I would if she'd let me. I regret it because I'm coming to the conclusion that in kissing her, I might've lost her. And that's not something I'm ready to accept.

I clench my jaw, hoping that maybe I'm just overreacting. Maybe she's just still processing what happened and needs time.

"I wasn't planning on hosting anyone tonight," I grit out, keeping my eyes pinned on her.

I want to plead with her to look at me. I miss the familiar feeling of her warm brown eyes on me. When she looks at me, it feels like she actually sees me. Not Callahan Hastings, the billionaire heir to Hastings Inc. She doesn't see the man who's been called cold and ruthless on the internet or the one with more money than he can ever dream of spending. She sees me.

Just Cal. And I want that back more than I want to kiss her again.

Lucy's back stiffens at my argument. She keeps her eyes trained in front of her, way too focused on organizing the grocery haul for it to be believable. "Why not? The weather is beautiful today. I found so much fresh food. I could really make an amazing menu."

"Because I don't want to see anyone else but you today," I answer, my words coming out blunt but strained.

Out of all things, that's what finally gets her to look at me.

Her brown eyes meet mine, and I realize that it might not just be attraction I feel for the woman staring back at me. I might be developing feelings, something foreign to me. I've always been too busy with school and work to ever deal with feelings, but something is different inside my chest when she looks at me.

Lucy runs her palms over the front of her jeans. She sighs before tucking her hands into her pockets. "We really don't have to talk about what happened, Cal."

I try not to show any kind of reaction to her words, no matter how much I don't like them. They hurt. "Yeah, well, I do want to talk about what happened."

"It shouldn't have happened. You're my boss, and I don't know what I was thinking. We'll just pretend nothing ever happened."

I shake my head. "I don't want to pretend nothing happened." I *can't* pretend, but I keep that part to myself.

Lucy closes her eyes for a moment as she lets out a frustrated exhale. "Cal."

My heart hammers in my chest as I take a step closer to her. I don't close the distance between us fully, no matter how much I want to. I let her have her space. "I don't regret what happened between us," I confess. Being honest and vulnerable like this is new to me, but I don't shy away from it, hoping it helps her see I'm telling the truth.

Her eyes scan my face. "You don't?" The question comes out a little shaky. It takes everything in me not to pull her body into mine. We've never embraced, not really, but for some reason, all I can think about is hugging her right now.

"No. I couldn't regret that for a second."

She pulls her bottom lip between her teeth. I wish I could lean in and press my lips to the spot where her teeth dig in, but I don't. She's finally looking at me, talking to me. I don't want to cross a line and risk losing either. "It just feels like we shouldn't have lost control like that. You're my boss and Oliver's brother. We don't have to pretend like we didn't kiss, but we should at least not do it again."

She's close enough that she can probably hear the sound of my teeth grinding against each other. My jaw is so tense that it's painful. If it was anyone else, I'd stand here and argue, but I've learned enough about Lucy to know that right now, her mind's made up. I don't want to push her too far.

So I nod, even though I can't imagine going the rest of the summer—seeing her almost every single day—and not kissing her again.

Her eyes get wide. It's obvious she wasn't expecting me to agree so easily. If only she knew I'd agree to just about anything right now if it meant her not shutting me out.

"Okay," she breathes, her eyes focusing on my lips for a fraction of a second.

Maybe the reminder of what happened between us is running through her mind like it is mine. My tongue peeks out slightly, wishing to taste her again.

Her chest hitches as a small gasp leaves her lips.

My lips twitch with the hint of a smirk. She can say we shouldn't kiss again all she wants, but her body betrays her. I know she wants to; she's just fighting it for some reason I don't think she's fully shared with me yet.

I'll give her the time she needs to admit it to herself.

She puffs her cheeks out with a loud exhale before plastering on a smile. "So does that mean you've changed your mind about guests tonight?" she asks, her tone curious and hopeful.

I return her smile. "Nope. But you will be teaching me how to cook with all of these incredible and fresh ingredients you brought back. And we're going to record it."

twenty-five

LUCY

My heart hammers against my chest. I don't know if it's nerves about Cal getting ready to press Record or if it's because of Cal himself.

After he insisted this morning that I teach him to cook, he left me alone for the most part. Every now and then, I'd hear his voice filtering out from his office as he took meeting after meeting, but he rarely came out. At one point, he even went to Pembroke for a couple of hours, but now he's back, and it's time for his cooking lesson.

I'm so nervous I could throw up.

"Take a deep breath," Cal tells me from across the kitchen. I was nowhere near prepared to start recording myself, so I didn't bring a tripod or any kind of fancy equipment to record with. He built a makeshift stand for my phone out of different things he found in his kitchen.

"I'm nervous," I admit, giving him a shy smile. His tall frame hunches over the phone as he waits to press Record. Or maybe he's already started recording. The thought makes my stomach drop.

Cal runs a hand through the hair at the top of his head. He's wearing a cream-colored polo shirt and a pair of dark jeans. With him in the video, maybe I will actually get some views. No one will care about the cooking lesson—they'll be too focused on how good he looks.

Or maybe that's just me.

I should've fought him harder on teaching him to cook. With the setting sun outside and the candles he lit for video ambience, it's feeling a little too romantic.

"Stop freaking out." Cal's words snap me out of my thoughts. When my eyes meet his, I find him watching me carefully. There's a hint of a smile on his lips.

"I'm not freaking out," I lie, wiping my hands down the front of my apron.

His laugh sends tingles down my spine. I don't know how there can be an entire kitchen island between us and the man still manages to send shivers throughout my entire body. Despite agreeing this morning that we won't kiss again, the tension is still there.

The sound of my vibrating phone fills the kitchen. Cal looks down at my screen. "It says it's your mom calling. Do you want to take it?"

There's a sinking feeling in my stomach as I nod. "Yeah, I probably need to take it real quick."

Cal grabs my phone and reaches to hand it to me. My pulse spikes with anxiety as I take it and swipe to answer.

I turn and walk to the opposite side of the kitchen, trying to get as far away from Cal as possible.

"Is everything okay?"

My mom knows my work schedule pretty well at this point. I try to give it to her every week, when I know the days and times I'll be working, so she can have an idea of when I might not be able to answer my phone in case of an emergency. The fact she's called has my stomach in knots.

My mom takes a deep breath on the other line, only further

fueling my nerves. "Yes, honey, it's just that I'm at the pharmacy picking up your father's prescription." She pauses. There's a rustling sound as she seems to say something to someone. I wait anxiously for her to keep talking. "Our insurance is getting denied again, and they're telling me the only way I can get it tonight is to pay out of pocket. I'm so sorry to ask. I know you just sent money for the store's rent, but is there any way you could—"

"I'll transfer the money," I say, trying to keep my voice quiet so Cal doesn't overhear. The last thing I need is for him to ask questions I'm not ready to give answers to.

I can picture my mother's face so easily. I know the wrinkles between her brows are probably more pronounced than normal. Anytime she gets stressed, they deepen. And the stress in her shaky exhale is obvious on the other line. "I'm so sorry to ask, honey. You know I wouldn't if I had another option."

I nod, trying to swallow the lump in my throat. "It's fine, Mom, I promise. I'll get it sent right away." Sometimes I feel guilty for taking this time to pursue my own dream. I've left my mom to deal with all of Dad's stuff on her own, but I try to remind myself that the money I'm making this summer is far more than what we bring in at the store. Finishing up this job before returning home is the best thing for everyone. It allows me to earn enough money for us to have actual savings. "Are you sure? I can see if we have extra cash. I just—"

"Mom, I'm going to transfer it immediately. It'll be okay, promise. Just make sure you get a receipt so we have it for our records with the insurance." I speak slowly and quietly, trying to not only calm my mom's nerves but ensure that Cal doesn't hear anything.

"I will," Mom answers, the relief evident in her voice. "Thank you, Lu. I promise we'll pay you back."

I shake my head, even though she can't see it. Guilt washes

over me at the thought that she thinks I'd ever ask her or Dad to pay me back anything. They gave me time to follow my dream before coming home. The least I can do is give them some of my paychecks. "Tell Dad hi for me." I try to keep my voice composed, but it's hard. Emotion clogs my throat, making me sound more hoarse than normal. "I love you both," I add, barely above a whisper.

"I will. We love you. I'm going to tell the pharmacist to go ahead and fill the medication now."

"Bye, Mom."

"Bye, honey," she responds before hanging up the phone.

I stay there, facing away from Cal, for a few seconds to compose myself. I don't know if he heard any of the conversation or not. I hope he didn't, or if he did, he'll pretend he didn't.

With a loud exhale, I try to loosen my muscles. I still feel a little stiff as I turn to face Cal, but I plaster a smile on my face anyway.

He hasn't moved, but his furrowed eyebrows and the intense way he keeps his eyes trained on me tell me enough. Even if he didn't hear the extent of my conversation with my mom, he's still worried. "Everything okay?" he asks, his voice low and sincere.

I try not to think too deeply about the concern written all over his face. It's better if I think this tension between Cal and me is only physical. The last thing I need is to convince myself that he actually cares about me.

"Everything's fine," I assure him, walking back over to where I've prepped the ingredients for the meal.

Cal watches me carefully. His blue eyes track my every move as I rearrange the items on the counter just to give myself something to do.

He clears his throat. I meet his gaze as he grabs the edge of the countertop and leans forward. The intensity with which he stares at me, his lips set in a hard line, makes my pulse spike. "You know you can talk to me, right?" His voice comes out gruff.

I nod, my face feeling suddenly flushed. He stares at me like he cares, and that's dangerous for my heart. I give him what I hope is a believable smile. "I do. Like I said, everything's fine. My mom just needed help with something, but it's all good now."

He sighs. His knuckles tap against the countertop with a second deep exhale. "Okay. If you say so. You good to record?" He gestures to the film setup.

I nod my head, walking over to him and looking down at my phone. I don't have any more notifications from my mom, but I turn the ringer on just in case she calls while it's recording. "Hopefully you won't regret offering to do this with me," I tease, trying to lighten the mood.

He scoffs. "Wouldn't dream of it, Lucy Rae." I watch quietly as he carefully places my phone in his makeshift camera setup.

His eyes find mine as one corner of his lips lifts. "I'm going to press Record now so we can get started."

Nervous butterflies take flight in my stomach. Even with him here, I feel anxious about talking while the camera's recording. I try to push that to the back of my mind. "I'm as ready as I'll ever be," I answer with a groan.

Twenty-six

CAL

"Okay, just like that," Lucy says softly from my side. She leans over the counter, watching me closely as I grate parmesan onto the platter in front of me.

"Is that enough, or should I add more?" I ask, loving how natural it feels to be in the kitchen with her. I've never been particularly interested in cooking. I'm all about being efficient. It's always made sense for me to hire someone to prepare meals for me so I can focus on work. But being in the kitchen with her tonight and learning from her has turned out to be a better time than I expected.

"Personally, I love the way fresh parmesan elevates bread-crumbs, so I'd say you can do more."

I nod, doing exactly as I'm told. She stands by my side, using a spoon every now and then to mix the breadcrumb mixture around.

"Next, we're going to take our pounded chicken breasts, dip them in egg, and then we're going to coat them in the bread-crumbs." Lucy looks at me as she explains what we're going to do, but at the end, she gives the camera a shy smile.

I can't help but smile too. It's obvious the further we get

into this lesson, the more comfortable she becomes speaking in front of the camera.

"Got it," I respond, watching carefully as she shows me exactly what to do.

"And once it's nice and coated, we're going to place it on our lined pan before repeating with the rest of the chicken." It's quiet as she lets me take over coating the chicken breasts in the egg wash and breadcrumbs. I don't miss that with each minute that passes by, her shoulders loosen little by little.

It struck something deep inside me to see the concern written all over her face when she got the call from her mom. I'm not sure what happened, and it was obvious Lucy didn't want to tell me either.

However, whatever it was, it worried Lucy...which means it worried me. From the moment she took the phone call, I've wanted to ask what was wrong, but I've kept myself from doing so.

If Lucy wanted to tell me, she would. And for some reason, it's bothering me that I'm not someone she trusts enough to confide in, even though it makes sense why she wouldn't. We haven't talked about a lot of personal things. What goes on in her personal or family life shouldn't be my business.

But I want it to be my business. I just don't have the nerve to tell her that yet because I don't want her to tell me no.

"Those look perfect," Lucy compliments as I finish putting fresh basil leaves atop the slices of mozzarella she had me place between each piece of chicken.

"Only because I have an amazing teacher." I fold my arms across my chest, basking in the warmth that comes from her smile.

"Chicken parmesan is pretty simple," she mumbles, tucking a piece of hair behind her ear as she focuses on the ground for a moment.

"Maybe some of the best recipes are simple but delicious."

It seems like she's forgotten all about her phone, which is still recording, by the way her entire face lights up at my words. "Simple but delicious. I like that. That's what I want my recipes to be."

I cock my head in the direction of the pan of food we need to put into the oven. "It seems like that's what they'll be. My stomach is already growling thinking about eating this meal."

She rolls her eyes before sliding the pan off the counter. Carefully, she walks it to the large oven range. "The trick to the perfect chicken parm is to make sure your oven is hot. You don't want to overcook the chicken, but you want the cheese to get nice and melted and the crust of the chicken to be crispy. A hot oven is key."

I nod. I probably won't ever be making this dish again, but she doesn't need to know that. Maybe I will one day just to reminisce about making it with her. I'll remember the way she smiled at me when I followed her directions correctly. Or the way she blushed when my arm would brush against hers.

I won't forget any of it.

Lucy slides the pan into the oven and quickly shuts the door. Her eyes meet mine, and for a moment, the rest of the kitchen fades away. I see nothing but her as she pulls her bottom lip between her teeth to fight a smile.

"I think it's going well," she whispers, her cheeks getting pinker by the second.

Fuck. I love the way she blushes so easily.

I'd love to see what other parts of her body flush because of me.

I squeeze my eyes shut for a moment, trying not to think of her like that right now. I need to keep my thoughts under control. If I don't, I'll do something stupid like lift her onto the counter and make out with her again. Except this time, there's no one here to catch or stop us.

"It's going better than well," I tell her. "Since the moment we started, you'd never know you don't like being recorded. You've done amazing guiding me—and your future audience— through the recipe."

She walks from the oven to me. Her palm finds the countertop as she rests some of her weight against it. "Well, you're not done with your lesson quite yet. I've still got some things to teach you...if you're okay with that."

I swallow, my mouth suddenly feeling incredibly dry. Thoughts run through my mind like a damn freight train of all the things I'd love to teach *her*. None of them have anything to do with cooking, making them inappropriate at this moment.

"I'm here as long as you want. Use me however you need." My words come out more and more rough with each one that leaves my mouth.

I turn away from her, having to adjust myself for a moment at the mental picture of ways she could use me. "Would you like some wine before we start the next part?" I rush to get my words out, trying to put as much distance between us as possible.

I thought it'd be easier for me to push my burning attraction to her aside. I didn't think it'd be too difficult to be a good student and pretend that the taste of her lips didn't haunt my thoughts all weekend. But it's harder than I thought it'd be. Maybe a few minutes away while I pick out a bottle of wine will help me get my thoughts straight.

"Everything okay?" Lucy asks from behind me, not answering my question. I keep my back to her as I take a deep breath to stifle my desire for her.

"Yes," I answer hoarsely. "Just thought it'd be the perfect time for a glass of wine."

I can't see her reaction to my words. But I can hear her deep breath. "Wine would be perfect. Whatever you think will pair well with the chicken parmesan and fresh spaghetti."

I nod, hoping she can see it even with my back to her. "I'll be right back," I respond, rushing away to give myself a moment to compose myself.

As I fuss over what bottle of wine will pair perfectly with this meal, I come to the terrifying realization that I don't just want Lucy at this point. I *need* her. I'm desperate for more.

More of the press of her lips against mine.

More of seeing a blush creep across her cheeks.

More of getting to know her.

More of her soft giggles.

Or more of her letting me inside that beautiful mind of hers.

I'm intrigued by everything she does, dying to know whatever she'll share with me. Now, all I can hope is that maybe she'll realize she wants the same things as me.

Maybe she'll want more.

Twenty-seven

LUCY

The first glass of wine took the edge off being around Cal.

The second glass of wine was probably a mistake.

I'm still fully aware of every decision I'm making. The problem is the wine has cleared my mind just enough that all I can focus on is the man sitting next to me at the kitchen island.

Cal insisted we sit here instead of at the kitchen table. He said he wanted to be closer to me so he could have a front-row seat to me trying the meal he mostly prepared by himself, with my guidance.

I didn't think much of his request, but now I'm wondering if I should've insisted on sitting at the table.

At least then, there'd be a barrier between us. His knee wouldn't keep bumping against mine. I wouldn't feel the press of his thigh against mine as he widens his stance in his chair.

I stare at my plate, more food left on it than I thought there'd be. It's not like I'm not hungry or the food isn't good. Cal's meal is very impressive.

I'm just too caught up in being so close to him to be able to stomach anything.

As if he can read my mind, Cal's voice breaks through my thoughts. "Is my cooking really that bad?"

I'm nervous to look at him. My body is buzzing with electricity, and I already know meeting his deep blue gaze will further light my body on fire.

I shake my head, staring down at my plate like it's the most interesting thing in the world. "The food's amazing, Cal."

He lets out a deep, throaty laugh. I remember when I felt the exhale of his laughter against my lips. I want to feel it again.

"You could've fooled me," he responds. "You've barely touched what I made."

I can't fight the pull to look at him any longer. My eyes meet his, and just like I expected, a bolt of desire runs through me.

"I promise what you made is perfect."

"You're perfect." His eyes slip to my lips. He doesn't hide the fact he's staring at them. In fact, he keeps his gaze pinned on my lips for far too long.

My heart pounds at his words—or maybe it's the way he stares at my mouth like it's the only thing that matters in the world.

"Cal," I get out, my tongue darting out to wet my lips.

"Don't," he rasps, his eyes meeting mine.

"Don't what?" My skin prickles with need. I want to feel more than the press of his thigh against mine, no matter how bad of an idea it is.

"Don't say my name like that." Apparently, he can't fight the sizzling tension between us either. He turns in his chair so that he's facing me directly. Our knees bump against each other with the new position, his legs suddenly encroaching on my personal space.

I don't fight it. I don't move. I can't. Not with the way he looks at me. All protests of why it's a bad idea to give in to my attraction to this man leave my mind the moment our eyes meet.

"How did I say your name?" I whisper, unable to make my voice any louder than that. My cheeks feel hot, and desire courses through my veins at the proximity of our bodies.

He tortures me by not answering my question. Or maybe the torture is the way he adjusts his body. He places his legs on either side of mine, caging me in completely. Now, his inner thighs press against my outer thighs.

"Like you're hungry for something that isn't this meal."

My eyes widen, and my cheeks flush. I know I'm toeing a very dangerous line right now. I'm the one who didn't want to talk about the kiss with him and pretend like it never happened. I'm the one who ran out in the first place. He hasn't hidden the fact that he wants to kiss me again. The problem is, I can't pretend anymore. Right now, all the reasons I felt we couldn't kiss again feel insignificant.

I straighten my back as my need for him takes over. For right now, I don't need to think rationally. I just need him.

"What am I hungry for, then?" I dare to ask, my entire body tight as I wait for him to answer.

He smiles, and I swear that cocky grin is like a caress against my skin. Heat runs from my head to my feet, making my toes curl inside my shoes. I wait with bated breath for him to speak, needing to know what his answer will be.

Instead of answering, he grabs onto the seat of my barstool and pulls me closer to him. The legs make a loud scratching sound against the hardwood.

At this point, I swear he's got to be able to hear the sound of my racing heart. It beats so loudly that there's a whooshing sound filling my ears.

"I still need to figure out what exactly you're hungry for."

His fingertips dance along my knee as he traces circles on my skin. "Is it my touch?" he asks, his voice deep and hoarse. My entire body shivers underneath his touch. I didn't know just the simple connection of skin somewhere so innocent could make heat pool low in my abdomen.

I don't know if I'm thankful for wearing a tennis skirt to work or if I regret it. Either way, the short fabric makes it easy for him to trail his fingers up my thigh.

"Tell me to stop if you don't want this," Cal says. His voice comes out strained. His eyes scan my face, searching.

I shake my head. "I can't."

His eyes darken at my response. I stifle a moan when he applies even more pressure against my inner thigh, his fingertips getting dangerously close to the part of me that's most desperate for him.

"Then tell me you want this. Tell me you're hungry for anything I'll give you."

My eyes flutter shut at his words. They aren't exactly dirty, but my body reacts like they are. "Yes," I manage to get out, my voice thick with lust.

I know it's a bad idea to do this with Cal. I'm already more attached to him than I should be. He's gotten underneath my skin and burrowed deep. The witty banter, prolonged looks, and unnecessary but wanted touches have broken me down. Nothing can change the reality that I have to go home at the end of this summer. We live two very different lives. Nothing can come of this attraction between us.

But is it really that bad to give in to the tension just for the summer?

Cal's calloused fingers inch higher and higher on my inner thigh and under my skirt. One of his knuckles brushes against my clit, making my hips buck in my seat.

He chuckles, the sound coming from deep in his chest. "You *are* eager for my touch." He touches me there again, but this time purposefully and with his fingertip. "Very eager for me with how wet you are. You're soaked through your panties, baby."

I let out a loud moan as I squeeze my eyes shut. It already feels like too much with him, and barely anything has happened between us.

His warm, big hands find either side of my waist as he lifts me off my chair and pulls me into his lap. I yelp, my eyes flying open in surprise. His hands slide down my back and grip my ass as he pulls my legs over him.

I'm straddling Callahan Hastings.

There are layers of fabric between us, but it's impossible to miss the way his length brushes up against my core. I moan at the feel of him there, immediately wishing there was nothing between us at all.

Our gazes lock. Cal's blue eyes stare deeply into mine as I rock my hips against his once.

His body goes tense underneath mine as he sucks in a deep breath. "Fuck," he mutters. He keeps one hand splayed on my ass while the other travels up my back. His fingers twist in my hair, directing me to keep my eyes pinned on him.

"I want this," I tell him. Something about the way he looks at me tells me he needs to hear the words. Maybe I need to hear myself say them. It's me accepting that this connection between us is undeniable, and I'm tired of pretending it isn't.

"Good fucking answer," he grits, leaning close and running his nose against mine. My entire body shakes with anticipation.

I didn't intend for this to happen tonight. I came to work thinking Cal and I could pretend everything was normal and nothing had happened between us at the pool party. I was foolish for thinking that. I've never had this kind of connection with anyone. I'm allowed to explore it—even if it's just for the summer.

"You hungrier for my touch or my lips?" The words are whispered against my ear, sending shivers down my spine.

"Both." I turn my head, trying to make our lips connect. He doesn't give in. He continues to tease me by just barely running his lips along the tender spot behind my ear.

"I meant here," he announces, moving his hand from my ass to between my thighs.

My head falls back in pleasure. "I want you to kiss me," I tell him. Or maybe it isn't me telling him—maybe it's me begging.

Cal shocks me by lifting me by the hips once again and placing me on the counter. A wine glass falls to the ground with the abruptness of his actions, and the chair scrapes against the floor as he stands to his full height.

The entire time, he keeps his eyes on me.

I love it when he looks at me like this—like I'm the only thing that matters to him. That's the thing about Cal. It's hard to get his attention, even harder to keep it, but when you have it, it's hard not to feel like the most powerful person in the world.

He spreads my legs wide open, cold air hitting my inner thighs. A loud, unfiltered moan leaves my lips when he slides his fingers underneath the fabric of my panties.

"Is this where you want me to kiss you, Lucy baby?"

twenty-eight

CAL

My entire body feels like a rubber band that's been pulled tight, just aching to be released. All I've wanted is to have Lucy like this again, but it wasn't something I was confident would happen.

Seeing her lust-filled, big brown eyes stare up at me as my fingers run through her wetness is my undoing.

I've never wanted something as badly as I want Lucy Owens. I'm desperate, ready to get on my knees and beg for her if that's what it takes to get her to see that this connection between us is undeniable.

By the way her body trembles underneath my touch, it seems like begging won't be necessary. Although, I might still get on my knees and eat her perfect pussy the way I've been dreaming of.

"Talk to me," I press, needing to hear her admit that she needs me. With each passing day I've spent with her, I've needed her more and more. I'm at the point where it feels like I'll combust if I don't have her. I almost did when I got that little taste of kissing her and had to pretend that the kiss didn't rock my world.

I drag my fingers through her wetness and circle her clit. I want to bottle up her moan that echoes through the kitchen. It's so fucking sexy I'd love to hear her moan like that all night tonight and every night after. I slide her panties to the side, getting my first view of her.

Fuck, she's perfect. I already knew she would be. Everything about her is.

I lean down and press a kiss to her inner thigh. "Do I kiss your lips or your pussy first? I'm fucking starved for both."

Her body shudders at my words. Or maybe it's the fact I still circle her clit at a slow pace as I wait for her to answer me.

"Kiss me," Lucy speaks up, her voice strained. She keeps her eyes on me, watching my every move as I decide what to do.

I continue to feather kisses along her thigh to tease her. I know it might be cruel, and it tortures me just as much as it does her, but I can't help it. She deserves to be teased just a little for walking out on our kiss and trying to pretend it never happened. "I plan on it, baby," I assure her, remembering her demand. "Tell me where."

She takes me by surprise by wrapping her fingers in the hair at the top of my head and pulling. She yanks, taking exactly what she wants as she pulls my head toward her.

"I want you to kiss me again like you did in the pool house. Like nothing else matters but me."

I smile, leaning in so my next words are said against her lips —the lips that haven't left my mind since the moment she's talking about. Hell, they were on my mind far before then. My hand not covered in her arousal reaches up to cup her jaw, angling her face up so she sees nothing but me.

"Nothing else matters to me, Lucy baby, I can promise you that." Before she can respond, I trap her lips with mine, reveling in tasting her again.

During our first kiss, she was hesitant. She needed a moment to let me in. Tonight, her mouth is wide open and ready for me. I groan, and she swallows the sound of my realization that she's had time to think it over. I can be confident this is exactly what she wants.

My tongue slides into her mouth, eager to feel hers against mine. I don't know how long we stay just like that, the two of us swallowing each other's moans as we give in to the passion between us.

I step between her thighs, pausing circling her clit so I can fully press our bodies together. My elbow hits something—I think another wineglass—as I twist her hair between my fingers, making sure to keep the one covered in her arousal out of the strands. Whatever it is hits the ground and shatters at my feet, but I don't pay it any attention.

It doesn't matter. Not when I'm finally kissing Lucy again.

Our chests rise in rapid succession as we take what we want from the other. We're teeth and tongues and wandering hands, the two of us desperate to get as much as we can from one another.

I rake my teeth along the hollow of her throat, nibbling slightly before easing the sting with my tongue. "You have no idea how many times I've thought of kissing you again," I admit. "God, Lucy, it feels like you're all I've thought about since the moment you left me alone in that pool house."

"Cal," Lucy whimpers, her head falling to the side as she gives me better access to her neck. "Don't say things you don't mean."

A growl comes from deep in my chest as I pause. I line my eyes up with hers, needing her to look me in the eye with my next words. "I'm not the kind of man who says things he doesn't mean." My words come out gruff, maybe even a little harsh, but I need her to know that anything I tell her is the truth.

No matter how frustratingly foreign the feeling is, I feel

something for her. It's more than something. It's a lot. How she could even question if I mean what I say is beyond me.

Before we do anything else, I gently wrap my fingers around her wrist and bring her fingertips to my neck. I press them against my skin with enough pressure for her to feel her effect on me.

"No one's ever made my pulse spike like this. When I tell you that you're all I've thought about, I mean every word."

Her fingers twitch against my skin. She presses even harder, her fingertips firm against my dancing pulse. The most beautiful smile spreads over her plump lips. "Good. Now, kiss me again, Callahan Hastings. You said you were hungry, after all."

I smile as my heart leaps in my chest. I've been so focused on my career throughout my adulthood that I never gave myself time to develop feelings for anyone. I was married to my job, and I liked it that way. I even thought it could never happen to me, that I would never be able to feel anything for anyone. But then came Lucy Owens, proving to me that it isn't impossible, that the right person just hadn't come along. I have no idea what any of this means or what will happen, but I know that I'll savor every moment I have with her. I won't take for granted the moments I get to have her just like this.

I lean in, capturing her lips with mine. I've never been happier to oblige her request. I want to kiss her all night and make up for the lost time between Saturday and today.

"I promise I was just going to teach you to cook tonight," Lucy tells me, pulling away just enough to get the words out. She's breathless from the kiss, the skin around her lips red from where my facial hair has rubbed against it. "I don't want you to think I had any ulterior motives...other than using you to be able to record myself teaching a recipe, of course."

Her rambling is adorable. I smile before gently moving a

piece of hair out of her eyes. "Have ulterior motives about kissing me anytime you want."

Her cheeks turn my favorite shade of pink. She lets out a little laugh before rocking her body against mine. "Your charm is impeccable right now. You're saying all the right things."

I give her a wolfish grin. My tongue peeks out to wet my lips as I take a step back and appreciate the sight in front of me. I've traveled all over and seen some of the most incredible sights this world has to offer. None of them hold a candle to the one in front of me.

Lucy, with her eyes on mine, her lips raw from kissing me. With her cheeks pink and her chest heaving in anticipation, there truly is no better sight in the world.

There's broken glass at my feet and splattered wine on the floor, but it doesn't matter. It's a mess I can clean up later. Right now, I'm more worried about eating her pussy so well there's a mess between her thighs.

I bite my lip as an intense sound of arousal comes from deep in my chest. I'm so fucking ready to have a taste of her, to feel her come against my tongue. I adjust my aching cock in my chinos at the thought.

My time enjoying just the sight of her is over. I take a step closer, placing my palms on her inner thighs. "Time for you to spread those legs open nice and wide for me, baby. I'm ready to finally get a taste of your pussy."

Twenty-nine

LUCY

"Wait," I call, stopping Cal as he lowers his face between my thighs.

My heart races faster than I even thought was possible with how much I want him right now. Wetness pools between my thighs at just the thought of what he's about to do. But there's one more thing I need to tell him before he does anything else.

I bite my lip, nerves buzzing through me. "I just wanted you to know that it can take me a long time to...you know..."

He lifts a dark eyebrow. How is something so simple so seductive when he's the one doing it? "Come?" he finishes for me.

My cheeks heat at the way he says it. I nod. "Yeah, and that's if I even do it at all," I mutter. Something about telling him this with his head between my thighs makes my words even more embarrassing.

His fingertips twitch against my thighs. He's silent for so long that I wonder if I should've stayed quiet. My stomach sinks slightly as I try to press my legs back together, but his hands digging into my skin prevent me.

"I just wanted to let you know in case you thought it was taking too long. You don't have to make me finish," I rush to get out, stumbling over my words. "I just didn't...uh..." I close my eyes for a moment out of mortification. Leave it to me to ruin one of the most erotic moments of my life to tell him that it can be hard for me to come if someone else is doing it. "I didn't want to fake it with you." The last words are said so quickly I don't know if he can even understand them.

A low rumbling sound comes from deep in Cal's chest. His fingertips dig into my skin as his heated gaze moves from my core to me. His eyes are narrowed. At first, I worry he's upset. Then, I realize they're hooded with lust. The cockiest, most dangerous smile spreads over his lips. "I'll stay here all night until you come against my tongue, Lucy baby."

Then...he winks.

He freaking *winks*.

"But I know it won't be long until you're moaning my name." And if I weren't seated on the counter, I'd be weak in the knees at his confidence. He uses my shock—or horniness at seeing him wink at me—to his advantage and hooks his thumbs in the fabric of my panties and tugs.

He effortlessly slides the fabric down my thighs and then bunches it in his palm. "I should've known they'd be pink. Can I tell you something, Lucy baby?"

"What?" I pretty much pant, my senses on overdrive by the way he looks at me. He looks like he truly is starving for me and only me.

"I think pink might be my favorite color. It's the color of your cheeks when you blush, your lips after kissing me, your panties, your pussy..." His words trail off as he swipes a finger through my wetness.

My hips buck off the counter at the feeling of having him touch me there. It's like my entire body is on fire with that one simple touch.

Maybe his cockiness is justified. He slowly inches a finger

inside me, and my vision blurs from how good it feels. My head rolls backward as a moan escapes me.

Cal laughs against my inner thigh. His breath is hot against me. God, he's so fucking close to being just where I want him.

"I'm so fucking hard just at the sight of you," Cal tells me, placing a chaste kiss on my hip. He's a tease, and I can't even be mad at him for it because I love it.

"I want to feel it." I lean back, placing my palms against the cold counter to help hold my weight. He's trailing kisses along my skin as he gets closer to putting his mouth on my clit. I know the moment his mouth finally connects, I'll need the extra support to keep me upright.

"Oh, you will. I can't fucking wait to feel your fingers wrapped around my cock. Fuck. I'm getting harder just imagining it." He presses his palms to my inner thighs and spreads them even farther apart.

Even though they're dimmed, the pendant lights that hang above the kitchen island shine directly over us. There's no doubt he can see all of me.

If it were anyone else, I'd be embarrassed to be on display like this. But I want him to see me, something I never expected to crave.

"Before I finally get a taste of you, just remember how much I love it when you say my name. Understood?"

I nod, unable to form words because he runs his tongue over me.

I moan, my toes curling at the feeling of finally having his mouth right there. He starts slowly, his tongue circling my clit. It feels so good that my entire body tingles with pleasure.

He slides a finger inside me. It feels euphoric to not only have him licking me but filling me as well. His tongue flicks against my clit before he lets out a low growl. "Fuck, you're the best thing I've ever tasted."

My head falls back when his mouth fuses against me again. "Cal." I moan his name just like he wanted me to. I can't help it. He eats me out like a man who's been starved, and it feels far too good to keep quiet. I knew things would be different with him because I've never felt this kind of raw attraction before. It's the reason I couldn't fight this thing between us any longer, even though I know it's bound to get complicated. But even knowing how much I wanted him, I didn't expect my entire body to feel like it was on fire so quickly.

He's going to make good on his promise. I'm going to come —and it'll be soon.

Cal slides another one of his thick fingers inside me. It's only his fingers, but I already feel so full I can't imagine what it'll feel like to have his dick inside me. For a moment, I worry if I'll even be able to take it.

All worries are wiped away as he hooks his fingers inside me at the same moment he pulls my clit into his mouth and sucks.

"Oh my God." I lift my hips off the counter, trying to find some kind of relief from the building tension deep inside me. It's like a spring has been pulled tight, just waiting to be freed. I'm so close. The buildup is intense as he continues to finger me and eat me out at the same time.

"Cal, I think I'm going to come." I pant, my hips circling as I try to chase the release I'm so close to. I don't know how long his mouth has been between my legs, but I know he's got me closer to coming faster than I can even get myself there.

He laughs—freaking laughs—with his tongue against my clit. "Yeah, you are. You're so fucking close I can taste it. Come all over my tongue for me, Lucy baby."

His words are my undoing. It's like my entire body explodes as the orgasm rips through me. "Cal!" I scream, moan after moan falling from my lips as the waves crash inside me.

He doesn't stop at all; if anything, his fingers and tongue work faster.

The orgasm overtakes me.

I can't focus on anything but the sensation of him between my legs as all the tension is freed, resulting in the most euphoric feeling in the world.

thirty

CAL

Lucy's hips buck up and down as she rides out her orgasm. Her moans and pleas, mixed with the way she repeats my name over and over again, have my cock straining in my pants.

She's so fucking beautiful when she comes. I haven't been able to take my eyes off her from the moment I tasted her.

Her thighs tighten around me, caging me in to breathe nothing but her. I revel in it, loving how she squeezes me and keeps me in place.

Her taste coats my tongue, and my fingers curl inside her. I milk the orgasm as long as she'll let me, wanting her to experience every delicious second of me making her feel good.

"Cal," she finally gets out, her thighs parting slightly, allowing me to move. Her voice is raspy from her screams. "That was..." Her words trail off.

I carefully slide my fingers out of her, reveling in the sight before me. "That was everything," I comment, my eyes trailing over her body.

I'll never be able to walk into my kitchen again without thinking of her on the counter, spread out just like this for me. Her chest heaves up and down as she regains her breath.

Nothing's ever been hotter than hearing my name while

tasting her come. Her entire body shook against me as her pleasure took over. I'm already looking forward to doing it again.

"I can't believe we just did that," Lucy mutters, her eyes darting around the kitchen. "That was so good."

I smile as I stand to my full height and bring our faces close together. "Just good?"

She smiles, her eyes tracing my mouth. I can feel her wetness still coating my lips, and I can't help but wonder if that's what she's focusing on. "It was more than good," she says slowly, her attention still fully on my mouth.

"Kiss me?" I ask, desperate to feel her lips against mine again.

She bites her lip and looks at me bashfully from under her eyelashes. "Is that okay with you?" she whispers, her gaze flicking to my lips for a moment. "It looks like you still have..." She pauses as her cheeks somehow get even pinker. "Well, you might still have *me* on you." Her words are said so low I wouldn't have been able to hear them if we weren't face-to-face.

I let out a low groan at how sexy her words are. "Kiss me so you know how good you taste," I demand, leaning close and running my nose along her jawline. "Then you'll understand why I might get addicted to having my face between your thighs."

She takes me by surprise by leaning forward and claiming my lips with hers. The movement is bold, and I can't even try to hide how much I fucking love her taking control. A rumble of a growl comes from deep inside me at how turned on I am by the thought of her tasting herself on me.

Her tongue swipes across mine as her hand slides down my chest. My stomach tightens as her hand snakes lower and lower.

"Lucy." Her name comes out choked as her fingers dance along the waistband of my pants.

She doesn't answer me. Instead, she continues to kiss me like her life depends on it. I kiss her right back, savoring the simple fact that I get to kiss her at all. The look in her eyes after we kissed in the pool house had me worried I might not get a chance to do it again.

I'm so fucking happy I did.

She slides her hand from my waistband, her fingers softly drifting over my cock.

My forehead finds hers as I try to take a breath, thinking about how good that one little tease of her touch was. She slides her hand over it again, her fingers tracing over the outline of my straining cock. Air hisses through my teeth as I suck in a breath at the feeling.

"I want to touch you," Lucy tells me, her voice raspy and needy.

I groan, rocking my head back and forth as our foreheads still rest against one another. "Fuck, I want that so bad."

She laughs, fully grabbing my cock through my pants this time. "Then let me."

"I didn't even think I'd get to taste you tonight," I admit, trying to keep it together as she continues to stroke me through the fabric of my chinos. "I don't want to rush things," I continue, but she doesn't listen to a thing I say.

"What if tonight is your only chance?" she counters. My eyes fall shut as her lips find my neck.

I wasn't expecting this from her. I wasn't prepared for it. I'd love to remove the annoying fabric preventing her from really touching my cock, but I truly don't want to move too fast. I'm afraid if I let her touch me—suck me—the way I'm desperate for her to do, it'll be too much too soon, and it'll scare her away.

I can't lose whatever is starting between Lucy and me.

Because of that, I let out a low groan of regret before

reaching between us and softly wrapping my fingers around her wrist.

"Tonight won't be the only chance, Lucy baby. Whatever we've started isn't stopping anytime soon. Let's take it slow. Tonight was about you."

Lucy pulls her head back. Her bottom lip juts out in the tiniest of pouts. "You don't want me to?"

Something deep in my chest aches at the question. I grab her chin and tilt her face up, making sure she's looking at me as I speak my next words. "Trust me, baby, there's nothing I want more right now than to feel your hand wrapped around my cock." I swallow, my mouth feeling dry at imagining how fucking good it's going to feel when she finally does. "Fuck, I'm hard and ready for you just by the soft little teases you're giving me. I just..." I sigh, not knowing how to explain what I'm thinking to her. "I just don't want to rush things and freak you out. I can't handle having you look at me with that look of regret again like you did in the pool house."

Her eyes soften as she moves her hand to my cheek. My body protests, wanting more of what she was doing, but my heart leaps inside my chest at the caring way she's looking at me right now.

"I won't regret this happening tonight," she assures me, her words coming out confident as her eyes scan my face.

I let out a sigh of relief. "I hope you mean that," I admit, cupping her face.

For a moment, we just stand there looking at each other. I'm the first one to move. I place a small kiss to her waiting lips before taking a step back. My eyes find the floor.

There's glass and wine everywhere. "Stay right there until I get this cleaned up," I command, already backing up to grab some paper towels.

"Cal, I've got on shoes. Let me help you. I think I'm the one who knocked them down anyway."

I shake my head, holding my hand up to point at her. "No. You sit right there until all of this is cleaned up."

Lucy rubs her lips together as she fights a smile. She leans forward a little, her legs dangling off the counter as she adjusts her position. "Your bossiness and ability to get what you wanted with a simple command used to push my buttons."

I crouch to the ground and begin to carefully move the glass to a central location. I'll need to use a broom to sweep up all the broken pieces, but first, I want to try and soak up some of the wine. "What about now?" I ask, looking up at her from the ground. "Do I still push your buttons?"

She lifts her shoulder in a shrug as she gives me a beaming smile. "Now, I think your bossiness is hot. I like it when you push my buttons." She goes quiet for a moment. It's almost like I can see the wheels turning in her mind as she thinks about what else she wants to say. "You bring out a different side of me. I like it."

I return her smile, pride blooming deep in my chest. Her words are exactly what I wanted—needed—to hear. I love that there's a side of her that only I bring out. I look down, focusing once again on cleaning up the mess on the ground.

The entire time I'm cleaning up, I fight the inclination to tell her how much I like her. She brings out a different side of me as well. I've never dealt with feelings or caring for a woman before. Not in the way I'm starting to care for Lucy.

It's refreshing and terrifying. I have no idea if she feels the same, and for the time being, I'm too nervous to even ask her. For right now, I don't need to know how she feels. Knowing she won't regret what's happened so far between us is enough for me.

"Okay, I think we should be good," I tell her, standing up

and looking at my clean floor. I took the vacuum to it as well, wanting to make sure there weren't any remaining shards of glass.

"Never did I think I'd see you on your hands and knees cleaning," Lucy notes, sliding off the counter. "It was kind of sexy."

I chuckle, grabbing her hand and pulling her body against mine. "Was it now?"

Lucy nods, her fingers twisting in the fabric of my shirt. "It was."

I playfully nip at her lips, loving the feel of her body against mine. "I couldn't risk you slipping or stepping on glass."

Lucy smiles before wrapping her arms around my middle. She squeezes as she hugs me tightly.

The gesture makes me realize I don't know if I've ever just *hugged* someone. Not like this. Her ear presses to my chest, and I wonder if she can hear how fast my heart beats in this position.

I've never been interested in embracing someone like this, but as I tuck my chin over her head and hold her close to me, I realize I'd stand here all night if she wanted to.

It feels right to hold her just like this. "Thank you," Lucy mutters, her words coming out a little muffled from where she talks against my chest.

"For what?"

"For tonight," she answers, her body relaxing further against mine. "For letting me teach you a recipe and cooking with me. I felt more comfortable in front of a camera than I ever have."

"You don't have to thank me for it. I loved cooking with you and seeing you in your element. You're meant to share your recipes with the world."

She laughs against me. "You have way too much faith in

me. The video we made tonight could still suck. I need to watch it and see."

I shake my head. "I'll have all the faith in you until you have it in yourself. What are we making tomorrow?"

Lucy pulls her head up and looks at me. "Cal, we can give it some time. You don't have to make another video with me tomorrow."

I don't know how it isn't obvious to her how much I want to be around her. I've been very clear about how I don't do anything I don't want to do. I want to cook more with her tomorrow. I want to spend time with her. "I know. So what are we making?"

Lucy purses her lips as she thinks about my question for a moment. "I'll have to think on it tonight. I like my trip to the farm stand to guide my recipes for the day as well, so I won't know for sure until tomorrow morning."

I nod my head before giving her a smile. "Can't wait to find out tomorrow, then."

"You're so stubborn. You really don't have to film with me tomorrow."

I press a light kiss to her lips. "I know."

"You're still going to do it anyway, aren't you?"

I smile and nod my head before pressing another kiss to her lips. "I sure am. I can't wait."

She sighs but doesn't stop beaming while doing it. Fuck, she's beautiful. "What am I going to do with you, Callahan Hastings?"

I grab her hips and pull her close to me, having the perfect idea. I know exactly what I want her to do with me before she goes home tonight. "Kiss me."

thirty-one
LUCY

"Thank you again for paying for the prescription, Lu. You know I hated having to call you," my mom tells me through my phone's speaker.

I sigh as I sit back in the seat of my Bronco, waiting for a group of joggers to pass in front of me. It's another beautiful morning in the Hamptons. There are a lot of people already out enjoying the weather despite the early hour as I drive to Dolores's farm stand.

"Mom, you don't have to keep thanking me. Of course I was going to make sure Dad got whatever meds he needed."

"I just feel bad with all this money you keep sending home. Are you sure you don't need it?"

I wince at the sadness and remorse in Mom's voice. I know how much she hates asking for money, but she doesn't understand that I wouldn't be able to have any of this if she hadn't let me pursue my dreams for a year before returning to Virginia. It's really nothing to send money home. I make far more than I could've ever imagined now that I work for Cal.

"I don't need it, Mom," I assure her. "I want to send it to you and Dad. If you don't need it now, put it in savings in case something comes up."

Mom's quiet on the other end of the line. I leave her alone with her thoughts, knowing she needs the time to gather them before saying anything else. I drive slowly toward the farm stand, the warm wind hitting my cheek through my open windows as I take the curves slowly.

"You know it's your brothers' birthday soon," Mom finally says. My foot hits the gas a little harder than necessary at her words. I wasn't expecting her to bring up my brothers or their birthday.

"I know," I answer, trying to hide the emotion clogging my throat over how much I miss them.

Not only is it almost their birthday, but that day also marks the anniversary of when we lost them both in a car accident almost seven years ago. Our family was big on birthdays until we lost my brothers to a drunk driver. Now, we pretend the day is just like any other. No one talks about Luke or Logan anymore. It hurts too much.

My mom sighs on the other end of the line. I imagine her standing in the kitchen I grew up in. Mom and Dad had the house long before my twin older brothers and I were ever born. I can see it so clearly, my mother hovering over the counter with the phone pressed to her ear. She loves to stand at the kitchen counter and talk on the phone while staring out the back kitchen window. I know just by the way she sighs that there's more she wants to say but is holding back.

"How's Dad doing today?" I ask her, wanting to change the subject to avoid the silence. Plus, I know her well enough to know she'd rather have a change of subject as well, even though she's the one who brought them up.

"He's doing good. Insisting that he should work all day at the store when I'm telling him that's a horrible idea."

I can't help but smile, even though it might be a bit of a sad one. "That sounds like Dad," I respond. "Is Alec there today?"

"Alec's here most days. Even on his days off, he comes in to check on your dad and make sure he isn't overworking himself," she replies, and I nod quietly to myself.

A little over two years ago, Dad had a heart attack. When it first happened, the doctors weren't sure he'd make it. But he did. It took countless rehab appointments and what felt like setback after setback, but he shocked everyone with his recovery. We didn't think he'd ever return to the family store he'd poured his heart into for decades, but he made sure he could.

Just, sometimes, it's too much on him, no matter how much he doesn't want to admit it. He's getting too old to run the store. I'll be back at the end of the summer to help him. I appreciate Alec, my brothers' best friend, who I've known my entire life, for stepping in and helping Dad as much as he does.

"Make sure to tell Alec 'hi' and 'thank you' for me. I can't wait to see him and Elaine when I come back."

Mom laughs, and it feels so good to hear the sound. Recently, it seems like our phone calls consist of reviewing Dad's medications and talking about the store. It's good to just hear her laugh and let go a little. "I will. Elaine's finally in her second trimester and feeling better. She doesn't totally hate being pregnant anymore."

For ten minutes, my mom and I have a normal conversation. We talk about her excitement over Elaine and Alec having a baby. Over the years, he's become another son to my parents. Alec was always with my brothers, meaning he was always at our house growing up. When the twins started working at the family furniture store, so did Alec.

He kept working for my dad even after Luke and Logan passed. Seven years later, I can't imagine what the store would be like without him. Mom's over the moon that he and his wife are having a baby. She jokes it's her way to get her baby fix in since I'm nowhere near having children of my own.

"Be honest with me. Is your boss nice to you? Are you happy? I worry how the people there treat their staff."

My cheeks heat at my mom's question. She asks it innocently. She has no idea that my boss is very nice to me. In fact, he was kind enough to give me the best orgasm of my life last night.

I pull in next to a big SUV and put my car in park. "Yes, I'm happy. My boss is fine. He treats me well, I promise."

"Are you sure he treats you well?" she presses, making my cheeks feel even hotter due to her line of questioning.

"Yes. It's a really good job, Mom. I'm happy. I promise."

Mom hums on the other end of the line. She's quiet for a moment, which gives me time to gather myself, her questions having taken me by surprise.

I woke up this morning excited to see Cal again. I'm also a little nervous to see him after he had his face between my thighs last night, but it's a good kind of nervous. I'm not sure what's happening between us, but I don't want it to stop. But before things progress any further, I should probably talk to him. I get attached easily, and getting attached can't happen since I leave at the end of the summer.

Although I doubt that's something he'll have a problem with. He doesn't seem like the type to get attached.

"Okay, Mom, I'm at the farm stand, so I'm going to let you go. I'll call back tonight once I'm off."

"Okay, honey. I love you. Thank you again for sending the money over."

"Stop thanking me, Mom. I love you. Tell Dad I love him too."

Mom listens to me. She doesn't mention the money again. "Bye, Lu. Have a good day at work."

I pull the phone from my ear and make sure the call has ended. Something in my chest feels lighter this morning. I hadn't realized how much I missed just having a normal conversation with my mom. As I grab my purse and my mesh bags, I make a mental note to have more conversations like today's with her. It was good to get a glimpse of who she was before Dad's heart attack.

I step out of the Bronco and slide my phone into the back pocket of my striped linen shorts. Paired with a baby tee and a pale yellow cardigan, it isn't the most professional outfit I've worn to work, but I didn't have time to do laundry over the weekend and was too busy doing other things with Cal last night to catch up either. Plus, he doesn't seem like the type to really care about more professional work attire. I think we left any professionalism behind the moment he kissed me in the pool house.

The cool ocean breeze lifts my hair off my shoulders as I walk toward the farm stand. Dolores isn't sitting in her normal chair keeping lookout, which means she must be busy helping customers.

I hear Dolores's laugh before I see her. I don't think I've ever heard her laugh so hard. It makes me smile as I walk up to the stand. I'm running through what items I might want to pick up for meals today when my footsteps falter.

My eyes connect with *who* is making Dolores laugh like a schoolgirl.

It's like he can sense me because Cal's gaze finds mine immediately. I try not to melt at the slow smile that spreads over his lips.

God, why does he have to look so good all of the time? He's still intently listening to Dolores, evident in the way he's still responding to her, despite the fact that his eyes never leave mine. My feet stay planted as I work through the shock of seeing him here this morning. It's early. While his schedule changes day to day, he usually uses this time in the morning to go for a run or to work.

Not go to the farm stand.

He looks too good to be shopping for fresh fruits and vegetables. He wears a pair of light-colored pants that are perfectly tailored to his body and has paired it with a cream-colored knit shirt. Everything about him screams wealth. He looks out of place next to Dolores's farm stand.

Speaking of, she notices that Cal isn't looking at her anymore. She looks over her shoulder and smiles widely when she spots me.

"There's the beauty we were talking about," Dolores croons, gesturing to me to close the distance between us.

I smile shyly as I follow her request. "Good morning," I mutter under my breath, looking between the two of them. I blink, wondering again if Cal really is here or if I've made it up.

No, he's definitely here. The smirk doesn't leave his face as he coolly tucks his hands into his pockets and keeps his attention on me. "Good morning, Lucy."

thirty-two
CAL

"What a surprise it is to see you here this morning," Lucy says sweetly, coming to a stop next to Dolores and me. She keeps blinking and looking at me, almost as if she's trying to figure out if I'm actually here or not.

"I love a good surprise," I respond. My fingers twitch inside my pockets as I focus on the woman who I couldn't stop thinking about last night. In fact, she infiltrated my mind so much that early this morning, I woke with thoughts of her, of looking forward to seeing her. Eventually, I accepted I wasn't going to be able to drift back to sleep, so I got out of bed two hours earlier than normal and went about my morning.

It's worked out perfectly.

"Cal was just telling me that you were teaching him how to cook. That's so kind of you, Lucy." Dolores places her hands on her hips as she looks between me and Lucy with a smile on her face.

Lucy narrows her eyes on me. "Is that all he's told you?" she asks, her face pinching together in confusion.

"Yes," Dolores offers.

Lucy nods before rolling her eyes. "He seems to have

forgotten that the only reason he's learning to cook is because he's helping me."

Dolores purses her lips as she stares right at Lucy. I smile, purely entertained by the interaction going on. Dolores shakes her head before she looks at me. "You seemed very interested in what Lucy likes to purchase and how often she's here to be the one doing her a favor."

I cough, not expecting to be called out. I go head-to-head with some of the most powerful men in the world and don't bat an eye. Why is this woman who's old enough to be my grandmother the one who's able to catch me off guard?

"Was just making conversation," I respond, looking over at Lucy. She stares back at me with her arms crossed over her chest and her eyebrows raised. It's clear she's still wondering why I showed up this morning.

I'm asking myself the same thing. All I knew was I wanted to see her as soon as possible. I didn't want to wait until she made it to my house, so I drove to the farm stand.

"So, what are we shopping for today, Lucy?" I ask, tilting my head and watching her with the corner of my mouth lifted.

"I haven't decided what I'm making yet. I was going to see what looks good here, unless you have any requests?"

I shake my head. "I'm excited to make whatever you want."

Someone walks up to the farm stand, pulling Dolores's attention from us. She walks over to greet them as Lucy stays where she's standing and stares up at me.

"What are you doing here, Cal?" she asks with a smile. She pulls her sunglasses from the top of her head and slides them over her eyes as she waits for me to answer.

I take a step closer to her. Everything in me wants to grab her by the hips and pull her body to mine, but I don't know if that's something she'd want. Because the PDA might make her uncomfortable, I keep my hands stuffed in my pockets, no matter how badly I want to feel her body against mine.

"Can I give you the honest answer, or do you want me to make something up?" I ask, watching her closely. No matter how excited I was to see her this morning, part of me has also been anxious. She assured me she wasn't going to regret what happened between us last night, but part of me wondered if she'd change her mind when left alone with her thoughts.

Her wide, radiant smile and the blush creeping up her cheeks tell me that maybe my worries were just worries. "I want you to give me the honest answer."

The tightness in my back loosens a little at her response. "I'm here because I wanted to spend time with you. You're always so excited to tell me about your finds here. This morning, I wanted to experience it with you."

Her lips part as her chest rises. She stares at me with her big brown eyes, the same eyes I went to bed dreaming about and woke up thinking about. "I was not expecting you to say that," she confesses.

I wasn't expecting to feel it. I keep the thought to myself, no matter how true it is. Everything with Lucy is unexpected, and I don't see the use in fighting my desire to be around her. I can either get what I want and be around her, or I can avoid her and think about her the entire time. If I'm with her or not with her, the fact that I've caught feelings for her remains the same.

"Well, while we're talking about things that are unexpected, I have a request," I begin.

Lucy adjusts the strap of her purse on her shoulder, her eyes narrowing on me. She wears a pair of blue-and-white striped shorts that I'm trying hard not to stare at. I can't help but picture sliding them down her sun-kissed thighs and kissing the sensitive skin on the inside of her legs before pulling her clit into my mouth.

"And what is your request?" Lucy's words break me from the dirty thoughts I'm having about her.

I scrub my palm along my face as I try to play it cool and pretend I wasn't daydreaming of tasting her again. "I'd like for you to take the morning off and spend it with me."

Lucy's jaw falls open. "It's Tuesday. I'm supposed to work today. Do you not need food?"

I shake my head. "Not breakfast or lunch. Spend the day with me. And then this evening, we'll film another recipe video."

Lucy rubs her lips together in an attempt to hide her smile. She looks over her shoulder to see if anyone is near, but Dolores is helping customers far enough away from us that she can't hear anything. Lucy's eyes meet mine again. "Are you asking me out on a date?"

"Only if your answer is yes."

"Do you not have to work today?"

I'm the CEO of Hastings Inc. My father passed it down to me on my thirtieth birthday. I could work every minute of my day if I *wanted* to. My schedule is filled with calls I was supposed to be on, but I don't tell her that. We've got a few investment companies we're looking into that I need to look over, but that can wait. "I'm the boss, and I make the rules. There's nothing on my schedule today but to spend time with you."

Lucy sighs before tucking a piece of her dark hair behind her ear. I love that I get to see it fully down like this. When cooking, she typically pulls it back. It's nice to see her out and about instead of in my house.

"Do I have a choice?" she asks playfully.

"Of course you do. You can tell me no, and I'll give you the morning and afternoon off, still paid. You don't have to spend time with me if you don't want to. What I want doesn't have to be what you want." The last words come out a little hoarse. I'd be disappointed if she didn't want to spend the day with me because I want to spend it with her so badly, but I'd respect her decision.

It seems like it takes forever for Lucy to answer. Her soft smile has me hopeful she wants the same thing as me, but I remain cautiously optimistic as I wait for her response.

"Yes."

Relief floods through my entire body as a smile spreads over my lips. "Yes, what?"

"Yes, I'll spend the day with you."

"It's a date?" I ask, wanting so badly to reach out and run my fingers along her cheek.

"It's a date," Lucy confirms, making me feel like the luckiest damn guy in the world.

I laugh, a foreign feeling of happiness and something I can't describe coursing through my veins. "Good," I get out, having to clear my throat because of how raspy the word comes out.

We stand there staring at one another for a moment. We wear matching smiles. The morning has barely begun, and it already feels perfect.

Lucy's smile falters for a moment. She reaches out and places her hand on my arm. "There's just one thing I want to say before we start our day date."

All the happiness that was running through me seconds ago turns to nerves at the look on her face. She chews her bottom lip anxiously, like she's dreading what she's about to say.

"What is it?" I ask, even though I don't want to know the answer.

"I know this probably goes without saying, and you don't even seem like the type to get attached. You're probably used to casual dates and hookups." Her words falter for a moment as a blush fans out along her cheeks at the mention of hookups.

"But I'm normally not a casual person—never have been. I'll be leaving at the end of this summer. I can't do complicated. So this thing between us is just casual, right?"

I'm quiet for a moment as I think through her words. I hate picturing her leaving at the end of the summer and never seeing her again, but I hate missing out on spending time with her while she is here even more.

"Just casual," I assure her, even though the words don't feel right when I say them.

Nothing about what I feel for her could ever be casual.

Thirty-three

LUCY

"Cal, you really don't need to do this," I insist for what feels like the tenth time.

Cal doesn't listen to me. He keeps his phone pressed to his ear as he talks to someone on the other end. We'd been looking over the vegetables at Dolores's farm stand when Cal had asked me why I drove instead of riding my bike. I told him that my basket was broken and I didn't have the storage I needed to get the food back to his house.

By the time we checked out with Dolores and were walking back to our cars, he declared I needed to ride with him because he had somewhere to take me.

Turns out that *somewhere* was a local bike shop, where he insisted I pick out a brand-new bike. We've been standing in the aisle for a while now as I wait for him to accept that I'm not letting him buy me a bike.

Cal turns and talks under his voice for another minute before he faces me once again. "Which bike are you picking out, Lucy baby?"

I stare at him with my mouth wide open. The man really is stubborn and not listening to a thing I've been saying.

"I'm not picking out a bike," I tell him as I fold my arms across my chest.

"Then I'll pick one out for you."

A strangled noise comes from my throat. "No, you're not doing that either."

"Are you two still doing okay over here?" one of the sales workers asks from a few feet away from us. He smiles nervously as he looks between Cal and me.

"The bikes here are beautiful, and I'm sure they're top of the line," I begin, my eyes scanning all the different choices the store has to offer. There are pink bikes and yellow bikes and bikes of any other color I could imagine. Ones that are retro and ones that are electric. If I needed a new bike and had money to spend, this would be the perfect place to shop. "But I don't need a new bike," I continue, narrowing my eyes at Cal in a look that I hope conveys to him that I'm serious.

I look at him for a few more seconds before focusing my attention on the worker. "Thank you for offering to help, and I'm sorry to waste your time."

"What about this one?" Cal asks, grabbing onto the handlebar of a light green bike with a cream-colored woven basket.

"No."

He sighs, keeping his grip on the handlebar as he looks the bike over. It's beautiful. If I were looking for a new bike, this one would be a contender. But I'm not looking for a bike.

Cal clicks his tongue as he continues to admire it. "I thought you'd love this one. The green reminds me of the apron you like to wear."

My heart melts at him bringing up my favorite apron. It was one my mom got me before I left for the Hamptons. I know it was a splurge for her to buy, so it's my favorite to wear when I cook. It touches me that he remembered it at all. "The bike is gorgeous, Cal. It doesn't mean I need a new one. If anything, I need a new basket for the bike I already have."

"This bike has a basket that looks good." He pulls on it gently. "Looks sturdy to me too. Could fit a pretty decent farm stand haul."

I shake my head. "You know you're supposed to listen to the person you're on a date with."

This makes him laugh. He walks away from the bike and closes the distance between us. With no one around, he cups my chin and tilts my head up to look at him. "Trust me, I hang on every word you say. I understand you don't necessarily need the bike, but I *want* to get it for you. The one you've been using is old and clearly falling apart since the basket came off. It isn't safe for you to be riding around the Hamptons on."

I roll my eyes at him. With each comment he makes, it's getting harder to deny his offer. "The basket came off, Cal. I'd hardly call the bike unsafe. I got it for a good deal since I don't need it for long. I'm leaving at the end of the summer, remember?"

He lets out a growl as his lips press into a thin line. His eyes track my face for a moment. "I'm well aware you're leaving. I'll pay to have it shipped to Virginia for you."

His calloused fingers scrape against my skin as he moves his hand from my chin to my cheek. Now isn't the time to ask, but I can't help but wonder where his callouses even come from. I know it can't be his job.

The two of us are quiet as I try to think of another excuse to give him about why I don't need to pick out a new bike. Some things come to mind, but I know by the hard set of his jaw and the way his blue eyes stare into mine that I'm not going to win this battle with him. He's made up his mind that I need a new bike, and he's determined to buy me one.

I let out a long sigh before leaning into his touch. I've tried to make sure to keep my distance from him, unsure about his feelings on other people seeing us like this, but the bike shop is empty besides the workers. I don't think we'll be caught here.

"I don't want you to think you have to buy me expensive things. My bike is fine."

Cal leans in and presses a kiss to my lips. It's the first time we've kissed since he walked me to my car last night.

I missed kissing him. He kisses me slowly but possessively, making my toes curl in my sneakers.

He pulls away before the kiss gets too deep. It's still intense enough to make my entire body heat with desire. "I want to buy you expensive things, Lucy. What's the point in having an ungodly amount of money if I can't spend it on the first woman to capture my attention like this?"

There's a whooshing sound in my ears with the intense spike of my pulse at his words. I don't think I heard him correctly. He's thirty-four years old; surely, many women have caught his attention. I know I've seen photos of some of them on the internet when I used to look up his family. His pinky gently presses against my pulse from the way he holds my face, making me wonder if he can feel the way my heart rate jumped at his words.

He doesn't take them back or elaborate. All he does is stare at me, his eyebrows raised expectantly.

I can't think of a response. I'm still too stunned by what he admitted—and questioning the truth of it—to come up with a witty remark. Seconds pass, maybe even minutes, as we stand in the middle of the bike aisle, staring at one another.

Finally, I accept that there's no stopping him. If he wants to buy me a new bike, he's going to. "Fine, you buy me the bike. But I want you to know I'm not used to people buying me things often, and I don't know how to properly accept them. If I act weird, that's why."

Cal smiles before moving to cradle my face with both of his hands. "That's okay. I'll make sure to spoil you so much in the time that I have you that you get used to it."

And before I can respond, his lips press to mine again. The kiss is perfect. He takes his time, kissing me right in the middle of the bike aisle for anyone to see.

When he's done, he's patient as I look at every single bike the store has to offer before deciding on the green one he found earlier.

thirty-four

CAL

"Have lunch at Pembroke with me today," I tell Lucy as I walk toward her in the back garden of my house. She hunches over one of the garden beds as she collects fresh basil.

Lucy turns to face me with a smile. It's been almost two weeks since my first cooking lesson with her. Almost two weeks filled with stolen kisses when no one's around and finding excuses to spend as much time as possible with her.

"It's Friday, and I'm supposed to be working," she states matter-of-factly. She plants her hands on her hips as she stares me down.

"Good thing I'm the boss. You don't have to work today. Come to the club and have lunch with me. "

"Cal, you already gave me all of yesterday off unexpect-edly. I don't need today off too."

She wears a floppy sun hat that makes me smile. Anytime she's out harvesting from the garden, she wears it. I find it adorable. It's so...*her*. I grab her by the hips and pull her body into mine, loving that there's no one here stopping me from holding her close.

"You had yesterday off because I had to fly back to

Manhattan for work. I didn't get to see you for a day, and I missed you. Have lunch with me."

Lucy wraps her arms around my neck. "I will have lunch with you." The mischievous smile playing on her lips tells me exactly what she means by that.

I shake my head before leaning in and playfully nipping at her bottom lip. "I mean a lunch you didn't prepare."

She sighs before rising to her tiptoes to plant a kiss on my lips. I know she's trying to distract me, but it won't work.

My hands travel down her back before I let them slide underneath the fabric of her dress.

It's also been almost two weeks since I've tasted her, and I feel starved. It's not because she hasn't tried to push things further. She's tried many times to repay the favor and touch me the way I touched her. I just haven't wanted to rush things with her and scare her away.

But my patience can only go so far. My hands cup her ass cheeks and squeeze as I pin her body to mine.

"You want to go to the club...just us two?" she asks, her voice hesitant. "Won't people find that weird?"

I hate the wrinkle of worry that appears along her forehead. I'd let anyone see us together if I knew she'd be comfortable with it. "Even if they found it weird, which they shouldn't because there's far more interesting gossip than us having lunch together, no one would say anything. I want to leave the house with you, baby."

"What if instead of lunch, we do a dinner and invite everyone to join us?" she offers, her fingers playing with the buttons of my shirt.

I try not to frown. I'd like to take her to the club and make it seem like a date. The only time we're ever alone together outside of the house is when we go to Dolores's farm stand. We go together just about every morning, a routine I've grown fond of and want to continue, but I also want to do more with her.

I keep all my thoughts to myself despite how hard it is. With anyone else, I'd be blunt about what I want, but things are different with Lucy. She makes me more patient, even if it doesn't feel good in the moment.

"If that's what you want to do, then that's what we'll do," I respond, keeping my voice controlled. I don't want her to hear the disappointment in it. I understand why she might not want people to get the wrong idea. She used to work at Pembroke, and she works for me now. The rumor mill can get crazy. People are bored and love any reason to talk. I just don't really give a damn what they say. But if she does, I won't push her to go on a date with me.

Maybe next time I approach it, I can ask her to go somewhere that isn't the club. Maybe that'll get her to say yes to an actual date.

"Are you mad at me?" Lucy asks, her voice cautious. Her honey-brown eyes nervously roam my face. She moves her hands to my chest and keeps them there, her eyes watching me expectantly.

I hate that her default is to think I'm mad at her. Something I've learned about her is that she's a people pleaser. From the little I've gathered during the rare times she talks about her family, she's responsible for taking care of them. She's a nurturer, and because of that, she's focused on asking how others feel instead of focusing on how she feels.

"I don't think I could ever be mad at you even if I tried," I admit.

She bites back a smile as her eyes dart to my chest. "Good, because I have a confession."

I raise my eyebrows. "And what is that?"

She pulls her hands from my chest and holds them up

between us. "I had no idea my hands were dirty before I touched your shirt." She wiggles her fingers a little, proving that they're dirty from the garden.

I let out a dramatic gasp as my eyes fall to my shirt. The pale blue linen now has two perfect muddy handprints on it.

"I'm so sorry," Lucy starts, her eyes wide with sorrow. "I forgot to grab the gardening gloves from inside, and I really didn't think I'd be out here long. I didn't even think about checking my hands before touching you and..." She pauses, her hands still dangling in the air between us as her eyes search mine. "And now you're actually mad, aren't you?"

A low chuckle leaves my throat. "What'd I say? I can't be mad at you."

Her shoulders fall as she lets out a sigh of relief. "Oh, thank God."

I smile. "But..."

"But what?"

"You're going to pay for that," I tease, lurching for her.

She's quicker than I thought. A loud scream comes from her chest as she dodges my grip just in time. "Cal!" she yells, running through the garden beds to escape me.

"I'm going to catch you, baby," I tell her with a laugh, running after her.

"No!" I love the sound of her laughter as she races around the garden. Her hat flies off with the sudden movements.

"It's only fair," I tell her, standing on the opposite side of the bed from her. "You ruined my shirt."

Her hair falls down her shoulders. It's messy and untamed, thanks to the hat. She looks so fucking beautiful. "I didn't mean to," she explains, twisting her hands in front of her before wiping them off on her dress. Her eyes move to the ground for a moment before she looks back at me. "I'm sorry," she adds with a radiant smile.

"Prove it. Let me catch you so I can get you back." Without warning, I try to lunge in her direction.

It happens fast.

She lets out an adorable yelp and drops to the ground for a moment.

As she stands up, she points the hose right at me. Before I can react, water hits me square in the chest.

Lucy lets out the cutest giggle I've ever heard as water continues to spray me in the face and chest. "I'll help you get clean!" she yells.

I smile, taking a moment to bask in the pure joy. The way she smiles freely as her entire face lights up is worth being sprayed in the face with cold water from the hose.

Fuck. The way I feel about her—the feelings she brings out of me—are unlike anything I've ever felt before. She might ruin me, and I can't even blame her for it. She's told me she wants this to be casual. The problem is, seeing her smile like this, hearing her laugh as she stops spraying me with water and drops the hose, makes me want things I know I can't have.

I sigh, trying to ignore the blossoming ache in my chest.

Her chest heaves up and down from her laughter as she watches me carefully.

A smile slowly blooms on my lips as I tuck my hands into my pockets. "You better run, Lucy baby. Because when I catch you, you're going to pay for that too."

thirty-five

LUCY

My heart races in my chest as I rush through the double doors that lead from Cal's porch into the kitchen. I can hear him running after me, but I don't look back.

I run as fast as I can, my laughter echoing off the walls of his house as I run down the hallway. I don't even know where I'm going; I just know I'm trying to prevent him from catching me for as long as possible.

It doesn't work. I'm halfway down the hallway that leads to his room when his arm snakes around my waist.

"Got you," Cal growls against my ear.

"I really didn't mean to get your clothes dirty," I tell him, my lips twitching with a smile he can't see from behind me.

His chest shakes against my back with a throaty laugh. "That might be true, but you knew exactly what you were doing when you got me all wet."

Taking me by surprise, he grabs my waist and spins me to face him. In one fluid motion, he steps forward and presses my back into the wall.

My eyes flick down to where his wet shirt clings to the outline of his toned abs. I swallow, my throat suddenly feeling dry at the sight. "I was just trying to help you get clean," I offer in my defense.

Cal leans in. My lips part eagerly, waiting for him to kiss me. Something about him chasing me was hot. Or maybe it's the way the fabric of his shirt sticks to all of his defined muscles that has desire coursing through my veins. Either way, my pulse spikes eagerly as I desperately hope this is the time he finally lets things progress between us.

He doesn't kiss me. Instead, he teases me by bringing his lips centimeters from mine before pulling away. His eyes flicker down to the muddy handprints on his shirt. "The shirt doesn't seem any cleaner. I'm still dirty, but now I'm also wet."

I try not to smile as dirty thoughts run through my head.

As if he can read my mind, Cal's hand finds my inner thigh. "I think it's only fair if I return the favor."

I moan at the scratch of his fingertips on the tender skin there. It hasn't even been two weeks since I've felt him touch me like this, but I've missed it. We've kissed plenty of times... countless times recently. But he's done everything in his power to keep it from going even a baby step past making out.

It seems like the wait has been just as hard on him as it's been on me. He wastes no time snaking his hand up my thigh and running his pointer finger over my aching clit through the thin fabric of my panties.

"Are these satin?" Cal asks, a choking sound coming from his throat as his fingers glide over the fabric.

I nod, my back arching off the wall at finally feeling his touch again.

I've missed it way more than I want to admit to myself.

"Yes," I pant as he inches a fingertip underneath the fabric. "I've been wearing cute underwear for weeks, hoping that something would happen between us again."

He presses his lips to mine as a sound of approval comes

from deep in his chest. His tongue traces the seam of my lips as he inches a finger inside me. He kisses me deeply for a moment before pulling away just far enough to speak. "Fuck. Now it's going to be my mission to see what panties you're wearing every day from here on out."

I want to laugh, but I'm too caught up in the feeling of his thick finger sliding all the way inside me to actually do it. "Don't make empty promises," I tease, feeling bolder than I typically do. Something about him encourages me to be this way. At first, I felt uneasy about Cal bringing out this sassier side of me, but now I'm happy he does.

Cal kisses along my jaw, and I moan at the way he playfully nips at my delicate skin before easing the pain with his tongue. "Trust me." His lips continue to trail along my skin as his finger works in and out of me. "I'm a man of my word. Every day now, I need to know what panties you put on just for me."

He falls to his knees slowly. On his way down, he trails kisses down my body through the fabric of my dress. Once he's on his knees, he keeps his eyes pinned on me as he lifts my leg over his shoulder.

My entire body trembles at the sight in front of me.

Cal on his knees. His wet clothes stuck to his body, showing off his perfectly defined muscles. The way his hair falls in his face as he stares at me with so much lust makes me eager for what's next. With my leg propped over his shoulder, he kisses the inside of my thigh.

"You wear these dresses and tennis skirts so often, they're such a tease," he says, using the hand not holding my thigh to push up the fabric of my dress.

"They're comfortable," I tell him, lifting my hips from the wall as he hooks his fingers into the side of my panties and begins to slide them down my legs. He moves my leg off his shoulder only long enough to get rid of them completely.

"Fuck, I missed this pussy," he mutters. The words are said gruffly but quietly, almost as if they were said to himself instead of to me.

He looks up at me from his spot on the ground. For a moment, my eyes flutter closed at the sight. Never did I think I'd have Callahan Hastings on his knees for me. I keep them closed for a moment, giving myself time to gather my composure before opening my eyes again.

It's the most perfect sight.

His piercing blue eyes are darker than normal, lust clouding them as he leans in and swipes his tongue against me.

I moan. The acoustics of the narrow hallway make the sound much louder than it was...or maybe I really am being that loud. I can't seem to care. Not when he slides his finger back inside me at the same moment his tongue circles my clit.

I sway on the one foot I have steady on the ground, my body too focused on what he's doing between my legs to stand up straight.

Cal's grip on me tightens. He slides one hand to my ass and squeezes. The movement presses me to his mouth as his tongue expertly works against my clit. He then pins me against the wall, ensuring there's no chance of me being unsteady again.

His finger speeds up inside me.

"You taste so fucking good, baby," he tells me, lifting his head to meet my gaze for a moment. "I missed it."

A rush of wetness pools between my thighs at the sight of *me* glistening around his mouth.

"You could've tasted me again a while ago. You were the one stopping it from happening."

A low growl comes from his throat. "I know, baby. I'm sorry. Do you forgive me?"

I moan at the softness of his tone. There's something about the way he said those words and seeing him on his knees in front of me, his lips wet with my arousal, that makes them ten times hotter than they'd be in any other scenario.

"Maybe," I tease. "Only if you forgive me for ruining your shirt."

His eyes flick down to the muddy handprints on his shirt. "Ruin anything you want of mine, Lucy Rae. If it ends with you moaning my name and my face between your thighs, you can destroy every material item I own."

He doesn't wait for me to respond. He fuses his mouth to me once again, and my head falls back against the wall with how good it feels.

Everything's different with Cal. In no time, the familiar buildup of tension and desire is seconds away from tipping me over the edge. It doesn't take long for the tension to snap and for my screams to ricochet off the narrow walls.

Cal makes sure I ride out the entire orgasm before he pulls his mouth from me. "Those moans were sexy. I'll have to work harder when I finally fuck you though. Your next orgasm will be around my cock, and I want it to be my name that's falling from your lips."

I suck in a breath at his words.

Does that mean we're finally going to have sex?

A shiver runs through my body at the idea. "Cal," I get out, not knowing what to say.

I didn't know it was possible to be so desperate for another human being. I've never felt desire or lust like this. I've never wanted someone inside me as badly as I want to feel all of him.

I'm still trying to figure out what else to say to him when he stands up and places his hands on my ass. In one easy move-ment, he lifts me up, my legs wrapping around his middle out of instinct.

"I've done everything I can to be patient with you, Lucy," Cal begins as he kicks the door to his room open. "It's taken everything in me to try and do things right. But I'm desperate for you. I can't hold back any longer. Tell me, can I fuck you?"

I moan at the way he says *fuck*. I didn't know a word could be so sexy, but coming from his mouth, it's the sexiest word to exist. "Yes," I respond, my hips moving up and down to get some kind of friction.

Cal gently places me on his bed. His hair sticks out in different directions from where I must've grabbed onto it when he was eating me out. "I'm so fucking relieved to hear you say that," he croaks, his brilliant blue eyes scanning over me. "Can I see you?" he asks, his voice quiet. "All of you?" he adds.

I nod, my skin heating at the thought of being completely naked in front of him.

"Only if I can see all of you," I answer, my words coming out just as hoarse as his.

He smiles and takes a step back, his eyes appreciatively roaming my body. "Clothes off, Lucy baby. *Now*."

thirty-six

CAL

My fingers quickly work at undoing the buttons of my shirt as my eyes stay pinned on Lucy.

There's no way I'll ever forget this moment. Her lying on my bed, her fingers wrapping around the hemline of her dress as she lifts it up her body and tosses it to the side.

She slides her feet out of her sandals and lets them fall to the floor.

I suck in a breath, my fingers pausing what they're doing at the sight of her. She lies on the linen comforter in nothing but a bra that matches the panties I've already stripped her of.

"You're so fucking beautiful," I declare, my eyes drinking in every perfect inch of her. I've wanted to see her like this for so long; I want to make sure I savor it.

Even Lucy's chest turns pink at my words. It matches the same color as her cheeks as she reaches behind her and unfastens her bra. The straps fall loosely down her arms, and I'm seconds away from finally seeing every inch of her.

She bites her bottom lip as her eyes rake down my body. Her hands hold the cups of her bra to her chest, taunting me.

"You can't see all of me until I can see all of you, Callahan."

I groan at the way she says my full name. It's sexy as hell, said slowly and sultrily. In a way that I'm going to think about when I'm alone, repeating it over and over in my head.

"It's hard to do anything but focus on how perfect you are," I rasp, moving to remove my clothes. "I've been dreaming of having you like this for over a month now."

Growing frustrated with the buttons of my shirt, I just yank it open, sending buttons flying. I shrug my arms out of the fabric and let it fall to my feet.

Lucy hungrily watches me take off my shoes and set them to the side. I'm quick at undoing my pants and stepping out of them. I pause for just a moment in nothing but my boxer briefs.

My palm runs along my cock to give myself some relief. I push the fabric of my briefs down my thighs and bare myself to her. I tug once along my cock, drinking in the sight of her while I do it.

"Your turn," I say to Lucy, reveling in the way she stares at me. She hasn't moved the entire time I've stripped off my clothing. All she's done is closely watch my every move. Desire for her courses through my veins at how obvious it is that she wants this just as bad as I do.

Her smile is timid and beautiful as she glances down to where her hands hold the bra to her body. She moves then, grabbing onto one of the straps and using it to slide it off and toss it to the side.

It's silent in my room as we both hungrily take in the other's body.

I've never been patient. I would've expected to already be inside her by now after wanting her so badly for so long, but I want to cherish every second of this moment.

"Are you going to come closer?" Lucy questions, her voice barely above a whisper.

I laugh, the sound filling the silence of the room. "What if I want to appreciate the view a little longer?" I've never had a woman in my own bed. I never wanted to. I've always gone to their house so I can leave whenever I want and not have someone in my personal space. Now, as I take in Lucy lying naked in my bed, her body flushed with desire, I realize I can't imagine ever *not* having her in my bed.

Lucy props herself on her elbows, her eyes focusing on my straining cock. I'd been so focused on memorizing every inch of her that I hadn't paid attention to it. With her eyes pinned on it and her lips parted, I can't ignore the ache for another second. My fingers wrap around my length, and I begin to stroke up and down.

"I want to touch you," Lucy breathes, her eyes wide as she hungrily watches my every move.

She rubs her thighs together before her fingertips dance along her skin, traveling to the apex of her thighs.

"You can touch yourself," I tell her, loving how the afternoon light shining through the bedroom window illuminates her perfect body.

"I'm waiting for you to touch me," she counters. She bites back a smile as she nods her head to where I continue to stroke myself. "Actually, I'm waiting to touch *you*."

A growl of approval comes from my chest. I love that she's telling me exactly what she wants.

"Before today, did you touch yourself while thinking about me since the last time I touched you?"

"Yes," she says on an exhale, her eyelashes fanning against her cheeks as her eyes close in pleasure for a moment.

"Show me how you did it, Lucy baby."

Her entire body shakes at my words. "Cal." My name comes out like a plea from her lips. I'm loving this view of her with her messy hair falling down her shoulders and her cheeks the color of pink I love so much.

"Do as you're told," I command, keeping my voice soft.

"Show me how you touched yourself. I bet you pretended it was me touching you, didn't you?"

Her eyelids flutter shut as a loud moan passes from her lips. She rocks her hips back and forth against the mattress, and all I can think about is how much I can't wait to have her do just that with my cock buried inside her.

"I'm waiting." This time, my words are rougher because of my desperate need to watch her slip her fingers between her thighs and touch herself. I want to study her as she shows me how she likes it. I think I have a good idea based on the two times I've had the pleasure of touching her, but I still want her to show me.

She parts her thighs slowly, her breathing speeding up as she glides her fingers along her skin from where they rested at her sides to now along the tops of her thighs.

"Play with your nipples first," I instruct, eagerly waiting to see how she plays with herself.

Will she gently tease the peaked buds, or will she pinch them because she likes it more rough?

Lucy does as she's told and slowly runs both hands up her sides before tracing the underside of her breasts. I stand there and study every one of her movements, my hand still moving up and down my cock.

My entire body aches with the need for her touch, for me to be inside her, but I don't rush it. Right now, I'm relishing in the view of Lucy playing with her tits just for me.

She rolls her nipples between her fingers before pinching them.

I smile, my heart slamming against my chest as one of her hands leaves her tit and drifts down. She's got to be worked up because she takes no time before she's touching herself. Her fingers circle her clit for a moment before venturing further down. I almost come undone just at the way she moans when she slides not one but two fingers inside herself.

"Fuck, baby," I manage to get out, my hand pumping even faster around my cock. "I can't fucking wait to be inside you."

Her head falls back at my words, but her eyes stay trained on me. "Then come do it."

Her words make me laugh. I fucking love the side of her that talks back. She doesn't do it all the time, but when she does, I feel on top of the world to be the one to bring it out of her.

"And I thought I was the impatient one." I take a step closer to her, my knees almost bumping against the edge of the mattress. "You're the one who scolded me just last week about it."

She laughs, her fingers stilling inside her for a moment. "You can't rush focaccia, Cal. It takes time."

"Me savoring every fucking moment of making you mine takes time."

Her mouth snaps shut, and her eyes go wide at my words.

Using my free hand, I grab one of her ankles and pull her to the very edge of the bed. She yelps, her fingers sliding out of her from the sudden movement, and she reaches to grab me.

"Wait," I say, pulling my hips back for a moment. I want her to touch me—desperately—but I need to be inside her more. Now that she's so close, with no barrier between us, I want to feel her sweet cunt wrapped around me.

I stop stroking myself and grab her wrist, my fingers wrapping softly around her as I guide her fingers to my mouth. They're wet with her arousal, and even though I can still taste her on my tongue from earlier, I'm ready for another taste, even if it is just a tease.

"Let me get one more little taste before I make you mine," I tell her before taking her fingers into my mouth.

Thirty-seven
LUCY

Cal's tongue presses against my fingers as he takes them into his warm mouth. He sucks hard, lapping my fingers clean of my arousal. The gesture makes me moan and the space between my legs throb.

He's busy twirling his tongue along my fingers, giving me the chance to reach between us and finally touch him.

I pull my hand from his mouth seconds before air hisses through his teeth as my fingers wrap around his length. He's so thick I can't even get my fingertips to touch.

"Fuck." He lets out a whimper when I begin to pump up and down.

The sound drives me wild, making me want to squeeze a little harder as I move up and down his length. I want to get more sounds just like that out of him.

"I don't know if you're going to fit inside me," I announce, voicing my fears out loud. He's big, both in length and girth. I don't know how I'm going to take all of him, but I desperately want to try.

He lets out a low groan at my words, or maybe it's my hand continuing to pump up and down his length. "I was made for you, Lucy Rae. I'll fit inside you perfectly."

His words make me pause, my hand stilling mid-stroke. It isn't the first time he's mentioned me being his, and I'm sure he didn't mean for his words to hold as much weight as they do, but to me, they mean a lot.

I try not to get stuck on them or overanalyze since he doesn't seem to notice he's even said them.

My thoughts quickly dissipate when he leans in close and hovers his lips over mine. I pick up the pace of my strokes along his length, moving up and down faster, wanting to take things even further. I want him in my mouth, to make him feel good like he's already done for me, twice.

"Can I tell you something?" he rasps. We're so close his eyes bore into mine.

"Yes," I breathe, my gaze falling to his lips for a moment. He's still covered in me, but it doesn't stop me from wanting to kiss him.

"Your hand around my cock feels so good, baby." His forehead falls to mine as he looks between us. We both watch the way my fingers move up and down his length. With his attention on me, I twist my grip a little, wanting to make it feel as good as possible for him.

"You're doing so fucking good that I could come just by the way you jerk me off."

"Not yet," I warn, my lips brushing against his with my words. "I want to have my turn tasting you first."

Cal closes the small distance between our lips. I open my mouth, expecting a deep kiss from him. It's the opposite. He presses a featherlight kiss to my mouth. "I want to watch you take my cock between those pretty pink lips of yours so fucking bad, baby. Trust me. But right now, I need to feel your pussy around my cock."

"Cal." His name comes out breathy and strangled as he slides his dick out of my hand. I miss the connection of our bodies immediately, but he doesn't keep us from touching for long.

He gently presses his hand to my chest. "Lie back," he instructs.

"But I want to—"

Cal's fingers find my lips. "I know you want to suck my cock, Lucy. You're such a good girl for wanting that. But what I need from you is to lie back so I can finally fuck you so good that you'll be screaming my name. I want you thinking about what's about to happen between us for days to come. You got that?"

All I can do is nod. When he applies a little more pressure to my chest, I let him, my body falling into the plush comforter.

Cal climbs onto the bed and in between my thighs. "I haven't been with anyone in a while, and my last test was normal. But if you're not comfortable with it, I can grab a condom. I don't have any in my room, but there's some in the—"

I shake my head. "I don't want anything between us, Cal," I rush to get out. My words come out like a plea. When I finally get to feel him inside me after making me wait for what seems like forever, I want all of him, with nothing in the way. "I'm on the pill, and my last checkup was also clear."

He takes me by surprise by running the tip of his cock through my wetness. "I don't want anything between us either."

I jolt at feeling him there. He's so close to finally being inside me, but not close enough. He drives me crazy by continuing to tease me, running his tip through my arousal but not actually sliding it in.

I lift my hips off the mattress, hoping the movement will encourage him to stop the teasing.

It doesn't.

Cal laughs, the sound deep and raspy. It's one that sends shivers down my spine at how sexy it is. "I love how ready you are for me," he growls, stopping right at my entrance.

I moan when he slides just his tip in.

"Just do it," I tell him, wiggling my hips to try and take him deeper.

Cal's hand falls next to my head. He leans down, his chest pressing against mine. He supports most of his weight, but I still love the feel of having his body fully against mine like this. "Who's the impatient one now, Lucy baby?"

I love the raspiness of his voice. It's raw and real, making butterflies take flight in my stomach.

"You've made me wait so long. Too long. I just want to feel you, Callahan." I'm well aware my words come off as begging at this point, but I don't care. I need him in a way I've never needed anyone. I know there are so many reasons none of this should be happening between us, but I just don't care about them anymore.

I want him. I need him.

Cal's fingers softly brush stray pieces of hair out of my eyes as he brings his face close to mine. The gesture is delicate. Paired with the way he's just barely seated inside me and how I can't see anything but the stunning depths of his bright blue eyes, the moment feels incredibly intimate.

"I'm just trying to take my time with you," he croaks. "I want to commit every single second of finally being inside you to memory." As if to drive his point home, he slides in a little deeper.

I moan, and my eyelids flutter shut from the feeling. He stretches me, and the sensation is incredible. I don't think he's even halfway in yet, and I'm full of him.

With my eyes still closed, Cal's lips find mine. He kisses me slowly as he slides another inch in. When I moan again, he swallows it, his fingertips digging into my cheek as he holds my face close to his.

He continues to kiss me, his lips warm as his tongue finds mine. My entire body feels like it's on fire from the intense way he kisses me as he coaxes himself more inside me inch by excruciating inch.

"Open your eyes, baby," Cal insists. "I want to look at you as I fill you with my cock."

His words bring out another moan. It feels so good, almost too much, to have him so deep. I feel like I could combust at any second from the different sensations taking over my senses, but I manage to open my eyes.

I find Cal's already on mine. Every time he's this close, I'm taken aback by just how beautiful he is.

When our eyes connect, he smiles. It's one I feel throughout my entire body...all the way to my heart.

"Good girl," he praises, rewarding me by sliding in a little further. At this point, I feel so full of him. He's got to be close to being all the way inside me.

"Cal," I pant while trying to keep my eyes open to look at him. I can feel myself stretching around him as he pushes all the way in, and for a moment, I wonder if I'll be able to handle all of him.

"I know, baby," he whispers against my lips. He kisses me softly for a moment while he gives my body time to adjust to him.

He stays still, but even without him moving, it hurts a little. I take a deep breath because despite the tinge of pain, nothing's ever felt better. It truly feels like we fit together perfectly.

One of Cal's hands stays on my cheek, his fingers splayed out as he keeps my face angled toward him as he props himself up on his elbow. The other hand softly pushes hair off my shoulder before he trails kisses along my shoulder and neck. He still doesn't move his hips, something I appreciate as my body continues to grow accustomed to him.

"You're doing so good," he praises, his lips hovering over my nipple. Even though his breath is hot against my skin, the sensation of having his mouth there sends shivers down my spine.

He pulls my nipple into his mouth at the same moment he rocks his hips in and out of me. I try to keep looking at him like he told me, but I can't keep my eyes open a second longer. My eyelids flutter shut from pleasure at the feeling of him sliding in and out of me.

"Cal," I moan, my back arching off the mattress as his tongue circles my nipple. His mouth is warm, and his wet tongue there feels better than I could've ever imagined. I wrap my legs around his waist to bring him even closer to me, needing to feel as close to him as possible.

"You're perfect," he announces, moving from one nipple to the other.

I love that he's being gentle. His hips move in and out of me at a pace that allows me to adjust to the size of him, but it still doesn't feel like enough.

"More," I plead, lifting my hips in an attempt to take him even deeper. My hands run up and down his back, trying to find something to hold on to.

"Careful what you ask for," Cal warns, his hips still moving at a pace that's teasing me. "I'm trying to be gentle and give you time to adjust, baby."

"Cal, I need more. Faster. Please fuck me." My thoughts come out jumbled. I can't think straight past how badly I want him. He's being slow and gentle, and I appreciate it, but now I need him to stop being gentle so I can feel the punishing rhythm of him thrusting in and out of me.

Cal groans. With my nipple still in his mouth, the sound

vibrates against my skin. He releases my nipple with a *pop* before bringing his forehead to mine.

"You sure that's what you want?" he asks, his voice almost hoarse. It's evident how much restraint he's showing just by how strangled his words come out.

I reach up and grab the back of his neck, bringing his face as close to mine as possible. "Yes." The single word comes out like a plea, and I don't even care. I *will* beg him to fuck me faster and harder if that's what it takes.

I need more of him. More of this.

A low growl comes from deep in his chest. "Just tell me if it's too much, baby."

I shake my head. I don't need him to be careful with me right now. He's already done that by not letting anything go past making out between us for almost two weeks.

Now's the time I want all of him.

"Don't hold back," I pant. "Fuck me, Cal. Fuck me, the way you've been dreaming of."

The sexiest sound of approval comes from deep in his chest. "If that's what you want, Lucy baby."

thirty-eight

CAL

I'm fucking gone for Lucy Rae Owens.

Deep down, I knew it before I was ever inside her, but feeling her wrapped around me only confirms that this woman owns me.

I pick up the pace, trying not to go too hard too fast. It took everything in me to be gentle with her, to give her however long she needed to adjust to me. But now that I know she's ready for more, I don't know how much I can hold back.

"You feel so fucking good," I tell her, pressing my lips to hers before she can even respond. Her lips are pillowy soft as her tongue eagerly meets mine. With each thrust inside her, I move my hips faster and faster.

Eventually, my room is filled with the sounds of our skin slapping against each other, mixed with our needy moans.

"I'll never get enough of this," I continue, needing her to know how perfect this feels.

Lucy Rae Owens has absolutely ruined me for anyone else.

"Oh my God," she moans, and the sound only turns me on even more, something I didn't know was possible. I've never been this turned on in my life, and I haven't been inside her very long.

"Tell me this is everything to you too," I beg, thrusting into her.

"Yes," she answers before trailing her hands down my back. Her nails scratch my skin, and I love the feeling. I want her to leave whatever marks she wants. She can permanently brand me at this point; there's no one else for me but her.

"Fuck." I groan, sheathing myself all the way inside her. This time, I pause, savoring the feeling of being completely buried inside her for a moment.

"Cal," she protests, her nails biting into my lower back.

I laugh at how needy she is. It's so fucking hot how desperate she is for this. I love it because I know I'm even more desperate for her.

I pull out slowly before quickly thrusting back in, repeating the motion a second time. Her pussy greedily hugs me tighter with each thrust.

"Fuck."

I thrust deeply inside her, forcing her to take all of me.

"You're."

Another thrust.

"So."

I thrust again, eating up the way she moans with each one.

"Goddamn."

Another thrust, this one quick and hard.

"Perfect."

"I'm going to come," Lucy cries, her pussy clenching around me. Her fingernails bite into my skin as she squirms from the pleasure.

"Good. I need you to come all over my cock, baby." I continue to fuck her at the same pace, wanting to send her over the edge.

It doesn't take long until I feel her clamp down around me so tight it's almost painful.

"Cal," she cries out, her head rocking back and forth as the orgasm takes over her body.

I let out a moan of my own at feeling her come around me. My body sticks to hers from the effort, but her coming with my cock inside her is the sexiest thing I've ever seen or felt.

"Good girl," I praise, kissing down her neck and moving my hips in a slow circle to try and milk her orgasm for as long as possible. "God, you coming on my cock is the best thing I've ever felt. So tight and needy. You're so fucking wet you're soaking me."

Lucy's eyes flutter open and shut as her entire body trembles from the orgasm. One moan after another falls from her lips as she rides out the waves.

I commit every single second of it to memory. I never want to forget her just like this. Her body underneath mine. Her lips red and swollen from my kisses. Her cheeks flushed from my dirty words and the passion between us. For the rest of my life, I'll remember her desperate pleas for me to fuck her harder and the way it felt when she came around my cock.

I couldn't forget any of it, even if I wanted to.

Once her moans dissipate and her body stops trembling, I slow down my thrusts. Her eyes open and find mine, the slowest of smiles spreading across her face.

"That was..." Her words trail off.

I nod. She doesn't even have to finish her thought for me to know what she's thinking. "That was everything," I confirm.

I lean in and kiss her, keeping my hips still but not pulling out of her.

My tongue traces the seam of her lips for a moment before she eagerly opens her mouth for me. Her tongue slips out to meet mine. I'm not done with her yet. I know by how reactive she still is that I can get another orgasm from her before finding my own release. I reach between us and circle her clit with my fingertips.

"Cal," she whines. "I've already come twice."

I smirk against her mouth. "And you'll come a third time, baby. Give me one more. I want to feel you tighten around me as I empty myself inside you."

She groans before fusing our mouths together. Her hands grab either side of my face as she takes the lead in the kiss. I let her, my hips beginning to rock in and out of her once again.

She gets wetter with every thrust, proving that I'll be able to get another orgasm from her. Pride spreads through my entire body remembering how she mentioned how hard it can be for her to come.

But not with me. Not for us, because joined together like this, we're perfect.

Lucy's the first one to pull away. Her eyes search my face for a moment before she bites back a nervous smile.

I rock in and out of her slowly, unable to resist returning her smile. I didn't know it was possible to be so fucking cute and so goddamn sexy at the same time, but of course, anything's possible when it comes to her.

"You didn't let me suck you this time...I at least want to ride you."

Tingles run down my spine at her words. I groan, wanting nothing more than to have her ride me.

I don't need her to tell me twice. If she wants to ride me, who am I to stop her?

I move my arms behind her back and lift her off the mattress, making sure I stay inside her the entire time. She lets out a yelp of surprise when I spin our bodies so it's now me against the bed and her on top.

My cock stays inside her the entire time.

Lucy's hands fall to my chest due to the sudden movement.

She steadies herself for a moment, a sultry smile on her face the entire time.

"You actually listened to me," she notes, circling her hips once as if to test out her power on top.

Air hisses through my teeth at how good it feels. The new position makes it feel like I'm even deeper inside her.

I give her a cocky grin, even through the rush of lust overtaking my senses. "I did. Now, show me why I should do it more often. Ride me, Lucy baby."

Thirty-nine

LUCY

Being on top has never felt good for me before. It always felt like a lot of work and killed whatever buildup I had for an orgasm.

But with Cal, I already know it won't be like that.

I move my hips up and down once, testing what it feels like in this new position. A soft moan leaves my lips as my eyes roll back in my head from the pleasure.

Being on top is a totally different feeling. He stretches me all over again, but this time, I feel even more full of him. The position puts him even deeper inside me—something I didn't think was possible.

It's almost too much.

My hair falls down my back as I begin to rock up and down at a steady rhythm. The one I pick must be good because Cal lets out a moan that I feel throughout my entire body.

I didn't know a man could make noises that sounded so sexy, but every raspy moan and groan from him makes me come undone.

"You're so deep," I tell him, my words coming out breathless. Until now, he's done all of the work, but I still feel like I've run a marathon. Each orgasm he gives me is better than the last.

They overtake my entire body, leaving me gasping for air by the end of it.

Cal's hands move down my waist and grab onto my hips. He holds them there, applying enough pressure to keep me from going too far but still allowing me to choose the pace.

"Fuck, baby," he croaks. His eyes move from mine to where our bodies are joined. "Look at you taking me so well."

I moan, my eyes moving to the spot he's focusing on. I follow his lead and watch as I move up and down his length.

It's hard to keep my hips moving when it feels this good. I want to fall against him. My entire body feels like it's on fire, and it almost feels like I've ridden one orgasm into the next. Tingles break out all over my skin because of how incredible it feels.

I spin my hips a little as I continue to rock up and down. A loud, unfiltered moan leaves my lips at the feeling it elicits. I just feel so full of him. He's taking me to my limit, and nothing's ever felt so right.

"Cal," I pant, picking up speed. My thighs shake from using muscles I don't typically use, but it doesn't stop me. I can't stop, not when it feels this good. Not when Cal's making the sexiest noises of pleasure from what I'm doing to him.

His fingertips dig into my hips as his eyes meet mine. I love that I'm getting to see him like this. He isn't holding back. All the time, he seems so composed and put together, but not right now.

Right now, he looks like a man crazed, and it's because of me. Power blooms in my chest at the thought.

His hair sticks out in every direction, completely opposite to the clean, slicked-back look I'm used to seeing on him. His jaw clenches every time I move up and down. His lips part, and his eyes close every now and then as he gives in to the pleasure.

But my favorite part is when his eyes are open and he looks

right at me. It feels like he says so much while saying nothing at all with the way he stares at me. His pupils are so dilated that I can barely see his deep blue irises.

I move even faster, letting out a moan when one of his hands moves up to cup my breast. He takes my nipple between his fingertips and rolls it between his fingers, making my core ache with desire.

"Keep taking what you want from me," he grits out. "It's so fucking sexy watching you do exactly what you need to come again."

He pinches my nipple. It stings, but the pain only fuels my pleasure.

"I'm close again," I tell him, needing him to be close as well. I want to feel him come while he's still inside me. I want to hear what noises he'll make when he finds his release. I really just want to finally make him feel as good as he's made me feel.

"I am too," he growls. "I can feel you tightening around me." His words come out strained, but they're all it takes for the orgasm to rip through my entire body.

I moan—or maybe it's more like a scream—as the sensation begins at my clit and radiates through my entire body. It's so intense I can't move. My hips still, and my body falls against Cal's.

We're chest to chest and forehead to forehead as the orgasm still overtakes my senses.

"Lucy," Cal gets out through gritted teeth. His hands find my hips again as he keeps me pinned to him. Even though he's underneath me, he begins to thrust up and down, fast and rough.

"Fuck, baby," he groans, fucking me so hard that it only intensifies my own orgasm.

"Come for me," I plead, desperate to make him feel what

I'm feeling. "Come inside me," I add. I want to feel every second of his own orgasm.

Cal's fingertips bite into my skin as he continues to drill into me. "Luc—" My name falls off as he finds his own release, only heightening my own.

For a moment, the room is filled with our moans and heavy breaths as we get lost in the moment together.

Time drags on in the most delicious of ways. It's like time comes to a standstill as we both ride out our orgasms. I don't know how long it takes for us to regain our breathing, but eventually, my eyelids flutter open to find Cal already staring at me.

"Lucy Rae," he rasps. He clears his throat after, as if he didn't mean for me to hear the emotion clogging his throat.

I push myself up just enough to be able to see him better. I wish I could stop time so I could memorize everything about this moment with him. I never want to forget the way Callahan Hastings stares at me like nothing else matters in the world.

There's so much emotion in his face. His features are soft—his eyes, his smile, the relaxation of his jaw. The two tiny creases that almost always appear between his brows are gone. Instead, his forehead is smooth, and the only lines on his face are the ones appearing around his eyes from his smile.

"Was that worth the wait?" Cal asks, his voice thick.

I laugh. "I'm still mad at you for making me wait. We could've been doing that for two weeks already."

His hands move from where they rest on my hips. I shiver underneath his touch as he softly brushes his fingertips along my arms. He traces this path until both of his hands grab mine. Our fingers intertwine before he tugs, pulling my body flush to his once again.

I gasp, using our clasped hands to help steady myself.

Cal nuzzles his nose against mine, the gesture far more intimate than any kiss could ever feel. "We'll make up for lost time," he assures me, reminding me of what we were talking about.

I smile at the sexiness and the grittiness of his voice. "Is that a promise?"

He kisses my cheek softly. "Yes, baby, it is. I'm already looking forward to being inside you again."

I move my hips a little to prove a point. "You're not even out of me yet."

He gives me a cocky smirk before lifting his head and giving me a quick kiss. "Still looking forward to doing it again." The words are said against my lips.

I give his hands a squeeze before pushing off his chest slightly. My senses are in overdrive from the multiple orgasms, and having him still inside me begins to tickle. I slowly inch off him and slide off to his side, missing the feeling of him inside me the moment he's out. I look down, finding my thighs damp from our arousal.

"I probably need to shower," I say with a nervous laugh. I hadn't thought about the after part with him. I just knew I was desperate for him to finally fuck me. Now that it's over, are things going to be awkward? I don't think they will be. Nothing was awkward after Cal went down on me—other than the fact I begged for him to let me touch him and he said he wanted to take things slow.

Cal sits up, and something inside me melts when he places a tender kiss on my shoulder. "Then let's take a shower," he offers.

My eyes go wide for a moment. "Together?"

He continues to press featherlight kisses to my shoulder and collarbone. "Yes, together. I love that my cum is leaking out of you, yet you're blushing at the thought of us showering."

My cheeks heat even more at his comment. I rub my lips together as I fight a shy smile. "We don't have to," I begin, my eyes anxiously darting around the room. "You know, if you don't want to or that isn't your thing."

It's silent for a few moments. Each passing second that he doesn't say anything feels like torture. Finally, I look at him, finding him staring at me with a wide smile on his lips.

"What?" I whisper.

"Just so you know, anything with you is my *thing*. Haven't you learned that by now?" He reaches up and tucks a piece of my hair behind my ear. "I can't get enough of you."

Forty
CAL

Lucy and I are walking hand in hand down the sidewalk when I come to a stop.

"Let's go in here," I offer, gesturing toward the house to our right.

Lucy looks at the house with the gray shingles. "Cal, you're joking."

I shake my head as a slow smile spreads over my lips. "I'm not joking. Let's go inside."

"That's the Chanel house. I don't need anything from Chanel."

"Does anyone really *need* anything from Chanel?" I counter, lifting an eyebrow. "I want to get you something."

Her jaw falls open. She looks adorable standing on the sidewalk, her hair pulled back in some sort of clip she had in her bag, her mouth hanging open in disbelief. Her wide eyes stay pinned on me, no words leaving her mouth for a bit, as if she's waiting for me to tell her it's a joke.

It isn't.

I've had the best afternoon helping her pick out an outfit for dinner tonight with some of our friends, and I don't want it to stop. I've quickly learned how much I enjoy buying her things. I want to buy her anything she shows even the slightest interest in, just because I can. I'm still waiting for her to open up to me more about her life before this summer, but from what I've gathered, she hasn't ever had anyone spoil her the way she deserves. Knowing that makes me want to be the man to do it.

Lucy gestures to the bags I'm holding in the hand not holding hers. "Cal, you've already bought me plenty. You don't need to buy me anything else, even if it is something as special as a Chanel bag."

I take a step toward the landmark house. You typically need an appointment to get a private shopping experience, but last time I came here with my mom to pick out a gift for her, they gave us the private experience upstairs with no need for an appointment. I doubt today will be any different.

"I want to," I tell her, tugging on her hand to pull her closer to the store. "Let me."

Lucy shakes her head. "You already bought me an outfit for tonight, plus three new pairs of shoes, and let's not forget the cooking set you *insisted* I needed."

I squeeze her hand while lifting my shoulder in a casual shrug. "You did need the set. The green matches the apron from your mom perfectly. It was kismet we found them since they were limited edition and all."

"And it was so thoughtful of you to get them for me, Cal. Truly." She takes a step closer to me and cups my cheek in the hand that isn't intertwined with mine. "You've already spoiled me more today than I've ever been spoiled. I don't want you to think you have to buy me anything else."

I lean into her touch. Feeling her skin against mine is now something I crave. Even when she stepped away from me this afternoon to try on clothes or when she was sitting across from me at the restaurant, I hated every second our bodies didn't have some sort of connection.

I've never felt like this about someone. I've never even come close. It's so new and foreign to me I can't even fight it. I don't want to fight it, despite all the reasons I know I probably should. She's my brother's ex-girlfriend, she's under my employment, and she hasn't shied away from the fact she's leaving at the end of this summer and isn't interested in anything more than a fling.

It'd be best for me to fight the feelings I'm developing for her, but I can't bring myself to do it. I think it's too late, anyway.

"Do you want a Chanel bag?" I ask, savoring the feeling of her fingertips against my skin.

She sighs and gives me a timid smile. "That's a silly question. Everyone wants a Chanel like everyone wants to win the lottery. Of course I want it, but it's not something I ever actually saw myself having. And I'm okay with that."

"Then let me buy one for you. We have time to kill before we need to get ready for tonight, and buying you something here is the perfect way to do it."

She laughs and shakes her head at me. "I can't believe you just said that. You don't just kill time by shopping at Chanel."

"Today, we can. C'mon, baby." I drop her hand and point to the purse she's always carrying around. "You've retied the strap of this one because it keeps breaking."

She raises her eyebrows defiantly and gives me a sly smile. "Maybe I did it on purpose."

"It wasn't broken at the start of the summer."

Her lips part in shock. "How do you know that?"

I don't tell her I've noticed everything about her for a while now. She lays her purse on the corner of the counter every morning before bringing the farmer's market bags to the island and taking out the contents. Twice, I've seen her fuss over retying the strap of her purse together so she can still use it.

I've also noticed that every time she unloads her farmer's

market haul from the mesh bags, she narrates everything she's doing. It's like she's recording a video that isn't even there. I could go on about the things I know about her, but I choose to not go into detail at the moment.

I lift a corner of my mouth in a side smile. "I just noticed your purse was broken. It's probably a sign you need a new one."

Lucy huffs as she dramatically rolls her eyes at me. "You know you really don't have to do this, right? I don't even want to know the price tag on them, and I really am happy with the bag that I have." She lets out the most adorably nervous laugh. "Can you tell I'm not used to expensive things?"

"I know I don't have to do anything. But I want to, baby. I like buying you expensive things."

She shakes her head. The movement causes a stray piece of hair to fall from the clip and into her eyes. "You're ridiculous, Callahan Hastings. You know that, right? I don't think anyone else but you would ever insist on spending this much money on me."

Good. I hate the thought of anyone else seeing the way her entire face lights up when she's getting spoiled.

I use my free hand to push the stray strand of hair from her eyes. Leaning in, I press a kiss to the tip of her nose. "I'm only ridiculous for you, Lucy Rae Owens." I wink at her before grabbing her hand and leading her to the Chanel boutique house.

———

Lucy stares at me with a determined look in her eyes. Her eyebrows are drawn in, and her lips are puckered in the most adorable of scowls. "Absolutely not," she clips, trying to keep her voice hushed.

"Absolutely," I immediately respond.

"No."

"Yes."

The private shopping attendant clears her throat nervously from a few feet away as Lucy and I argue on the couches of the second-floor private shopping room.

"Cal, I said no," Lucy mutters. She looks over at the attendant, Samantha, and gives her a tight smile. "Do you maybe have anything that doesn't cost as much as a brand-new car?"

Samantha lifts an eyebrow and smiles at Lucy. "If a man is willing to buy you a purse, even with this price tag, you shouldn't tell him no."

I laugh at Samantha's words. Immediately, I try to cover it up with a cough when I see the dirty look that Lucy tosses my way. I haven't had her look at me like that in a very long time. It's as cute as ever.

"Ugh," Lucy grumbles, twisting her hands in front of her. "You can't buy me a purse that costs twenty thousand dollars."

"It's under twenty thousand," I counter, fighting the smile threatening to take over my lips. "And yes, I can. It's the purse you like and the purse you're going to get."

We've been shopping for about an hour. Samantha's shown us multiple beautiful handbags, but I could tell that the one sitting on the table in front of us was Lucy's favorite. She gasped when Samantha brought it out. The moment I saw her eyes go wide and her lips part in awe, I knew I had to get the bag for her. She looked at the purse like it was a prized possession. I want to buy it for her.

I just need her to agree to it.

"Cal, it's *barely* under twenty thousand. You can't buy it for me. What if I ruin it? My job is messy. I'm messy. It's not practical for me to have a purse worth this much."

"You can always get it professionally cleaned. Just let your boyfriend buy you the purse," Samantha adds at the last minute.

Lucy lets out a strangled noise as she looks at me wide-eyed. "Oh, he's not my boyf—"

"Yeah, Lucy, just let me buy it for you," I cut her off with a smug grin. Being called her boyfriend made satisfaction wash over me. I realize I *like* the sound of it.

Lucy adjusts her position on the couch, crossing one leg over the other. "This isn't fair. It's two against one."

I lift my shoulder in a casual shrug. "I guess you should just let me buy it, then."

Lucy stares at me through narrowed eyelids. "What if that one isn't my favorite?" She pulls her eyes from mine and points across the room, where a tiny purse sits by itself on a white shelf. "That one's my favorite." She pushes her shoulders back and sits up straighter, clearly proud of herself for lying and saying that her favorite bag is the one that's a fraction of the price of the one I know she likes best.

I lick my lips as I form an idea. My eyes track over the private room as I remember the other items Lucy had her eye on while shopping. A wide smile spreads over my lips as my attention returns to Samantha.

"We will take the large bag, the small one my girlfriend just pointed out, and..." I point to a tan-colored crochet bag hanging across the room. It looks perfect for Lucy's farmer's market hauls. "We'll also take that one as well."

Lucy hits my thigh with the back of my hand. "No, we won't," she hurriedly gets out.

Samantha doesn't listen to her. She places the bag I know is Lucy's actual favorite back in its cloth dust bag and picks it up off the table.

"Wait," Lucy calls after her, trying to get Samantha's attention.

Instead, I place my hand on Lucy's thigh and squeeze. "Baby, look at me."

Lucy focuses on Samantha, who's already made it across the room. "No, I need her to stop before she rings everything up and it's too late. You're spending way too much money on me."

"Look at me," I repeat, gently grabbing her chin and coaxing her to face me.

Lucy listens, her beautiful brown eyes connecting with mine.

Before she can protest me buying her things again, I clear my throat. "I know you're not used to it, but I want to change that. You deserve to be spoiled, Lucy Rae. Will you do me a favor and let me be the one to do it?" My voice cracks a little at the end. I let it. I need her to know how badly I want to be the man to spoil her for as long as she'll let me.

Her eyes soften as she leans deeper into my touch. I resist the urge to lean in and press a kiss to the freckles at the tip of her nose.

"Well, when you put it like that, how can I say no to you?" she asks, her voice soft.

I smile before leaning in and pressing a kiss to her lips. "Spoiling you is quickly becoming my favorite thing to do, so you don't."

"You're spoiling me too much."

I shake my head, kissing her again because I feel like it. My words are said against her lips. "There's no such thing, Lucy baby."

Forty-one

LUCY

"Oh my God, you had sex," Charlotte declares the moment our eyes meet.

A blush immediately creeps over my cheeks as my eyes dart around the dinner table at Pembroke Grill.

Jude barks out a laugh at Charlotte's words while Cal coughs in surprise.

All I can do is stare at my best friend in horror, wondering how she could tell with just one look at me and why she decided to announce it to the entire table the moment Cal and I walked up to it. Luckily, the only people seated at the table are her and Jude right now.

"Charlotte," I scold, my voice tight as I look around the restaurant. Everyone here used to be my coworkers; I don't need them knowing that I've slept with Cal.

Charlotte narrows her eyes on me. "What? You can't tell me I'm wrong. You have that *I've just been fucked* flush to you."

I groan, embarrassment coursing through my veins.

"Come with me," I demand, grabbing her by the arm and pulling her from the chair.

"Whoa," Charlotte mutters with a laugh, thankfully letting me pull her away from a snickering Jude and a smirking Cal.

My grip on Charlotte's wrist stays firm as I lead her to the bathrooms. I try to keep my eyes down, not wanting to get stuck talking to any former coworkers before I can lecture my best friend about what's appropriate to yell in public and what should be discussed in private.

"Lucy, if you move any faster, you're going to make me fall on my ass because of these heels."

I sigh but slow down just enough to keep her steady on her feet. I have no idea if any Pembroke employees look our way or not. I keep my focus on the floor as we close the distance to the private bathrooms.

As soon as we make it there, I pull her in and slam the door shut behind us.

When I turn to Charlotte, a knowing grin is plastered on her face. "Speaking of heels, those look new and expensive." She nods her head to the new pair of heels Cal bought me while shopping today.

"Charlotte, quick question. Has anyone ever told you about keeping some thoughts to yourself?"

Charlotte shrugs before tossing her perfectly curled hair over her shoulder. "Don't get mad at me for stating the obvious. You've got it written all over you."

I groan, my eyes closing for a moment. I wasn't going to keep this new development a secret from Charlotte. I definitely wanted to talk about it with her, but I just thought I had more time before I had to explain how everything is strictly casual and nothing more.

"Lucy, shut the fuck up. Is that a Chanel bag?"

Charlotte closes the distance between us and carefully grabs my purse. She crouches down and pulls it closer to her face to inspect.

I can't help but smile when Charlotte looks up at me with her jaw wide open.

"Yes, Cal might've bought me the shoes and the bag today," I answer, trying to keep my voice nonchalant.

"Why are you living my dream? Good sex and a rich man spoiling you? Sign me up."

I laugh. "Who said it was good sex? Plus, don't pretend Jude isn't flirting with you all the time."

Charlotte rolls her eyes before standing up once again. "Everything about you tells me you've had hot, sexy, toe-curling sex. You've got a flush to your cheeks that won't go away, and your lips look plumper than normal, probably from all the making out you've been doing. And to your second comment, Jude flirts with everyone. I'm nothing special. He would not be buying me a Chanel bag."

I sigh, deciding that since she's already onto me, I might as well not lie to her. "The sex with Cal is incredible. It's new... like, *today was the first time* new."

Charlotte's perfectly lined lips spread into a smile. "Good for you for not letting your stupid ex get in the way of having mind-blowing sex with Callahan Hastings. I want to know all the juicy details. "

I bite my lip. I don't feel guilty for sleeping with Cal, even if he is Ollie's brother. It's been so long since Oliver and I dated, I know he wouldn't care, but I know if people knew that I also dated Oliver and was now sleeping with Cal, they might judge me. And if they weren't judging me for that, they might judge me for sleeping with my boss.

I push the thoughts from my mind. Cal and I are adults who can sleep with whomever we want. No one outside of our close inner circle even needs to know. Once I'm gone after Labor Day, it won't even matter.

"Things with Cal were too intense to let anything hold us back," I answer honestly. "I tried fighting it as long as I could, but it was only a matter of time until things happened between us."

Charlotte nods giddily. She grabs my hands and jumps up and down a couple of times, a beaming smile still on her lips. "I love this so much. I'm glad you finally gave in." She points to the brand-new purse. "Looks like it's working out for you very well."

I laugh. The purse is the nicest thing I've ever owned. I still can't wrap my mind around the price tag that came with it, but since Cal was insistent on purchasing it for me, it felt only right to use it tonight. "Yeah, we'll see how things go. I have to remind myself to not get attached to him," I admit with a resigned sigh. "It's easy for me to lead with my heart instead of my head, and I can't do that with him. I leave at the end of the summer, and we both live incredibly different lives. All we can ever be is casual."

Charlotte lifts her eyebrows. "If you're going to do casual, doing it with Cal seems like the perfect choice. He doesn't seem like a total raging asshole. You, my beautifully lucky friend, have hit the jackpot."

I let out a small laugh as I wave my hand through the air dismissively. "I am lucky, aren't I?"

She nods excitedly. "Yes! I'm so happy I told you to accept the job with him. Can you imagine what your summer would look like if you'd made the wrong choice and turned him down?"

Her question makes me pause. Time has flown by since I started working for Cal. I haven't really had the time to stop and think what my last summer in the Hamptons would've looked like if not for him.

I swallow, feelings that absolutely shouldn't be there blooming in my chest. The summer is almost halfway over, and it's already been the best one of my life.

"It really is crazy to think how different it would've been if I was still working at the Grill and cooking on the side for rude men like Laurent Hughes."

Charlotte lets out a grunt of annoyance before turning around and stepping in front of the bathroom mirror. She fluffs her hair before rolling her eyes. "He was seated in my section two nights ago. The man really is intolerable."

I nod before stepping next to her and looking at my reflection. A small gasp falls from my lips as I take in my appearance.

"Well, now I know how you immediately knew something had happened between me and Cal." I've never been the best at makeup, but I had tried applying a nude lipstick while getting ready for tonight. I've had the occasional lunch with Cal and our friends here at Pembroke, but I haven't had dinner here. Dinner at the club is different. It's fancy. I wanted to apply a little more makeup than normal for it. But I hadn't really thought much of it when Cal and I made out in the front seat of his car since we showed up to Pembroke a little early.

Charlotte snorts before pointing to my new purse. "Did you bring any makeup to touch things up? I can help if you did. No one else at the club will know you're getting hot and heavy with a member. And not just any member...*the* Callahan Hastings."

She wags her eyebrows playfully at her comment. In return, I give her an eye roll. Luckily, I had thrown my lipstick and some powder in my purse before leaving because I was trying to find things to fill my new bag with.

"The 'no sex with members' rule doesn't apply to me since I don't work at the club anymore," I throw back at her as I search for my makeup.

"Oh, so I can go ahead and tell all of your former coworkers, then?"

I aim a dirty look in her direction immediately. "Charlotte!

No, absolutely not. It's none of their business. I want things with me and Cal to be private."

She gives me a triumphant smile. "Then the 'no sex with members' rule does kind of apply to you."

I smile, handing her the makeup, knowing she'll be better at helping me clean it up than I would be. "Fine," I begin with a laugh. "You win. Just help me get fixed up so not everyone knows about my pre-dinner make-out session?"

Charlotte grabs a paper towel and takes a step closer, the smile still on her face. She gently grabs my face and wipes at the smeared lipstick around my mouth. "I just can't believe my best friend has Callahan Hastings falling at her feet."

I try to hold still but roll my eyes at her words. "He's hardly falling at my feet, Char."

She freezes, the paper towel still pressed to my skin. "I know you don't believe the words coming out of your mouth."

"What do you mean?"

"I mean, the man is spending thousands upon thousands of dollars on you, and don't even get me started on the way he looks at you in those cooking videos you've been posting. He's a puddle at your feet."

She throws the paper towel away before opening up the powder and gently dabbing it against my skin with a makeup sponge.

"No he isn't," I rush to get out. I don't want Charlotte to make this thing between Cal and me seem like more than it is. That'll only lead to me getting hopeful, and I can't think that way. We'd never work anyway, and that's okay as long as we both recognize that now, from the beginning. "It's just a fling," I add, trying to put as much conviction in my words as I can.

The sigh that Charlotte lets out tells me everything I need to know. She doesn't believe me. "Whatever you say, Lucy," she mutters with a hint of resignation in her tone.

I keep quiet as she finishes fixing my makeup. The only thing running through my head is how I don't know if I believe me either. Things with Cal feel far too intense to only be casual, but that's a problem I'll deal with later.

Because no matter what, that's all we'll ever be...temporary.

Forty-two
CAL

"What are you smiling at?" I ask Lucy, walking into the kitchen to find her sitting at the counter, looking at her phone. The smell of garlic and herbs fills the entire room.

Lucy looks up at me, almost taking my breath away with how stunning she is. It's been a week since we had sex, and I can't get enough of her. Every night, when she gets ready to leave, I want to ask her to stay the night. There's nothing I want more than to hold her all night and wake up to her in the morning, but I haven't told her that yet because she reminds me any chance she can that things are casual between us.

So, no matter how badly I want her to sleep next to me, I'm scared she'll say no.

I've never really felt scared to do anything, so all of this is new territory to me.

"I was going through our videos I've been posting, checking for comments and responding to them, when I realized there's this account that's liking and commenting on everything I've posted. Even my old photos." I close the distance to her as she holds up her phone to show me.

I smile, paying attention to the account she's pointing out. The account is mine, but I don't tell her that. "I love that, baby.

You have a fan." I lean in and press a kiss to her cheek, reveling in her familiar scent I've become far too attached to. "Do I need to figure out how to get on there and tell them I'm still your number one fan and they can't take my place?"

She rolls her eyes before setting her phone on the counter. She stands on her tiptoes and wraps her arms around my neck. "Dolores asked about you this morning."

I raise my eyebrows and smile. "Oh, did she?" I had a meeting I couldn't miss, so I couldn't go to the farm stand with her. It's become a little tradition ever since that first time I showed up and surprised her there. Sometimes, she convinces me to ride bikes there together; other times, we drive and revel in having the top down on one of the sports cars I own and keep here for the summer. "She did. You'll never believe what also happened this morning."

I wrap my arms around her waist and pull her body flush with mine. "What happened?" I ask, my gaze traveling over the constellation of freckles on her cheeks.

"Mr. Fred agreed to meet me at the farm stand this morning. He finally got the courage to ask Dolores on a date. They're going out tomorrow night."

I give her a wide smile as my arms tighten around her. "Seriously?" I don't hide the shock in my voice. I've only met Mr. Fred a few times when I've accompanied her to her place to grab her things. In the times I did talk to him, he seemed too nervous to actually ask Dolores on a date. I didn't know if he'd ever do it, but apparently, today was the day he was brave enough to finally ask. I never thought I'd be so invested in a potential love story between two people old enough to be my grandparents, but because of Lucy, I've been telling Dolores to give Mr. Fred a chance every morning.

My smile gets even wider at the realization she actually listened to me.

Lucy nods her head. Her gaze flicks to my lips for a moment before her eyes return to mine. "Seriously. We're about to be the best matchmakers, babe."

Her eyes get wide for a moment at the slip of the nickname. She stills in my arms, her brown eyes pinned on me.

Pride radiates through my entire body. I love that she just called me babe. "Babe, huh?" I give her a smug grin, finding the shocked look on her face absolutely adorable.

I live for moments just like this. Moments where it seems like maybe one day, I'll be able to convince her that this thing between us is far more than a fling.

Lucy gives me a nervous smile.

God, she's so fucking perfect that it makes my heart hurt to even look at her.

"It kind of just rolled off my tongue," she confesses before burying her face against my chest. I love holding her in my arms like this, but I'm a little sad to not be able to see the beautiful blush creeping over her cheeks from the slip-up.

"Was it too much?" Her words come out muffled against the fabric of my shirt.

I squeeze her tighter before tucking my chin over her head. "Hell no," I answer immediately. I want her to do it again. I'm desperate for any inkling of affection she'll give me that shows she doesn't see me as just some summer fling. "Baby, you can call me babe all you want. I fucking love it."

She pulls her head from my chest and smiles up at me. "Really?"

I nod, leaning in to press a kiss to her lips. I was planning on keeping it soft and fast, but she changes my plans when her tongue skirts against the seam of my lips. I open my mouth for her, welcoming the feeling of her tongue slipping against mine.

My hands find the side of her face as the kiss deepens. I don't know what it is about being alone in this kitchen with her that makes my entire body heat. Maybe it's the fact that so much of our time is spent in here, or maybe it's the memory of having her spread wide open for me on the island. Whatever it is, my cock gets harder with each swipe of her tongue against mine.

Her breath is hot against my lips as she pulls away, a sultry smile forming. "*Babe*," she repeats, saying the word nice and slow.

I groan. "Say it again."

Her hands move to my chest. She runs her palms along the button-up, her fingers moving south. "Babe," she says again, her voice lowered. She begins to undo the buttons of my shirt.

"What's in the oven?" I ask, my words coming out hoarse. I was inside her only a few hours ago. I shouldn't feel this desperate for her, yet I do.

Lucy pulls her head back, her eyebrows slightly furrowed with confusion. "A summer vegetable quiche. Why?" She finishes unbuttoning my shirt before pushing both sides open. I love the appreciating look she gives my body as her eyes roam up and down my torso.

"How much longer does it have?" I ask, my voice tight. I want her so fucking bad, and I don't want to wait any longer. I know her well enough that she won't spare whatever dish she's making for breakfast—even if she got an orgasm in exchange.

Her eyes light up, and a smile graces her lips once again. "Probably like ten minutes. Why do you ask?"

My hands skirt down her back and grab her ass. "Ten minutes is all I need."

I'm about to lift her onto the counter when she shakes her head. "No. Ten minutes is all *I* need."

Before I can protest, she drops to her knees, her fingers quickly working at the button of my pants.

"Lucy..." I grit out, savoring the view of her on her knees and her big, brown eyes aimed up at me.

"You're not going to stop me this time," she begins, undoing the zipper and not wasting any time pushing my briefs and pants out of the way.

"But, baby," I argue, the rest of my protest dissipating on my lips when her hand wraps around my cock.

She pumps up and down, a hungry look in her eyes as she moves her attention to my length. "I've wanted to do this for days now, and you haven't let me. You're always distracting me by making me feel good." She looks up at me again, her hand still moving up and down. "Now I want to make you feel good, *babe.*"

I know there's no way I can deny her when she licks her lips and pushes her hair off her shoulders and out of the way.

My head falls backward, and my fingers tangle in her hair the moment I feel her hot breath against the tip of my cock.

"Fuck, baby, I don't think I've ever been so turned on in my life," I confess, my entire body tight with anticipation over what she's about to do. It's not like I haven't wanted to feel her mouth on me; it's just that I've been so obsessed with burying my face between her thighs or sliding into her that we haven't done this yet.

Her tongue swipes along my shaft. "It's about to get even better." Without saying anything else, she takes me into her mouth and proves all over again that I'm ruined for anyone else but her.

Forty-three
LUCY

"Do you know what you're doing tonight?" Charlotte asks on FaceTime as I get ready in Cal's bathroom.

I shake my head. "I have no idea. I was making lunch when Jude showed up acting weird. He and Cal kept whispering to each other. I have no idea what's going on."

Charlotte shrugs, a suspicious smile forming on her lips. "I can't wait to find out what they're conspiring about."

I narrow my eyes at her for a moment, my tube of mascara hovering in front of my face. "Did Jude tell you what they're planning?"

Her mouth falls open as she vehemently shakes her head. "Jude didn't tell me anything. Why would you think that?" Her voice goes up an octave at the end of her question.

She still holds the phone in front of her face, but she looks away, staring at something I can't see as she takes her break in the Pembroke Hills employee locker room.

"I think that because you're acting very suspicious," I tell her. I raise my eyebrow at her, waiting for her to come up with another lie about how she knows nothing when it's obvious she does.

"Just finish getting ready so you can find out the surprise and report back to me."

I roll my eyes before focusing on the mirror again. "It seems like I don't need to report back to you. You already know what's happening."

This morning started pretty normally. Cal couldn't come to the farm stand with me because of a meeting, but I picked up everything I needed for meals today. I then got to Cal's place and made breakfast, but when I was busy preparing lunch, Jude arrived unannounced.

That's when things got weird.

Right after the three of us ate lunch, Cal announced I wouldn't have to worry about dinner tonight and that I'd need to be ready by six for a surprise.

Never did I expect Charlotte to also be in on whatever the surprise is, but one FaceTime with her, and I'm convinced she knows exactly what's happening.

"What are you wearing tonight?" she asks, trying to keep her voice smooth. The thing about Charlotte is she's an open book. You can always read all of her reactions. You know her mood by the look on her face and the tone of her voice. And the tone in her voice right now is telling me it's taking everything in her to keep whatever this secret is. It didn't take me very long into our friendship to learn she's terrible with them.

I finish applying mascara to my eyelashes before I look at her. "Does what I wear really matter?" I push, trying to get more details out of her.

Charlotte somehow manages to maintain a straight face, even though I can tell it's killing her. She keeps her lips pressed into a thin line in an attempt to fight a smile. "Wear whatever you want," she gets out, her voice high-pitched and tight. "Just be comfortable."

"Charlotte." I sigh, wondering what they're all keeping from me. It's not like it's even close to my birthday or anything of that nature. I'm dying of curiosity about why I'm even being surprised to begin with. "Should I be nervous?" I ask cautiously.

She gives me a warm smile. "No, Lucy. You should be excited. I promise this is something I know you'll be excited about."

"So, you *do* know!"

Her eyes go wide for a moment before she tosses her hair over her shoulder and shrugs. "I have no idea what you're talking about. I'll call you once my shift is over! Love you!"

Before I can ask her anything else, she ends the FaceTime and leaves me staring at my phone with a million questions running through my head.

Since Charlotte is no help at all, after I finish getting ready, I decide to slip on a simple dress I picked out on my shopping date with Cal last week. Even though I've never stayed the night with him, I've learned to keep an extra bag of clothes here just in case. Sometimes in the middle of the day, Cal decides we need to go golfing, or he wants to have people over for dinner or even grab food at the club. Because of that, I needed a few options to keep here for when those things come up. And tonight, I'm very proud of myself for being prepared.

I think the new dress should be perfect for whatever secret thing Cal has planned. It's a simple black halter dress with small white polka dots all over it. The fabric feels like butter against my skin, making it comfortable, but it can also pass as a little dressy if needed.

I'm busy searching my purse for a clip or a headband to help pull some hair out of my face when Cal walks into the primary bathroom.

"Fuck, I forgot how much I love you in that dress," he notes.

My entire body flushes at the way he stares at me. He leans against the opening to the bathroom, one ankle crossed over the other as his heated gaze drinks me in.

"That's a good thing, since you're the one who bought it," I respond, giving up on finding anything in my purse and tucking my hair behind my ear.

I give him a smile through the mirror before doing a quick spin in the dress to show it off.

A low hum of approval passes his lips as he pulls my back to his chest, his eyes still pinned on me through our reflection. "You're beautiful," he tells me, his voice low.

A shiver runs down my spine at the tender way he holds me, mixed with the grittiness of his words. It's the small moments just like this that make me wish things were different.

From the moment I came to the Hamptons, I've known my place was always back home. I'm okay with that. Although taking over the family store was never my dream, I'd do anything for my parents. They've already gone through so much, it wouldn't be fair for me to ask them to keep working just so I can stay here in the Hamptons. And I'd never ask my father to sell something he's poured his entire life into, but it doesn't mean that when Cal looks at me just like this, I don't wish there was a way I could move back to Virginia and also keep him.

"Tell me what you're thinking about." I love the deep, throaty sound of his voice, even if there's no way I'll answer his question honestly.

"I was just thinking about how lucky I feel right now," I answer. It's kind of the truth. I wouldn't want things I can't have with Cal if I didn't feel so incredibly lucky to have the short amount of time I do have left with him.

He presses a soft kiss to my neck. I love the scrape of his stubble against my sensitive skin and the way his scent surrounds me because of the proximity of our bodies.

"Baby, I'm the lucky one," he responds huskily.

My eyes flutter shut as he peppers the softest of kisses along my neck. I keep my eyes closed, trying to ignore the sinking feeling settling throughout my entire body as I realize I'm doing exactly what I said I wouldn't.

I think I'm falling for Callahan Hastings.

The realization is terrifying. I try to push the feeling away, pretending that if I don't think about it or dwell on it, maybe it'll go away.

When my eyes open and I find him watching me through our reflections, I know that as much as I'm going to try and ignore the feelings, it won't take away the fact that they're there. That what I feel for him is real and getting deeper with each day I spend with him.

"You ready for your surprise?" he asks, breaking me from my thoughts.

I nod before turning around so I can wrap my arms around his neck. "Should I be nervous?"

He shakes his head. "No, you should be excited for this surprise. I'm confident you'll love it."

I search his face for any clues about what it could be. "Really? You're confident? Now I'm even more intrigued."

He gives me his typical cocky smirk that makes me melt every time before grabbing my hand and taking a step back. "Let's go find out."

I let him lead me down the hallway, my heart picking up speed, getting more excited with each step we take. He seems to be leading me to the kitchen. The closer we get, the more I hear the faint sound of music filling the space.

We're just about to turn the corner and walk into the

kitchen when Cal turns around. For the first time, I see a nervous smile on his lips.

"Close your eyes for me, Lucy baby," he instructs, his voice soft. I know I must still be confused about my feelings for him because the gentle tone to his words and the look in his eyes tricks my mind into thinking he might actually be falling for me too.

"Do I really need to close my eyes?" I ask, shifting anxiously from one foot to the other. Excitement courses through my veins at whatever this surprise is. Just by Cal's demeanor, I can tell that whatever it is, he's nervous about revealing it to me. But it's a cute kind of nervous. Almost like he's put a lot of thought into it and is anxious to see my reaction.

"Yes, close your eyes. The sooner you do it, the sooner you can see your surprise."

A smile spreads over my lips, but I do as I'm told. I close my eyes. I expect Cal to start walking again, but instead, he presses a quick kiss to my lips.

"Okay, keep them closed," he tells me, his lips moving against mine. He keeps them there for a moment before the warmth of his lips against mine is gone.

He starts to walk, his steps slowing as he carefully guides me the rest of the way to the kitchen.

The music gets a little louder and filters through the surrounding space. I don't recognize the song playing, but it reminds me of something you'd hear while summering in Italy.

"I'm going to count down from three. When I make it to zero, open your eyes."

I nod in understanding, my lips twitching with a budding smile. I don't know if anyone's ever taken this many steps to surprise me. I have no idea what he's hiding in his kitchen, but I know I'll love it because he cared enough to plan it in the first place.

"Three," he begins, keeping his voice steady.

My heart slams against my chest in anticipation. I'm so excited that I can't even wipe the wide smile from my face.

"Two..."

I swear he's counting slowly just to torture me. I'm dying for him to make it to zero so I can see.

"One..."

"Zero..."

I open my eyes immediately, not even waiting for him to tell me to do so, and the loudest gasp leaves my lips, and I cover my mouth in shock.

"Cal," I get out, my voice barely above a whisper as I take in the sight in front of me.

I don't even know where to look. His kitchen has been transformed into a filming area. Lights have been set up in every corner to perfectly illuminate the kitchen, and on the counter, there's a tripod with a nice camera connected to it. There's even a microphone attachment on the camera as well as an iPad that shows exactly what the camera is filming.

"What do you think?" Cal asks, his hand finding my back.

I want to look at him, but I can't. I can't pull my gaze from the sight in front of me. Also on the counter are the new dishes he insisted on buying me a week ago, along with some new items I've never seen before. Cutting boards, knives, and bowls are all lined up on the counter.

He's created the perfect setup.

It's the most thoughtful thing anyone's ever done for me, and I have no idea how to even form coherent enough words to tell him that.

"This," I begin, my voice cracking with the emotions clogging my throat. My eyes sting with tears of gratitude. I don't know if I want to continue to take in every thoughtful item in front of me or if I want to look at him and hope he sees in my eyes all the things I'm too overwhelmed to say.

Cal reaches out and runs his knuckles along my cheek. There's so much softness in his face, even despite the hard lines of his perfectly chiseled features. "There's one more thing," he says, using the hand that was just pressing against my skin to point across the kitchen.

"Lucy, I'd love for you to meet Enzo Russo. His restaurant in Italy has been awarded three Michelin stars. He so graciously accepted my offer for him to fly out here and teach you some of his most popular and authentic dishes. He's also agreed to allow you to film the entire experience."

I think the chef steps into the kitchen, but I don't see him. Not really. One minute, my feet are on the ground; the next minute, I'm catapulting my body against Cal's and trusting he'll catch me. My arms wrap around his neck as his wrap around my middle.

I tuck my face against his neck as my body shakes from being so happy and overwhelmed. "Cal, I have no words," I say, my voice coming out muffled.

He laughs, the sound of it vibrating against my body. "Does that mean I did okay?"

I nod, hoping he can feel it. "Yes," I mutter, still in complete awe of the sweet gesture. I woke up this morning thinking it was going to be a normal Thursday, and here he was, planning the sweetest surprise anyone's ever done for me, just because.

If I wasn't already falling for him, this would've done it. But who could blame me? How was I not supposed to fall for Callahan Hastings when he does things as thoughtful and sweet as this?

"This is the best gift I've ever been given, Cal," I say, my voice barely above a whisper from the emotions still overtaking me. "Thank you," I add, looking at him with a smile so wide my cheeks hurt.

"Only the best for you, baby, since you're the best gift I've ever been given." He cocks his head to the side and brings attention to Enzo before I can even analyze what he just said. "You ready to get cooking?"

Forty-four

CAL

"I still can't believe you planned all of this for me," Lucy whispers, a beaming expression on her face.

"Why is it hard to believe someone would want to plan a special surprise for you?" I counter, my attention solely focused on her. I lost track of the time when she and Enzo were cooking. I was in a trance, watching her in her element, learning from one of the best chefs in the world. It took a lot of convincing—and money—for Enzo to fly out here just for the evening with Lucy, but I would've paid anything to see her as happy as she's been tonight.

Lucy takes a sip of her wine as she gathers her thoughts. I give her all the time she needs, curious to know the answer to my question. She and Enzo finished cooking over two hours ago. He sat and ate with us for a bit, answering any questions Lucy had for him before he eventually excused himself and left Lucy and me to enjoy the food they'd prepared.

She lets out a long sigh, her eyes focused on me. A candle flickers between us, the light reflecting in her big brown eyes. "I guess it isn't hard to believe someone would want to. It's just that no one has before."

"You deserve all the special things, Lucy Rae," I begin, having to clear my throat because of the emotion clogging it. If she could just spend a minute in my head, she'd realize just how special she is and how much she deserves more than what she's used to.

Even in the candlelight, I can see the flush creep upon her face. She looks down, her eyelashes dancing across her cheeks as she stares at her wineglass. "I don't even know what to say back to you when you say sweet things like that." Her words come out softly and directed at the table.

I reach across the table and take her hand in mine. My thumb brushes over the top of her hand as I wait for her to look at me again. "You don't have to say anything, as long as in your head, you know just how special you are." I want to add to that sentence and tell her how special she is to *me*, but I keep it to myself.

I've never been one who's open with my feelings because I haven't felt anything close to what I feel for Lucy. I didn't have to be open about feelings that weren't there in the first place. But now that I feel so deeply about her, it's terrifying. She's the first person to ever capture my attention—and my heart.

She has all the power, and I've never been a fan of giving people power over me.

But for her, I'll always make an exception.

Her eyes find mine again. I could never grow tired of staring into her chestnut-brown eyes. Looking into them is beginning to feel like home, and that's a dangerous realization. "You know, if you would've told me that night we were reunited at Laurent Hughes's that this is where things were headed, I would've never believed you."

"What do you mean by that?"

"I mean, I never would've guessed that you'd be personally flying a three-time Michelin-star chef out just to teach me how to cook Italian dishes because of something I mentioned once. Or that you'd spend I don't even want to know how much on filming equipment for me just because of a silly hobby of mine."

My lips press into a thin line at her comment. She's one of the most talented people I've ever met. Enzo was even impressed by her cooking, and he didn't strike me as the type who's impressed often. My thumb traces circles over her knuckles. Although the touch is light, even the small amount of contact between us makes my entire body heat.

I give her hand a squeeze before letting out a long sigh. "For one, you're a phenomenal chef, baby. Don't discredit yourself and call it a silly hobby. Your recipes deserve to be recreated around the world, and nothing about that is silly. And for two, you should've known the lengths I'd go to just to see you smile after that night at Laurent's. Because the moment I heard Thomas was trying to hire you for the summer, I gave the private chef that I've used for years a paid summer off just so I could tell you I needed one."

Lucy's jaw drops as she looks at me wide-eyed. "You what?"

I smirk before lifting a shoulder. I hadn't planned on telling her about Randall's sudden summer off, but it isn't something I care to keep secret anymore. It's got to be obvious to her how crazy I am about her.

"I've had the same private chef for seven years now, maybe even eight. Randall is like family, but he also has his own family. When I found out you'd be interested in taking a private chef job, I didn't want it to be with anyone but me."

Lucy stares at me from across the table. She shakes her head in disbelief. "So you've been paying me all summer and Randall as well?"

I nod before picking up my own wine glass with my free

hand. I lift the glass to my lips and take a sip before carefully setting it back on the table. "Yes. And I'd do it again in a heartbeat. I don't even want to think what my summer would've looked like if I hadn't made the decision to give Randall a long vacation and have you take the spot."

A tentative smile builds on her lips as her surprise sinks in. "So that's why people were shocked when I said I was working for you for the summer. Both Jude and Dolores had mentioned Randall. I wondered if something bad had happened with your chef before me."

I keep my eyes trained on her, watching her carefully to see if my confession upsets her. It doesn't seem to. Her eyes still stare at me with a softness to them. The doe-eyed way she's always looking at me makes me want to be the best version of myself for her. "Nothing bad happened with Randall. Once I return to Manhattan in September, he'll be back to cooking for me. Honestly, it was about time he got a break from me. But he still checks in all the time and sends me pictures of him visiting his nieces and nephews in California."

Lucy leans forward and props her chin up with her hand. I love that it gives me an even closer view of her beautiful face. Her big, round eyes and perfectly plump lips. The freckles that form constellations on her cheeks and the tip of her nose, which always seems to be sunburnt. Everything about her is absolutely radiant, and I'll take any close-up view of her I can get. Especially tonight, as I'm battling with myself about whether I should just admit that I have real, deep feelings for her or keep pretending that all we are is just a fling.

"How is it possible you're so perfect?" she asks.

"The only perfect one between us is you, Lucy baby. And I ask myself almost every second of every day how I got so lucky to have someone as perfect as you even give me the time of day."

She playfully bites her lip as she shakes her head. "No, you're perfect, Callahan Hastings. Everything you do. The night you planned tonight, the way you even recruited Jude and Charlotte's help. The way you still paid the chef you've had for years for an entire summer and then paid me double what my other offer was just so I'd say yes. God." Her words fall off for a moment as she stares at me in disbelief. "You really *are* perfect."

"It's just because I'm crazy about you," I admit, my heart racing inside my chest.

Saying the words out loud feels vulnerable. I can't imagine it's something she doesn't already know because I feel like everything I do makes it obvious how much I care about her. I haven't even tried hiding how I feel about her from my friends or anyone else.

I can't fight what's happening. Now, I just need to know that she feels something for me too, but I'm too afraid to ask, scared to have her tell me again that we're just a fling.

I swallow, my pulse spiking with the thoughts racing through my head. All I want to do is pull her close to me and get answers. I want to beg her to admit that there's more between us and that she's even half as crazy about me as I am her. I want to ask her if she'd ever consider moving to Manhattan or if there's any part of her that thinks things could work between us past the summer. There are so many things I want to know, but all the questions get stuck in my throat from fear.

I scrub my hand over my mouth, so many feelings rising to the surface. I don't know if I can handle the answer to all of the questions running through my mind, but I'm feeling brave enough to ask one.

"Can I ask you something?" I get out, my voice hoarse.

She smiles. "Ask me anything."

"Could you see yourself with me...even after this summer?"

My heart drops the moment she pulls her hand from mine and sits back in her chair. Whatever she's about to say, I know it isn't going to be what I want to hear.

And that realization tears me apart.

Forty-five

LUCY

My mind races with different ways I can answer Cal. Whatever I was thinking he was going to ask me, this was not it.

I wish I knew what to say back to him, but my mind is at a loss. Tonight has been so perfect I don't want to ruin it. But I also don't want to lie to him. Not when he's staring at me so vulnerably, almost like it killed him to even ask me the question to begin with.

"I wish that were an option for me," I whisper, not knowing how to tell him that I can't change my future, no matter how badly I want to.

How horrible would it be for me to admit that I don't want to take over my family's store? It's everything my father has worked for. It's his legacy. He literally almost worked himself to death, working so hard that he had a heart attack, to keep the store afloat. It was his dream to pass it down to his sons. When we lost my brothers, I knew whatever future I saw for myself didn't matter anymore. I had to take over so we could keep the store in the family despite not wanting to.

But I can't tell that to Cal. Even admitting that I don't want it makes me feel horrible, and I don't want him to see me as a bad person.

Cal sits up as his eyebrows draw together. "Why isn't it an option?"

"Because I have to go back to Virginia. I'm the only one left to take over my family's store, and it's time to give my dad a break. It's time for me to run it, not him."

His lips press into a thin line as he thinks about my answer. I hate that I can tell I've hurt him. He's normally full of confidence, his head held high and his shoulders pushed back. Right now, it's the opposite. His entire posture is stooped as his facial features set in a grimace.

"Is that what you want?" he asks, his eyes pinned on me.

I nod, unable to speak the words and lie out loud to him. "But if I had the choice, if I didn't have to go back, then the answer to your question is yes. I'd want to be with you after the summer, Cal."

A sad laugh escapes him as he runs his hands through his hair. "I don't know if that answer makes me happy or incredibly sad."

I slide out of my chair and close the distance between us. I hate the sad, pained look in his eyes. I never thought I'd be the one to make Cal feel that way, but I hate that what I've said has hurt him. He's quickly become one of the last people I'd ever want to hurt, and I don't know what to do to prevent it from happening again.

I tried telling him all we could be was temporary. I tried telling myself the same thing. But whatever's happening between us, it seems that our hearts haven't paid heed to the warnings from our heads.

And I don't know if there's anything I can do to stop the pain that is inevitably coming at the end of the summer.

"You have me for the summer," I tell him, not knowing what else to say. I straddle his legs and lower myself onto his lap, my eyes searching his face for any sign of what's running through his mind.

He leans into my touch when I grab both sides of his face, needing to feel his skin against mine. "That won't be enough for me." His voice is hoarse and filled with emotion, hitting straight to my heart.

I stroke his cheek, savoring the feeling of the scrape of his facial hair against my fingertips. "It has to be," I whisper.

Cal shakes his head. "I wish you'd be honest with me, baby. I know there's more to why you need to go back to Virginia. You're just not telling me what it is."

I swallow, my eyes searching his. There's so much pain in the blue eyes staring back at me that I almost tell him everything. I almost tell him how devastated both my parents were when we lost Luke and Logan. There were times I would sit at the top of the stairs and listen to my parents sob into each other's arms. Often, they'd fall asleep right there on the couch, their bodies so exhausted from the tears that they couldn't even make it to their room. I'd tell him how the lawsuits against the drunk driver completely drained the little money my parents had and that we almost lost the store in the legal process just to be able to pay the bills.

I'd tell him how the night before I left for college, my dad sat me down at the table and told me he needed me to be the one to take over the business. He cried in front of me—something he'd never done. He always saved those moments for times he thought I wasn't around. Tears had run down his face when he said he couldn't lose the store on top of losing my brothers.

The moment I arrived on my college campus, I changed my major to business. I swore I'd do whatever it took to never see my father that defeated again. I got the degree I needed to make sure I did all his work justice when he passed down the company to me. I thought I'd be well into my thirties before I was ever faced with having to actually take it over, but then the heart attack happened.

I'm having to take it over far sooner than I ever imagined, and I almost confess to Cal that despite all of that, I still wish deep down I didn't have to. I'm terrified I'm going to fail and ruin the legacy my dad so desperately wants to uphold. From the moment we got the news of the accident, I've tried doing everything possible to take care of my parents and be the perfect daughter.

They've gone through enough. I never want them to worry about me.

If I could, I'd admit to Cal that I feel guilty for not wanting my father's legacy and that, because it isn't my dream, some-how, I'll mess it all up. That I'll let him down, and he'll have not only lost Luke and Logan, but he'll have lost his store too—because of me.

"Why aren't you saying anything?" Cal asks, his words breaking me from my thoughts. I hadn't even realized I'd been so lost in my head that I hadn't responded to him.

I lean in and place my forehead against his. For a moment, we just soak each other in. His eyelids flutter shut, and so do mine. Our breaths fall in sync, and I don't know how much time passes while we stay like that.

Eventually, I let out a long sigh. "No matter what I tell you, it won't change anything, Cal. I have to go back to Virginia, and you'll go back to Manhattan, and what I want won't change that. It wouldn't work."

I expect him to argue, but when I open my eyes and find his already on mine, it seems like he doesn't have it in him to argue anymore. We stare at each other for a few seconds before he lets out a long sigh.

"I'm going to spend the rest of the summer trying to change your mind, baby. You'll see."

Before I can tell him it's no use, his lips are crashing against mine, and his fingers are tangling in my hair.

The moment our lips collide, I let out a satisfied moan. Nothing has ever felt more right than when Cal's lips are on mine. I know for a fact no kiss in the future will ever compare unless it's from him.

Because of that, I throw myself into the kiss. I greedily push my tongue into his mouth, wanting to deepen the kiss as much as possible.

My hips grind against him. I search for some kind of relief for my throbbing clit. The possessive way he kisses me and keeps my mouth pinned to his turns me on. I can't get enough of him.

Cal rips his mouth from mine. His fingertips press against my scalp as he makes sure I can see nothing but him with his next words. "You've ruined me, Lucy baby. I need you to know that."

He leans in to kiss me again, not even giving me the chance to respond. Maybe he does it on purpose. Maybe it's that he thinks he can't handle my answer. Whatever it is, I welcome the distraction.

It'll just hurt us both if I admit to him he's ruined me too.

I think I'll spend the rest of my life comparing every kiss— every man—to the one holding me right now.

Cal's hands move from my hair. They slide down my back before cupping my ass. He continues to prove to me that no one else will ever kiss me as well as he does as he stands up. I don't ask where he's leading us because it doesn't matter.

I'll go wherever he leads as long as he keeps kissing me just like this.

Forty-six

CAL

I taste Lucy's moans as I gently lay her on my bed. I give the kiss everything I have, funneling every single one of the feelings running through me into it.

My feelings for her. Intense and only growing stronger with each day I spend with her.

My frustration. I can tell there's something she's hiding from me, and it's eating away at me. She doesn't trust me enough to tell me why she's giving up her passion for cooking to run a family business she never even talks about.

My fear. Deep in my gut, I know I'm going to lose her. Just by the look in her eyes and the defeated way she answered my questions, I know no matter how she feels, she's going to go back to Virginia, and she has no intention of including me in her life there.

For the first time in my life, I feel helpless. I've always been able to get my way—sometimes easier than others. I've always been able to bulldoze my way to an outcome I wanted.

But with Lucy, I can't.

And that fucking kills me.

All I can do now is try to use the time I have left with her to change her mind.

And that's what I try to do with the way I kiss her. I kiss her slowly, pretending that I have all the time in the world with her.

Eventually, we both grow desperate for more. Lucy's fingers pull at my clothes as she tries to get them off me without breaking the kiss.

I pull away, a smirk blooming on my lips. "Are you greedy for more, baby?"

She nods, and her lips, red and raw from the kisses and the scrape of my facial hair, turn into a perfect smile. "Yes. I need you," she adds, her voice breathy as she grinds her hips against me.

I let out a low chuckle, my eyes raking over her body. I love the dress she's wearing. She took my breath away when I first saw her wearing it tonight, but I'm ready to see it gone.

My hands fist the fabric of the dress as I slowly begin to push it up her body to remove it.

A small gasp leaves my lips when I push it up far enough to find she isn't wearing anything underneath. "Have you not been wearing any panties all night?"

She bites back a playful smile. "I ran out. I thought I still had extra pairs in my bag, but I didn't. The dress was long enough that no one would know."

I glide my finger over her, finding her already wet and ready for me. "Now *I* know. And that's all I'll be able to think about every time you wear this dress."

"Good."

I don't waste time pulling the dress off her and tossing it to the side. My clothes come off in a rush next, joining her dress on the floor. There have been plenty of times when I've taken my time with her. Tonight is not that night.

Our conversation after dinner has left me both nervous and determined. I'm anxious I might actually lose her, that somehow, she'll be able to walk away from us. Because of that, I'm determined to show her how perfect we are together.

It seems that Lucy is as eager to feel the joining of our bodies as I am. The moment I'm undressed and my body is back between her thighs, she's lifting her hips.

"Cal," she begs, circling her hips to line me up with her.

"Yes, baby?"

"Please." She lets out a low moan when I guide the tip of my cock through her wetness. Typically, I like for her to have one orgasm before I even slide inside her, but tonight is different. I'm too desperate to be enveloped by her to do anything else. I need that connection between us.

When I'm inside her, she can't hide from me. Her walls come down, and it's obvious that she's feeling everything I am. After our talk tonight, I need that more than ever.

"I know, baby," I assure her. I slide inside slowly, wanting to give her time to adjust since I haven't given her as much time as I normally do.

Lucy moans.

I moan.

We both get lost in the feeling of joining our bodies.

I keep my rhythm slow, savoring the way Lucy moans every time I fully push inside her, filling her with every inch of me. She makes the sexiest noises, and I commit every single one of them to memory.

"You feel so fucking good, baby," I grit out, trying to keep ahold of myself so I don't come too early. I don't want this to end so soon. Now that I'm inside her, I want to draw this out for as long as possible.

Lucy's eyes open and focus on me. She doesn't have to say anything for me to know exactly what she's thinking.

"I know," I tell her, leaning in and pressing my lips to hers.

I move my hips, rocking in and out of her as we get lost in the kiss.

As good as it feels, it still doesn't feel like enough.

I need more from her. With my lips still against hers and my tongue in her mouth, I slide my hands behind her back and pull her off the mattress.

I keep pulling her up and lean back. Now, she completely straddles me, putting me even deeper inside her.

"Oh my God," she moans as her hands find either side of my face. I love that she holds me so tightly. Even with our lips apart, she keeps our faces as close as possible as I continue to rock in and out of her.

It's on the tip of my tongue to tell her how much I care about her.

To tell her that despite her warnings, I've fallen in love with her.

She's it for me.

I pick up the pace to avoid saying any of it. I don't want to scare her away, and I can't handle having her tell me another time how things between us are just temporary. It'll break my fucking heart, and tonight, that's not something I can deal with.

"Babe, I'm close," she pants, her lips finding my neck as she presses kisses along my skin.

I almost come undone just because of the pet name. She says it with a moan, driving me absolutely fucking crazy.

My thrusts get even faster and deeper. I know she's taking me to her limit, but her moans and pants tell me that's just how she likes it.

"Me too," I tell her, my fingertips pressing into her sides as I keep her pinned to me.

"Come for me," Lucy pleads, her voice high-pitched and needy as I feel her tighten around me. Her nails dig into the back of my neck as she holds my face close to hers.

The begging tone of her voice just about sends me over the edge. My entire body heats with the beginning of my orgasm.

"You first," I demand, keeping the fast pace. "Come for me, baby, and then I'll fill you with my cum."

Lucy throws her head back. "Cal," she screams, her pussy holding me tight as her orgasm takes over.

The feeling of her coming around me is all it takes. My own orgasm rips through me.

I fuse my mouth to hers, needing even more of a connection with her as the most intense orgasm of my life takes over. My tongue tells her all the things I can't say out loud.

That I fell for her.

That I want to be with her.

That I can't imagine my life without her in it.

The kiss, mixed with the punishing rhythm of my hips, is intense. I don't stop until both of our moans die down and her body goes lax against mine.

Our chests heave up and down as our eyelids flutter open and we focus on each other.

The moment our eyes connect, a thought pops into my head.

"Stay with me tonight," I beg, not even caring how desperate my words sound. "Sleep next to me. Let me hold you all night and wake up next to you in the morning. *Please*, baby."

Lucy nods as she still regains her breath from the intensity of the sex. "Okay," she gets out through her labored breathing.

I let out the biggest sigh of relief. "Yeah?" I ask, needing the reassurance that I understood her correctly. The hint of a hopeful smile blooms on my lips.

"Yes," she responds, giving me a timid smile. "There's nothing I want more than to wake up next to you tomorrow morning."

"I'm so fucking happy you said that," I confess, pressing a

soft kiss to her lips. I can't wipe the goofy smile from my face at the thought of being able to hold her all night and see her radiant smile first thing in the morning.

There's still so much I want from her, but for tonight, it's a win to finally have her spend the night with me. I have the rest of the summer to show her how things are too perfect for us to be temporary. Eventually, I'll tell her I've fallen in love with her. But for tonight, I'll accept the small win.

Tomorrow, I get to wake up next to Lucy Rae Owens.

I can't fucking wait.

Forty-seven

LUCY

I wake up with my cheek pressed to Cal's chest. His heartbeat is steady against my skin as I rouse from the most peaceful night of sleep I've ever had.

The slow rhythm of Cal's breathing tells me he's still fast asleep. I smile, loving that I've woken up before him. If I can slip away without disturbing him, I want to make him breakfast in bed. My smile gets even wider at the idea. I've made him breakfast countless times, but something about making him breakfast after being next to him all night makes it seem more special.

I slide out of his hold inch by inch, moving incredibly slowly so I don't wake him up. The moment my feet hit the soft material of the rug, I let out a sigh of relief.

I'd gone to bed without a hint of clothing on. My dress still lies on the floor next to his discarded clothes, but I don't feel like putting it back on. Instead, I tiptoe to his closet and pull one of his button-ups off a hanger. I also grab a pair of his briefs before quietly putting both items on. The shirt is so long on me that it falls just above my knees, while the briefs are big enough that I need to roll the waistband once to keep them on my hips.

They don't fit right, but I kind of love it.

I leave his closet as quietly as I can and tiptoe my way to the bedroom door. Before I leave, I turn and commit the view of Cal fast asleep in bed to memory. I love how every single one of his facial features is relaxed. There's no hard set of his jaw or the intense pull of his eyebrows together on his forehead.

He looks at peace. When he first asked me to be with him after this summer, I didn't know how the rest of our night would go. I was terrified I was going to lose him before the summer even ended, but he seemed to have accepted my answer.

He never asked about Virginia again. After we had sex, we showered together, both of us giggling like little kids as we helped clean each other's bodies. I don't know how long we lay in bed talking about the most random things, but it was the best night of my life.

His surprise and the thoughtfulness behind it.

The way the sex between us felt different. I've never felt more connected to someone than I did last night. It was incredible.

My favorite part might've been falling asleep next to him. We talked until we both got so sleepy that our words became slower and slower until we both drifted off. The last thing I remember is Cal telling stories of him and Jude in boarding school before sleep pulled me under.

I manage to sneak out of Cal's room without waking him up. Once I make it to the hallway, I hurry to the kitchen and try to come up with a plan for breakfast.

I'm shocked to find the kitchen clean. Cal's housekeepers must've already come by for the morning. I've always wondered how often he has people help with the house. Every morning I show up to work, it's obvious the house has been cleaned; they're just always gone by the time I get there.

I blush, relieved that Cal had shut the door to his room after we'd taken a shower. If he hadn't, his housekeepers would've gotten a show this morning since both Cal and I went to bed naked.

I'm trying to think of what ingredients I know we have when I spot my phone on the counter.

Guilt washes over me as I realize I'd gone all night and morning without checking it.

I rush over to my phone, turning it over to find countless missed calls from my mom.

My stomach sinks as I click her name to call her back. I'm filled with more and more dread with each ring she doesn't answer.

The call goes to voicemail. I immediately call her back as I pace Cal's kitchen, waiting for her to pick up.

"Lucy," my mom answers, her voice raw. I know just by the tone of her voice that something is very wrong. "Are you okay? I've been calling all night."

"Mom, I'm fine. I'm sorry, I don't know what I was thinking." I take a deep breath, trying not to let my voice break. God, I can't believe I'd gone all night and into this morning without checking my phone. "What happened?" I ask, my voice breaking.

"Your dad was closing the store last night. When I hadn't heard from him, I called Alec to see if maybe he had. He hadn't either, so I drove to the store and found your dad unresponsive."

My hand covers my mouth in shock. "Oh my God," I cry, my eyes frantically darting around the kitchen as I try to process what my mom's saying.

I'm terrified to ask my next question because I don't know if I'm prepared for the answer.

"Is he okay?" I ask, my voice breaking.

"We're in the hospital now, just waiting for answers. They

don't know what happened, but as of right now, it seems like he's going to be okay. I don't really know. No one will tell me anything."

I let out a breath of relief as I run through the things I need to grab. I've got to get home.

"I'll be there as soon as I can," I tell her. It'll take me hours to get to the closest airport and get a flight out, but there's nothing I can do about that. Before I can even start the three-hour drive to the airport, I'll need to run by my place and grab some clothes.

"Oh, honey, I can handle it," my mom assures me.

I shake my head immediately. The exhaustion is clear in her voice. There's no way I'm making her handle this alone. "No, Mom. I want to be there. I want to see Dad, and I want to be there for you. It just might not be until tonight that I arrive."

"Are you sure?"

"Yes. Please just keep me posted if you get updates. Tell Dad I love him and I'll be there soon. I'm going to book a flight out as soon as we hang up."

"Okay. Be safe. I love you, Lu," Mom responds. I hate how worried she sounds, and I hate myself for being irresponsible enough not to have checked my phone since last night. She's had to worry about Dad all alone while I was being selfish.

"I love you too, Mom. I'll be there soon, I promise."

I hang up the phone just as tears begin to rush down my cheeks. I try to stop them, but the guilt of not being there when my parents needed me and the fear of not knowing if my dad is going to be okay overtakes me. I'm so upset with myself. I've always been so good at keeping my phone on me at all times in case of an emergency.

I just got so swept up in the night with Cal that I forgot all about it.

And I hate myself for letting that happen.

"Baby, what's wrong?"

I jump, turning to find Cal walking into the kitchen. He slipped on a pair of sweatpants and nothing else.

A sob rips through me just at the sight of him.

His entire face falls as he rushes to close the distance between us. Without any questions, he pulls me against his chest and holds me as my body shakes from the sobs coming out of me.

Cal's hand cups the back of my head. He just holds me as I try to regain my composure enough to talk.

Eventually, I let out a shaky breath as I pull my cheek from his chest.

"I have to go home," I announce, wiping underneath my eyes. "I need to get back to Virginia."

"I'll go with you," he responds immediately, his thumbs swiping at the tears still streaming down my cheeks.

I shake my head. "No. I need to get home. It's my dad. Something's happened, and I need to help my mom and—"

"And you can do all of that, baby. I'm not stopping you." His eyes are full of concern as they scan my face. "I'm just saying I'll go with you so you don't have to go back alone."

I let out another cry at how sweet he's being. I can't ask him to drop everything and come back to Virginia with me. I don't know how long I'll be there. Deep down, I wonder if I should just stay in Virginia for the rest of the summer. I don't know if I'll be able to leave again after hearing the fear and exhaustion in my mother's voice and not being there to help her.

"I don't know how long I'll be there for," I begin, stepping out of his arms. "I know it's unprofessional for me to quit like this, but I don't know if I'll be back to work this summer. My mom will need help, and I can't leav—"

"Lucy, we're not talking about work right now," Cal interrupts. There's frustration laced with worry in his words.

"I work for you," I remind him, my voice shaking. "It's my responsibility to let you know if I won't be able to work, and with my dad in the hospital for I don't know how long...I just don't think I'll be able to work anymore this summer."

"Your dad's in the hospital?" There's so much concern in his voice that it kills me. He doesn't even respond to the fact it's unlikely I'll be able to finish out the summer working for him.

I nod, trying not to let my emotions get the best of me. "Yes. He's in the hospital, and my mom's there handling it alone, and I just need to get home as soon as I can. I can't work for you anymore. I can't be here."

Cal's hands find the sides of my face as he steps closer to me once again. "Baby, I don't care if you can't work for me. What I care about is *you* and making sure you're okay."

"I'm okay," I lie, ducking under his arm. "I just need to book a flight home." I take a deep breath, trying to compose myself. After I make it to Virginia and I get things figured out, I'll be able to fully break down. Right now, I need to push all my emotions to the side and get back home.

"I'm coming with you." Cal's tone makes it seem like it's not up for discussion.

"No, Cal. You stay here."

He lets out a low growl. "I'm just supposed to stay here and do nothing while the woman I'm falling in love with is left to handle her father being in the hospital all alone?"

I gasp at his words.

Did he...did he just admit that he's falling in love with me?

My vision gets even blurrier after his admission. No, he can't be falling for me. Maybe I heard him wrong. I'm stressed and not thinking clearly. It's got to be that I didn't hear him right.

"Cal," I whisper, and it feels like my entire world is closing in on me.

My dad's in the hospital.

My mom is scared, tired, and shouldn't have to bear the burden of dealing with this alone.

I'm the one who's supposed to be there for my parents, and I'm states away, completely helpless.

And now, Cal might be saying things like he's in love with me, and all that means is I'm going to hurt him when I go back to Virginia—alone.

His posture is stiff, and his face is set in a grimace. "I've got a plane. I'll call my pilot right now, and we'll be able to fly out in an hour."

I shake my head. He's a distraction. Missing all the phone calls from my mom last night is proof of that. If I hadn't been with him, I would've answered the first time my mom called. She wouldn't have had to worry about why I wasn't answering on top of dealing with my dad being hospitalized. The last thing I need is for Cal to come back with me.

"I have to go alone. I'll be there a long time, and you have stuff you have to do here."

He scoffs. "There's nothing more important to me than being there for you through this. Let me help."

Tears freely fall down my face. "I don't need you to be there for me."

His head rears back as if I'd slapped him. The hurt is written all over his face as his blue eyes scan my face. "Why do you feel like you have to handle everything on your own?"

Forty-eight

CAL

I don't know what a broken heart feels like. I've never cared about someone enough to give them the power to break my heart.

But the dull throb beginning in my chest right now has got to be close. It's all because of the look on Lucy's face. She doesn't have to say a word for me to know that this conversation isn't going to go how I want it to.

I so desperately want to be the person Lucy leans on when she needs help. I want to be there for her like I want my next breath. My entire body aches at the thought of her going back home to deal with things by herself.

I want to be there for the woman I fell for, but it's becoming more and more clear that as desperately as I want to be the one for Lucy to lean on, that isn't what she wants.

"For once, just let someone be there for you, baby," I croak, not caring how vulnerable I sound. This woman owns my heart, and I need her to know and hear in my voice how badly I want to be there for her.

Her lips tremble, and I hate that tears still stream down her face.

I reach out to try and wipe them from her cheeks, but she shies away from my touch.

And that one simple movement obliterates my heart.

Her entire body shakes as she aims her gaze to the ground. "I'm the only person my parents have, Cal. I have to be there for them, and I don't need you there to distract me."

My mouth snaps shut so quickly I wonder if she hears the impact of my teeth slamming together. I rub at my chest, a pain radiating through me from her words. "Is that what I am to you? A distraction?"

She kills me with one simple nod of her head.

Blood drains from my face as I slowly nod. All this time, I've been envisioning what a life with her could look like. Every time she's opened her mouth, I've waited with bated breath, hoping this would be the time she'd open up to me. I was hoping for a future with her, and to her, all I am is a *distraction*?

Her eyes meet mine, and I can see that she's put her walls back in place. It's been so long since I've seen them like this. She's staring at me blankly like she did that night at Laurent's when she pretended not to know me.

"Maybe it's best we end this now, anyway, before things get carried away," she whispers. "We were only supposed to be temporary. With you being Oliver's brother and me having to leave, this is what's best."

My jaw tightens. I hate that she even brought up Oliver as if he is any kind of reason we can't be together. The only person preventing me and Lucy from being together is her.

And it seems like there's nothing that'll change her mind.

As someone who is used to getting what they want, it's a hard pill to swallow. I can have anything in the world, but I can't have her.

"Say something," Lucy begs. Her voice breaks a little, and I hate how that little hitch in her voice gives me the tiniest ounce of hope that maybe she'll realize she's making a huge mistake.

I shake my head. I run my hand over my mouth as I try to think about what to even say to her. Just as her walls have come up, I can feel mine doing the same. I never wanted that to happen with her, but I can't help it. I have to protect myself the best I can as she breaks my heart.

"What is there to say? I told you I'm falling for you, and you told me I was a distraction. I don't know what else to say to you, Lucy, other than I wish you'd stop trying to carry the world on your shoulders all alone. I've never even been close to falling in love, but now that I know what it feels like, I think you feel it too. But for some reason, you're scared of me loving you, and if you don't even trust me enough to tell me why, then there's nothing else I can do to change your mind. Until you're ready to trust me and let me be there for you, then there isn't much for us to talk about."

I try to deliver the words softly. I'm not trying to fight or do anything to hurt her. Even so, she winces at my words. She's got a lot on her plate, and the last thing I want to do is add more to it, but she wanted me to say something, so I did.

"You're only a distraction because I've never felt for someone what I feel for you," she finally gets out. Her words come out shaky, and she doesn't even look at me when she delivers them.

I swallow, not knowing how to process her words. A sarcastic laugh leaves me as I realize how depressing this entire scenario is. "Apparently, whatever you feel, and hell, even what I feel, isn't enough. You're still not going to let me go with you and be there for you, are you?"

She lets out a sob as she shakes her head.

I nod as pain takes over my entire body. Nothing's ever hurt this badly, and no matter how hard I try to rub my chest to make the pain go away, it doesn't subside.

I close my eyes for a moment as I force myself to accept defeat. No matter how much I want to, I can't fight for someone who doesn't want to be fought for. I can see she feels the same as I do, but I'll never force her into something she doesn't want, even if it's absolute torture to have to let her go.

When I open my eyes, I let out a shaky breath as a numbness I hadn't felt in a long time creeps into my veins.

"While you gather your things, I'll call my pilot. We'll go by your place so you can grab anything you need, and then I'll drop you off at the airport."

"You don't have to do tha—"

"Will you please just let me do this one last thing for you?" I plead, my voice hoarse. I'm sure I look ridiculous to her right now. It feels like all the color has drained from my face, and my entire body feels clammy. I can't stop rubbing at the pain in my chest, and my jaw hurts from how much I've been grinding my teeth.

Thankfully, Lucy allows my last request. She nods, and it's all the answer I need. Before I can beg her to change her mind about me, I turn to head back to my room to grab my phone.

She doesn't say a word to me the entire ride back to her place.

Nothing's said as I help her pack her things into a small purple suitcase.

We're both silent as I drive her to the private airport.

Finally, I can't take the silence for another second. She's broken my heart and ripped it into a million pieces, but I can't let her get on that plane without saying goodbye.

We stand by my SUV, the both of us staring at one another.

"I meant what I said. I'm falling for you, Lucy Rae, and I want to be there for you. It's killing me not to get on this plane with you, but for once, I'll accept not getting my way. But if you find yourself ever needing me, I'm one call away. You got that?"

Lucy's chin trembles as she nods. "I'm so sorry. I wish things didn't have to end this wa—"

Her words get cut off as I pull her against my chest and just hold her. I'm well aware that people are watching us, but I don't know the next time I'll ever get to hold her like this—if ever. I just need a few more moments to commit this to memory.

I don't know if it's her or me that trembles, but our bodies shake as we hold each other.

I'm the first to pull away. I'm afraid if I hold on to her any longer, I'll never be able to let go. And right now, she's made it obvious that she needs to go—and she needs to go alone.

I have to let go, no matter how much it fucking kills me to do it.

My hands find either side of her face. We just stare at each other for a moment. My eyes trace the freckles along her cheeks, committing every single one of them to memory. I run my thumbs along them, hating how final this goodbye seems. There's so much uncertainty about if she'll ever change her mind about us and if I'll ever see her again, and that destroys me.

"Goodbye, Lucy baby," I rasp, trying to hide my hurt from her. I don't want to make her feel any guiltier than she already does. It's clear she's carrying enough about not being in Virginia, so I want to do my best not to add to the guilt that's clearly consuming her and preventing us from being together.

She rises to her tiptoes and presses a kiss to my lips. My entire body relaxes for a brief moment at the connection. My eyelids flutter shut, and for a few prolonged seconds, I pretend this isn't a goodbye.

My hands tighten against her cheeks as I keep her close to me just a little longer.

She pulls away, and I hate how swollen and red her eyes are from all of the crying. "Goodbye, Cal."

She steps out of my grasp and walks to the plane. I count every step she takes away from me. With each one, I hope that she turns around and tells me she's changed her mind. If she just asked me to get on that plane with her, I would.

She doesn't.

She doesn't even look back at me.

Not when she greets the pilot, Brian.

Not when she gets to the top of the stairs.

And not even when she steps into the open door of the jet.

As soon as she disappears, I look at my pilot. I clear my throat to make sure my words don't come out sounding too pained. "You take care of my girl. I want to know the moment you land."

He nods. And then, before I can make a fool out of myself and run inside to beg her to change her mind, I turn around and walk away from the only woman I'll ever love.

All I can do is hope that our feelings are strong enough for her to realize just how perfect we are together.

I sit in my car and watch the private jet take off with a lump in my throat. I watch as my entire world flies away as I come to terms with the fact that I have no idea when I'll see her again.

It's only when the plane disappears behind some clouds that I wipe a single tear away from my cheek and drive away from the private airport with a broken heart and an intense longing for a woman who doesn't want to be mine.

Forty-nine

LUCY

"Lucy, you're making me nervous. Stop hovering," my dad scolds. He stares at me over his wire-rimmed glasses. His dark, bushy eyebrows pull together on his forehead as he gives me a deep scowl.

I give him an apologetic smile. "You just got back from the hospital, Dad. I'm just making sure you're okay."

He waves his hand through the air dismissively. "I'm fine. Now that they've got my medications sorted out, you don't have to worry."

I narrow my eyes on him. No matter how much it annoys him, it's my job to worry. He was in the hospital for a week while they tried to figure out what was happening with him. He was having an abnormal heartbeat rhythm, a complication that can happen after heart attacks.

It feels like I didn't sleep for that entire time; I was so sick with worry. His team of doctors is amazing, but every time we felt like we had a handle on things, he would have an episode with his heart that sent us right back to square one. Eventually, they felt good enough about his new medications and care plan to let him go home.

"You know I'm going to worry, but I'll try not to hover.

Mom should be back soon from the pharmacy, but do you need me to get you anything?" I place my hands on my hips and wait for my dad to answer as he tries to get comfortable in his leather recliner.

"You could take me to the store. I want to check everything out," he grumbles. It's obvious that it's eating away at him that he hasn't been able to return to the store since his incident, but his doctors were very firm that he needs to take it easy.

"You were just released from the hospital this morning, Dad. Maybe we should give it some time before we try working again?"

He lets out a disgruntled growl. The man doesn't know how to relax, but now that I'm back and in charge of keeping an eye on him to give my mom a break, he's going to learn real quickly how serious I am about listening to his doctors. I never want to get a phone call like that from my mom again.

"Maybe *you* should go check it out," Dad offers as I hand him the TV remote.

His warm brown eyes focus on me, the hint of a smile forming on his lips. Every time Dad smiles, it's a reminder of how Luke had his exact smile. It's bittersweet.

I flip through the channels, trying to find something Dad will like, as I can't help but return his smile with one of my own. It feels like smiles have been few and far between the past week, so it's good to see Dad giving me one.

Especially with how close it is to Luke and Logan's birthday.

"Are you trying to get rid of me?" I ask.

"Yes," he responds immediately, making me laugh. Being grumpy is a personality trait of his. I forgot how much I missed it. His personality is coming back after being so out of it in the hospital. "I haven't been alone in forever. If I can't get to the store, then I can send you and maybe have some peace and quiet before your mother gets home and fusses over me."

"We're both just worried about you," I explain, reaching out and placing my hand on his shoulder. Dad's always been grumpy, but his exterior only got rougher after losing my brothers. Then, after the heart attack, it got more intense. I hadn't realized how dim his personality had been in the hospital this past week until now, when his normal demeanor started coming back.

"Stop worrying about me and go check on Alec. I'll be fine here."

I stand there for a moment, wondering what I should do. I've been trying my best to go to the store when I can to give Alec a break, but almost every time I'm there, he ends up staying anyway. Alec knows how to run things far better than I do, but I'm trying to learn.

"Let me call Mom first and make sure she's okay with it," I offer, deciding it might be good for me to stop by and learn more of the ropes from Alec. Plus, it keeps me busy, and keeping busy is the only way I've been able to survive the last week.

I miss Cal terribly. There's an ache in my chest that settles deep in my bones at losing him. I've kept myself so busy that I haven't even been able to really think about what happened between us.

I want to keep it that way. If I think about the pained look in his eyes when he told me he loved me and how I reacted to it, all I feel is burning pain. I know I didn't handle things right, but there's nothing I can do to fix it now.

I'm still scared that if he was here, I'd get lost in him again, and I can't have that. Not when Mom needs help juggling Dad's appointments and keeping up to date with his medications. Or how Dad needs me to take over the store. In the small breaks of handling those, I've stayed busy by prepping and freezing nutritious meals for Dad that are good for his heart and preparing extras to give Alec and his wife too.

While Mom stayed at the hospital, I came home and cleaned the house from top to bottom. I went to the store to get groceries to make sure everything was stocked and I have already started a family calendar so she doesn't have to remember all the countless appointments by herself.

I plan to keep doing all of that, now, with Dad home. These things are what I need to focus on, no matter how much I miss Cal and wish things were different.

"Are you going to keep standing there and blocking the TV, or are you going to go check on Alec?" Dad asks in a teasing tone, breaking me from my daydreams.

I push all the painful thoughts of Cal from my mind and give my dad a tight smile. "I'm checking with Mom first, but yes, if she's okay with it, you'll get rid of me."

"Finally," Dad whispers under his breath, but he says it with a smile. I don't blame him. He's used to being fiercely independent. I'm sure being forced to rely on others is hard for him.

I don't tell this to Dad, but Mom is almost done at the pharmacy. She tells me to go ahead and head to the store. Dad will get his alone time—but it'll only be a few minutes.

As I drive to the store, I try to keep my mind busy with any thought that doesn't involve Cal.

I start planning what food I want to make for my family this week.

I remind myself that I still need to get Dad in to see his physical therapist next week.

I make a list of what bills need to be paid.

I even make a note to call around to some nearby florists to get some arrangements made for the anniversary of Luke and

Logan's death. I want to put fresh flowers on their graves but also get Mom some flowers too. I know it'll be a hard day for all of us. Mom's always been a fan of fresh flowers but won't spend the money to buy them for herself.

At first, I'm able to keep my mind free of Cal, but it doesn't take long for my thoughts to drift to him.

I don't know when it happened, but I fell in love with him. I tried fighting it. While in the moment, I thought I had a good handle on things. I thought both my mind and heart knew that everything between us was only temporary.

I should've known that falling for him was inevitable. Week after week, we spent almost every day together. Little by little, he stole my heart. And it's only when I got on that plane after breaking his heart that I realized how much he owned mine.

A tear runs down my cheek as I give myself a moment to miss him. Anguish washes over me at the reminder of how much I hurt him. It's obvious he's not a man who enjoys being vulnerable, and I can't help but hate myself for how I handled his vulnerability. I could've confessed to him why it was so hard for me to open up to him, but I didn't.

And now, it haunts me.

Fifty
CAL

I'm never falling in love again.

I always thought people were dramatic when they complained about a broken heart. I'm a grown adult; I didn't think anything had the capacity to make me not want to leave my bed or even eat a meal.

But then I fell in love with Lucy Rae Owens.

It's been thirteen days since I watched her step onto that plane, taking my heart right along with her.

Thirteen mornings I've woken up and not wanted to get out of bed.

Thirteen nights I've lain awake talking myself out of calling her and reminding myself that if she wanted to talk to me, she would.

I fell in love with a woman who wasn't ready to be loved, and I'm paying the price for it.

It doesn't help that everything reminds me of her. I used to love the Hamptons and Pembroke. Being here for the summer was my escape. Now, being here without her is torture.

I barely want to step foot in Pembroke Grill, thinking of all the times we sat around a table with our friends.

Speaking of friends, I've rejected every invite to see them. I don't want to have to explain Lucy's sudden disappearance to anybody. Jude's the only one who hasn't let me avoid him. The fucker shows up every morning and forces me to get out of bed. He even makes me eat by hitting up different local spots and bringing breakfast in the morning. He doesn't ask about Lucy, but he gives me updates about her dad, thanks to Charlotte.

I'm happy that they're back at home and he seems to be recovering, but I can't pretend I'm not devastated that she hasn't reached out. Part of me was holding out hope that once her dad was out of the hospital, she'd call or text me.

She hasn't.

And now, I'm just left in a house that reminds me of her.

I walk into Pembroke's gentleman's lounge, wishing I was anywhere but here. Even this club reminds me of Lucy. I don't want to be here, but I'm also a curious man.

When Ollie reached out and told me he was in the Hamptons for the weekend and wanted to meet, my first thought was to tell him no. I'm already reminded of Lucy enough. I hate that even looking at my brother will remind me of her as well.

My eyes scan the dark room before I find my brother sitting in a back corner. He sits in a large leather armchair with an empty one right across from him.

I sigh, still far enough away that he hasn't noticed me. If I turned around now and left the lounge, he'd never know.

I weigh my options for a moment and ultimately decide that I'm too curious to walk away before talking to him. We don't have a close relationship. He never reaches out, and I can't help but wonder if Lucy is the reason he did. It can't be a coincidence.

I close the distance to Ollie before stopping right in front of him. His eyes go wide when he spots me.

He takes me by surprise by standing up and giving me what looks like a genuine smile. "Cal, good to see you."

I try to wipe the surprise from my face at his friendly demeanor. "*Ollie*," I respond, saying his name slowly.

Ollie points to the empty chair across from him. "Want to sit? I ordered you a bourbon, but I'm still waiting on it. Is that still your drink of choice?"

I watch him carefully as I take a seat, wondering what the hell is going on.

"That's perfect," I answer, keeping my voice even.

Ollie nods. "Cool," he gets out before joining me in taking a seat. I don't even know the last time we saw each other, but somehow in that time, he looks different. He's dressed better, more maturely. And that annoying, overly cocky demeanor he normally has is nowhere to be found.

"Why did you want to meet today?" I ask, not wanting to beat around the bush. I'd much rather be at home throwing myself into work to avoid the gaping hole in my chest left by Lucy.

Ollie's eyes go wide for a moment. He takes a sip of his drink, seemingly trying to buy himself time to get his thoughts together. "You're getting right to the point, aren't you?" he mutters under his breath.

I nod, my focus still on him as I try to figure out what he wants before he can even ask it.

Is he here because he somehow heard about me and Lucy? Surely not. I'd expect him to be more hostile if that was the reason for him setting up a meeting.

He could be here asking me for money, but it doesn't feel like that either. If he needs money, he goes to Dad, not me. I don't think he's stupid enough to think I'd ever give him a loan.

For once, I can't predict someone's next move, even if it's my brother.

"Listen, there's something I wanted to talk to you about today," Ollie begins, his tone becoming more uneasy.

I sigh. "If this is about Lucy, I don't want to hear it," I respond, cutting him off as he opens his mouth to say something else.

His mouth snaps shut, and his eyebrows rise to his hairline. "Lucy?" he asks, his voice full of disbelief. He stares at me, completely dumbfounded, making it clear that whatever he came to talk about, it wasn't her.

I pinch the bridge of my nose between my pointer finger and thumb. I'm so exhausted that I spoke before I should've. I reacted instead of waiting for him to tell me the reason for wanting a meeting.

And now I have to pay the price.

"Are you talking about Lucy Owens?" Ollie pushes.

I gladly accept the bourbon from our server, buying myself a little time to gather my thoughts as I suck down a large drink of the amber liquid. With a sigh, I set the bourbon down on the little table between our chairs and nod.

"Yes. The only Lucy we know."

Ollie slowly nods as he tries to understand where this is going. "Why would I be here to talk to you about Lucy?"

"Because I ran into her at the start of the summer. Did you know she was working as a private chef here in the Hamptons?"

Ollie raises his eyebrows. "I knew she enjoyed cooking, but no, I had no idea she was working here. Why would I want to talk to you about that, though?" he adds at the last minute.

I wave at Ryker and a man I don't recognize as they walk into the lounge. I half expect to see Camille walk in after them since it seems that this summer, everywhere Ryker is, Camille is close behind. But no one else walks in, and I return to looking at my brother.

"I hired Lucy as my private chef and then fell in love with

her," I blurt, not wanting to drag this out. I don't really care about his opinion of my feelings for Lucy.

Ollie chokes, pulling his crystal tumbler away from his lips as a coughing fit takes over his entire body.

I shrug, taking another sip of my drink while he collects himself. Even saying her name out loud cuts right through me.

"I'm sorry, I'm trying to play catch-up here. Lucy worked for you? And you fell in love with her? You're talking about *my* Lucy?"

I scoff at the way he says *my*. "Please. She's not yours and never was. She's mine. But yes, we're talking about the same Lucy."

Ollie blinks a few times. He slowly begins to nod and I can almost see the wheels turning in his head. "Um, okay," he begins. He clears his throat, clearly still not recovered from choking on his own drink. "Well, I didn't know what to expect from seeing you today, but hearing you fell in love with my ex-girlfriend was not something I could've ever expected."

Jealousy runs through me at him being able to call her his ex-girlfriend. It's unreasonable, but I'm jealous that he ever got the title of being her boyfriend.

It's not a title I ever had, despite how madly in love with her I am.

Right now, it's not even a title I think I'll *ever* have. Although, I'm so in love with her at this point that I'd be happy with foregoing boyfriend and going straight to husband if she'd let me.

I shake my head for a moment, trying to dull the ache in my heart of letting my mind wander to fantasies of being anything to her but temporary.

"I'd rather pretend you were never her boyfriend, to be honest," I mutter. "You never deserved her. And before you get mad at me for falling for someone from your past, just save your breath. I don't give a damn if you don't like that I fell in love with her."

Ollie raises his hands defensively. "Look, I was young and a terrible boyfriend to her. There were absolutely things I could've done differently, but my feelings for her were never what they should've been. Who you love is none of my business, Cal."

His words take me by surprise. I was ready for a fight, or at least for him to make some kind of snide comment.

"How is she?" he asks. There doesn't seem to be any hint of anger in his tone. His question seems genuine. Before I can answer him, he clears his throat before speaking again. "Fuck, I just realized what this month means for her. Is she doing okay?"

My eyebrows furrow together on my forehead. I try to hide my confusion at his question, but I can't. "What are you talking about?" The question leaves my mouth before I can think better of it.

Ollie frowns a little as he stares at me, his eyes searching my face. "What do you mean? I can't remember off the top of my head how many years it'd be, but I know this month is the anniversary of her twin brothers' death."

Pain slices through me at his words. For a moment, I can't even think straight. It hurts too bad to know that she experienced a loss of that magnitude and I had no idea. She never once told me about them passing.

She never even told me she ever had brothers.

There was so much more I still wanted to learn about her, but I hadn't expected her to have something like this in her past. She holds herself with so much strength, I never would've guessed if Ollie hadn't told me.

My heart aches for her and what she's been through. It kills me that she didn't trust me enough to tell me about that part of her life.

And it hurts even more to know Ollie knows, and that she trusted him enough to open up about them but never once mentioned their death to me.

"You didn't know?" Ollie annoyingly pushes. He sounds genuinely shocked that I had no idea. I'm still too stunned by what he revealed to even pretend to have known.

I grunt and shake my head. "No," I admit, my voice hoarse. "She never..." My words drift off as sadness seeps through my veins and takes over me.

Ollie, to his credit, doesn't gloat or revel in knowing something I don't. Maybe he *has* matured. His features might actually pull into a look of remorse as his eyes watch me carefully. "For what it's worth, I found out one day in college because of Sophia. Lucy had told Sophia, and Sophia brought it up one day. We were all eating lunch, and Sophia accidentally let it slip. Lucy told me more after."

I meet my brother's eyes. His words bring a small amount of relief, but it still hurts that he knew and I didn't.

"I wasn't trying to start anything by asking. I just wanted to know how she was doing. I didn't treat her right, and we weren't meant to be, but I'll always hope she's doing okay. I'm sorry to have mentioned it to you."

I down the rest of my bourbon, needing the drink just to get a hold of myself. It makes a loud clinking noise as I set it back down on the table between us. "It's fine. I actually believe you." A sad laugh leaves me because this isn't the direction I expected the conversation with Ollie to go. "It might not matter, anyway. I told her I was falling for her, and she told me I was a distraction. She went back to Virginia to be there for her parents, and I really don't think she has any intention of coming back."

"Don't you have a private jet? Why don't you go there?"

I sigh, wishing it were that simple. "I told her I'd go with her. I begged to go with her, really. She told me she didn't want me to."

Ollie laughs. "Of course she did. She doesn't know how to ask for help. Put yourself in her shoes, Cal. Her older brothers died when she was just a teenager. The weight of the world was put on her shoulders after. She's all her parents have now, and I think she takes that to heart. But if you love her, just go to her and show her that she doesn't have to carry the weight alone anymore."

My throat feels clogged as I look at my brother and really see him. We've never been close, largely thanks to the over-a-decade age gap between us and him being insufferable in his younger years, but now as I stare into his eyes, I realize that maybe things can change between us.

Maybe he's right.

Maybe it's time I go get my girl.

No one's ever shown up for her before, and it's about damn time someone did.

"I've got to get to Virginia," I mutter, the words barely coming out above a whisper.

Ollie nods. "Yes, you do."

I hurry and push myself out of my chair. I can't believe I've gone two weeks sulking here and feeling bad for myself when I could've been in Virginia, proving to her that it's okay to need someone else.

Now, I don't want to waste another second.

"Wait, is there something you needed?" I ask, wondering if I should hug my brother. I've never once thought of giving him a hug, not since he was a child. But something was different today, and now I feel like I should at least thank him for talking sense into me.

Ollie smiles. He stands up and lifts a shoulder in a shrug. "We'll have to do a rain check until you're back, but I wanted to meet to ask you to be my best man at my wedding. Me and Sophia are engaged, and I know things haven't always been great between us, but I want you standing up there with me...if you will."

"That's amazing. Congrats, Ollie." I wrap my arms around him and give him a hug. It's awkward, and we're both a little stiff, but a genuine smile graces my lips at the possibility that things might get better between us. "I'd love to," I add, surprising myself by meaning the words.

Ollie points to the exit. "I'm relieved to hear you say that. Now, leave. I've never seen you talk about a woman like you do Lucy. Go get her."

I nod, not needing any more prompting to go after the woman I love.

It's clear there's still a lot I can learn about Lucy. There's so much I hope she opens up to me about. I still need to earn her trust, but I can't do that from here in the Hamptons. I want to prove to her it's okay to lean on someone and that even when things are hard, she has me.

I'll spend forever proving to her she doesn't have to handle things alone anymore.

And I'm ready for that forever to start right now.

Fifty-one
LUCY

"How's your dad doing today?" Charlotte asks, unable to hold still and almost making me nauseous with how much she moves her phone while we're FaceTiming.

I give her a smile as I sit back in the old office chair in the back room of my family's store. It's getting late in the evening, but I still have so much to do before I can go home for the night.

"Dad's doing good. Still grumpy that we're not letting him work, but we haven't had any mishaps since he got back from the hospital."

Charlotte nods.

"I know where you get your stubbornness from," Charlotte quips. "I haven't had the pleasure of meeting your dad in person yet, but it's obvious that you're set in your ways just like he is."

Through FaceTime, she and my father have struck up a friendship. I've never heard my dad belly laugh, but that all changed the other day when Charlotte and I were video chatting. She was catching me up on what was going on in her life—leaving out details about Cal—when she made some kind of joke that my dad overheard. After that, he's asked every day when I was going to talk to my funny friend. He'll be upset I talked to her tonight without him being able to say hi.

"Hi, Luce!" Jude calls, his face appearing on the screen next to Charlotte.

I smile, feeling sad that I'm not there with them. Jude and Charlotte seem to be spending a lot of time together recently, and I miss them both terribly. I didn't expect them to become close friends, and I'm a little jealous that Jude's getting to spend so much time with Charlotte. I miss my best friend.

"Jude," I call, giving him a wave. "What are you doing with Charlotte?"

"Annoying me like always," Charlotte pipes up, rolling her eyes as Jude grabs at his chest dramatically.

"Not surprising," I respond, trying to keep a smile on my face despite the sadness washing over me. I'm glad I'm here with my parents. I need to know they're taken care of and things are running smoothly. My place is here, but it doesn't mean I don't miss the life I had in the Hamptons. I hadn't realized how happy I was there until it was taken from me.

"So, how's the store going? Are you getting the hang of things?"

I groan, thinking of the mess I made today. "No." I let out a pathetic laugh as I push away all my intrusive thoughts about how I'm not cut out for this. "I'm terrible at selling things, Char. I almost messed up three sales today. We would've lost them if it wasn't for Alec coming in to save the day."

Charlotte purses her lips as her eyes soften. I love that even through the phone screen, I can read every single one of her emotions. "You're still figuring it out," she begins, keeping her voice reassuring. "You'll learn the ropes."

I shake my head. "I don't know, Char. I'm trying, but I just suck. I was tasked with ordering some pieces from a new distributor, and I kept messing up the count. I keep track of supply numbers all the time when preparing meals for parties of people. I don't know why I suck at it when it comes to furniture."

"You're learning a lot at once. I promise you'll get better at it." Charlotte holds the phone closer to her face and gives me a comforting smile. "Love you, Lucy. Take a deep breath. You're doing the best you can."

My eyes sting with the threat of looming tears. "I really needed to hear that," I respond, talking through the lump in my throat.

It's on the tip of my tongue to ask about Cal. I want to know how he's doing. Has he already moved on from me? Does he talk about me? Is he doing okay?

The questions are at the forefront of my mind, but I keep them to myself. Today's already been a long, hard day. I don't know if I'm ready for the answers to those questions.

"We miss you here," Jude says, grabbing the phone from Charlotte and saving me from asking things I shouldn't.

"Hey, that's *my* best friend, not yours!" Charlotte scolds. I can see her try to grab the phone in the background, but Jude holds it out of her reach.

"It's my turn to talk to Luce," he declares, using his free hand to keep Charlotte from grabbing the phone.

"I miss you guys too," I respond with a smile. Even Jude became someone I grew attached to, something I hadn't realized until I was back here in Virginia.

"When are you coming back?" Jude presses, not paying any attention to Charlotte's protests about giving her the phone back.

I let out a sad sigh. Most of my belongings are still in the Hamptons. I need to figure out if I should just hire movers to pack it all up or if I can make it down there for a couple of days just to get everything packed up and sorted out.

"I don't know if I'll be coming back," I answer honestly. "I'm still trying to get things running smoothly without my dad here at the store. And then I don't know if I can leave my mom to handle things on her own."

Jude nods, giving me his normal grin. "You just let me know how to help. I want to be there for you, Luce. We all do."

Emotion overtakes me again. Now that I'm away, it's obvious how I'd built my own little family there. Charlotte, Jude, Mr. Fred, Dolores, Margo, Winnie, Emma, Camille...and most importantly, Cal. I don't know when it happened, but all of them became my second family.

And I miss them like crazy.

But I can't do anything about it because my own family needs me here.

"He misses you, you know," Jude chimes in, keeping his voice soft.

"Jude!" Charlotte yells from out of view of the phone screen.

He looks at her with wide eyes. "What?" he asks innocently. "It's true. I have to talk him into getting out of bed most mornings. He's lost without Lucy, and I think Lucy should know that."

"Give me my phone," Charlotte demands. Her hand appears in view as she tries to wrestle the phone from his grip.

Their words fade away as I focus on what Jude said. The guilt flooding me is overwhelming.

He can't get out of bed?

Tears prick my eyes at the image of him being so heartbroken he can't even get up in the morning. I never wanted to cause him pain. He's the last person in this world I wanted to hurt, and I still did.

A tear runs down my cheek. I try to wipe it away before

either of them can see it, but Charlotte wrestles the phone back from Jude just in time to see me do it.

"I'm so sorry," she gets out, a little out of breath. Her shoulders rise and fall quickly from the effort it took to get the phone back from Jude.

He gently pushes her to the side, allowing his face to be in view as well. Charlotte shoots a dirty look in his direction, but she doesn't push him out of frame.

"Fuck, Luce, I didn't mean to make you cry," Jude says, his features softening as I wipe underneath my eyes again.

I shake my head, trying to regain my composure. It's my responsibility to close up the store tonight, but I wouldn't be shocked if Alec randomly dropped by to make sure I'm doing it right. He seems to be checking on me a lot since I've tried taking things over. I can't say I blame him.

"It's fine, I promise," I try to assure him. I don't miss the way my voice shakes. Knowing he's still not doing well two weeks after I left is taking its toll. My resolve to do the right thing and leave him alone is slowly getting chipped away.

All that's left is the intense way that I miss him and the desperate desire to hear his voice.

"You know...if you called, he'd answer," Jude prods. He keeps his voice soft but doesn't back down when Charlotte aims another dirty look in his direction.

"Would he?" I counter. I don't know if I'd blame him if he didn't want to talk to me. He opened up to me and confessed his feelings, and instead of me being honest and telling him I'm in love with him, I called him a distraction.

I'll never forget the anguish etched into his features. I don't know if I can repair the damage I did. Especially since I still don't know if we could ever make it work. At least right now. Not with me having to take care of things here.

"Luce," Jude begins, pulling me from my thoughts. "I've

known Cal almost my entire life. The only thing I've ever seen him really love was his job—until you. The moment he hired you, he changed. He loves you. And he's my best friend, so I'm allowed to say this, but he isn't built to love a lot of things. But when he does, he loves hard. I don't think there's anything you could do or say that he wouldn't forgive you for. Call him. Tell him you love him—because I know you do—and then together, you can figure out the rest."

Charlotte wipes at her eyes a little, looking at Jude with a shocked expression. "When did you become so sweet?"

Her comment makes me laugh. I mimic her, wiping at my falling tears thanks to what Jude said.

"I know I hurt him," I explain to Jude, my words coming out shaky. I'm sure I seem like a complete mess right now. I can't stop the tears from falling, and I'm not even trying to hide them at this point.

"I can guarantee you that not speaking to him is hurting him more than any words you have said or could say to him," Jude points out.

I let out a shaky sigh, realizing he might be right. I thought I was doing the right thing by ending things with Cal. We have two very different lives, and instead of figuring out with him how we could make things work, I pushed him away. I didn't think it was possible to juggle a relationship with him and my responsibilities here in Virginia.

In the two weeks since I last saw him, I've learned I don't know if it's possible to move on with my life without him.

I'm so in love with him that I miss him to my core. I thought loving him would be a distraction, but the more I think about it, maybe the real distraction is missing him.

If I had him to talk to at the end of the day and allowed him to be there for me, I think I'd be in a much better headspace to handle things here at home.

"I love him," I blurt, sitting straight up in my chair. It's so old it creaks because of the sudden movement.

Jude fist pumps in the air, letting out a long whistle. "Yes, Luce, you do. Now, hang up the damn phone and call him."

"Call him!" Charlotte interjects before she excitedly gives Jude a high five.

My heart hammers in my chest. It feels like my stomach has fallen to my feet at the prospect of talking to him again.

"I'm nervous," I confess, my words coming out hurried. "What if he doesn't want to talk to me?"

Jude lets out a sarcastic laugh. "Oh, he wants to talk to you. Call him. Now."

I look at both Jude and Charlotte on my screen, a wave of love and appreciation taking over me for both of them. "Okay, I'm going to call him. Thank you both for the little push."

"Stop stalling," Charlotte remarks with a raised blonde eyebrow.

Jude nods in agreement. "Goodbye, Luce."

He hangs up the phone before I can respond.

For a few moments, I stare at the blank screen, wondering if I should really call Cal. Jude made it seem like Cal wants to talk to me, but what if he's wrong? He wasn't there. He didn't see the light leave Cal's eyes the way I did.

I feel nauseous. I close my eyes for a moment and let out a loud groan. For a few fleeting seconds, I felt brave about calling Cal thanks to Jude and Charlotte.

Now, I feel like I could throw up. I want to talk to him so badly, and I'm terrified he'll ignore my call.

I wouldn't blame him if he sent me straight to voicemail.

"Call him," I whisper to myself as I try to hype myself up for it. I open up my contacts and scroll to his name.

I stare at his information so long his name goes blurry with unshed tears. I take a deep breath before clicking his name. I do it quickly, not allowing for time to psych myself out of it.

My hand trembles as I press my phone to my ear.

Hope blossoms in my chest with the first ring. As soon as he answers, I'm just going to tell him I love him. There are so many things I know I need to say to him—one of them being an apology—but the first thing will be that I'm madly in love with him.

It rings again.

I let out a slow breath, trying to keep my breathing even. He's a busy man. It's normal for him to not answer right away.

Another ring.

Please just answer, Cal.

I know he can't hear me, but now that I'm so close to being able to profess my love to him, I don't want to waste another second.

I'm about to panic that he's not going to answer my call when the phone stops ringing.

I suck in a breath of air, waiting for him to say something.

He doesn't.

Before I can lose my confidence, I blurt out the words I should've said two weeks ago.

"Cal, I love you," I begin, my words coming out so fast it probably sounds like one long word instead of a coherent sentence. "I love you so much, and I'm sorr—"

"You've reached Callahan Hastings from Hastings Incorporated. Leave me a message, and I'll get back to you as soon as I can."

There's a beep, but I barely hear it over the thrum of my pulse in my ears.

Hoping it's maybe a mistake, I press his name again to call back.

This time, he'll answer.

If he sees me calling twice, he'll understand how badly I need to talk to him.

He told me to call him anytime.

He'll answer.

He doesn't.

This time, it goes straight to voicemail.

My phone drops to my lap as the realization sets in.

It's too late.

He doesn't want to talk to me. I know his phone is always on him. He's on it frequently. He doesn't miss calls.

He just doesn't want to talk to me, and I can't even be mad at him for it.

A sob rips through me as I accept the fact that I've lost him. And I can't blame anyone but myself for it.

Fifty-two
LUCY

I pull into the driveway of my childhood home feeling completely empty.

I've called Cal twenty-two times in the last two hours.

He hasn't answered a single one.

All the calls go straight to voicemail.

Talking to Jude and Charlotte had made me feel so hopeful. Jude had made it sound like Cal would forgive me for anything if he just knew how I felt. Now, he won't talk to me, so I can't even tell him how I really feel.

I swallow, wincing at the soreness in my throat from my sobs. I spent the better part of an hour huddled in the back office of the store, letting myself finally break down at the loss of Cal. For two weeks, I've tried to be strong. I pushed all thoughts of him from my mind as I focused on being there for my parents.

But I can only be strong for so long.

And having hope that maybe I could make this work—be the daughter my parents deserve and also still have Cal in my life—just to have it ripped away from me was my breaking point.

I'm broken.

I've never had my heart broken, not really, and I hope to never feel something like this again. My entire body aches with regret and loss. It doesn't help that I know I wouldn't be feeling this way if I'd just been honest with Cal and myself to begin with.

I should've known the love we shared was too intense to just fade away with time and distance apart.

I thought I was doing the right thing. That's all I've ever wanted to do. From the moment we lost Luke and Logan, I tried stepping up to be the perfect daughter. My parents had already lost two children—the golden boys of the family—and I never wanted them to have to worry about me. I wanted to make sure I never gave them trouble. I wanted to make things easy on them.

I dropped all my dreams of becoming a chef and went to college for business and marketing. I worked as much as I could to pay for my schooling and kept the best grades possible. I thought the degree in business would set me up to properly run the store, but my recent failures show I must not have worked hard enough in school.

I've tried and tried to be there for my parents, but somehow, it still feels like it hasn't been enough.

I'm terrible at running the store.

We're still trying to figure out Dad's health.

It's obvious Mom is still stressed, even with me here trying to help.

And in trying to be the perfect daughter, I hurt the man I love, who just wanted to be there for me.

I rub the heel of my palm against my chest, trying to dull the pain.

It doesn't.

I grab my phone from the passenger seat, checking to see if Cal called me back and maybe I just missed it.

He hasn't.

With a resigned sigh, I grab my purse and open the door to the car I've owned since I was sixteen.

All the lights are on in the house, meaning Mom and Dad are still awake. It's a little surprising. Typically, they're both in bed by now.

Every step toward the door feels heavy. I was hoping they'd be asleep. I haven't even looked at myself in the mirror, but I'm sure it's obvious I've been crying. I wouldn't be surprised if my eyes are puffy and my face is splotchy from all the tears.

I'm so emotionally and mentally drained I won't even be able to pretend I'm okay if one of them were to ask.

I reach to unlock the front door, but the moment I grab the handle, I realize it's already unlocked. I guess if they're still awake, they haven't gotten around to locking it yet.

I push the door open and am immediately hit with the sound of my mom's laughter.

I pause in the doorway, wondering if I'm hearing things. I haven't heard my mom laugh like that in ages.

Another laugh from her fills the silence as I take a cautious step inside. Voices come from the kitchen, but I'm too far away to see who it is. It sounds like it might be more than just my mom and dad, but I can't be sure.

Quietly, I shut the front door behind me. I don't want to interrupt whatever is happening in the kitchen. It's been so long since my mom laughed like that, and I don't want to risk stopping her.

I slip off my shoes and leave them by the front door. I keep my footsteps light as I walk toward the sound of laughter and voices.

The smell of garlic and tomato hits me the closer I get. It smells amazing but makes me curious. None of the meals I pre-prepared should smell like this.

I turn the corner and stop in my tracks at the sight in front of me.

Mom and Dad sit at the kitchen table with warm, bright smiles on their faces. Their bodies are angled toward the small kitchen island, their focus on the man plating what looks to be chicken parmesan.

Cal.

For a moment, I don't move, wondering if I'm seeing things. I cried so hard at the store, is it possible I'd fallen asleep in the chair? Maybe I'm dreaming. He wears a pale blue button-up with the sleeves rolled up, and his attention is on trying to perfectly plate the food, giving me a few seconds to figure out if this is all in my head.

"Lucy!" Mom calls, and I swear the tightness in my chest loosens the smallest amount at the happiness in her voice.

Cal looks up, his entire body going still as our eyes meet.

I let out a gasp the moment our eyes connect.

He's here.

He's real.

"Cal," I whisper, unsure if he can even hear me. I'm so shocked at seeing him standing in my kitchen that I can barely get words out.

And for the first time in two weeks, I'm able to take a deep breath because the man I'm completely in love with steps around the small island and takes a step toward me. His lips turn up in a cautious smile.

"Baby," he rasps.

I don't give him a chance to say anything else.

My bag and keys fall to the floor as I close the distance between us. Trusting he'll catch me, I launch my body at his and pull him close to me.

He's ready. My arms wrap around his neck as his wrap

around my middle. I tuck my face into the crook of his neck and take a deep inhale, trying to figure out if I'm dreaming.

"Are you really here?" I ask, my words muffled against his skin.

His body shakes with the hint of a laugh. "I'm here."

I bury my face deeper into the crook of his neck as my arms tighten around him. I savor the feeling of his embrace, something I was terrified I'd never experience again.

My dad clears his throat from the table, reminding me that we aren't alone.

I let out a nervous laugh as Cal gently sets me back on the ground. We separate, but only barely. I make sure to grab his hand as I pull my eyes from him to my parents, needing some kind of contact just to prove to myself that he's actually here.

Although it was my dad who cleared his throat—a smile still, surprisingly, on his lips—it's my mom who speaks up.

"Lucy, you didn't tell us you had a boyfriend," she comments. She raises an eyebrow and stares at me expectantly.

A blush creeps over my cheeks as I feel like a teenager just caught in a lie.

My eyes dart to Cal. "Boyfriend?" I ask, my voice hopeful. I have no idea why he's here or how he ended up palling around with my parents in their kitchen, but I let my heart hope it means that he's mine again...that he's forgiven me.

"Yes, *boyfriend*," Cal confirms with a sly smile. "It seems you forgot to mention me to your parents." There isn't any bitterness in his tone at all. It almost sounds like he's teasing me.

"My mistake," I whisper with a smile. I look at my parents at the table. "Mom and Dad, meet my boyfriend, Cal." Butterflies take flight in my stomach at introducing him that way.

Cal squeezes my hand, as if he's telling me he approves of the introduction.

Dad swats at the air as he adjusts his position in his chair. "We already met him when he showed up at our doorstep insisting he was your boyfriend. I about slammed the door in his face, thinking he was some weird stalker."

I giggle at the mental picture, trying to imagine how that even played out. "I am kind of shocked you ended up letting him inside."

Cal's the one to speak up. "I showed him one of our cooking videos to prove I knew you. The chicken parmesan one is going viral, by the way. I'm not sure you've noticed. You haven't posted in a while."

"How do you know that?"

He lifts a shoulder in a casual shrug. "I've paid attention."

Dad clears his throat again. "It took a few minutes, but he finally convinced us to let him inside. The food he promised to cook—your recipe, he tells me—was what really sold me."

Mom sits up in her chair, leaning forward on her elbows. "Lucy, I'm amazed at how many people are watching these videos and recreating your recipes."

I blush. I haven't even checked any of my social media since coming back to Virginia. There were too many reminders of Cal. The videos I posted of us together were doing well, but I couldn't bring myself to watch them or share the ones we recorded that I hadn't posted yet.

Cal wraps his arm around me. "Wait until you taste the recipe. I'm typically terrible at cooking, but after following her instructions closely, you'll discover just how talented she is. She makes anyone a great cook, even me."

"Did you make it?" I ask, my eyes wandering to the four nicely plated chicken parmesans on the counter.

Cal gives me a proud smile. "I sure did. Now, let's eat. I've been talking with your parents, and we have some things to discuss..."

I pull my head back, looking at him through narrowed lids. "We do?"

He nods, pointing to the kitchen table for me to take a seat. "Yes. Sit. I'll get the food, and we'll get started."

Without leaving any room for discussion, he removes his arm from around me and closes the distance to the small kitchen table. He and my mom share a knowing look as he pulls the chair out from the table.

"What's happening?" I ask as I take a seat. Everyone's quiet and sharing looks with each other that I don't understand.

Mom reaches across the table and grabs my hand. I hold my breath, wondering what my parents and Cal could've possibly been talking about. She gives me a warm smile as she squeezes my hand. "Before we say anything else—" Her eyes move from mine to Dad's before she focuses on me once again. "—I just want you to know how much your father and I love you. We've asked more out of you over the years than we probably should have. And I know we probably didn't say it enough, but we love you, and we could never thank you enough for everything you've given up for us."

I swallow, my eyes beginning to sting. I didn't know I had any more tears to cry, but something about the tenderness in her voice, paired with her words, hits home.

"I haven't given up anything," I manage to get out. Cal places plates in front of us before taking a seat himself. I don't look at him, not right now. Not with the look in my mother's eyes. "It's you and Dad that have given up so much. I just want to help and make things easier on you."

Mom nods, her own eyes welling over with tears. "I know, Lu. You've been perfect. But...you're not the parent. We are. It isn't your responsibility to make things easier on us, and I think, over the years, we've put too much pressure on you."

I shake my head as my bottom lip trembles. Cal places his hand on my thigh, a quiet reminder that he's here.

"No, you didn't," I counter. They've had a lot on their plate over the years. I just tried helping where I could.

"We've asked too much of you, Lucy. And that's our fault," Dad speaks up. "But that stops now."

I shift my body to look at him.

He pauses to cut into the chicken parmesan and take a bite. His eyes close for a moment. When they open again, he immediately focuses on me. "Lucy, this is incredible."

I smile as Cal gives my thigh a reassuring squeeze. A small laugh leaves me as I tilt my head in Cal's direction. "Well, *I* didn't make it. Cal did."

Mom lets go of my hand before taking her own bite. She nods in agreement. "I've never had anything like this. This is amazing."

I blush, my gaze darting to my lap for a moment before looking back up. "The compliments should go to Cal for cooking it."

Dad grabs a napkin and wipes his mouth. He sighs, his palms hitting the table. "Lucy, I've been talking with Cal, and I think it's best you don't take over the store."

I gasp, my eyes moving from my dad to Cal and back again. "What? No. I'm trying my best, I promise. I'll learn the ropes and—"

Dad holds up his hand. "You're amazing at anything you put your mind to. I have no doubt that given the time, you'd do amazing things with the store. But you shouldn't have to, honey. Not when it's obvious your talents would be wasted there."

I look at Cal in confusion. "What did you tell them?" I ask, panic in my voice. If I don't take over the store, Dad will feel the need to run it. He'll overwork himself and jeopardize his health because of me.

"Cal didn't really have to tell us anything. He just showed us your videos, and that told us everything we needed to know. I don't think I've ever seen you light up the way you did in those videos."

"I can run the store and cook on the side," I offer, desperate for him to listen to me. I can't allow him to take over the store again, not when his health keeps declining. "I promise I'll be better at running it. Alec's teaching me so much, and I'll—"

Mom places her hand on my shoulder. "You don't have to be better, Lu. You're doing your best. We want you to do what you want with your life. As your parents, we can't ask you to give up your passion for us."

I choke out a sob. "As your daughter, I can't make you run the store by yourselves."

Cal clears his throat. "That's the thing, baby. They won't have to."

Dad nods as my eyes find his in confusion. "We have Alec."

"What?" I blink a few times, trying to understand what's happening.

"Alec's been with us..." Dad pauses for a moment as he takes a deep breath. "Well, he's been with us for a very long time."

I nod, my heart aching as my mind fills in what he isn't saying. Alec's been with us before Luke and Logan passed. He's been like family to us.

"It was never fair of me to ask you to run the store, Lucy," Dad continues. "You had dreams, and I took them away from you because I didn't know what else to do."

"You didn't take anything from me," I rush to say. "Everything I've done, I wanted to do. I'd do anything for you."

Dad nods in understanding. For a few seconds, he just stares at me. His lips press into a thin line, and I swear his eyes get a little glossy. "It's not your job to fill the void left by their deaths. And it was really unfair that we made you feel like you had to. The only thing we need from you is to be happy."

My bottom lip trembles as I try my hardest not to cry. I want to be strong, but I hadn't realized how badly I needed to hear those words until he said them.

I look over at my mom. All she does is nod. "We love you, Lu," she manages to get out through her own tears. "And we think it's best if you follow your dreams and we ask Alec to take over the store. He's earned it, and we should've thought about him—and you—sooner."

Before I can say anything, Cal wraps his arm around me and pulls me against him. "We've come up with a really solid plan that should make everyone happy. Want to hear it?"

I stare at him wide-eyed, wondering how I got so lucky to be so fiercely loved by a man like him. All I can do is nod at first, so overtaken with love and appreciation for the man sitting next to me. "Tell me everything."

Fifty-three
CAL

"So, this is it," Lucy tells me with a bashful grin as we step into her childhood bedroom.

I laugh, my eyes scanning the room, not knowing where to look first. "This is amazing."

Lucy softly shuts the door behind us, making my pulse spike a little, remembering the scowl on her father's face when Lucy said we were going to go upstairs to talk some more.

I clear my throat, my eyes focusing on the shut door. "Your dad was very clear he wanted that door open."

Lucy laughs and rolls her eyes. "I'm twenty-three years old. He'll get over it. Plus, he's going to bed. No one sleeps deeper than him."

I nod, feeling like a teenager again, afraid of a father on the other side of the house. I take a step closer to a wall of photos. It showcases photos of Lucy at different ages, making me smile. I point to one of a five- or six-year-old Lucy in a full chef's costume. "So you knew you wanted to cook from a young age?" I ask.

She nods as her attention shifts to the photo as well. "You could say that."

I continue to look at the photos as she takes a step closer to me, closing the distance between us. Her arms wrap around my middle.

"I can't believe you're here," she says against my chest.

My hands travel down her back and rest at the small of her waist. I keep her body close to mine, reveling in the feeling of holding her once again. "There's nowhere else I'd rather be," I tell her honestly.

Her chin presses into my chest as she angles her head up to look at me. "So, quick question. Where's your phone?"

I cock my head to the side. One hand leaves her waist to grab my phone from my pocket. I tap the screen, but nothing happens. "It must be out of battery. Why?"

She chews her lip as her brown eyes search mine. "When you plug that in, don't be alarmed by the amount of missed calls from me."

I smile, my heart warming at the knowledge she finally called me. "Really?" I've been attached to my phone for two weeks without her. I checked it way more than I should've, just hoping she'd call. It figures when she finally did call, I missed them.

Lucy nods, her teeth still digging into her bottom lip. "Yeah. I called you...*a lot*. There was just something I really needed to tell you."

Something about the look in her eyes makes hope bloom in my chest. We just spent two hours discussing a plan with her family where Lucy got what she wanted but felt that her parents were taken care of as well. She made it clear she wanted me in her plans for the future, but the more validation I got from her that she's ready to tackle anything life throws at us together, the better.

"What did you need to tell me?" I ask, my words coming out low and raspy. My heart lurches in excitement at the smile spreading across her lips.

Lucy runs her hands along my chest. I love feeling the press of her touch against me again, even if there is a layer of fabric between us. I feel like I barely breathe as I wait for her next words.

Her brown eyes find mine. "I love you, Callahan Hastings," she says, her voice strong. Her smile gets even wider as she moves her hands to cup my cheeks. "I love you so much that these last two weeks have been torture without you. I don't know what I was thinking, and I'm sorry for hurting you and pushing you away, but I love you."

I smile at her words, closing my eyes for a moment as I let them sink in. Happiness radiates through my entire body at finally hearing her confess her love. I let out a happy sigh as my hands find her face. I press my forehead against hers as we both hold each other's faces. "You have no idea how much I've been dying to hear you say that."

"I love you," she repeats.

The last two weeks have been pure hell. I didn't know it was possible to think about another person so much, but it seemed like my mind was full of nothing but her. There were mornings I woke up and feared I'd never get to hold her again. I didn't know if I'd ever get to tell her how much I loved her again, and I didn't even let my heart hope to hear her tell me the same.

But she's here in my arms.

She loves me.

And nothing else matters in this world.

"I love you too," I tell her, my grip on her face tightening. I look into her eyes, hoping she can see the love I have for her written all over my face. "I love you so fucking much, Lucy Rae. My love for you is the kind that only comes once in a lifetime. I've been so lost without you."

She nods. "I know. Jude told me. I'm so sorry to have put you through that. I think I just needed—"

My head pulls back. "Jude told you?"

She gives me a hesitant smile, as if she doesn't know if she was supposed to tell me that or not. "Yes. He was with Charlotte when she called me. It was actually them who finally made me see reason and realize I needed to call you and tell you how I felt."

"I'm so happy they did," I note, feeling immensely grateful for the two of them. Who knows how things would've turned out if she hadn't talked to them and decided that she wanted to make things work with us? Me showing up at her house unannounced and making a plan with her parents before she even got home could've gone very differently if she was still thinking I was more of a distraction than someone she wanted to spend her life with.

Lucy lifts to her tiptoes and presses a kiss against my lips. It starts out timid, but I end that quickly. We may have spent the last couple of hours together, but I haven't had the chance to kiss her yet. We were busy making plans with her parents about the next steps.

Now that her lips are against mine, I need more. I slowly slip my tongue into her mouth, waiting to see if she'll allow it.

I fight a smile when she immediately opens for me. Her hands move from my face as they slide down my arms and then find my chest. She grabs the fabric of my shirt and pulls my body flush to hers.

I don't know how long we stand there in her childhood bedroom making out. Time seems to stand still as we both get lost in the moment. Our hands in each other's hair, on the other's body, pulling at clothes. Neither one of us can get enough.

"I have a confession," I tell her, breaking the kiss for a moment.

"Yes?"

"I also got a little push to stop wallowing and to do something about it."

She smiles. "Was it also Jude?"

I shake my head, for some reason nervous to tell her the truth. "It was Ollie. He asked to meet at the club. We got to talking, and I told him how I felt about you. He's the one who pushed me to come here..."

My words fall short as I try to gauge her reaction. She stares at me for a moment with an unreadable look on her face. Finally, her lips spread into a genuine smile. "That was nice of him." She stands on her tiptoes again and places a soft kiss against my lips. Her mouth moves against mine with her next words. "I'm glad he did."

I let out a breath, not realizing how tight my entire body was as I told her that. "The reason he wanted to talk to begin with was because he wanted to mend things between us. He seemed older, more mature. He asked me to be the best man at his wedding to Sophia."

The last sentence comes out rushed. I'm nervous to see her reaction. I know she loves me, and she's made it clear things with Ollie were never as serious as she once thought. I just don't want her to be upset that he's marrying her old best friend.

The smile doesn't leave Lucy's lips. Her hands tighten on the fabric of my shirt. "I'm happy for them, Cal. I can't wait to be the hot best man's plus-one."

All the tension leaves my body at her words. "I'll have the hottest date there."

Her fingers begin to undo the buttons of my shirt. "I love you," she tells me, her eyes focusing on her task.

"I love you too, baby," I respond, groaning when her palms hit the bare skin of my chest. She slowly pushes the shirt off me.

"I choose you," she adds with conviction. "I promise to always choose you." Her fingers roam along my abs as she reacquaints herself with my body.

"Baby," I rasp, trying to hold myself back as her fingers play with the waistband of my pants.

It appears she's being a tease because her hands travel up my body before she wraps her arms around my neck. "I know I said this when my parents were with us...but thank you. For tonight. For everything."

I tuck her hair behind her ear and really look at the woman I love. I'd do anything for her, and tonight was just the beginning of us planning a life together. "Don't thank me. We're in this together, Lucy Rae. I'm just so fucking relieved you're letting me shoulder some of the responsibility with you."

Her answer is to kiss me all over again, a small moan leaving her lips as my fingers tangle in her hair.

We're still working things out, but it was clear after talking with her parents that the right thing to do is to ask Alec to take over the furniture store. He's been with them all along and has more than earned his right to take it over. I told Lucy's parents I could get them with the best business lawyers to talk about a partnership between them and Alec. I even already have ideas of some suppliers they could get into the store that would really make business boom. Lucy seemed relieved to pass on the store to Alec, mentioning that he deserves it more than she does and is far more equipped.

When we'd gotten to the discussion of Lucy coming back to the Hamptons for the summer and then to Manhattan to continue her work and be with me, she seemed unsure. Both her dad and mom insisted she get back out of Virginia, but I could tell it made her uneasy. Finally, we came up with the idea of hiring help for them around the house as well. That way, Lucy's mom can get a break when she needs it and won't have to handle everything on her own.

I haven't mentioned this to her yet, but I also plan on buying a house here in Virginia, close to her parents. That way, with a house nearby and my private jet, Lucy can come visit her parents any time she wants. I don't want her to think that being together means she can't spend time with them. Now, she'll be able to do whatever she wants, whenever she wants.

"Want to break some rules with me?" Lucy asks, pulling away from the kiss. Her fingers skirt across the waistband of my chinos again.

Her father's warning pops into my mind. He'd been adamant about us keeping the door open if I were to stay here with her tonight.

I groan, my head falling back as her fingers drift underneath my waistband. "I just met your dad. I don't want him to hate me."

Lucy laughs, her fingers undoing the button of my pants. "He won't hate you. He loves you, I promise. Plus, we'll be quiet." Her eyes meet mine as she playfully bites her lip. "I've missed you, babe. I need you."

I can't say no to her. I grab the fabric of her shirt and hastily strip her of it, needing her just as badly as she needs me.

Neither one of us says a word as we continue to pull each other's clothes off until we're left with nothing between us.

We get lost in each other, in the feeling of being together once again. And once our desires are satisfied, at least for the moment, we lie awake all night talking. She tells me all about her life, her brothers, and answers any questions I ask. Neither one of us holds back as we fully get to know one another. We're both honest and open, and by the time we both drift off to sleep, I'm more in love with her than I've ever been.

Something I didn't even know was possible.

Fifty-four
LUCY

"I have a gift I want to give you before we head out," Cal announces, his arms wrapping around my middle as he brings my back to his front.

I stare at him in the mirror with a smile on my face. "A gift for me? What's the occasion?"

"The occasion is you're back, and I missed you." He presses a kiss to the base of my neck, making my entire body shiver. He continues to trail kisses along my skin as I attempt to put my earrings in. His skin is soft against mine, something I'm not typically used to.

We're going to Pembroke Hills tonight for their annual Black-Tie Event. From what I understand, the club goes all out for the evening, and I'm excited to experience it.

It's my first time back at the club since returning to the Hamptons. After Cal surprised me by visiting, we spent a week getting everything settled for my parents. It was amazing having him at home with me, and I fell even more in love with him as I watched him create a bond with my parents. He eventually had to go to Manhattan for some work while I stayed in Virginia for another week, but we both arrived back in the Hamptons last night, and I can't wait to see all our friends.

I already miss my parents, but for the first time in forever, I'm at peace being away from them. I know they're okay, and I don't feel the same weight I used to when it comes to them. We had a lot of open discussions, and my relationship with them is better than ever.

"What are you thinking about, baby?" Cal asks, pulling me from my thoughts.

"Everything," I answer, giving him a soft smile through the reflection in the mirror. "I just can't believe I'm back and that we're here and everyone's happy."

"I've never been happier," he responds, his hands splaying out along my abdomen.

I take time to soak in the moment with him. He's never looked more handsome than he does right now. He wears a black suit that's perfectly tailored to his body with a black tie that sticks out against the white button-up he's paired underneath it.

"I like you in white," he comments, catching me staring at him through the reflection. I can't help but stare at him sometimes, still in awe that this man fell in love with me.

"Technically, it's cream." I smile, admiring the dress I picked out via FaceTime with Charlotte. I was all the way in Virginia and didn't have time to pick out a nice dress, and Jude had asked her to be his plus-one for the event, so she was already out dress shopping. When she showed me this one, I fell in love. It's a cream dress that almost feels like satin. It has a halter neckline and clings perfectly to the small curves I do have.

Cal playfully nibbles at my ear. "I don't care what it's *technically* called. I love you in white, and now I'm wondering how soon I can get you in a white wedding dress walking down the aisle toward me."

I roll my eyes at him. "We've had one night officially living together. You can't already be wanting to marry me."

It was sad to give up my place attached to Mr. Fred's store, but it was time for me to let someone else rent it. Plus, I was giddy about moving in with Cal.

"Oh, I knew I wanted to marry you from the moment we first kissed," Cal states matter-of-factly.

"Cal," I respond, shaking my head. "No, you didn't."

He confidently nods in the mirror. His hands move from around my waist, and I miss the warmth from them immediately. I watch him through the mirror as he pulls a small rectangular box from his tuxedo pocket.

I gasp, recognizing it as a jewelry box.

He laughs at my reaction, his eyes finding mine in the mirror. "Don't worry, Lucy baby, it isn't a ring...yet. Although, you tell me when you're ready for a ring, and I'll buy one immediately. Better yet, we could just skip the engagement altogether and just go straight to being husband and wife."

"Let's live together for at least a year before we talk about that," I tease. I love how much he loves me out loud. He says exactly what he's thinking, never once making me guess how he feels about me. It's incredible to be loved by him. I can't wait to feel it for the rest of my life.

"A year?" he asks, his arms coming around me as he holds the box in front of my face. "I was thinking we could maybe discuss it after...a month?"

I take the box from his hands and turn to face him, not bothering to hide how I roll my eyes at his comment. "Babe, you're ridiculous."

"Ridiculously in love with you," he easily responds, a cocky smirk on his lips.

God, I love this man.

He taps the box in my hands. "Open it."

I look down at the gift, wondering what's inside. He already told me it isn't a ring, but it's got to be some kind of jewelry by looking at the box. I run my hands along the top, excited to see what's inside. Softly, I pop open the lid, my breath hitching.

It's a necklace. The most beautiful necklace I've ever seen.

"Cal," I whisper, my hands shaking as I run my hands over the giant diamond pendant. "This is beautiful."

I stare at the large diamond that's in the shape of a heart. The diamond itself is massive and pink, and it sits on a sparkling chain.

"This pink is my favorite shade of pink," he tells me, his voice thick with emotion. "The same pink your cheeks turn when you blush."

I look up at him, my eyes welling with unshed tears. I don't know how he's so good at giving gifts, but I appreciate it beyond words. It's so thoughtful I don't even know what to say to him.

Luckily, he saves me from attempting to come up with the right words to properly show how much I love and appreciate the gift.

He gently lifts the necklace from the box and holds it in front of my eyes. The diamond sparkles underneath the closet light, showcasing just how stunning the piece of jewelry is.

Cal focuses on the necklace as well, his lips turning up in a half smile. "It's a heart because, like my heart, it's yours to keep forever, Lucy baby."

I try to blink to stop my tears from falling and ruining my makeup, but it's no use. A single tear runs down my cheek as my heart swells with love for the man standing in front of me.

"It's perfection," I manage to get out through my clogged throat. I look at him and hope my face conveys how thankful I am for him and the gift. "I love you so much, babe."

This makes him smile even wider. "I love you too. Now, turn around so I can put this on you, and you can show everyone tonight that my heart is yours."

I do as he instructs, turning to see our reflection in the mirror once again. He slowly places the necklace around my neck and fastens it.

For a few seconds, we both just stare at the piece of jewelry on me. It's cold and heavy against my skin, proof of just how large the diamond is. I have no idea when he bought this, but I don't even want to think about how much he spent on it.

"It's beautiful," I marvel, carefully touching the diamond. I feel like I shouldn't be allowed to wear something so nice.

"You're beautiful," Cal responds, his hands finding my hips. "There's one more thing," he whispers, pressing a kiss to my shoulder.

"Yes?"

"Our friends have been waiting in the driveway for ten minutes."

I gasp, hurriedly turning toward him and looking at him with wide eyes.

"What?" I ask in shock, my eyes scanning the closet for the purse I want to bring tonight. Of course, I have to go with the small Chanel bag he bought me not too long ago. I begin to stuff lip gloss and other touch-up items in the bag. "How come you didn't tell me that? They're going to be upset we've made them wait."

He laughs, handing me my phone that I was just about to start looking for. I make sure I don't have any missed calls before stuffing it into the bag as well. "They're not going to be upset, I promise. The limo probably has the nicest champagne possible, and I'm sure they're just enjoying everyone being together again."

I hope his words are true as I take one last look in the mirror before running as fast as I can in heels to the front door. Just like he said, a long black limousine is parked in our driveway.

"Finally!" Charlotte calls from the sunroof.

Emma's head pops out next to hers. "Were you guys getting in a pre-event quickie?" she yells.

I blush, shaking my head at how unfiltered Emma is as I make my way to the limo. I can feel Cal following me closely.

"Someone didn't tell me you were waiting for us, or I would've finished getting ready quicker," I toss out, looking over my shoulder and giving Cal a playful look.

All he does is shrug. "You can't rush perfection."

His words make me smile. I turn back around, nearing the limo. As soon as I get close, the driver opens the door for me.

I slide inside, smiling at all of our friends waiting for us. Cal was right—most of them are holding champagne flutes, careless smiles on their faces as we get in.

"Sorry for making you guys wait," I mutter sheepishly, sliding into the seat next to Jude.

He swats at the air. "No big deal. We were having fun." His eyes find Charlotte as she stops hanging out of the sunroof and takes her spot on the other side of him.

"Let's do this!" she cheers excitedly, clapping as the limo begins to pull away. "I can't wait to experience this Black-Tie Event as a guest."

I give her a smile, feeling equally as giddy as she does.

Everyone breaks into their own side conversations as the limo heads to the event. I probably look crazy to anyone looking at me, but I can't wipe the smile from my face as I look around.

I swallow back happy tears as I think back to the beginning of the summer. My only friend was Charlotte. I worked all the time and didn't know what it was like to find a family outside of my own. My eyes skirt over the people that I've gotten to know as summer passed by. Some I'm closer with than others, but they're all people who contributed to the best summer of my life. Charlotte, Jude, Beck, Margo, Emma, Preston, Ryker, Camille, Winnie, Archer, all people I've grown closer to.

I've never had close friends like this. We've already discussed plans in Manhattan once the summer ends, and for the first time in my life, I've been so excited about what the future looks like.

My future is my own and not dependent on things out of my control, something that feels like a huge relief.

My eyes find the man sitting next to me, gratitude overwhelming me at how things have changed throughout the course of the summer with him.

When I first saw Cal at Laurent Hughes's dinner party, I wanted nothing to do with him. Now, I don't want a life that doesn't include him in it.

He's my home.

My love.

My teammate.

Callahan Hastings.

My former boss and my ex's older brother.

My heart.

Mine.

For as long as I can remember, I've felt like I've had to carry the weight of the world on my shoulders. I wanted to be the perfect daughter for my parents and make sure they were taken care of. I didn't want to mess up, and I wanted to do everything in my power to make life easy on them, knowing they'd already been through so much. I hadn't realized how much carrying that weight was getting to me or how hard it was for me to let someone in because of the weight I was carrying.

It wasn't until Cal loved me fiercely and with no need for anything in return that I learned to let someone be there for me.

He taught me that love can make us stronger and that it's okay to need someone else.

Loving him is the best decision I've ever made.

I smile, realizing our life together has only just begun. This summer has been the best summer of my life, and I can't wait for many more. I'll be in good company with him by my side for all of it.

Epilogue
LUCY

My body trembles with excitement as the bridal coordinator plays with the hem of my wedding dress.

From a few feet away, someone else helps fix the knot of my father's tie. He smiles at me from across the entryway of the villa, giving me a wink as they continue fussing over the tie he insisted on tying himself.

I take a deep breath, trying to calm the jitters.

I'm getting married today.

I smile, still in shock that today's my wedding day.

It feels like it took forever to get here, but it also came so fast. At the end of our first summer together, Cal proposed. It was magical, and I didn't know it was possible for me to be so happy. At first, we were going to do a small wedding as soon as we could. But after thinking about it, I knew my dream was to get married in front of all our friends and family. We thought about doing something at Pembroke, but when Cal was able to book my dream villa in Lake Como, Italy, for our wedding, it seemed like fate. We were engaged a little longer than we first thought we'd be, a little over a year, but I already know it'll be worth the wait.

Plus, it has already felt like we're married in the year we've been engaged. We moved in together the moment I came back to the Hamptons. With anyone else, it would've been fast, but with Cal, it felt right. I just wanted to be with him. When we got engaged at the end of the summer and Cal had to go back to Manhattan, I went with him. We bought a brownstone in the city with the most magical kitchen that was also close to our friends. I continued to film my cooking recipes there. Each one got more views until finally, they became so popular Emma set me up with her talent agency.

I'm in the process of writing my very first cookbook—an actual dream come true. While we're here in Italy, we're also shooting photographs for the cookbook.

I smile, letting out a shaky breath, thinking how none of this would be happening if the man I'm about to marry hadn't shown me how to believe in myself.

Dad's arms wrapping around me to pull me into a hug break me from my thoughts. "You ready?" he asks, holding me tight. He's careful not to touch my hair that the stylist took an hour curling into perfect waves down my back.

I nod, giving my dad a nervous smile. "I am. Are you?"

I reach up to wipe underneath his eyes, where tears are forming. He laughs, trying to swat my hand away, embarrassed at being caught crying.

"As I'll ever be," he answers, his brown eyes—the same color as mine—roaming my face. His broad shoulders rise and fall as he lets out a strong exhale. I don't try to fill the silence, giving him the time he needs to say whatever's on his mind. In the last year, my parents and I have become closer than ever. Cal surprised me by buying a house a few streets down from my childhood home, so we visit them a lot, and because of that, the last year has been really healing for us as a family.

We talk freely about Luke and Logan now and even about the little things in life when our conversations always used to revolve only around the family business. The store is thriving more now than it ever has, and we're able to just enjoy each other's company, something I don't take for granted. Luckily, Dad's health is also better than ever. Forcing him to take it easy has really allowed his body to heal the way it needed to.

"I love you, Lucy," Dad manages to get out, his voice thick. He wipes a tear away the moment it hits his cheek. "And I might not say it enough, but I'm so proud of you. Your mother and I both are. And I know Luke and Logan would be too. You've built a beautiful life."

I blink, trying to prevent the tears from falling, knowing the makeup artist had spent a good chunk of the morning perfecting my makeup for my big day.

The blinking only helps for a bit before tears fall at my dad's words, paired with the adoration in his eyes. "I love you too," I whisper. "So much," I add, needing him to know that.

He nods, his eyes moving to the wedding coordinator, who cautiously steps closer to us. "We're about three minutes away from when the orchestra will start playing your entrance song. Are we ready?"

"We are," Dad answers for me, giving me one final squeeze before he weaves his arm through mine. His hand squeezes mine in encouragement.

Arianna, our head wedding coordinator at the villa, flies into the room with a clipboard in her hand. "Almost show-time!" she excitedly says, stopping in front of me. "You're as stunning as ever," she gets out with a smile.

I return her smile. "Thank you." I glance down at my wedding dress. I thought it'd be really easy for me to pick a dress, but it took four bridal salons before I finally found one I envisioned myself walking down the aisle in.

It's made of delicate lace with a beautifully intricate pattern that took my breath away. The dress has an off-the-shoulder neckline and sleeves that go to my wrists. The lace fabric clings to my skin and gathers at my feet with a gorgeous train.

I take a deep breath, reminding myself that this moment is real. I'm about to walk down the aisle to the love of my life.

"You've got about thirty seconds until the doors will open," Arianna declares, handing me my bouquet of flowers.

I try to get words out to thank her as she pulls my veil over my face and makes sure I'm ready for the grand entrance, but I'm not able to say anything.

I'm too excited to see Cal. We tried to do the traditional thing where we slept in separate rooms, but we both lasted until about midnight, and then I was texting him and begging him to sneak into my room. We're not used to spending time away from one another, and it didn't feel right to not sleep next to each other, even the night before our wedding.

But it's still been hours since he slipped out of my room this morning. I've missed him, and now I get to see him and call him my husband for the very first time.

"It's time," Arianna announces, a beaming smile on her face.

I look over at my dad, my chest constricting with love at the look in his eyes.

He doesn't have to say it again. His face tells me everything I need to know. He's proud of me. I squeeze his hand before looking forward.

Arianna gestures for us to begin walking, and with each step, the nerves start to leave my body. I know with every step, I'm getting closer to the man of my dreams.

The large, old wooden doors of the villa open up. Our loved ones all stand up as my dad leads me down the aisle.

For one split second, I look at our friends and family all gathered here to celebrate with both Cal and me. Our villa is big enough to accommodate all of them, and we've all been here for a week, enjoying Lake Como together while staying in the villa.

It's been the best week of my life, but the next two weeks will give it some competition. Our loved ones will return home while Cal and I take off on our honeymoon.

Speaking of Cal, my eyes finally connect with his.

My steps falter for a split second at seeing the man I fell in love with during a summer in the Hamptons waiting for me at the end of the aisle.

Luckily, Dad guides me forward, making sure I don't miss another beat as he leads me to my Cal.

All nerves leave my body as I focus on Cal. He's my safe space, my other half. I was always scared to depend on someone else, but I just hadn't found the right person. Cal's never let me down. He's been solid and steadfast in his love for me from the beginning of our relationship.

And now he's about to be my husband.

I want to pay attention to all the details everyone put into our dream wedding. Huge, gorgeous floral bouquets line the aisle, guiding me right to Cal. There's a stunning lakefront view right behind the floral-covered altar.

But all I see is him.

We're about halfway to him, and happy tears are already falling down my cheeks.

Cal looks incredibly handsome in a tailored black tux. It fits him perfectly, his frame standing out against the white floral background.

He smiles, his hand moving to cover his mouth as he stares at me from down the aisle in awe. He mutters something to the officiant, but he's too far away for me to know what he says.

"Oh, wow," Dad mutters in awe from next to me. I pull my

gaze from Cal just long enough to see what's caught Dad's attention.

Right next to Mom in the first row are two empty seats, each with a picture frame.

Luke and Logan.

Dad and I lean on each other to keep walking down the aisle.

My heart bursts at the sentiment. I never wanted to imagine my wedding day without the two of them. Now, I don't have to. They're right here with us.

I meet Cal's eyes again and know that it was his idea to save the spots for them. Leave it to Cal to make me fall even deeper in love with him, even on our wedding day.

My heart beats faster with each step closer to Cal. He's so close now I can make out the brilliant blue of his eyes.

Another step.

I can't believe I finally get to marry this man.

He smiles, making my heart leap in my chest. God, I can't wait to see that smile for the rest of my life.

Another step.

I'm close enough now that I can see the reason his eyes look so blue is because they're glossed over with his unshed tears.

"Hi, baby," he croaks, meeting us at the edge of the altar. His eyes roam over my body as he drinks me in. I love that after he snuck out this morning, we kept it on the traditional side and waited to see each other until right now.

Nothing will ever top this moment.

The love and reverence in his eyes as he looks at me.

The way he shakes my dad's hand before my dad takes his seat next to Mom.

The way he grabs my hands and doesn't listen to the officiant for a moment, allowing himself time to look me over from top to bottom.

"I love you," he whispers, his back still to the officiant as he leans in and presses a kiss to my cheek through the veil.

"I love you too," I whisper back, my hands shaking with excitement as he leads us both to the altar.

We stop in front of the officiant as the orchestra plays the last notes of the song.

The officiant clears his throat. "Friends and family, we've gathered here today to..."

I hear what the officiant says, but not everything registers. I'm too lost in looking into Cal's eyes. Now that the day and moment is here, I'm just ready to officially be announced as his wife.

I stare at the man in front of me, tears pooling in my eyes at how much I love him. I didn't know a love like we share even existed, and I don't know what I did right in life for fate to align for us to meet not just once but twice, but I'm so happy it did.

I give him a smile before mouthing the words "I love you."

He winks and squeezes my hands before mouthing the same thing back to me.

The ceremony is perfect. When Cal finally lifts my veil and presses his lips to mine as our first kiss as husband and wife, pure joy overtakes my entire body.

He cries.

I cry.

Both our families cry.

And I swear even some of our friends cry too.

I've had a lot of amazing days with Callahan Hastings. From the very beginning with our early morning farm stand adventures to cooking with him in the kitchen of our home in Manhattan while snow blanketed the city in white. Even some of our most recent amazing days, like the one where I got the call from my agent that my cookbook was going to be published, or even the other night where Cal and I sat on the terrace of our room at the villa and planned out the next few years that are hopefully filled with lots of love, cooking, and babies.

We've shared many incredible days together.

But as we kiss in front of all those we love most as husband and wife for the first time, I count this moment right here as the best moment of my life.

Callahan Hastings is my husband.

He pulls away, that cocky grin that made me fall for him on his lips. I can't wait to keep falling more in love with him every day for the rest of my life. "You're my wife, Lucy baby."

I nod. "And you're my husband. I love you, Callahan Hastings."

He leans in and presses one more kiss to my lips as our loved ones cheer in front of us. "I love you too, Lucy Hastings."

DO YOU WANT MORE
Lucy and Cal ?

Join Cal and Lucy on their honeymoon and subscribe to my newsletter to receive the extended epilogue for *In Good Company*.

Join here: authorkatsingleton.com/#newsletter

DO YOU WANT MORE
Pembroke Hills?

Make sure to pre-order *Bad for Business,* book two in this series, now. We will be going back to Pembroke Hills for Ryker and Camille's book. *Bad for Business* releases on September 23rd.

ABOUT BAD FOR BUSINESS

- *enemies to lovers*
- *billionaire*
- *black cat x golden retriever*

PRE-ORDER BAD FOR BUSINESS:
https://geni.us/badforbusiness

ADD BAD FOR BUSINESS TO YOUR GOODREADS TBR:
https://geni.us/badforbusinessGR

Acknowledgments

Starting a new series is absolutely terrifying. It'd been so long since I'd introduced new characters to readers, that I didn't know what to expect for this book. From the very first page of writing *In Good Company*, I knew Cal and Lucy and everyone at Pembroke Hills would steal a piece of my heart. Instead of being scared to start over with a new series, I was thrilled. Writing about a country club has been an idea of mine for years, and I'm over the moon that the time has finally come where I can be in my Pembroke Hills era. Cal and Lucy quickly became my favorite characters I've written so far. I put so much of myself into this book, and I hope you fell in love with them as much as I did.

There are so many people who helped me along the way while I was writing *In Good Company*. Without them, this book wouldn't be what it is now, and I'm eternally grateful for their support.

To my husband, thank you for your endless support, and for being my rock. I know I don't say it enough, but I appreciate everything you do to help make my dreams come true. From being a supportive husband, a present father, and a business partner, there's so much you do behind the scenes that I'm eternally grateful for. I love you forever.

Lauren and Chasity, thank you for being there every step of the way while I was writing this book. The two of you were crucial in making this story what it is, and I'll never be able to say thank you for being my alphas. You're stuck with me forever, I hope you know that. Thank you for being the very first people to read this book in its rawest form and for cheering me on when I wondered if the book sucked. I love you so much and am so happy this community led me to both of you.

To Kristie, thank you for helping me plot this book and talking through the jumble of ideas I had for Cal and Lucy's love story. I'm so happy with how the book turned out and appreciate your help so much.

Kelsey, thank you for holding my hand throughout the many breakdowns I had while writing this book. I'm so fortunate to be able to work with my best friend and I appreciate everything you do to keep all things Kat Singleton running. I wouldn't be able to function without you. I love you.

To Tiara, thank you for not calling me crazy when I asked (begged) you to come work for me. I'm so grateful that our love of books brought us together and that I not only get to work with you, but call you one of my best friends as well. I know it isn't keeping me organized, but I appreciate everything you do to keep my life together. I love you.

Summer, my cover queen, thank you for being patient with me throughout the many renditions of this cover. I'm so freaking obsessed with the final result and I appreciate you working with me to create magic for this cover.

Mikaela, thank you for everything you do to help market my books. I know we ask a lot of you and I'm so grateful for all of your help.

To my friends who cheered me on every day while writing

this book. I wouldn't have finished this book without you. I love you.

To Holly, Salma, Sandra, Alexandra, and Briana, you're my dream team of editors and proofers. Thank you for all your help in making this book perfect for release. I appreciate your help so much!

To Nina, thank you for being my agent. Working with you is a dream and I'm so lucky to have you. You're always championing my books and I appreciate it so much. I can't wait for all the amazing things we'll do together!

To Valentine and everyone with VPR. Thank you for everything you do to keep me in check. It's not a secret that I'm a constant hot mess, and all of you are the reason I'm able to function. Thank you for making all things Kat Singleton run smoothly and amazing. I'm so thankful to call VPR home and for your help in getting *In Good Company* out to the world.

To the content creators and people in this community that share my books, I'm so eternally grateful for you. I've connected with so many amazing people since I started this author adventure and it means the world to me to have all of you to connect with. I'm appreciative of the fact that you take the time to talk about my stories on your platform. I notice every single one of your posts, videos, pictures, etc. It means the world to me that you share about my characters and stories. You make this community such a special place. Thank you for everything you do.

To the amazing humans on my own personal content team, thank you for making every release amazing. You babes are forever blowing my mind with the unique content you create based on my words and I'm so grateful to have all of you on this journey with me. I love and appreciate you so much.

I have the privilege of having a growing group of people I can run to on Facebook for anything—Kat Singleton's Sweethearts. The members there are always there for me, and I'm so fortunate to have them in my corner. I owe all of them so much gratitude for being there on the hard days and on the good days. Sweethearts, y'all are my people.

And last but certainly not least, thank you to *you,* the reader. Whether this is the first book you've read of mine, or you've been around for many releases, your endless support means the world to me. It is you who is the lifeblood of this community. It is you that keeps me going even on the hard days. You're the reason I get to wake up every single day and work my dream job, and for that, I'm so freaking grateful. Thank you for choosing my words to read. Thank you for supporting me. You've given me the greatest gift by choosing *my* book to read. I love you so much. I hope I made you proud with this book.

ALSO BY
Kat Singleton

BLACK TIE BILLIONAIRES

Black Ties and White Lies: https://amzn.to/4oPOdqu

Pretty Rings and Broken Things: https://amzn.to/3Ponrlc

Bright Lights and Summer Nights : https://amzn.to/48d9Kgg

PEMBROKE HILLS

In Good Company: https://geni.us/InGoodCompany

Bad for Business: https://geni.us/badforbusiness

SUTTEN MOUNTAIN SERIES

Rewrite Our Story: https://amzn.to/3KNni8W

Tempt Our Fate: https://amzn.to/3WoK2XW

Chase Our Forever: https://amzn.to/3PIj85V

THE MIXTAPE SERIES

Founded on Goodbye

https://amzn.to/3nkbovl

Founded on Temptation

https://amzn.to/3HpSudl

Founded on Deception

https://amzn.to/3nbppvs

Founded on Rejection

https://amzn.to/44cYVKz

Keep reading for the first chapter of Beck and Margo's story in
Black Ties and White Lies...

"Margo, Margo, Margo."

A familiar voice startles me from my computer screen. Spinning in my office chair I find my best friend, Emma, hunched over the wall of my cubicle. Her painted red lips form a teasing grin.

Pulling the pen I was chewing on out of my mouth, I narrow my eyes at her suspiciously. "What?"

She licks her teeth, flicking the head of the Nash Pierce bobblehead she bought me ages ago. "Who did you piss off this time?"

My stomach drops, and I don't even know what she's talking about. "Are you still drunk?" I accuse, thinking about the wine we consumed last night. We downed two bottles of cheap pinot grigio with our roommate and best friend, Winnie. Split between the three of us, there's no way she's still tipsy, but it's the best I could come up with.

She scoffs, her face scrunching in annoyance. "Obviously not. I was refilling my coffee in the lounge when *Darla* had asked if I'd seen you."

I stifle an eye roll. Darla knew I'd be at one of two places. I'm always either at my desk or huddled in front of the coffee maker trying to get the nectar of the gods to keep me awake.

Darla knew *exactly* where to find me.

She just didn't want to.

You accidentally put water in the coffee bean receptacle instead of the carafe and suddenly the office receptionist hates you. It's not like I meant to break it. It's not my fault it wasn't made clear on the machine what went where. I was just *trying* to help.

"I haven't heard from her," I comment, my eyes flicking to Darla's desk. She's not there, but her phone lights up with an incoming call. Darla rarely leaves her desk. It isn't a good sign that she's nowhere in sight. The sky could be falling, and I'm not sure Darla would leave her perch.

Emma rounds the wall of my cubicle, planting her ass on my desk like she's done a million times before, even though I've asked her not to just as many times.

"I'm working." Reaching out, I smack her black stiletto, forcing her foot off the armrest of my chair.

She laughs, playfully digging her heel into my thigh. "Well, Darla, that *amazing woman*, told me the boss wants to see you."

"I thought Marty was out for meetings all day today?"

Emma bites her lip, shaking her head at me. "No, like the *boss*, boss. The head honcho. Bossman. I think it's somebody new."

She opens her mouth to say something else, but I cut her off. "That can't be right."

"Margo!" Darla barks from the doors of our conference room. I almost jump out of my chair from the shrill tone of her voice.

Emma's eyes are wide as saucers as she looks from Darla back to me. "Seriously, Mar, what did you do?"

I slide my feet into my discarded heels underneath my desk. Standing up, I wipe my hands down the front of my skirt. I hate that my palms are already clammy from nerves. "I didn't do anything," I hiss, apparently forgetting how to walk in heels as I almost face-plant before I'm even out of the security of my cubicle.

She annoyingly clicks her tongue, giving me a look that tells me she doesn't believe me. "Obviously, I knew we had people higher up than Marty, they're just never *here*. I wonder what could be so *serious...*"

"You aren't helping."

There's no time for me to go back and forth with my best friend since college any longer. Darla has her arms crossed over her chest in a way that tells me if I don't haul ass across this office and meet her at the door in the next thirty seconds, she's going to make me regret it.

I come to a stop in front of the five-foot woman who scares me way more than I'd care to admit. She frowns, her jowls pronounced as she glares at me.

Despite the dirty look, I smile sweetly at her, knowing my mama told me to always kill them with kindness. "Good morning, Darla," I say, my voice sickeningly sweet.

Her frown lines get deeper. "I don't even want to know what you did to warrant his visit today," she clips.

Your guess is as good as mine, Darla.

"Who?" I try to look into the conference room behind her, but the door is shut.

Weird. That door is never closed.

"Why don't you find out for yourself?" Grabbing the handle, she opens the door. Her body partially blocks the doorway, making me squeeze past her to be able to get in.

Whoever this *he* is, doesn't grant me the luxury of showing me his face. He stands in front of the floor-to-ceiling windows, his hands in the pockets of the perfectly tailored suit that molds to his body effortlessly. I haven't even seen the guy's face but everything about him screams wealth. Even having only seen him from behind, I can tell that he exudes confidence. It's in his stance—the way he carries his shoulders, his feet slightly apart as he stares out the window. Everything about his posture screams *business*. I'm just terrified why *his* business is *my* business.

When they said boss, they really meant it. *Oh boy.*

What have I done?

Even the sound of the door shutting behind me doesn't elicit movement from him. It gives me time to look him up and down from the back. If I wasn't already terrified that I was in trouble for something I don't even remember doing, I'd take a moment to appreciate the view.

I mean *damn*. I didn't know that suit pants could fit an ass so perfectly.

I risk another step into the conference room. Looking around, I confirm it's just me and the mystery man with a nice ass in the empty space.

Shaking my head, I attempt to stop thinking of the way he fills the navy suit out flawlessly. From what I've been told, he's my boss. The thoughts running through my head are *anything* but work appropriate.

"Uh, hello?" I ask cautiously. My feet awkwardly stop on the other side of the large table from him. I don't know what to do. If I'm about to be fired, do I sit down first or just keep standing and get it over with?

I wonder if they'll give me a box to put my stuff in.

His back stiffens. Slowly, he turns around.

When I finally catch a glimpse of his face, I almost keel over in shock.

Because the man standing in front of me—my apparent boss—is also my ex-boyfriend's *very* attractive older brother.

KEEP READING HERE: https://amzn.to/4oPOdqu

About the Author

Kat Singleton is a bestselling romance author best known for her Black Tie Billionaires series. She loves writing elite banter and swoon-worthy men that bring the heat. Her readers enjoy the authentically raw love stories she pens and know to expect a romance filled to the brim with heartfelt emotion and sizzling spice before a happily ever after.

Kat lives in Kansas with her husband, her two kids, and her two dogs. She recently built her dream office, spending her days writing love stories and pinching herself that this is her job. When not writing, you can find her surviving off iced coffee and sneaking in a few pages of her current read off her never ending TBR. She is very active on her social media platforms and loves connecting with her readers.

links

PLAYLIST:
https://geni.us/ingoodcompanyplaylist

PINTEREST:
https://geni.us/ingoodcompanypinterest

Made in United States
North Haven, CT
15 April 2025

67905777R00231